THE ANCIENT ONES

by
Edward F. Topa

PublishAmerica
Baltimore

© 2003 by Edward F. Topa.
All rights reserved. No part of this book may be reproduced in any form without written permission from the publishers, except by a reviewer who may quote brief passages in a review to be printed in a newspaper or magazine.

First printing

ISBN: 1-59826-088-5
PUBLISHED BY PUBLISHAMERICA BOOK PUBLISHERS
www.publishamerica.com
Baltimore

Printed in the United States of America

PREFACE

Men of science, such as archaeologists and anthropologists, are continually examining the development of primeval man. From these efforts, many theories have been formulated regarding the evolution of the cultures in the 'old world', Europe, Asia and Africa, and the 'new world', the Western Hemisphere.

During most of the Tertiary and Quaternary periods, 66 million years ago, a land bridge extended from Siberia to Alaska serving as a passageway from the old world to the new world which kept man's cultural development coequal. As the sea level rose the land bridge disappeared and the development of the culture of the new world became independent of the old world. It remained this way until man developed the ability to navigate the oceans.

There is no historical record of the old and new world cultures visiting each other before the birth of Christ. According to scholars, the first explorers to the new world arrived in the fifteenth century. However, there are theories that man may have traversed the oceans in the millennium before the great explorers. Some men of science continue in their to attempts to prove this theory.

CHAPTER ONE

Somewhere in the mountain jungle of Guatemala, very near the Mexican border, a convoy of military trucks, loaded with men and supplies, was bumping and rolling along a road barely adequate for their passage. The commander of the convoy had to occasionally halt the trucks and order the men to clear fallen trees from the road, so they could pass. At one of these stops, Oberst Wilfred Keitel stepped from his vehicle and spread a map on the hood. He wore a jungle fatigue uniform with the military rank of colonel on the collar. He also wore a webbed belt and holster around his waist. The skin on his face was so tight it gave him a skeletal appearance. His nose was thin and protruded out to a point. His eyes were bright blue, and when he smiled, it usually was a sardonic smile. A captain and a sergeant joined him while he studied the map.

In an authoritative voice Keitel said, "Kapitan, we must be very close to the Mexican border, and I'm concerned about running into some patrols. I would like you to send out six two-man recon groups in thirty-degree intervals, which will provide us with a secure one hundred eighty degree arc. We will give them four hours to complete the assignment. Two hours out and two hours back. Tell the remaining men to check the loads and the trucks while they are waiting."

"Jawohl Herr Oberst," said Captain Mueller. He then turned to the sergeant and said, "Select the men, Sergeant, and I will brief them."

"Jawohl Herr Hauptner."

As they waited, the Captain turned to Keitel, "Oberst, you haven't been very specific about our mission. As you requested, I told the men we are going in to train the local native revolutionaries to use some of our more sophisticated weapons and we are the vanguard of our army. But you have not said why our entire army is leaving Guatemala or what our subsequent mission will be."

"Kapitan, as I said, we are going to train these aborigines and, at the same time, prepare a place for the rest of the army. We, then, will help these aborigines take control of the Mexican state of Chiapas. This is our mission."

"So our home base will no longer be Guatemala?" asked the captain.

"No, Guatemala is no longer a friendly environment for us," said Keitel angrily.

"We have been through this a number of times before, always looking for a friendly country to take Mr. Brabant's army."

"Kapitan, you will not use Mr. Brabant's name so freely in connection with this force of men."

"Yes sir. So, will we support the revolt as we did in Panama?"

"Yes, but this time will be different. This time we will not rely on some revolutionary government to take control. We will be in charge."

"What do you mean, 'in charge'?"

"All I will tell you now is that Chiapas will be our new home, and there will be no Latinos or aborigines trying to tell us what to do. I will tell you more, later. Now get the men moving," the Colonel said crisply.

After the captain briefed the teams on their mission, six pairs of mercenaries in jungle fatigues and all carrying M-16 automatic rifles, began a trek through the thick jungle growth to cover the area assigned to them. Corporal Joseph Beck and Private Werner Happler were one of the six teams of men. They were continually diverted by thick undergrowth, as they made their way through the jungle. The heat was oppressive, especially since they were carrying a rifle and backpack. Sweat ran down their necks and, in no time, their shirts were wet. The straps of their packs began to rub the wet fabric against their shoulders. Beck continually checked his compass to ensure they stayed on the course assigned to them.

After the first hour, Private Happler stopped and turned to the corporal. "Joseph, what the hell are we doing in this god-forsaken place, and where are we going?"

"Werner, you are a soldier, and you should know we just follow orders."

"Yes, true, but why here?"

"I understand we are setting up a camp on the other side of the border in Mexico and we will be training the Indians."

"What for?" asked Happler.

"Werner, you are a mercenary, and you do as you are told without question in this army."

"Army. What army? Keitel acts as if this is the Wehrmacht. Many of us are ex-soldiers from the GDR, but with the others, especially the locals, well, it's not the same."

"No, it isn't the Wehrmacht or the GDR, but you are a very well-paid mercenary. I heard the officers say Oberst Keitel and General Von Papen want this army to be like the Verfügungstruppen Waffen SS of the Third Reich, and they will have it their way. You have not been with us long, but I have seen Keitel beat those who disobey orders and execute those who try to desert, and he seems to enjoy it. Do not fall into disfavor with him. Now, we have a job to do, so let's get going."

"I will do as I am told, but we must take a break. I'm tired."

"I'm tired, too. After all, we were loading the trucks until three in the morning. We will stop for a break soon."

After walking for another ten minutes, the two men came into a small clearing, and Joseph said, "Okay, Werner, let's take a break."

The men took off their packs and sat with their backs to a tree. Joseph took a drink from his canteen, leaned back against the tree, and closed his eyes. As Werner was drinking from his canteen, he looked out at the jungle. There was a very dense growth of underbrush with a dark area, which could be the entrance to a cave.

He looked at his partner. His head was back against a tree, his eyes were closed, and he was breathing heavily from his mouth. Joseph had fallen asleep. Werner walked to the opening, took his flashlight from his belt, and shined it into the cave. As he looked in, he realized it was not a cave he was looking into, but a room.

He looked more closely at the outside, and he could see there were walls behind the brush. This was a building which, over time, became completely covered by jungle growth. As he moved inside, he adjusted the flashlight to a broad spread of light, but he could only make out some very gray-looking walls.

The coolness of the interior was a welcome change to the heat of the jungle, but it made him shiver not with cold, but with uneasiness. The noises of the jungle faded as he moved into the room. There were many shadows created by his light, but nothing he saw took definite shape. As his eyes adjusted to the darkness, he could make out faint figures painted on the walls. One looked like a man's body with a jaguar's head and claws. He adjusted the light to shine on the painting with a more direct beam. As he looked more closely, the figure seemed as if it was preparing to leap out after him. Werner turned his head quickly, as he thought he heard the scraping of feet on the floor. He began to perspire profusely, despite the coolness of the interior.

His inquisitiveness began to turn to fear, so he decided to get out quickly. As he began to back up, he unexpectedly bumped into a wall and dropped his rifle and flashlight. The clatter of the rifle hitting the floor sounded like a cannon, and the light spun around as it hit the floor, creating a myriad of shadows. His heart was pounding in his chest so hard he could hear it. His breath was coming in gasps, and he thought to himself, just find your rifle and get out!

He picked up the flashlight and swept the beam back and forth searching for his rifle. As he bent down to pick up his rifle, he saw a flash of something shiny out of the corner of his eye. He turned his flashlight in that direction and ,suddenly, in the pool of light were two bare feet. As he rose, he heard a voice, which froze his body in place with terror.

"This is the temple of the Ancient Ones."

He began to raise his light as he heard a hissing sound and saw a shiny object flashing toward him. As the object swept into the light, he realized it was a blade. Before he could react, he felt a sting as the blade plunged into his abdomen. The sting became a fire as it ripped through his stomach and sliced up to his chest. The breath rushed out of him as he felt something hit bone. He screamed, dropped the light, and grabbed his stomach in agony. His hands felt like someone had poured a thick liquid full of slippery eels in them. He tried to cough but could not because his mouth was full of his blood. Werner was conscious of a strong odor and realized he was holding his intestines. He fell forward in a heap on the floor.

Joseph suddenly awoke to what seemed to be an echoing scream. When he looked around and did not see Werner, he got up quickly and grabbed his rifle. He thought the scream came from his right, but he was not sure. Maybe Werner went into the jungle to relieve himself and killed an animal. Yes, he thought, that could be it. After all, the lieutenant told them there were jaguars in this jungle. He waited and looked for Werner to come out of the brush and then called to him. "Werner, where are you?" Nothing. "Private, answer me."

Joseph walked across the clearing in the direction from which he heard the scream. He, too, noticed the opening. He looked in and convinced himself Werner had entered the cave and surprised an animal. Yes, he thought, he killed a big cat! However, suddenly he said aloud, "I didn't hear a gunshot."

He gripped his rifle harder as if holding it tighter would somehow give him more protection. He called out, "Werner, are you in there? Answer me." He heard the echo from his own voice, but nothing else. With his left hand, he reached for the flashlight on his belt, while his right hand was holding his rifle pointed straight ahead, his finger on the trigger. He turned on the light with his left hand and grasped it to the barrel of the rifle, so wherever he shined the light, he would also be pointing his rifle.

He slowly entered and could see the floor and the walls were stone slabs, like the ancient Indian temples he had seen in Guatemala. He waited for his eyes to adjust to the low level of light. There was a large stone table at one end, which could be an altar. This was not a cave. It appeared he had entered an ancient temple. He passed his flashlight beam around the room and then down to the floor, where he noticed something in a pile.

Joseph walked toward it, looked down, and realized it was a man on his knees slumped over to the ground. There was a strong odor, and he knew something was wrong. His chest constricted and his body tensed as he looked up. He heard a whistling sound and felt a sting as something struck him in the right side of his neck. His head involuntarily turned to the right, and he had a feeling of floating. He looked straight ahead at a camouflage uniform, like his own, and with his name-tag above the left pocket. As he gasped, his head hit the floor and then his body fell forward.

*****

Later that day, an Indian named Tucanil came to the top of the hill above the same temple. He knew where the temple was because his grandfather had been a minor priest in the consanguinity of Maya priests known as Ah Kins. He had taken Tucanil there to receive the sign of the followers from the chief priest, the Ah Kin Mai. His grandfather had warned him that it was forbidden to enter the temple without a priest, but his reasons for being there today were desperate.

Tucanil needed money, and he needed a great deal of it. He could no longer stand to see his wife suffer, and without the operation she needed, she would continue to suffer the rest of her life. The only way he knew to get that much money was to find some of the ancient statues in the temple and sell them. His grandfather had told him ancient warriors protected the temples, and they would not hesitate to kill intruders. His love for his wife overcame the respect and fear he had of the temple and its guardians.

Cool air was drifting down from the mountaintop, creating a dense fog. As he made his way down the hill, he suddenly saw a bright ring of light, which dissipated into a glow in the fog. The light came from a number of men carrying torches. They were very large men wearing headdresses of feathers. He stopped and hid in some bushes so he would not be seen.

He knew the legend of Jacatez, the 'Jaguar Lords', who guarded the temples. According to Mayan legend, the Jacatez were to spend eternity guarding the sacred treasures of the ancient ones and protecting their culture. They were supposed to be superhuman.

The men began marching up the hill in his direction. Fear gripped his heart. He turned and ran into the jungle, as fast as he could, not knowing where he was going. After running for a while, he stopped to catch his breath. He looked back and could no longer see the lights from the men. Suddenly he realized he had no idea where he was and could not see for more than a few feet because of the night and the fog. He would have to wait until morning.

He found a tree with a large crotch well off the ground to protect him against wandering jungle animals. He climbed up and spent a sleepless night thinking about the warriors he had seen and wondering if his idea of coming to this place was wise. Just before dawn, he fell asleep, but the morning sounds of the jungle animals and birds woke him. The day was clear, so he climbed higher up in the tree to see where he was and saw the trail to the temple.

He thought about the protectors of the temple and the fear he had felt the night before. But there was nothing else he could do. Since it was daylight, he decided it might be safe to go back. As he came to the entrance, he approached cautiously and peered inside. It was very dark. He grabbed a handful of dried grass, twisted it, and lit it with a match. He entered, holding the burning grass with his arm outstretched so he could see in front of him.

The light from the burning grass was faint. He could see shadows in the room but could not make out what they were. He felt his way along a wall and bumped into a flat, hard surface, like a table. As he ran his hand along the table he felt a flat round piece of pottery that had protrusions sticking up from the edges. He picked it up and put it in his sack. He began to perspire.

Above the tabletop, there was a small ledge of stone. He slid his hand along the ledge until he knocked something off onto the table. He jumped at the sound. He could not see what had fallen, but when he reached for it, he thought it felt like a small statue. He put it into his sack. As he walked along the wall adjacent to the table, the light from the burning grass began to diminish and die.

He turned to leave to get some more grass to light his way. As he walked toward the light of the door, he stumbled and fell over a large object on the floor. He reached out with his right hand to push himself up and touched something wet and sticky. He quickly drew his hand back. He got to his knees and reached out again carefully to see what was on the floor. His hand touched the fur of an animal. There was no movement and no breathing. He moved his hand across the animal and touched some bare skin and then a nose. "La Madre de Dios!" he gasped with terror, as he realized he was touching a face.

He jumped up, and ran to the opening. He looked down, and his hands were covered with blood. With terror in his heart, he ran through the jungle. The leaves and branches of the trees and brush hit him in the body and the face, but it did not slow him down.

He ran until he was at the top of the hill overlooking the temple. There was no one following him. When he got to a stream, he immersed his head in the water and then washed the blood off his hands. His heart was still pounding. He looked around to see if anyone was coming and, then, thought about the pieces he had put into his sack. He took them out and examined them. The round disk had raised protrusions all along the edge of the disk, but it also looked as if there was something carved into the surface. The other piece was a statue encrusted with soil. He washed the object in the stream, and parts of it glistened a beautiful green in the sunlight.

He was beginning to breathe more easily. He sat back and studied the figure. It looked like the legendary protector of the Maya's, Jacatez; half cat, half man. He, again, became tense and frightened. He could not go back to the temple. Jacatez had killed and would kill him, too, if he went back. He looked around in fear and decided to go home.

When Tucanil's wife saw what he had in his sack she asked, "Have you gone to the forbidden place?"

"No, no, I found them in a cave in the mountains," he lied. "I will sell these and get money to fix your leg. Soon you will have no more pain."

*****

Back at the convoy of trucks, Colonel Keitel asked, "Kapitän, have all the patrols returned?"

"All but Corporal Beck and Private Happler," the captain responded.

"What? Have you tried to contact them by radio?"

"Yes sir, I have. But, you know, in these mountains the transmission and reception can be poor."

"What do you think happened to them? Are they the type to desert?"

"No sir. Becker and Happler are good Hessian soldiers who served in the army of the GDR. They would not desert. Maybe they are lost. After all, compasses can be misguiding in these mountains. They will probably be here soon."

"We cannot wait, Kapitan. Radio the convoy following us to keep an eye out for them. Let's get moving."

CHAPTER TWO

Alek Roman was sitting on the veranda of his rented house in one of his favorite places in the world, the Pacific coast of Mexico, thinking of his past and where his future would take him. He had been in this tropical paradise for the last four weeks, soothing the pains in his battered body and psyche from the past ten years of abuse. Abuse brought on by a profession that put him in places and situations constantly fraught with danger, where people were disposable commodities, and lawless and barbaric actions were common in the pursuit of wealth and power.

As he sat back and thought about the many dances he had with death, the scar on the bottom of his foot began to itch. The wound had been caused by a poisoned punji stake that could have killed him. Luckily for him, whoever put the stake in the underbrush did not get enough urine on the point. As he rubbed his foot, he thought about the scar on his face, which was hidden by his eyebrow. It had come from an axe hung in a tree, meant to decapitate the person who tripped the lever. His quick reflexes saved him from anything worse than a minor wound.

The only other prominent scar was low on his abdomen. The scar could not be seen unless he was being examined medically or intimate with someone. When those intimate moments occurred, there was always the question of how it happened. It was interesting to see the expression on the lady's face when he would tell her a ten-year-old had shot him. All of these incidents, over the years, had hardened Alek to a degree where he trusted no one and accepted nothing at face value.

Yet, on his last assignment, he came close to death because he hesitated to act quickly and decisively and allowed his pursuers to gain the advantage. He survived, this time, because he was lucky, but it seemed the hard veneer he had developed, which was his protection, was beginning to melt away. If he continued on this way, he might end his career and his life, prematurely.

Therefore, he had decided it was time to change his life. He began taking inventory of things like his education, work experience, life style, and training. This was déjà vu. He remembered doing the same thing when he was about to graduate from college. He never had a specific plan for his education. His friends chose their academic major with a career as their goal. His goal in college had been to merely get a degree. When he graduated, he had no idea what he wanted to do, so he returned home to discuss his future with his best friend, his father.

Mikhail Roman's, Mike to his friends, first job was in the U.S. Army. When World War II broke out, he had just finished high school. He, like so many others, joined the U.S. Army because he considered it his duty to fight for his country. He liked the army and even considered making it his career, but he had to come home to care for his aging father.

When Alek arrived home, he and his father discussed Alek's future. It was obvious that Alek had no goal in mind for a career. Mikhail knew the Army would force a career direction for its recruits. So, after some discussion, he suggested his son enter the military service, and Alek agreed because he could not come up with a better plan.

His OCS training was primarily on how to be an officer and how to lead men. The concepts were not difficult for him to learn, but they were difficult for him to apply. He discovered that, when action was required, his tendencies were to rely on himself. After graduation from Officers Candidate School as a Second Lieutenant, he thought he would get some training, which, along with his college education, would provide a future career for him. Instead, he was selected for advanced training in Intelligence, then in counterinsurgency. Not exactly, what he had in mind. After finishing his training, the Army sent him anywhere the U.S. had interests to protect.

Alek's army career was successful, with a number of aberrations. Some were moderate highs, brought on by acts of valor, some were lows, usually caused by improvising instead of following orders. However, there were more lows than highs, with the most significant aberration a downward blip right near the end of his enlistment. That is when the Army and Alek decided to part company.

After his release from the military, and with some coercion from a friendly politician, the government hired him to do similar work to what he had done in the Army. As his career progressed, he became one of the most expert counterinsurgents in the government service and a highly paid employee. This had been his career for the last ten years.

When Alek decided it was time to leave government service, he notified his controller. He was directed to report to Washington and was told, by the head of his department, that he could not just quit. All agents stayed with the agency, in some capacity, for their entire career. Alek contacted his father's best friend, Senator Paul McGruder, who had helped him before. Eventually, Alek got a call from the head of his agency saying that they would not discharge him, but they would put him in an inactive status.

Over the years, he had spent little of the money he had earned, since he was usually on Uncle Sam's expenses. He had invested his earnings and his inheritance and, now, had sufficient funds invested to support himself.

So here he was on the veranda of his beachfront house. He had sublet his apartment in Washington and gave away or stored all of his worldly possessions. It took a number of weeks for him to unwind. He slept late, read, walked on the beach, and totally ignored the world. No newspapers, radio, or TV, just solitude. He did call Senator McGruder to let him know where he was and to thank him for his help. McGruder said he was happy to help the son of his best friend.

He had been in Mexico for five weeks, and as he looked out at the ocean, he thought it was time to begin to plan what he would do in his new life. However, it was another perfect day here in paradise, so why not let the planning go for another day.

Alek was a people watcher, and he liked to make a game of what was going on at the beach. He would look at the tourists and guess who they were and what kind of life they had. He looked at an elderly couple as they walked along the shoreline, probably retired. She was looking for shells, and he was exercising his neck muscles by rotating his head to watch the young girls walking by. Each seemed focused on what they were doing and accepting of each other.

Closely following was another couple, who looked to be on the lean side of their fifties. They were rather ordinary. They were both milky white, and the man looked to be the type that never broke into a sweat from physical exertion. His wife trailed slightly behind, and she, also, looked like she avoided exercise. She had on one of those bathing suits with a little skirt, an attempt to hide her middle age spread, but it was a poor attempt.

The next was a man who looked like a successful businessman, with a cigar in his mouth and a stomach protruding enough that if it were on a woman, it would be a sure sign of being pregnant. His wife had on one of those gold shiny bathing suits, which was only meant to be worn outside of the water. Alek decided to have a closer look, so he picked up the binoculars and focused in on them. He had originally brought the binoculars to look at the sea life and the birds, but they had quickly become part of his people watching. As he focused on the woman, he saw a diamond ring as big as her knuckle on her left hand and a bracelet full of diamonds on her wrist. They were probably staying in the opulent hotel up the beach. He moved the binoculars up to look at their faces. Her husband looked deep in thought, as if he were wondering if any of his subordinates were planning his overthrow while he was on vacation. Suddenly the couple started to walk much faster, probably so she could get in the shade, and he could call the office.

He finally decided he had enough people watching. As he turned to readjust the chair to a reclining position, he caught a movement out of the corner of his eye. A woman was walking, not across the beach as the others were, but down to the beach from somewhere to the right of his beach cottage. She was wearing a long beach dress and, under her hat, he could see jet-black hair. She was carrying a bag and a folding beach chair. He could not see much of her, since her dress was up to her neck and down to her ankles, but when she moved there were some interesting ripples in her dress.

His curiosity got the best of him, so he decided to see where she was going. She stopped halfway down to the water's edge, unfolded her beach chair, and spread out a towel. She, then, took out some items from the bag and set them next to her chair. She took off her hat and bent down in order to lift the beach dress over her body. As she removed the dress, he could see her legs were well muscled, but smooth, shapely, and lovely.

The next thing he saw was her derriere. Each side was like a drop of water rolling down a windowpane. As she continued to lift up her beach dress, he saw the woman's pale orange bathing suit, which was backless and bright in contrast to her dark skin. He grabbed his binoculars quickly, in order to see what he considered a very important part of her, before she sat down. As the binoculars focused on her he moved them down to see the curvature at the base of her back where it met her derriere. He was suddenly preoccupied with an image of his hand sliding down the woman's back until it found the most marvelous part of her anatomy.

As if to interrupt his reverie, the woman finished removing her dress and shook her head until her hair flowed back and forth on her shoulders like silk. She reached back, grabbed her hair, and tied it into a knot on the top of her head. He kept expecting her to turn around; instead, she just sat down in the beach chair and reached for a magazine.

Alek sat back for a moment, looked up at the sky, and wondered how he could get this beauty to turn around. His curiosity was highly aroused. He decided that if the rest of her was as good as what he had seen, he wanted to figure out how he could meet her.

When he looked back at the woman, he noticed the men, walking along the water's edge, and some of the women, were looking up at his beach lady. His curiosity finally peaked, and he decided to go and see her for himself. He got up and climbed over the low wall of the veranda. The sand was hot on his feet, and as he walked toward the shoreline, he was trying to think of something clever to say. As he approached her, he opened his mouth to speak and instead yelled, "Ouch," as he stepped on something sharp in the sand. He grabbed his foot in pain and ungracefully fell on his derriere in the process.

The woman heard Alek yell out and looked up with surprise. This is when he saw her face. Wow, he thought. Her eyes were as big and black as night, and her lips were full and a deep orange color. As she turned to look at him, the material in her bathing suit was stretched across her breasts. Very nice, he thought. Not big, but beautifully shaped, almost too beautifully shaped. The look of surprise left her face, and a smile bordering on laughter began to appear. She had apple cheeks from being pushed up by a perfect smile.

As he got up, he looked down and realized he had stepped on her hairbrush. "Sorry," he said, as he picked it up. "I hope I didn't break it."

"No, it's alright," she said looking at the brush. "I'm sorry. It must have dropped out of my bag. I hope you didn't break anything else," she said with a smile.

"Well, I guess we're both sorry, and no one got hurt, and nothing got damaged, so I guess everything is alright."

"Are you sure? You certainly came crashing down on your...um...well...did you hurt yourself?"

"No, just my pride," he said. "I usually try to make a better impression."

"Who were you trying to impress?" she asked teasingly.

"Well I didn't quite mean it that way. I was sitting up there on my veranda, and I thought I would go for a swim," he said.

"Isn't the water kind of cold this time of the day?" she asked with a coy smile.

"Yes, I usually...ah...ah...well, no, I was not going swimming. You're right; the water at this time of the day is cold. To tell you the truth, I saw you setting up your chair on the beach, and I thought I would welcome you to my beach."

"Oh," she asked, "is this your beach?"

"No, I didn't mean it that way either. Look, I have been staying here for a few weeks, and I kind of look at it as my beach. It's a public beach, and anyone is welcome, especially you," he said.

"Really. Is that your standard line or just your beach line?" she asked again with that great smile.

"I don't have a standard line or a beach line," he said with a smile of his own.

"Well, you sure seem the type who has a line for all occasions, although I must say, your entrance could use some improvement," she said as she tittered.

Alek returned her smile and said, "Oh no, my entrance was fine; it was my landing that could use some work." They both laughed, and he was captivated by the look in her eyes.

"Well, you could start over again," she said.

"No, no," he said quickly. "I wasn't even sure how I was going to get to talk to you, and, now that I'm here, I'm not going to lose the ground I literally gained," he said with a laugh.

"So you came down to talk to me."

"Sure," he said. "I always greet the most beautiful ladies on the beach. You were lucky you chose this spot."

"Really," she said indignantly.

"What do you mean?" he asked.

"Men are so controlling, they think everything that happens is because they want it to," she said.

"You mean this meeting was not my idea?" he asked.

She smiled smugly and said, "Sure, it was your idea."

"Well, if that's so, why do I suddenly feel like I'm the spider caught in his own web? Or was it my web?" he asked.

She avoided the answer and said, "My name is Cara Amelot," as she offered her hand.

"I'm Alek Roman," he said as he took her hand in his.

"Alex, as in Alexander?" she asked.

"No, it is Alek, with a 'k' at the end, as in Aleksey."

"Hmm, very different. Is it a family name?"

"Well you might say so. I'm of Russian descent, and my great grandfather was also named Aleksey. He was named after his great grandfather, so the name kept skipping a generation, and I happened to be the right generation."

"Oh," she said, "but Roman doesn't sound Russian."

"When my grandfather came to the United States, he decided not to use his real name on his immigration papers. Since he was a supporter of the Czar Romanoff, he decided Roman would be a good American adaptation to use."

"That's very interesting. Are you going to save Aleksey for your great grandson?" Cara asked.

"Sure, that would be nice. But first I have to have a son," he said with a smile.

"Oh, you're not married."

"No, not yet," he said.

"Not yet? Do you have plans?" Cara asked.

"No, but who knows what will happen," Alek said as he laughed. "And is Kara with a 'K' like in Anna Karenina?"

"No, it is Cara with a 'C' not a 'K.' My father named me after a flamenco dancer named 'Caracol,' but it's also the name of an ancient city. Amelot is Spanish, and my abuelo a few generations back was a Duke, Serrano Francisco Amelot."

"I have heard of the Caracol, but I know it as a city in northern Chiapas."

"Have you been in the village long?" asked Cara. "From the darkness of your tan, it looks like you've been here for some time."

"Yes, for a few weeks," he said. "You look like you've been here for some time, too."

"Oh, not long," she said. "I tan easily. I'm in a condo up the beach, and I've been spending my time either indoors or catching rays on the balcony. This is only my second time on the beach."

"Your second time? I didn't see you here before," he said.

"Well, the beach in front of my condo is next to the hotel and is very busy. So, I tried to sit near the rocks yesterday, but there always seemed to be a group of kids or adults who think they are climbing Everest. It's much quieter here," said Cara.

"I'm glad you picked this part of the beach to spend your day," he said. As he looked up at the sun, high in the sky, he realized they had been talking for quite awhile. He felt the rumbling in his stomach, which told him it was lunchtime. He turned to Cara and said, "I usually have lunch about this time. Would you like to join me?"

"What did you have in mind?" she asked.

"The hotel up the beach has a restaurant on the water which is open to the breezes off the bay. You can sit and watch the sun, sea, and people while you have a great lunch. They have excellent grouper and shellfish. Do you like seafood?"

"I like most seafood as long as it's not still crawling or swimming," Cara said.

"They have both. So shall we go?" Alek asked.

"Alright. Is it very far?" asked Cara.

"No, it's just about a half a mile down the beach."

"I'll have to take my things back to the condo first. I don't want to carry them all over the beach," she said.

"You don't have to. You can put them on my veranda. They'll be fine there, and, then, I will have an excuse to walk you back here," said Alek with a smile.

"I guess that's okay," she said.

He helped Cara gather her things, and they walked up to the beach cottage. They put them on the veranda, and she reached into her bag and pulled out a wrap-around skirt to put over her bathing suit. He grabbed the T-shirt, which was on the chaise, and they left.

They made some small talk as they walked up the beach. When they got to the restaurant, the hostess came to seat them at Alek's favorite table, overlooking the ocean. The hostess handed them a menu, told them about the specials for the day, and then left.

Cara turned to him and said, "Nice table. She seemed to know you wanted this one in particular."

"Yes," Alek said, "I come here every day, and they have gotten used to me asking for this table."

The waiter arrived, and they ordered drinks. Cara asked for a Pina Colada, and Alek, a Mexican beer.

They looked at the menu, and Cara said, "Oh, shrimp ceviche, one of my favorites. I think that is what I'll have."

"I guess I'll have a grouper sandwich. It really is very good. They serve it on the Mexican version of a sourdough roll."

They ordered and, then, looked out at the pelicans that were also having fish for lunch. Neither of them said much of anything until the food came. They ate their lunch and exchanged comments about the food and the surroundings. When they were finished, he turned to Cara.

"So this is your second week here. Is this your annual vacation?" he asked.

"No actually, it is more like a business trip," she said.

"Oh really, what kind of business?" asked Alek.

She looked at him and said, "I'd rather not get into that right now. I'm enjoying the restaurant and the company. I don't want to talk about business now."

"That's great," said Alek, "would you like to take a walk on the beach?"

"Alright," she said. "I need to walk off some of that lunch."

As they walked out of the restaurant, he looked at her from behind and thought, okay, but be sure not to lose too much of those good parts. As they strolled, they got closer and closer until their movement made them touch, now and then. He loved it. He looked at her a number of times and thought about how lucky he was to have met such a beautiful woman.

Cara noticed he kept looking at her and finally said, "Do I have something left on my face from lunch? You keep staring at me."

"No, not at all," he said, "I was just thinking about a game I play when I'm watching people walk by my beach."

"Do you try to guess what they do and what their life is like?" asked Cara.

He looked at her with surprise and said, "Yes I do. And do you do the same thing?"

"Yes, it's fun. Of course, I'm not as sophisticated as you are with this pastime."

"What do you mean?" asked Alek.

"I saw the binoculars on the chair when we went up to your cabana. Are they for watching people, or are you a bird watcher too?"

"Well," he said, "I guess a little of both. I was wondering if any of the people sitting on their verandas along the beach were looking at us and making any suppositions."

"And, if they were, what do you think they'd come up with?" asked Cara.

"I'm sure they would be looking at us with envy and thinking I have great taste, being with such a beautiful woman."

"And the women are thinking about how fortunate I am to be with such a handsome man," she said with a smile.

"Well, since we are both so lucky, we should stop worrying about what they think and just enjoy ourselves," he said.

About that time, they arrived at Alek's cabana. "Would you like to have a drink? We could collaborate on people watching," said Alek.

"Okay," she said. "It's so hot. I could really go for one of those nice, cold Mexican beers, if you have one."

"We always have cold beer available here. Just have a seat, and I will provide the best beer and a fresh lime to go with it."

He went into the kitchen, got two beers, and cut up some lime. When he arrived out on the veranda, Cara had removed her wrap and was laying on one of the lounge chairs. He placed the tray with the beer and lime on a table between them and handed her a bottle. He took off his T-shirt and sat in the other chaise.

She watched him as he took off his shirt and thought, nice back, good shoulders, good tone in the arms, and a nice slope to the waist. Not a weight lifter, but certainly in good shape.

He noticed her watching him but did not respond. Instead he said, "I'm sorry I forgot to bring glasses. Would you like one?"

"No problem," she said.

He held out the plate full of limes, and she took two pieces. She put one in the bottle of beer and took the other to suck the juice from it.

"So you like lime." Alek asked.

"Yes, I hope you don't mind. They're so refreshing."

"I know," he said, "I do the same thing."

"You didn't do it at the restaurant," she said.

"Well, I was just trying to be on my best behavior," he said. "No sucking limes, no slurping food, and no eating with my fingers. Well, I guess I did eat my fries with my fingers."

"Your manners were impeccable," Cara said.

They sat for a while, not talking. They just looked out at the blue sky, the white caps on the ocean, and the birds flying overhead. He could not believe how they had just met and could just sit like this. When he was with a woman, he usually felt he had to be entertaining and witty. With Cara, however, he was quite comfortable just being there with her. As he looked over, she turned to lie on her stomach. There were those beautiful mounds of pleasure. "Stop it," he said to himself, "you sound like some kind of trashy love novel." He also turned on his stomach, looked over at her, and closed his eyes.

CHAPTER THREE

Some time later, Alek slowly opened his eyes and jumped up when he realized he had fallen asleep. He looked over to the other chaise and saw Cara was gone.

When he noticed her beach things were also gone, he mentally kicked himself. "What an idiot I am," he said. "Here, I finally meet a beautiful woman, who is so easy to be with, and what do I do? I fall asleep. Well, she's gone. I can't believe I was so comfortable with her that I just dozed off." He looked at his watch. 5:30PM. He must have slept for at least an hour.

"So, what do I do now," he said to no one in particular. "She said she was staying at a condo down the beach, but which one? There are only fifty or so in the area. Well, I'll just have to check out each one until I find her."

As he got up to go in, he noticed a piece of paper on the table. He picked it up and read, "Hi, sleepy. You looked so relaxed I didn't have the heart to wake you. If you're not busy tonight, how about letting me make you dinner. I'm at 9734 Baja Boulevard, apartment 310. If you want to accept, be there at 7:00. If not, call me at 71860 and have a good excuse."

"You are one lucky SOB, Alek Roman," he said aloud.

He quickly went inside and turned on the shower. He took off his shorts and stepped under the warm spray. The spray of the water made him feel the effect of the day's sun on his back. He finished his shower quickly. As he rubbed his body with a towel, he could feel the old scars again, but these were not the things he wanted to think about now. He had a hot date, and he was really looking forward to it. "Listen to me," he said to himself, "a hot date, where did I get that from?" He smiled at the idea that things were working out, and he would get to see Cara again.

He looked at the clock and saw it was 6:30. He put on a pair of old faded jeans that looked more white than blue, and then he slipped a navy blue shirt over his head. He brushed his hair vigorously as he looked into the mirror.

"Well, you don't look too bad for someone coming up on 35," he said. He stuck his feet in a pair of sandals and went into the kitchen to get a good bottle of wine he had picked up at the local liquor store.

He walked out the front door and headed down the road. From the address she had given him, he guessed the condo she was staying in was located a few buildings down the road. As he walked, he savored the coolness of the early evening air and the beautiful flowers growing along the way. He stopped in an open field and picked some wild lilies.

When he reached her building, he looked at his pocket watch. It was 6:55. He entered the building, found the elevator, and punched the number 3. When he got off on the third floor, he looked for 310 and rang the bell. The door opened, and Cara stood there in a flowery silk sun dress, which seemed to caress each curve. It had thin straps and was just low enough to allow him to see the outline of the tops of her breasts. Her black hair glistened, her skin glowed, and the deep red on her lips accented the colors in her dress. He was captivated by her.

"Hola," she said, "welcome to mi casa, Senor."

He looked at her, wanting to say something clever, but, instead, he stood there with the wine in one hand and the flowers in the other.

"Are you going to come in", she asked, "or are you just here to deliver wine and flowers?"

"Uh, yes," he said, "I mean, no. I mean, no, I'm not here to deliver, and, yes, I'm coming in." He felt a little rattled, which was most unusual for him. He had been with many women and none ever rattled him like this. Somehow, Cara seemed to affect his sensibilities by just standing there.

He entered a large room, which had white upholstered chairs and a sofa with muted multi-color patterned pillows strewn about. There was a white rattan dining table and chairs in front of the door which led out to a balcony. A light green carpet covered the floor. There were green plants everywhere, and he felt like he had just walked into a garden.

"You have a beautiful place," he said.

"Thank you. Let me take the wine and flowers."

"The wine is a Pinot Noir, and the flowers are wild, from the vacant field down the road."

"Thank you very much, kind sir," she said. "Would you like a drink?"

"Yeah, that would be great," said Alek.

"What would you like? I have gin, vodka, rum, and beer. I'm having a martini."

"Vodka on the rocks with a peel of lime would be great."

"Okay, coming up. I'll put the flowers in water and make you a drink. If you'd like, you could go out to the balcony, and I'll bring the drinks out there."

"Okay," he said.

He walked out on the balcony and listened to the soft music. Since the balcony faced the ocean, there would be a wonderful view of the sunset. There were two chairs, a coffee table, a sofa, and a telescope on the balcony. He walked over to the telescope and thought it would be great for checking out people on the beach.

He bent over, took a look and his fists clenched involuntarily. He felt an uneasy twinge in his stomach as he realized the telescope was zeroed in on his veranda. He could almost read the headlines on the newspaper he had left on the table. To Alek, being suspicious was a normal reaction, which came from years of being suspicious of everything. That is what helped to keep him alive. He shook his head to clear his mind.

Wait! That was the past, he thought, as he relaxed his body. Why should he be suspicious? It could be a simple explanation. She probably came back and decided to see if he had awakened.

Cara came out onto the balcony with two drinks. "Here you are. I hope you like the vodka. It's not Russian; it's Finnish," she said.

"I'm sure it will be fine," he said. "I noticed you have a telescope. I took the liberty of looking through it, and I must say that's a rather interesting view you have targeted."

Cara blushed slightly and said, "I saw you on the beach the other day and thought I saw you going into your cabana. I just checked it out when I got back."

"Any particular reason other than my good looks?" Alek asked.

"Can we talk about that later? Dinner will be ready in a few minutes, and it cannot wait. I'd hate to spoil it," Cara replied.

"Sure," he said as the feeling of trepidation emerged again, "why not a little mystery after dinner."

She ignored the remark and said, "I have a few things to do in the kitchen, so enjoy your drink, and I'll be right back."

He sipped his vodka like any good Russian would and made an effort to enjoy the ocean view. However, his suspicious mind kept wandering back to what Cara had said about talking later. At that moment Cara came back onto the balcony and said, "Dinner's ready now."

They walked into the dining room where Cara had lit the candles and placed a salad on the table.

"I hope you like paella," she said. "It's in the oven and should be done by the time we finish the salad."

"Paella is one of my favorite dishes," he said.

"Why don't you open your wine? There's a corkscrew on the counter."

Alek opened the bottle, poured each of them a glass, and joined Cara at the table. As they ate dinner, they made small talk about where they were from and where they had been. She said she was from Washington D.C. and attended George Washington University. He told her he grew up in New York and attended Columbia University. They talked about school, but neither offered any information about their current background. Cara produced another bottle of Pinot Noir at some point during the meal, and as they finished the second bottle, he began to feel mellow. They both reached to pour the last of the wine at the same moment. As their hands touched on the bottle, Cara felt a tingling sensation go through her body. She turned to him, and they looked into each other's eyes.

They both began to feel uneasy, and he finally said, "That was a great dinner. I never had paella better than this."

"Thank you for the compliments," she said nervously.

"I thought I was the only one who made paella with just seafood. Where did you learn to make it that way?"

"I learned to make paella when I was in Spain. In Valencia I met a grand lady who taught me how to make paella with the fresh seafood harvested locally. She told me to leave out the meat in order to enjoy the full flavor of the seafood." Cara nervously said, "Would you like to have some coffee on the balcony?"

"I sure would, and if you hurry, we can see the sunset. There is nothing like the sun setting on the ocean. And with the elevation of your condo, the view should be magnificent."

"Okay," said Cara. "I'll be right out."

He went out to the balcony, took a deep breath, and looked up at the sky, not focusing on anything. His body began to feel warm as he thought about the feeling he had when his hand touched hers. The vodka and the wine mellowed him. Any suspicious thoughts he might have had earlier in the night were gone for now. At that moment, Cara came out with a tray and set it on the table. She had brought coffee and a carafe of cognac. She poured two snifters and handed him one. She began to serve the coffee.

"Wait," he said, "don't pour the coffee yet. You'll miss the sunset. The colors keep changing as the sun sets further in the sky."

They stood at the railing sipping their cognac and looking out at the ocean and the sky. The colors began as pink and gray, but they quickly deepened and spread into the low hanging clouds.

Alek put his arm around Cara's waist without thinking, and she did not move away as he pointed down to the water and said, "Don't just watch the sky. When the ocean is this calm, the best colors are across the water."

"On the water?"

"Yes, the ocean is just like a palette for an artist who is painting the sky," he said.

"Beautifully put," she said. "Did you read that somewhere?"

"Yeah, I have to admit I did read it somewhere, but it just flowed out of me because of those two bottles of wine we shared."

"We really did finish both of those bottles of wine, didn't we," she said. "I know I feel a little light headed. Maybe, I'd better forget this cognac."

"Well, I'm not going to. It tastes too good," he said with a smile.

"Good thing you don't have to drive to get home," she said.

The sun began to sink, and they stood close to each other, enjoying the rest of the sunset. Soon, darkness was on them.

"Right now, I feel like I have been transported to another world," said Cara. "It must be the combination of the sunset, the wine, the drinks, and the beautiful evening making me feel like we're in Elysium."

He turned to face Cara with his arm still around her waist. He touched her cheek with his right hand, leaned over, and softly kissed her lips. She put her hands on his shoulders and moved closer to him. They leaned back for a moment, looked at each other, and then he took her face in his hands and kissed her again. Their mouths opened, and they began to explore each other. As he moved his hand down to her waist, it brushed against her breast, which felt warm and soft under the silk of her dress.

She felt the slight touch of his hand, and it created a tingling feeling that traveled through her. He then placed both of his hands on her waist and held her close enough so her breasts were just touching his chest. The sensation to Cara was electrifying. He then moved his hands down her sides to the spot where her waist flared into her hips. They looked at each other again and kissed softly. As he moved his hands to her back, she put her arms around his neck. All inhibition seemed to be lost as they pulled each other's bodies closer.

Cara then grasped his hair in her hands and pushed her lips into his so hard it almost hurt. He squeezed her body even closer to his and she inhaled quick and hard. His hands again slid down her back as he felt the beautiful firm roundness of her and then pulled her lower body to his. They pressed themselves together. She began to kiss him on the neck while she let her hands fall to his waist.

He moved his hands slowly upward until he reached the softness of her skin above the back of her dress. He slipped his fingers under the straps of her dress and pulled them over her shoulders. He put his lips on her neck, shoulders, and then down to her breasts. He trailed the front of her dress downward and as his lips exposed more, he felt the soft warm skin and the firmness of her. He pulled the dress down over her breasts.

He leaned back and looked at her breasts. There was a tan line low on them, and they were round and firm with dark nipples. His mouth moved down to her nipples. As he touched them with his tongue, she gasped and pulled his head hard into her breasts. Then, suddenly, she pulled his hair back and lifted his head back to her mouth. They kissed feverishly.

She leaned back and pulled her arms from the straps of her dress, which then fell to her waist. She lifted his T-shirt up and over his head and pressed the bare skin of her breasts into his chest. She kissed his neck and chest while she slid her hands down to the button on his jeans. She undid the button, slid the zipper down, and reached inside to feel his hardness in her hand. He gasped and caressed her back.

He reached for the waist of her dress, slipped it down over her hips, and let it fall to the floor. He reached down again and slipped his hands inside of her panties.

She tugged downward on his jeans and they fell down over his hips. She slid her hands into his briefs, then reached around and grabbed his buttocks, which flexed even harder as he pulled their bodies closer together.

He lifted her off her feet and put her legs around him. He placed her down on the sofa, bent over her body, and gently pulled down her panties. He knelt down next to her and began to kiss her lips, her chin, her neck, and her breasts. He slowly moved his hands over the soft skin and felt the hardness of her nipples as he held them in his hands and caressed them with his tongue. His lips moved down over her stomach brushing her skin until he kissed the soft insides of her thighs. Her skin was warm and very soft.

Alek stood up and removed his briefs and jeans. Cara looked at his body in the moonlight as he slowly lowered his body to meet hers. He reached down and gently massaged her between her legs. She was already wet and hot. She moaned and gasped for breath. He began to enter her, and as he did, he felt her warmth engulf him. As he lowered his body, he pushed harder and he felt the warmth deep inside of her surrounding him. He was now flat against her body and moving his hips gently in a circular motion. With each motion, she felt him move deeper inside of her. They kissed harder and harder as the rhythm of their bodies increased. He lifted his head and raised his chest up and away from her while maintaining the rhythmic motion. He looked down at her. Her breasts glistened with perspiration, and she breathed heavily. They began to turn their bodies until she was on top.

He lay there motionless for a moment until she adjusted her body. She sat straight up on top of him, and he admired her breasts. They looked lovely in the moonlight. She began a rocking motion and thrust her hips forward and into him. Her body swayed in a sensuously undulating motion. She leaned over and he took her breasts again into his mouth. She gasped and straightened up again while moving her hips faster and faster. He began to move his hips upward and into her, joining in her rhythm. She was now breathing very fast and was making louder sounds that seemed to come from deep inside of her. Suddenly, she seemed to hold her breath as she thrust into Alek as hard as she could and he felt a flood of warmth as she gave one last gasp and fell on top of him.

He held her close and continued to move his hips up and down slowly. She lay against his body for a time just feeling his warmth. She then began to kiss his neck, his lips and his chest. He slid back and up until he was sitting, and she was straddled on top of him. He held her breasts in his hands as he began to thrust upward. She began to control her motion and their bodies came together in a rhythmic motion. They moved harder and faster and he felt himself growing larger inside of her.

He felt his tension rising higher and higher as he pushed every muscle in his body to the maximum. He suddenly reached the point where his body felt like it would burst, and he exploded inside of her. He wrapped his arms around her body, and she did the same as they held each other as tightly as possible. He shuddered and moaned in ecstasy, and they both trembled as they pressed their bodies together.

They were soaked in perspiration, and huddled together in a state of total exhaustion. She gave a little gasp as he withdrew from her body. Alek held Cara gently as she turned until they were side by side. She found a niche in his shoulder and snuggled into it. She lay against him until she fell asleep. After a time, he gently lifted her head and set it on a pillow. He carefully rose so as not to disturb her. He felt a chill as the air cooled with the setting sun. He pulled on his pants and shirt, went into the living room, and found an afghan to cover her.

He returned, covered her, and then sat in the chair watching her sleep. He sat there looking at her and considering the new feelings growing in him. Meeting her like this was so lucky, he thought.

Then, he began to think about how they met. He was always cautious about chance meetings. As he thought, he remembered a few things she had said which aroused his anxieties further. He leaned back in the chair and looked up. The evening sky was full of stars and the moon made it seem as bright as day. It was incredible to see. After a short time, Cara moved slightly and looked up at him.

"Hi," she said, "I guess it was my turn to fall asleep." She stretched her body under the blanket and asked, "Have I been out long?"

"No," he said, "just a short time."

"And you just sat there all this time?"

"Sure, I was looking at the beauty of the night and you."

"Now you're embarrassing me," she said. "I'm not used to drinking so much wine, and I don't know what got into me. I'm sorry I fell asleep."

"That's okay. I love to look out at the night sky and reflect."

"Will you share your thoughts?" she asked.

"Some of them, like how lucky I am to have met you out of all the people wandering on the beach. Being with you is so natural. We talk without having to look for something to say, and even when we don't talk, there's no uncomfortable silences."

"Well, that's good, isn't it?"

"Yes, but I have the feeling our meeting was more than just luck," Alek said sardonically.

"What do you mean?" she asked.

"Well, I thought I was arranging a meeting with you when I came down to the beach today. Now, I'm not so sure. Then, there's the telescope on your balcony pointed at me and what you said we would discuss after dinner."

"Boy, you don't forget a thing do you?"

"No, I have been trained for years to see everything, hear everything, and not to forget."

"I know you have," she said.

"What?" Alek asked with a start.

"I do have something to confess. I knew who you were before we met. I also know what you do, or did," Cara said.

"What? What the hell are you talking about?" he asked as he sat upright in his chair.

"I know that up until a short time ago, you worked as some kind of an operative for the government in various capacities and much of your work was in Central America," Cara replied.

He now understood his meeting with this beautiful lady was a planned mission, and he began to get angrier.

"So, our lovely interlude was staged by you." He looked hard at her and knew the anger in his voice was mirrored by the anger in his eyes.

"No, yes. I mean, no, not all of it. But I can't talk to you like this. Please let me go in and change, and then I'll explain. Please trust me. I'll just be a minute."

Alek's instincts told him to leave, but his emotions told him otherwise. Besides, his curiosity was aroused, and he could not just walk away from her. "Okay," he said, "but make it quick, and I certainly hope you have a good explanation for all of this."

She got up with the afghan wrapped around her and quickly went in through the door. He saw a light go on in the bedroom window of the balcony. He decided it was best to be cautious, so he walked over to the bedroom window. He saw her walk in, throw the afghan on the bed, and stand there naked. He looked at her and, once again, realized how beautiful she was.

She rummaged through some drawers and came up with a pair of sweats and a shirt. When she put them on and turned off the light, he returned to his chair. He heard her moving around in the kitchen. After a few minutes, she came out with a fresh pot of coffee and set it on the table.

"Will you have a cup of coffee?" Cara asked.

"All right," he said indignantly.

Cara handed him the coffee and sat back in the chair.

"I guess I don't really know where to start," she said.

"The truth is always good. How about starting with why you arranged our meeting and why you lured me up here," Alek demanded angrily.

"Look, I did try to meet you, but what happened here tonight was not planned. I only wanted to have a chance to talk to you alone and to try to get you to help me. Then, things got, well, sort of out of hand," she said sheepishly.

"Help you with what?" asked Alek.

"My father," she replied.

"Are you going to tell me what this is all about," Alek said demandingly.

"Okay. My father is Edward Amelot. He's an anthropologist. He was in Mexico City on business. He left there some time ago to go to Chiapas to meet with a man who had sold him some artifacts. Then, he planned to search for an ancient ruin somewhere in southern Mexico, Belize, or Guatemala. I heard from him before he left, but I haven't heard anything since. Neither have any of his friends or associates. He just disappeared."

"So what's that got to do with me?" asked Alek.

"First let me explain something. I came here for help. I was told you were familiar with the area where my father was last seen, and you could direct me to the people who could help me to search for him," she said.

"What are you talking about?" he demanded again.

"I was told you knew people in Mexico, Guatemala, and the rest of Central America who could search for my father without regard for borders and governments. But, I was also told you would not want to get involved, something about your not wanting to reconnect with your past. I was even told you probably wouldn't talk to me about it," Cara said desperately.

"I still don't understand," said Alek.

"Based on what I was told, I felt if I came directly to you to talk to you about my problem, you would not listen. Therefore, I decided to try to meet you socially first, so you would know who I was and give me a chance to talk. Then, something happened here tonight between you and me. It wasn't planned. I guess the wine and the moonlight... well, I'm sorry for what happened."

"Why not go to the authorities?"

"When my father disappeared, I went to the U.S. State Department, and they contacted the governments of Mexico, Belize, and Guatemala. Each said they would do what they could. I asked why the US State Department would not just have someone look for him. I was told the State Department would not send anyone because it was within the domain of the local governments. I tried and tried through the right channels, but it did me no good."

"One of my father's oldest friends is Senator Paul McGruder. I went to him, and he tried to intervene with the State Department and with officials he knew in Mexico. He couldn't get any further, so he told me about you and that he had been a friend of your father. He said you could help me. He said you were the best at what you did, but I'm not exactly sure what that was. He did tell me to remind you everyone needs help sometime, and if you did help me, he would be most grateful, whatever that means."

"McGruder," Alek said under his breath.

"So, you do remember him," she said.

"Remember him? I guess so. He is like family. He was a one of my father's closest and dearest friends. They served together in the Marines in World War II. My father saved his life, and he saved my life, in a way. That's when we became friends, too."

"Will you help me?" she asked.

"First, let's get something straight. What happened between you and me is still suspect. Second, I'm out of the covert operations business for good. Period."

"Please, I'm only asking you to put me in touch with people in Chiapas who could help me find my father," she pleaded.

"Lady, you don't know what you are asking for. In the area you are talking about, the kind of people who could help you are not the kind of people you can deal with. This is not bartering for a pair of sandals on the beach. These are the kind of people who would take your money, your life, and whatever else they want. In addition, there is the political turmoil caused by the MYLN They are a group of local Indians who tried to secede from Mexico in an armed rebellion. The government stopped them, but they will try again. I happen to know they have been buying arms, and next time, it could be an all out war," Alek said.

"If you are trying to scare me, you don't have to. I'm already afraid," she said angrily. "But I'm even more frightened for my father. I have no choice but to try to contact anyone I can to help me find my father. I'm willing to pay for help. Please, can't you just make a call? Give me an address, a name, a letter. I promise I won't bother you anymore," she begged.

"Whoa. First, the senator knows I would not just give you some phone numbers and let you go. He was counting on me being chivalrous, and I am sure he asked you to call him to let him know how our meeting went. Is that right?" Alek demanded.

"Yes, he did tell me to let him know how it went," she said.

"Right, and if you report back that I would not help you or I sent you off with only some names, he'd be in touch with me even if he had to send everyone he knows to find me."

"But I'll tell him anything you want if you just help me make the necessary contacts," Cara pleaded.

"Look, I couldn't have you tell the Senator anything that's a lie. It would be like lying to my own father."

"Then you won't help me?" Cara asked dejectedly.

"I didn't say that. Besides the fact my father and McGruder were best friends, I owe the senator. However, right now, all that has happened today is just rolling round and round in my head. I need time to think. I'm going home now. I have your number. I will call you in the morning," Alek said as he got up to leave.

"Please believe me," she pleaded, "when I say what happened here was not part of a plan. I did conspire to meet you, but that was my only goal when I met you on the beach. I'm not that devious."

"Well, I need time to think. I will call you tomorrow."

As they walked to the door, Cara asked timidly, "What time? I'm sorry, but I just need help so desperately, and I don't know how much time I have."

"I'll come by at noon to talk."

"Please do. I know we can work this out."

CHAPTER FOUR

When Alek left, Cara went back out to the balcony. She thought about what happened with him and, at first, tried to blame it on having too much to drink. The alcohol may have had the effect of relaxing her, but that was not the reason she had been attracted to him. She had never felt like this before. Now, she had one more problem to deal with.

In the meantime, she had to think about what she would do if he said he would not help her find her father. She was at her wit's end. She had approached all of the influential people her father knew, including a number of high government officials. They were all consoling and told her how much they admired her father. They promised to get something done, but there was no urgency in their response. They all passed her off to some subordinate who made gestures, but they carried no influence.

Senator McGruder was the only one who had honestly tried to help. He was an old friend of her father's, who helped the museum with federal grants for research. McGruder knew time was of the essence. After some quick attempts to garner help, he told Cara that Alek was her best option but that he would be hard to convince. He said he would keep on trying from Washington, and he wished her luck.

She had a bad feeling about Alek, after his reaction to the way she contacted him. She had to consider that he might refuse to help her. She was not used to having people say no to her. Throughout her childhood, her father doted over her, and in her adult years, she could get her way with her looks and charm.

Cara's mother, Maria, died when she was four, and her father raised her with the help of a number of au pairs. Edward Amelot was so engrossed in his work, he always felt guilty that he did not spend more time with his daughter. Therefore, unconsciously he made it up by giving her just about anything she asked for.

As a teenager, she could easily be in with any group she wanted because of her beauty and her charisma. But she was taught by her father's example that living up to high standards brought its own rewards and attracted people who had substance, people she liked, people she could trust.

After finishing college with a degree in fine arts, she managed, with her father's help, to get a job with one of the leading commercial galleries in Washington D.C. She spent the first year doing all the menial tasks she thought were meant for underlings, but she always gave a maximum effort in her work.

As she was given some minor artists to preview, the results of her efforts attracted the attention of Madeline Provile, a senior staff member who befriended her. Madeline came from Paris and had worked at the gallery for fifteen years. She saw Cara was, in many ways, like herself; a spirited woman who aspired to much more. She, also, saw Cara had an eye for art, which could be developed for commercial use. She taught Cara to find art wealthy people wanted to buy and to display in their homes. Cara became her protégé, and they traveled all over Europe in their quest for art.

Cara became very successful and eventually developed a following of her own, which included a list of wealthy clients who would call her when they wanted new art to go with their expensive décor. She always kept prospecting for new artists, whose work she would introduce to her clientele.

In her business and travels, she met many men who were wealthy. She had a few affairs but none were serious. Usually these relations started because of her interest in the man, but the interest would eventually wear off. Some men were persistent and wanted more than she was willing to give. She would end those relationships as quickly and painlessly as possible.

Now, there was Alek. She had just met him, but she felt things for him she had never felt for another man. She didn't even know him. He could be a bad person. Then again, Senator McGruder would not offer someone to help who wasn't trustworthy. He said Alek was like a son to him. Besides, she did not believe she could feel this way about anyone who was really bad or evil. She wanted to tell Alek about the feelings she had for him, but right now, helping her father was the most important thing.

She leaned back and thought of her father. Edward Amelot was the best father a girl could have. Because of his work, he was not always there, but when he was needed, nothing stood in the way. He was more than a father; he was her best friend. He was warm, caring, intelligent, and entertaining. They traveled to great places together and had great times. She loved the trips they took to the warm places in the winter and the resorts in the summer. What she did not realize at the time was that all of their excursions were selected by her father, not only to give her a good time, but also a good education. These trips helped her to learn geography, cultures from different parts of the world, and languages. Her friends always thought she was very lucky, and their mothers thought her father was very handsome and witty. She just had to find a way to help him.

He had called her a few weeks ago from Cancun and told her he was going to visit Renaldo Armando, Director of the Museum of Anthropology in Mexico City. He said that he was going to do some research on the new artifacts he had acquired from a man named Castillo. He was very excited about this new discovery and said he thought this could help him prove a theory he had been pursuing for years. He was, then, going to meet with Castillo, and they were going to a secret temple somewhere in the area of Chiapas or, maybe even, Guatemala.

He cautioned her not to tell anyone about the ruin because, if the Mexican Government knew, it would take over, and he wanted an opportunity to see this ruin first. Besides that, he also told her that buying the artifacts from Castillo was illegal, but he would give them to Renaldo's museum when he was finished with them.

When she arrived in Mexico, she immediately attempted to contact Renaldo Armando. He had gone to Europe, and she kept trying to locate him there. She also tried to contact any other people she knew her father might visit in Mexico City. Most had heard from him while he was there, and a few had seen him, but no one knew where he was going when he left Mexico City.

She, finally, located Renaldo in England and talked to him.

"Mr. Armando, I am so worried about my father. I haven't heard from him in some time. I know he is working on some new artifacts he bought. Please, when did you last see him?" Cara asked of Renaldo.

"Your father visited with me for about ten days," said Renaldo. "He told me about the artifacts and the ruins he thought were in Chiapas. While he was here, he worked in the museum, daily looking through old records of ancient cities trying to find a lead to the ruins."

"Do you know when he left and where he was going?" Cara asked.

"Yes, he was going to Tapachula, in Chiapas, in search of the temple. I tried to stop him, but he was adamant about going to meet the man who sold him the artifacts. I have a very good friend in Tapachula who is a retired professor and a prominent man in the community. His name is Antonio Dega. I gave your father Dega's name, address, and a letter of introduction. I called Dega and told him your father would be contacting him to assist him in establishing the origin and age of his artifacts. I also told Dega your father was going to be looking for a man in the area and asked that he try to help him find the man."

"Do you know if he contacted Dega?"

"Yes, I received a note from Dega that said they had met and were planning to meet again. Since then, I have tried to contact Dega by phone, but to no avail. The phone service in Chiapas is not very good. I don't know if they met again, or if he met with Castillo. Cara, I tried to talk him out of going, but you know him. Once he gets an idea and a direction, he is resolute in his quest," Renaldo said caring.

"Since I have not heard from my father, I will probably go to Chiapas to see if I can find him."

"Cara, it is a very remote area of Mexico, and there have been political problems recently, which have become violent. Please, I know your father would not want you to go there."

"Thank you Mr. Armando, but I have to go. I will be careful, and I will leave a number for you when I get there."

"I will do everything I can to contact Dega, but the communications lines there are often out for weeks at a time for many reasons. Please, Cara, be careful," Renaldo said paternally.

The conversation with Renaldo was not the most comforting thing Cara had heard. She had to go to Tapachula, but she knew she needed help. Alek was her only hope. If she had just called him and approached him on a purely business basis, none of this personal involvement would have occurred.

Why didn't she just tell him about her father? That was her intention, but she wanted to get to know him first. Then, when they did meet, she felt so comfortable with him that she had let it become too personal. She always took the lead in her relationships and controlled the situations. All of a sudden, she was not the one in charge.

She knew she had to find a way to help her father and make Alek understand she was not being devious. She had to convince him to help her even if it meant destroying what could be a wonderful relationship.

CHAPTER FIVE

Alek left Cara's condo and walked toward the deserted beach. As he walked along, he noticed the brightness of the moon and the shadows of the palm trees. He needed to clear his head and to consider what had happened today, so he walked until he got to the rocky breakwater. He walked out to the end of the rocks and sat watching the waves thrashing below thinking about his day.

He had just had one of the most incredible and contradictory days of his life. Cara was the most enchanting woman he had ever been with. He was totally at ease in her presence and fascinated by her beauty; however, she did deceive him. He looked up at the sky and thought, what should I do? Since McGruder had sent her, he could probably trust her. After all, McGruder would not have told her about him if he didn't trust her.

Senator McGruder… Alek thought about what this man he had meant to him. There was a time when he was in really deep trouble, and McGruder was his savior. He could remember the string of events that brought him to this dilemma.

He was nearing the end of his enlistment, and he was not sure he wanted to continue his career as a counterinsurgent in the Army. After completion of each assignment, he would end up at some out of the way U.S. military base, assigned to the transient company until he got new orders. After his last assignment in the Mekong Delta, he was sent to Taiwan. The commander of his transient company was of one of the most despicable people he had ever known, Major Kurt Epling.

Major Epling believed in the Aryan myth that 'his kind' was morally superior, and he looked down on everyone who was not exactly like him. Black, Jew, Hispanic, and Oriental; he hated them all equally. However, he was a closet bigot who brought his hatred out only when it would not be seen by anyone in authority, especially his superior officers.

Alek had observed Epling's and his friends' bigotry in various drinking establishments in proximity of the Army base. One night, at one of these local bars, Epling and some of his cronies were tormenting an old Chinese man who was bussing tables. Their endless tormenting so upset the old man that he dropped a tray of dirty dishes; as a result, he was berated and kicked by the owner of the bar. Alek intervened with the owner and then told Epling exactly what he thought of him and his fascist behavior. Epling was drunk and turned his tirade on Alek. He told Alek he should be more concerned about his own kind ,and then he ranted about the inferiority of the yellow race. Sitting, unseen, in a booth nearby was the regimental commander and his adjutant, who had overheard Epling's entire speech. When they arose and confronted him, he did a quick song and dance about being misunderstood. The colonel left, but he let Epling know he would not forget the incident. Epling blamed Alek for exposing his bigotry to his superiors.

He turned to Alek and said," You will pay for this, Lieutenant." His friends quickly got him out of the bar. He later told his staff he was going to get even with Alek, and he did. While Alek was waiting for an appropriate assignment, Epling took the opportunity to send him to The Rock, and it was a young recruit, Private John Cody, who had the bad luck to be sent there with him.

Alek knew about The Rock, an island on the edge of hostile territory where Army intelligence had a two-man post. Those assigned to the island acted as communications' observers and analysts. This was not what he was specifically trained to do, but he had enough knowledge, so Major Epling could get away with sending him there under the guise of not having a trained senior person available. Alek didn't raise any objections since the normal tour on the island was two weeks followed by an R&R period and then reassignment. He could do the two weeks and would then make contacts to get him out of Taiwan.

The work on The Rock was all very secretive, and John Cody was there because he was trained as a radio intercept operator. John and Alek met briefly at their departure by boat, and when they arrived, the crew they were replacing greeted them. The boat dock was on the far side of the island. A large hill separated the dock area from the bunker that was to be their new home. The men whom they were replacing helped carry their gear and supplies to the bunker.

They told Alek and Cody the island was shelled by artillery fire almost every day from the mainland miles away, but the shells couldn't penetrate the bunker even with a direct hit. They briefed them on the daily maintenance and told them not to stray too far away from the safety of the bunker. They rushed through their briefing and, then, couldn't get off the island fast enough. Alek and Cody stowed their gear, settled in, and began monitoring the radio broadcasts while they waited for the first shelling to come.

When the first shelling came, Alek heard its telltale whistling. He knew that as long as they stayed in the safety of the bunker and took the appropriate precautions, they would be safe. However, this was John Cody's first experience with being shelled, and no amount of reassurance by Alek could make him feel secure.

Some men could face death when it came to them in battle with a visible enemy. However, here there was no enemy to fire back at and there were no comrades to share the battle. When the first shells landed, he could see the terror in Cody's face as he cringed with fear and looked for a place to hide. After the initial exposure, Cody would curl up in the corner, as if to make himself small enough, so he would be safe.

The passing of time didn't help because the constant waiting for the next shelling could drive a man insane. Cody was irritable for the first few days of the shelling, and, then, he became sullen. His skin became ashen from fear and lack of sunlight. He never smiled and talked only after a prolonged break from the shelling. The monitoring of the radio transmissions was a welcome break because it made him focus on the work at hand.

Alek settled into a routine. He and Cody had four-hour shifts to monitor the listening devices and send forward pertinent information. The rest of the time he used to exercise, to do daily chores, to write letters, to keep his diary, and to sleep.

Cody was afraid to go outside, so Alek took over all the duties outside the bunker. The routine each day was to check the generator, the antennas, and air intakes, but mostly he emerged to stretch his legs and breathe some fresh air. He varied the time of day he performed these functions in case he was being observed, but despite this precaution, the enemy seemed to know when he came out. The shelling didn't necessarily happen as soon as he came out, but when it did happen, he would get back into the bunker as fast as possible. He would find Cody in a fetal position in one of the corners. Alek tried repeatedly to get Cody to talk about his family and his home to no avail. When he did finally get him to talk, it was good therapy because it took his mind off the shelling and his fear.

John Cody was a nice kid from a farm family in southern Iowa. He told Alek he enlisted because he wanted to save enough money to buy a farm. There were no jobs in rural Iowa that could pay him enough to support his wife and save money for land, so when he and his girl, Cindy, got married, she stayed at home with her parents, and he enlisted. He sent his entire pay home, and she saved all she could so that they would have enough to buy their dream home. He figured that after one hitch, he would have enough money saved to buy a small farm. All he ever talked about was getting home to Cindy and working their farm.

Somehow, Cody lived through the two weeks, and as they prepared to leave, his spirits were higher. However, as they waited for the boat, there was no relaxation of his tension. When the supply boat arrived, there were two military police on board. The sergeant got off and handed Alek an envelope. Inside was a military order from Major Epling extending their duty on the island indefinitely because there were not any suitable replacements available. Alek told the sergeant he should take Cody back with him, but the sergeant said his orders were that they both stayed. The boat crew unloaded the supplies and left. Cody stood there until the boat was out of sight. Alek finally told him they had to get into the bunker before more shelling started.

He looked at Alek with terror in his eyes and said, "Why are they doing this to us? What have we done?"

Time passed slowly, and Cody became worse. When the shelling came, he would cringe in the corner and wait fearfully for it to end. After each shelling, he seemed to become more withdrawn. It was clear he was on the edge of losing it totally. Once he woke up screaming and tried to crawl into the airshaft. On other occasions, he would try to run out the door during the shelling, and Alek would have to physically restrain him.

The supply boat now came once a week, and it always had a Military Police guard. Alek told the boat chief, again, to let the major know about Cody. He told them Cody was going crazy, and they had to take him back with them. The MP's said the major explicitly said they were not to bring either of them back until he gave the order. Alek understood the boat crew and the MP's could only do as they were told.

After the sixth week, Cody seldom talked to Alek and barely ate. He decided he was going to get Cody on the next boat by getting the drop on the MP's. After the number of trips they had made to the island, they had become very casual. He was sure he could do this without any casualties. He told Cody not to worry anymore; they were going to leave in two days when the next supply boat came.

Cody just looked at him sullenly and said, "No, I know I'm never going to leave here."

He tried to reassure Cody, but he wasn't even listening. His shoulders hung down, and his eyes had the vacant look of someone with no hope. Alek knew it was only a matter of time before Cody went completely out of his head.

Alek usually slept for a few hours each night, but he stayed awake through the next two nights because he didn't want Cody awake and alone. Cody kept asking him when his four-hour tour was to begin. He would tell Cody to sleep, and he would call him when it was time to pull his duty.

Sometime, during the pre-dawn hours of the last day, Alek dozed off. Cody had awakened and silently went out and set up a machine gun and his personal weapons on the shoreline of the island facing the 'enemy'. He then waited and readied himself to return fire. The shelling started, and Alek woke up to what was an unusually loud noise from the shelling. He realized it was because the door was open, and Cody was gone. He went to the door and yelled to Cody to come inside. He waited for Cody to come rushing in. He waited and waited, and another shell landed. A pause came, and he thought he heard small arms fire. Could it be a force was trying to land on the island?

Alek grabbed his weapon and ran out the door. About a hundred yards off to his right, he saw Cody on the shoreline standing straight up and firing his rifle into the night. Alek looked hard out at the water, but there was nothing there he could see. Suddenly, he heard the familiar whistling sound signaling that another shell was coming in. He yelled to Cody to hit the deck and dove behind some rocks. The shell exploded somewhere in front of him and sent hot shrapnel and rocks everywhere. Alek hugged the ground and waited. After a minute, he looked up and saw Cody face down on the ground. Another shell was coming, and he ducked again. Two more came and, then, silence.

He couldn't wait any longer. He got up and ran to where Cody was lying. As he ducked from behind one rock to another, he yelled to Cody to get his butt inside before another round came in, but Cody did not move. He finally got to him and turned him over. What had been Private John Cody's face and chest was now a mass of blood, flesh, and dirt. Alek put his hand on Cody's chest, felt warm blood, and heard him moan. Cody tried to say something, but all that came out was a bubbling foam and blood. He tried to raise himself up, made one last gasp for air, and collapsed. Alek carried him back to the bunker and set him on his bunk.

This was not the first death Alek had seen in the Army, but it certainly was different. Cody was not killed during a battle, or while trying to protect his comrades in arms, or even while trying to prove he was brave. He died because he was pushed to the brink of madness and to an irrational act. He died because of one man's bigotry and hatred for another. Alek looked at

Cody and saw a person who just wanted to live a simple dream.

He spent the rest of the night with Cody, and the feelings of pain and sorrow engulfed his whole being. As he began to think about why this had happened, his feelings turned from sorrow to rage and, finally, hatred. The hatred was building in intensity, like a giant storm that intensifies into a hurricane.

He felt the tremendous force of his rage, physically building like the storm, but at the same time, his mind, like the eye of the storm, was calm. However, his mind could only focus on how much he wanted revenge for John Cody. He wanted revenge for this boy who died because of a man with a twisted mind, a man who had no compassion, no mercy for those who got in his way.

Alek stood, looked down at Cody, and said in a cold and lethal voice, "John, I promise you Epling will pay."

When the supply boat came in the morning, he was waiting. The crew and the MP's didn't even get up as the boat bumped the dock.

The boat chief yelled out, "Hi Alek, where's Cody?" Alek didn't respond. Instead, he jumped on the boat with his forty-five in hand and ordered the chief and the deck hand to get off. He told the MPs to unbuckle their cartridge belts and to drop their weapons over the side, one at a time.

The sergeant looked at Alek and said, "Don't do this, Lieutenant. Epling would love to be able to court-martial you."

Alek looked coldly at the sergeant and said, "Look, Sergeant, I don't want to hurt you or your partner, but if you don't do what I say, I will have no choice."

The sergeant looked at Alek's cold stare, turned to the other MP and said, "Do what he says." They slowly undid their holsters and dropped them into the water. "Alright," Alek said, "put Cody's body in the boat."

The men looked surprised. "Yes, he's dead," said Alek, "and someone is going to pay." They put John Cody's blanket-wrapped body on the boat. Alek walked over to the boat's radio, pulled the mike off, and threw it into the water.

The boat chief turned to Alek and asked, "What happened to him, Lieutenant?"

"He died, Chief. For no good reason, he died. Alright, get back on the boat, and let's get back to the base."

"Lieutenant, I've been making this run for almost a year, and I know what was going on between you and Major Epling. If I can be of any help, in any way, my crew and I will do it."

Alek said, "Thanks, Chief. Now, Sergeant, I want you and the Private to cuff yourselves to the boat rail and give me the key."

The sergeant looked at him with disbelief.

"I said now!" Alek snapped.

They did as he said, and he took the keys from the sergeant and threw them over the side. It took about an hour for the boat to return to the base. When they tied up at the dock, he put his pistol into his holster and jumped off the boat.

He turned to the boat captain and said coldly, "Don't follow me, Chief."

Then with a calm, but deliberate pace, he walked down the wharf to the major's office. There was only one thought in his mind. Epling! As he walked, it was as though he was in a glass tunnel that made everything around him blurry. He passed people who said things to him, but he heard nothing. Suddenly, he found himself in Major Epling's outer office. He walked past everyone into the major's office. Now, he could see out the end of his tunnel, and there was Epling, clearly visible, sitting at his desk.

He looked up with surprise and said, "What the hell are you doing here? I'm going to have your ass court-martialed."

Alek dove across the desk, knocking Epling to the floor. Alek got up on top of Epling, and as he struggled to get up, Alek hit him several times in the face. Tears were coming down Epling's face, and he did not move. Alek slowly and deliberately removed his pistol from its holster. He shoved the barrel into Epling's mouth. The major was bleeding and slobbering all over himself, and Alek looked at him with all of the hate he had inside of him. As he pulled the hammer back, he felt a blow to his head, and the lights went out.

He awoke in a cell in the stockade. He moaned and tried to sit up.

"Man, your butt is in a shit load of trouble," said the corporal of the guard. "Do you know what you did?"

"I know what I didn't do," Alek said. "I didn't kill the SOB. One more second, and he would have been gone."

At that moment, a captain from the Judge Advocate General came in and said he wanted to talk to Alek.

"Lieutenant Roman, I am Captain Miller from the JAG. I'm here to try to help you."

"Captain, I'm afraid there's not much you can do for me," Alek said.

"I am the counsel assigned to defend you. As I understand it, you and a Private Cody, had duty on The Rock for an extended period, and he was killed there by shellfire. You commandeered a supply boat that came to the island and tried to kill Major Epling. Why, Lieutenant? Why were you trying to kill Major Epling?"

"I exposed Major Epling as a bigot in front of Colonel Smith. He got in trouble with the Colonel over this, so he sent me to duty on The Rock. John Cody had the bad luck of being assigned with me. The normal tour on The Rock is two weeks. He was on The Rock with me for seven weeks. He couldn't take the constant shelling and finally cracked and got himself killed."

"You were on The Rock for seven weeks? Why?" Captain Miller asked.

"It was Epling's way of getting even with me. Cody was just an innocent bystander," said Alek.

"Lieutenant, are you sure about this?" Miller asked.

"Yes, I am sure Captain. Can I call my father in the States?" Alek asked.

"Yes, Lieutenant, I will inform the sergeant of the guard. You are going to have to stand a court-martial, Lieutenant. You can tell your story there," said Captain Miller.

That night Alek talked to his father.

"Hi, Dad, I guess you know what is happening to me," said Alek.

"Yes, son, I was contacted by an old friend of mine, Colonel Peters. We served together during the war. He is in the JAG's office in Taiwan and heard about your incident. He told me what you told your counsel. He also told me about Epling. Apparently, he may also be court-martialed."

"I'm sorry you have to get involved in this, Dad," Alek said with remorse.

"Alek, you are my son, and whatever you do, I will be at your side. Is it true you tried to kill Epling?" Mikhail Roman asked.

"Yes, I'm afraid it's true, but I had good reason," said Alek.

"So I heard. I am sorry about the young man that died. I understand he died needlessly," said Alek's father.

"Dad, they are going to transport me to the States for trial. I will need some legal counsel. I hate to have you involved."

"Alek, as I said, you are my son. Whatever you have done, we will face it together," said Mikhail Roman with a strong conviction. "I will do everything I can. I have already contacted a few friends that might be able to help."

"Thanks, Dad. I knew I could count on you," said Alek.

What happened next was a whirlwind of activity. Instead of a court-martial in Taiwan, Alek was taken on a military plane and transported by Military Police to Washington D.C. Two federal marshals met them there and took him into custody. They escorted him to an office in the Senate building, where he met with his father's friend, Senator McGruder.

McGruder came out from behind his desk and shook hands with Alek.

He looked up at the marshals and said, "Please wait in the outer office gentlemen. We will be a little while," said McGruder.

McGruder motioned him to a chair and said with a smile on his face, "Alek, it is good to see you again. I think the last time I saw you was when you graduated from college. Your father was very proud of you."

"Thank you for intervening for me Senator. I'm sorry my father had to call you for help," said Alek.

"Alek, you know I would do anything for your father. He saved my life twice during the war, and I can never repay that debt. Besides, you know me, I like a good fight," said McGruder. "Now, Alek, your father told me what happened, and I talked to Colonel Peters and to Major Epling's commander, but I would like to hear what you have to say."

"Well, it began when I got in trouble with Major Epling. Before I had even met him, I ran into him at a bar where he was harassing an old Chinese man. He is a dyed-in-the-wool bigot. I intervened on behalf of the old man, and he started spouting his supremacy diatribe. It just so happened his commanding officer was in a booth and overheard everything. I don't know exactly what happened between him and his commander, but it must have been bad. Epling was furious with me and sent me to what they call The Rock," said Alek.

"I understand it was not a very pleasant place for you or your partner, Private Cody. I went through being shelled in the war, and I can't believe you had to put up with it for seven weeks straight," said McGruder.

"Yes, it was difficult, especially for Cody; he just couldn't take it. He finally cracked and ran out into the shellfire and was killed. I just couldn't contain my anger, and that's when I went after Major Epling," said Alek.

"It's too bad the Army can't keep scum like him out. Do you have any proof of what happened?" McGruder asked Alek.

"I told you about Epling's commander. I'm sure he would testify to Epling's bigotry and his vengeful character. In addition, the supply boat captain and the Military Police said they would testify about how Epling kept us out on that island much beyond normal military protocol. I also kept a diary, and I got someone to send it to my father before Epling got a hold of it," said Alek.

"Alek, give me a few minutes," said McGruder.

He got up and made some phone calls while Alek sat and listened. The first was a call to what Alek assumed to be the Secretary of the Army.

After a lot of conversation, all during which McGruder kept getting louder, he finally said, "If you don't help me get justice done immediately, you will hear me all over Washington. Moreover, I will see to it the Army never gets another one of their programs past my committee. And further, I plan to call every senator on the hill and, also, the White House."

When McGruder finished, he turned to Alek and said quietly, "Don't worry Alek, usually the government is very inflexible, but now and then, if enough noise is made by the right people, we can get even the stodgy old Army to bend and look at itself."

"Senator, thank you for all of your help," said Alek.

He spent the night in a military detention cell. The next day, the marshals brought him back to McGruder's office. As he entered, McGruder was on a speaker phone, and he was talking to the Secretary of the Army, who was pleading with McGruder to end the calls he was getting from his supporters. McGruder finally hung up and smiled at Alek.

"Well, Alek, it seems there was enough evidence against this Epling to scare the Army into doing something about him. The secretary said he was not sure what punishment Epling would receive, but he did say he would no longer be in the Army. And the charges against you will be dropped," said McGruder with a big smile on his face.

"I don't know how to thank you Senator," said Alek.

"Oh, don't worry. There is a captain outside who is going to take you to the Pentagon for discharge. When that is over, come back here," said McGruder.

Alek was discharged, honorably, about four months before his enlistment was over. At his separation, the Judge Advocates Office told him his record would be clean if he talked to no one about what had happened. He asked about Major Epling and was told he was no longer his concern and that the Army would deal with him.

The next day, he went back to McGruder's office to thank him.

"Senator, I just don't know how to thank you enough. I am amazed about what you could get done and so quickly," said Alek.

"Sometimes the wheels of justice just need to be pushed into the right direction."

"And you certainly know how to do that, Senator. It is too bad that a good man had to die in order for someone like Epling to get what he deserves."

"Well, Alek, have you learned anything from the experience?" McGruder asked.

THE ANCIENT ONES

Alek smiled and said, "Yes, next time I won't be so slow to pull the trigger."

McGruder laughed and said, "It certainly would have been much more difficult for me if you had shot the SOB. But then again, if you did, the Army wouldn't have to worry about getting rid of him."

"Seriously, Senator, you are a great friend, and I won't forget what you did for me," said Alek.

"Now that you are unemployed, so to speak, what are you going to do with yourself?" McGruder asked.

"The things that I learned in the Army don't exactly qualify me for a job in a business office, unless they need armed covert actions," said Alek.

McGruder looked at him and said, "You might be surprised at the demand for your talents. I knew you would need a job, so I contacted a few friends of mine in the government."

"I don't know if I want anything to do with the military again," said Alek.

"Oh, don't worry. It has nothing to do with the Army or any of the other military branches".

McGruder then handed Alek a business card and said, "Contact the person whose name is on this card, and he will help you find appropriate work."

"I don't know what to say, Senator, but thank you again," Alek said.

Then, McGruder laughed and said, "I have to get to the Senate for an important vote on Army appropriations."

Alek remembered going to Virginia for orientation and training. He possessed most of the skills required to become a covert operative. However, the orientation was eye opening, since he was never aware of the places and types of operations in which the U.S. Government was involved. He was told to find a place to live in the area, and he would be sent word in a few days as to where to report for his first assignment. He got an apartment in Georgetown and attempted to get the rest of his personal life in order.

Alek looked out at the sky that was turning gray, the indication that dawn was coming. So much had already happened in his life, and, now, here was a new chapter ready to unfold, if he let it. He turned his thoughts to McGruder, who was asking him to help Cara. Well, he certainly could not have sent a better suppliant. She was beautiful and so easy to be with, maybe too good to be true. But then again, maybe this was his time to pay McGruder back for what he had done for him. Well, right now he needed sleep. He would postpone any decisions until he talked to Cara tomorrow. He made his way up to his house and fell into bed.

CHAPTER SIX

Alek woke up at 10:00AM and thought ruefully about sleeping late. Then, he remembered it was almost 4:00 A.M. when he got to bed. Even then, he lay awake thinking about everything had happened that day before he fell into a troubled sleep. Now as he lay there in the calm of the morning, he thought about Cara. His body got a warm feeling thinking of how beautiful she was, and how comfortable he was with her. He had to remind himself that their meeting was not by chance, she arranged it, and now she was asking him to risk his life. He really didn't know anything about her, her father, or what he was doing in Chiapas. From what she said, he may have been dealing with some questionable characters. Anyway, all of this intrigue and illicit activity were exactly the things he was trying to remove from his life.

Alek went into the kitchen, and as he was making coffee, his mind again drifted to Cara. He couldn't remember ever having feelings like this for any woman in his life. Last night he was ready to tell her things he had never told anyone. He thought about the feelings she expressed for her father and her concern for his welfare, a concern any daughter would have for a parent. What was he thinking? Why couldn't he just trust someone who was in trouble and looking for help? He thought of his own father and knew that he would always help someone in need and had taught him to do the same.

Alek knew that the world he had lived in for the past 10 years had changed him. Now, he questioned everyone and everything. He no longer could see innocence in people, only the evil that might come from anyone. However, he was starting a new life and couldn't keep judging people based on the life he led. Yet, he would always be careful because his past was never far away.

As he drank his coffee, he thought that there was probably nothing deceptive about Cara or the story about her father, especially since McGruder had sent her to him. He looked out at the ocean, thought of her and the warmth returned. He would go to see her as planned, ask some questions, and decide what else to do. After all, he had spent a great deal of time in Belize, Guatemala, and Mexico, and he could still contact his past associates there.

He finished his coffee and got dressed in shorts, a T-shirt, and sandals. He

THE ANCIENT ONES

walked back to her condo, and it was about 12:00 when he rang her doorbell. She opened the door before the bell stopped ringing.

"Hi," she said apprehensively, "I was waiting all morning, and I saw you coming."

"Oh yeah, I forgot. You have your own spy tools," He said sarcastically.

"Look," she said with great sincerity, "I was not spying on you. I just couldn't sleep, so I kept waiting for you to come. Could I make you some coffee?"

"No thanks, I already had some, but since it's after noon, I will have a beer while we talk out on the balcony."

"Okay," she said, "I'll be right out."

Cara scurried off into the kitchen and he went out to the balcony, looked around and considered what he would say to Cara.

Cara came out with a tray with one beer and some lime.

"Nothing for you?" Alek asked.

"No, I don't feel much like drinking today. I'd like to talk about getting help for my father, if that's okay with you. Have you decided if you will help me?" She asked and waited for his reply.

"Before we get into that," he said, "I would like you to tell me about your father and what this mess is all about."

"As I told you last night, my father is Edward Amelot. He works for a museum in Washington D.C. as an anthropologist. His research has always been centered on the natives of Mesoamerica. Just before his disappearance, he had acquired some artifacts, which he said could help him prove a theory he had regarding contact between an ancient culture from Mesoamerica, and another ancient culture from a different hemisphere."

"So, do you think these artifacts had something to do with his disappearance?" Alek asked."

"Yes, I do," she said emphatically. "My father wrote me that he met a man from Chiapas named Castillo, who had apparently removed these artifacts from an undiscovered ancient ruin which was located somewhere in the area bordering Mexico and Guatemala. He said that Castillo was evasive about where he had obtained the artifacts but admitted later he had gotten them from a Mayan Indian who lived in the area of the ruins."

"I know the area," Alek said gravely. "The Indians, the bandits, and the smugglers know the jungles of the area and travel back and forth across the border freely. The jungle is so dense that no army could stop illegal travel, even if it wanted to. I also know the government has concerns about smugglers taking national treasures out of the country."

"Well, my father would not do anything illegal," she said indignantly. "I know he bought artifacts before that were illegal; however, he always gave them to the government of the country they came from, when he was through with them. This time he said that he knew they came from an unknown ancient temple, and if he could find the temple, it would be a huge benefit to his research. He said Castillo agreed to take him to the temple for the right price."

"Okay," Alek said in capitulation. "So, what I know is your father's work is studying these ancient cultures, and he decided to find the source of some artifacts he obtained from a man in Chiapas. Did you try to contact Castillo?"

"Yes, I found a number for an import/export business in his name. I tried repeatedly to contact him by phone," she said, "but I found out that the phone system there rarely works. I do know from my father's associates that he did reach Tapachula and met with an Antonio Dega," Cara added. "My father's life long friend and associate Renaldo Armando from the Museum of Anthropology in Mexico City, sent him to Dega for help."

"Have you heard from him since he reached Tapachula?" Alek asked.

"Yes, he called, but I wasn't in. He said he would contact me soon, but he hasn't called or written since. I have tried everything I know to find him. I tried to phone Dega and had the same phone problems. I'm really afraid something has happened to him," she said in a tone filled with grief.

"Do you know exactly what it is he was looking for?" asked Alek.

"I know you are not going to like this," she said sheepishly, "but he asked me not to tell anyone."

"What? You want me to help you, but you won't tell me what it is he wants to find. Well, why should I do anything?" Alek demanded.

"First of all, you must understand how much I care for my father. From what you told me, you seemed to have had a similar relationship with your father," she said. "Secondly, you apparently felt close enough to me last night to talk of the future. And lastly, I desperately need your help."

"Listen, what happened last night has nothing to do with this. At least that's what you told me," said Alek.

"You're right, I did say that," said Cara, "but it is very hard right now to separate my emotional feelings for you from the problem I have with my father."

"One of the things I learned in my business is you cannot bring personal feelings into what you are doing," Alek said. "You can not make good judgments if you're involved personally with your problem."

"Oh, I'm sure you're right," Cara said despairingly.

Cara looked at him tearfully and said, "Alek, in the very short time I have known you, I have made a number of mistakes. I should have just called you and presented my problem on an honest business-like basis from the beginning. Instead, I became emotionally involved. That was wrong. However, based on what Senator McGruder told me about you, I felt that I had to get to know you, first, in order to ask for your help. It went farther than I had planned."

"You were probably right about just calling me. I am no longer in the covert operations business, and I would have brushed you off," Alek confessed.

"Well, I thought up the idea of meeting you on the beach. The day we met, I was going to sit there until you came down to go for a walk or a swim. I guess I didn't know how, but I knew I was going to approach you. After we did meet, and went back to your place after lunch, I thought we could talk candidly, but you fell asleep. So, I invited you for dinner, so we could be alone. My plan was to get to know more about each other, and, then, I could ask for your help. I didn't plan on what happened between us after dinner. I guess it was a combination of too much wine and moonlight."

"Well, it was a great day and evening," he said.

Cara smiled weakly and asked, "Does that mean you forgive me?"

"I guess there really is nothing to forgive," Alek said. "You were trying to find a way to accomplish your mission. Besides, I'm very familiar with giving your all for your mission."

Cara's smile changed to a look of horror. "I cannot believe you said that. I may have been devious in my plan to meet you, but I could not fake the feelings I showed for you. I am really sorry you think I could. I, also, am sorry I took up your time. Please leave," she said angrily with tears in her eyes.

"Wait a minute, don't get so upset."

"What! Don't get upset? You just told me I seduced you to get you to do what I wanted," she said as she tried to suppress her tears.

"Hey, I'm sorry. I didn't mean it that way," Alek replied sheepishly. "First of all, I was just talking about the meeting on the beach and how you arranged it. Hell, it wasn't too hard. The minute I saw you, I came running, or should I say, falling," he said trying to evoke a smile. "Secondly, I understand you were concerned about your father, and you were just trying to get to know me before you told me what you wanted. I know what happened last night was not staged."

Cara had tears streaming down her face and said, "I'm not sure how to take all of what you said."

"Look," said Alek softly, "I think we got off to a great start, which turned bad. It's me. I'm suspicious of everything and everyone. I understand you were trying to help your father. Why don't we try to start again? If nothing else, I owe Senator McGruder a great deal."

"You keep saying you owe him. What did he do for you?" Cara asked.

"I'll tell you another time," Alek replied. "For now, let's just say he's like a second father to me and concentrate on your problems."

"Alright," said Cara.

"If I'm going to help you, I have to know what's going on. Like, is what your father looking for worth a lot of money?"

"Yes, I'm sure it would be. Anything that coming from a new archaeological find would bring a lot of money from collectors," She said.

"Don't governments control discoveries like this?" Alek asked.

"Sure, if they know about them. The key here is that, apparently, only one man knows where this ruin is located," Cara answered.

"Okay. Well, why did your father's friend in Mexico City send him to this Dega in Tapachula?" Alek asked.

"Dega has worked with Renaldo dating artifacts, and he thought Dega might be able to help my father with his artifacts. Also, Dega, apparently, is an influential man in Chiapas, and that could also help my father."

"Do you know if he helped your father?" Alek asked.

"Yes," she said. "My father left a message for me. He said Dega had helped him to determine the origin of the artifacts, and they had become friends. He also said I could try to call Dega if I didn't hear from him."

"Did you call Dega?" Alek asked.

"Yes, many times, but as I said, the phones in Chiapas are not too reliable," She said.

"Did your father make contact with the man he bought the artifacts from, Castillo?" asked Alek.

"He said he was going to, so I can only assume he did," Cara answered.

"And you haven't heard form your father since. Well, it seems that Dega and Castillo are the places to start," He said.

"Since my father became friends with Dega, I'm sure that he will tell me what he knows, but it seems that Castillo is venal and might be a more difficult."

Alek's brow furrowed as he looked to be deep in thought and said, "Yes, he may be harder to convince, but the right person would know how to deal with someone like him."

Cara breathed a deep sigh and said, "Does that mean you'll help me? Could you make some calls, send a telegram, or give me a letter of introduction to whomever I need to contact in Chiapas?"

"A letter of introduction? You really don't know the kind of people you would be dealing with. In order to search over the borders and to get information from the kind of people that might know something, you have to deal with the dregs of the earth. My dear, if I sent you to the kind of people who could help you, Senator McGruder would have my hide," Alek replied.

"Look I will deal with anyone I have to in order to help my father. I only asked for contacts in Chiapas. I will tell McGruder that you helped me as much as you could," she said.

"Sure, that may be what you asked, but that's not what he's expecting of me. He's a foxy old guy who gets what he wants through charm, diplomacy, or outright bullying."

"I'm not sure what you mean," Cara said.

He looked at Cara with a smile, put his hands on her shoulders, and said, "Let's just say I'm in the game, and let's make plans to go to Chiapas and find your father."

CHAPTER SEVEN

Edward Francisco Amelot was born in Washington D.C. on July 27, 1945. His parents came to the United States preceding World War II. As the political pressures increased in Spain, and war became imminent, Carlo and Luisa Amelot immigrated to the United States. Carlo was a famous cellist. His music was his passion above everything else in his life except for Luisa, who was dedicated to Carlo and to Edward.

Carlo was physically a small man, who seemed even smaller when he was bent over his cello. Edward was very different. He was slightly taller than average, and he always seemed even taller because of the almost regal manner with which he carried himself. His hair started out black but grayed early on, as did his fathers. He had large dark eyes and high cheekbones like his mothers. When he matured, all of these features combined to give him the look of a distinguished man.

Edward didn't have his father's passion for music, but, like his father, he did address all things in his life with unbridled enthusiasm and dedication. Whether it was his studies, his work, or his leisure activities, he was always very engrossed in whatever he did.

He was drafted into the military after completing his undergraduate degree. He could have used graduate school as a deferment to being drafted, but he decided to go in the Army. His parents were aghast, especially his father, who had fled his homeland to avoid a war. However, Edward felt he had a duty, and as in all other things in life, he did what he thought was right. After OCS and infantry training, he spent six months in Vietnam.

After being wounded for a second time, he was sent to Thailand where he reveled in the country's history and culture. Compared to the death and destruction of Vietnam, this country was so sacred and serene. He spent all of his free time in the ancient temples, shrines and palaces, which harbored the artifacts of their ancient civilization. Here he developed a passion for studying the antiquities of man.

When he returned home, he decided to change his educational direction to anthropology. As he returned to the academic life, he discovered the history of Mesoamerica was to be his life's work, and he would have been consumed by this work had he not met Maria.

Maria de la Cruz was born in Valencia, Spain on October 22, 1948 and came to the United States when she was sixteen years old. Her parents worked in the Spanish embassy in Washington D.C. She was a beautiful and intelligent woman.

Edward met Maria at George Washington University in 1970. He was immediately captivated by her. Her hair was black, and she had dark, almond shaped eyes, and her skin was a milky white. However, her beauty was not the most significant thing about her. She had warmth of character and the gift of being able to transmit that warmth to those whom she loved. They were both in graduate school, and Edward pursued Maria, sometimes, to the detriment of his studies. One year later, before they had finished school, Edward proposed, and they were married, against the wishes of their parents.

After marriage, he found it difficult to find the time to spend with his work and his wife. He was always consumed with feelings of guilt that he didn't spend more time with his family, and when he gave time to his loved ones, he felt he was not giving enough time to his work. So, he was in a constant struggle to balance his life.

There would be times in his office when he would be completely engrossed in his work, and Maria's face would come into his mind. He would have a tremendous urge to go to her, at that moment, to tell her he loved her. However, with some difficulty, he would overcome these compulsions and turn his attention back to his work.

Maria understood Edward's passion for his work and continually forgave him when he was late for dinner or invitations with friends. A little over one year after they were married, Cara was born. Cara filled her days, and she was happy and content raising their daughter.

Maria would never leave Cara with anyone, and she and Edward took her everywhere with them. Edward would get daily calls at the museum from Maria letting him know when Cara sat up, crawled, walked, said her first word, said her first phrase, or said her first sentence. And all of these significant events were recorded by photos or on audiotape.

There was no doubt in his mind his life was perfect, so perfect that there were times when he actually felt a fear inside of him, a fear he would lose Maria. One day when Cara was five years old, Edward stayed with her while Maria visited a friend. She thought it was important for Edward and his child to have time together to bond. As they waited for Maria to come home, he got a call that Maria had been in a bad accident. He rushed to the hospital in time to hold her hand and to tell her he loved her. She looked at him, told him to take care of Cara, and that she loved him. Then, she squeezed his hand, and it was over.

After Maria's death, he was lost. He no longer had her as a friend to confide in, as the counselor to discuss his problems, or as the lover with whom he shared unbridled passion. His beautiful world had been shattered, and part of him had died. His only consolation was Cara. When he looked at her, he saw the same beauty that was in her mother. As Cara grew older, he spent many evenings with her looking at photographs of the wonderful times he and Maria had when she was a baby. He told Cara about the gentleness and caring in her mother, and the great love she had for her daughter.

He felt remorseful that his daughter no longer had her mother's warmth and nurturing. Therefore, he tried to spend more time with Cara to make up for the loss of her mother. However, it was difficult to do this and to continue his dedication to his study of the cultures of Mesoamerica. Somehow, he managed to become an expert in his field and to successfully raise a daughter who grew into a beautiful young woman.

CHAPTER EIGHT

Edward Amelot's career flourished. As he continued his studies, he uncovered some information which led him to develop a hypothesis that an ancient culture from China and Mesoamerica had made contact before the birth of Christ. Moreover, because of recent facts he uncovered, he was convinced the contact between the two cultures occurred in Mesoamerica. The scientific community had never considered that Chinese explorers had sailed across the Pacific Ocean because they were not known as seafarers.

The information that led to this recent revelation was some grainy old photographs of Olmec artifacts from a private collection that had been lost in the shuffle of heirs. There was no written record of the identification of each of the artifacts in the photographs, but Edward was sure that one of them was an azimuth circle. The azimuth circle was used in navigation to determine true azimuth and astronomic latitude. This could mean the Olmecs had developed or were given an instrument to help them navigate the oceans. This was not the kind of evidence that he or the scientific community would consider conclusive. However, he kept finding other evidential information, which nurtured his theory enough for him to continue the search.

Then, one day he received a telephone call from Jose Sucre, who was a curator for a small museum in Flores, a small town in northern Guatemala. This call was the beginning of a most promising adventure for Edward.

Whenever Jose was offered some newly discovered artifacts that his museum could not afford to buy, he would contact Edward or Renaldo. Sucre had always been honest with him about the origin and the validity of the pieces presented to him. Most of the pieces he got were from Indians who would come back and forth across the border from Mexico, so he was never exactly sure of their origin.

The telephone connection was very poor. "Edward, it is very nice to talk to you again." Sucre said.

"And the same, Jose. How are you doing with your museum's progress?" Edward asked.

"Not as well as we would like Edward, but you know funds are limited for us. That is why I am calling you. A man named Arno Castillo has brought me some old Indian pieces that are very interesting. One is made of clay in the shape of a circle with a number of protrusions along the top. The two others are unique feline figures carved in jade. Edward, I believe they are very authentic, and although I have not yet date tested them, I am sure they are definitely pre-Columbian and probably much older. My museum cannot pay the price asked for them."

Edward thought the clay piece sounded like an azimuth circle. He was not only interested, but also very excited. "Jose, I am always interested in anything you feel is authentic," said Edward trying to retain his composure.

"Good, I would hate to see them fall into the hands of a collector who would want them only for their economic value. I told Castillo you would call him."

Sucre then gave Edward a number in Chiapas, Mexico, where he could call Castillo.

He immediately placed a call to Castillo and was unsuccessful. The operator told him there was trouble on the line in Chiapas. After trying for a number days, he finally got through to Castillo's import/export business.

"Senore Castillo, my name is Edward Amelot. I believe Senore Sucre told you I would call."

"Si, he said you would call. You are calling me all the way from Washington in Norte American?" Castillo asked in amazement.

"Yes. I understand you have two jade figures of cats and a clay piece. Can you tell me anything about them and where they came from?" Edward asked.

"Si, two are as you say, el gato, although, they look different, and one is like a clay plate with pointed edges."

"I am very interested in these. If you will send them to me, and if they are verifiable, I will pay you."

"I do not send these anywhere without the money first," said Castillo.

"Can you tell me where they came from?" Edward asked.

"They came from an old temple deep in the jungle," said Castillo.

"Where is the temple?" Edward asked.

"No, I cannot tell you that. No one else knows where this temple is, but me."

"Will you make a photograph of the pieces and send them to me?" asked Edward. "Then, I can see if I want them."

Castillo was nervous. He definitely did not want to take pictures and send them through the mail. He would not give anyone proof that he had illegal artifacts. "No, Senore, no pictures. If you want them, I have to know now. I have others who want these pieces and will pay me now," said Castillo.

Edward didn't think this was true, but he would act quickly since he thought these artifacts could be the ones to help prove his theory. "I cannot pay for these until I see them; however, I will come to Mexico. Could you meet me in Mexico City?" Edward asked.

"No, Senore, that is too far from Chiapas." Castillo said, but in truth, he did not want to go to Mexico City because he was afraid to be around so much police.

Edward thought for a moment. He could fly easily to Cancun, which would also be an easy driving distance for Castillo. "I can meet you in Cancun in two days, at the Casa Magna Hotel," said Edward.

Castillo hesitated and asked, "You will bring the money with you in Norte Americano dollars?"

"Si, Senore," said Edward.

"Then, I will be there," Castillo said.

Edward thought that he had better not let anyone know why he was going to Mexico, especially his colleagues. Dealing with illegal artifacts was something many archaeologists did, but they did not advertise it. He decided, in order to keep his real reasons for going to Mexico from his colleagues, he would simply say that he was making this a trip to do some research.

After he met Castillo, he would arrange to visit with his friend Renaldo at the Museum of Anthropology in Mexico City. He told his colleagues that after his visit at the museum, he was taking a two-week vacation. His plan was to meet with Castillo, and if the pieces were what he thought they were, he would then go to Mexico City to verify their age and then get Castillo to take him to the temple. He made all of his travel arrangements, took care of his personal business, and left for Mexico.

Castillo had seldom been out of Chiapas State except to cross the border illegally into Guatemala. Cancun was in Quintana Roo State, and in order for Castillo to get there, he would cross Campeche State. The army had checkpoints at every road leading out of or into Chiapas. He was very nervous as he drove down the road with the illegal artifacts in his jeep. He had hidden the jade figures in a large container of a powdery substance used to clean floors and he hid the clay figure inside another container of soap powder. He was stopped a number of times but passed as a salesman for sanitation supplies.

When he arrived in Cancun, Castillo was amazed with the opulence. He called Edward at his hotel, and they planned to meet at the hotel restaurant where he was staying. He walked into the restaurant, and Edward got up and shook hands with Castillo.

"Hola, Senore. I am very pleased we could meet," Edward said.

"Hola," Castillo said nervously.

"Can I offer you a drink?" Edward asked.

"Si, I can use a drink. Here are the pieces," Castillo said as he handed a bag to Edward.

"We should not show these here. Let's go up to my room, and you can have your drink there."

"You are right. It is best not to transact business in public," said Castillo, as he looked around nervously.

They went up to Edward's suite, which had a sitting room and a bedroom. After Edward made Castillo a drink, he removed the pieces from the bag. The disk-shaped piece definitely could be used for determining azimuth. It was in very good condition and could easily be tested for age. The jade pieces, which he thought would be just the normal carvings, were even more exciting. One was carved in the shape of half-cat, half-man, like the 'were-jaguar', from the Jaguar Cults of the Olmecs.

The other carving was definitely not from this region. The color and texture of the jade, also, seemed to be different. The cat-shape seemed to be more like a lion than a jaguar, a Chinese lion! My god could this be? How did it get into an Indian temple in Mesoamerica, and when did it get there?

He would have to determine the age and composition of the pieces and, then, the origin of each. Could he finally have the proof he needed to prove his hypothesis? He must find out more about the source of the artifacts and if there were more to be discovered there.

As Castillo gulped down his drink he said, "Do you like these pieces? I am told they are very old and very rare."

Castillo was presenting his best sales effort.

"We discussed the price, ten thousand Norte Americano dollars. You have the money?" Castillo asked.

Edward was so excited about the pieces that he didn't want to haggle over the price.

"Where did you say these pieces came from?" Edward asked.

"I did not say, but they came from an undiscovered temple."

"Are you sure? Have you seen it yourself?" Edward asked in amazement.

"Si, there were many carvings on the walls of the building. There were a number of rooms in the temple. The only room I saw was large and had a stone table. I did not get to go into all of them. That is all I will say," said Castillo.

Edward thought he could be describing an ancient temple with a sacrificial altar where the Ah Kin or high priests held rituals. These observations seemed to add to the authenticity of the artifacts, and he was hopeful he had found a potential source to assist in proving his hypothesis.

"I will require some time to test the pieces. I have the necessary chemicals in the bathroom. Please help yourself to anything in the bar while I am gone," said Edward as he disappeared into the bathroom. Edward had brought along a simple chemical test that could determine the relative age of the artifacts within a few hundred years. He also had photographs of artifacts he hoped would have been from the same period and geographic area. The relics proved to be as authentic as could be detected by such a rudimentary test. He would seek further proof when he reached Mexico City. In the meantime, he would pay the money for them. He knew he would be taking a great risk buying these artifacts since acquiring or removing of relics from Mexico was against the law.

Edward came back into the sitting room and said, "I am as satisfied as I can be with the tests I was able to accomplish. I will buy the pieces."

"Good, then you can pay me now," Castillo said.

"I will pay you $5,000 now and $5,000 more if you take me to the temple," said Edward.

Castillo was angry and said loudly, "you said you would pay me $10,000 for the pieces. You said nothing about going to the temple. The temple is deep in the jungle, and it is dangerous to go there. No, either pay me my money, or I will, I ah, I will leave," Castillo now said nervously.

Edward took five thousand dollars in cash from his inner jacket pocket and laid it on the table. He heard the nervous sound in Castillo's voice, but he also heard the anger and knew he had to be careful.

"I know I said I will pay you $10,000 for the pieces, and I will. If you will take me to the location where the artifacts came from, I will give you this $5,000 now, the remaining $5,000 when we go to the temple. I will also give you another $2,000 for taking me there."

Castillo thought about going back to the ruins and got very nervous. He couldn't go back to the ruins again because of the spirits that guarded the temple.

"No, the spirits guard the temple, and it would be risking too much. Besides, the local Indians keep threatening to rebel. I don't want to end up in the middle of a war," said Castillo worriedly.

"Are you speaking of the MYLN?"

"Yes they are fanatical," said Castillo.

"I know of that group. I understood that their efforts to revolt were put down by the government."

"Yes, but I also know that they will try again."

"Alright," said Edward. "Instead of an additional $2,000, I will give you another $5,000 for taking me to the temple. That is my final offer."

Castillo was nervous, but $15,000 was too much for him to turn down.

"Alright, you must meet me in Tapachula."

CHAPTER NINE

Arno Castillo was a small man with an arched back and eyes that darted around like a wild animal that was preyed upon. He was proud of being of pure Spanish blood and had great disdain for the Mestizo's and the Indians with whom he conducted a great deal of his business. He especially didn't like the Indians and easily took advantage of them.

He owned a building in Tapachula, Mexico, which is on the Pacific coastal plain about nine miles from the Guatemala border. The small building served as his place of business and his residence. The location close to the Guatemalan border was particularly convenient for his illicit business activities.

He was licensed as an importer/exporter, but he dealt primarily in contraband. Most of the time, he dealt in stolen shipments of medicines, equipment, or arms, which would turn a quick profit. He kept the illegal goods in an old building he purchased on an unused banana plantation in the jungle near the border of Guatemala. The irony was the plantation land, which surrounded the building, had been taken over by the government. His contraband was in the middle of government land where trespassing was forbidden.

There was a good business in munitions in Chiapas. The uprisings against the federal government by the Indians were most profitable for him, and as an additional benefit, he didn't mind seeing the government kill off the Indians. At the same time he was trading in arms or other stolen goods, he was also dealing in any 'artifacts' he would acquire from the uneducated Indians from the jungles of southern Mexico or northern Guatemala.

The Indians would bring him all sorts of pottery, statues, knives, arrows, and other goods they found when digging in their gardens or out in the jungle. Most of these were things, someone had thrown away and were not very old. However, he bought most of them because there was always some unsuspecting foreigners who would buy any dirty old piece of pottery if he could convince them it was pre-Columbian.

One day while Castillo was at his plantation building, an Indian came walking up the road to the building. Castillo quickly came out and said in an authoritative voice, "This is private property. What do you want here?"

The Indian meekly said, "Senore, my name is Tucanil. The Indians in town told me you would buy old pieces." Tucanil reached into his sack and brought out a carved figure.

Castillo took it and rubbed off some of the dirt. He had never seen a piece quite like it. It was encrusted in soil, but it was plain to see that it was jade and was carved in a shape, which looked like a cat. His covetous nature told him he might have something of value here.

"Yes, it is possible I might buy this piece. Where did it come from?" Castillo asked.

Tucanil suddenly looked frightened and said, "I found it in the jungle near where I live."

Castillo could see that the Indian was lying. He grunted and asked, "Do you have any more like this?"

Tucanil was surprised at how quickly this man showed his interest. Now, he knew he should have brought the other piece. "Si, I have another piece in my barraca," said Tucanil warily. "It is not the green stone like this one. It is made of clay."

Castillo looked at the piece again and thought he might be onto something good.

"I will buy this and any other pieces, but I must know where they came from, so I will know they are not fakes," Castillo demanded.

Tucanil hesitated. He was afraid to go back to the temple because of what he had seen there. It was a sacred place protected by the ancient ones.

"I found the pieces in the jungle, but I do not know where they came from. I must sell these now. How much will you pay for this piece?" Tucanil asked.

Castillo could tell this Indian was desperate and needed money.

"I will pay you the most I can. I will go with you to your barraca to see what else you have to sell."

"Alright, we will go," Tucanil, said.

They got into Castillo's jeep and drove away.

Tucanil wore the traditional white cotton shirt and pants of the peasant farmer. His skin had the hue of Indian Ocher, and he had dark eyes and black hair he tied behind his head. He was an uneducated and simple man. The kind which was easy prey for someone like Castillo.

After crossing the river, they arrived at his adobe barraca with its traditional thatched roof. There was a small estabal built alongside of it with one old lame horse in it. The house was small and had thick walls to keep out the heat. The windows were covered with oilcloth, and there was smoke coming out of the chimney. Outside one of the windows was a vegetable garden. Castillo walked boldly into the smoky room and saw an elderly Indian woman removing corn from the husk by rubbing two husks together. It was Tucanil's mother, his only living relative besides his wife.

Tucanil's wife, Monaxzial, was standing over a pot that hung over the hogar of their chimenea. She had the same coloring as her husband and the same lean look of the poor. Castillo saw she had a twisted leg and limped around the room with a stick she used for a cane. She went about her chores and said nothing to Castillo, since it was the custom of the Indian women not to speak to strangers.

Some time ago, she had broken her leg when she fell from a tree as she was collecting fruit. Tucanil took her on his horse to the local clinic. The medical aide set the leg and told him he would have to take her to the hospital to be operated on. Since he could not pay for an operation, she suffered with the pain.

Tucanil looked at his wife. She was in pain, yet she kept her stoic look and continued daily with her work. She was proud, and she was brave. He had to help her.

Castillo walked back outside and sat at a table. Tucanil went to get the other piece and brought them some mescal. Castillo didn't like mescal. It was a poor substitute for tequila, but he drank it to appease the Indian.

"Here is the other piece I told you about," said Tucanil.

The piece was round and had triangular points sticking up from various places around the edge of the piece. Castillo was not very impressed.

"Alright, I will buy both of these pieces," Castillo said.

"Senore, my wife needs an operation. I need money to pay for this. It will cost twenty thousand Pesos," Tucanil said almost pleadingly.

The corners of Castillo's mouth turned up in a faint smile. He knew he could barter whatever he wanted from the Indian. "I cannot pay that much for these pieces, but if you take me to the place where you found these, and we find more, I will pay you enough for your wife to get her operation."

Tucanil hesitated with a pained look on his face. The ancient ones protected the temple, but Monaxzial was with child. The Ah Kin said it would be a boy child. How could she take care of a child when she could barely walk?

Castillo counted out one thousand pesos on the table and said, "I will give you the rest of the money you need if you take me to the place where you found these pieces."

Tucanil was about to say 'no,' when Monaxzial came limping out of the door. He looked at his wife with her twisted leg and said, "I will take you there."

Castillo and Tucanil left in his jeep. After driving for some time, Tucanil directed him to turn into what was not much of a road. Castillo stopped to take a mental note of where they had turned off. They continued until the underbrush got too thick for the jeep. Castillo pulled the jeep into some brush, so it could not easily be seen. He took two lanterns from the jeep, and they continued on foot. They walked for over two hours, deep into the jungle. Suddenly, they came upon what looked like an opening to a cave surrounded by underbrush. It had to be the temple. Castillo felt a sense of excitement over what treasures might be inside the temple.

He lit the lanterns and handed one to Tucanil as they entered into what appeared to be a main chamber. The room was very large and with a ceiling which was at least twenty feet high. Directly across from the entrance, there was a doorway, which was probably fifteen feet high. As they entered, Castillo could feel a damp and cold feeling that went right through his body. He was looking at the carvings on the walls by the light of the lantern, when he noticed that Tucanil was going into the next room.

He moved slowly along the wall and studied the various forms and shapes carved into the walls. He came onto a large round stone, about the size of a soccer ball, which bulged from the wall. As he rubbed his hand across the stone, he felt it rotate as if on an axis. As the backside came forward, it was not round like the front. Instead, it was flat vertically halfway down, and then protruded flat horizontally, and then rounded again, as if half of the backside of the ball was missing. He ran his had along the flat portion of the ball, and he could feel that bottom of the ball was hollow. He lifted the lantern to see inside. The light reflected off a number of green objects, one of which he picked one up and wiped off on his shirt. The stone gleamed in the light of the lantern, so he put it into his pocket and turned back to the source of his new discovery. Castillo thought he had discovered an ancient wall safe.

He began to reach inside again when he heard a blood-curdling scream. The sound came from somewhere inside of the door which Tucanil had entered. The sound was like he heard when a pack of coyotes ran down an animal and began tearing it apart while it was still alive. He pulled his hand from the wall, quickly turned off the lantern so no one could see him, and pressed his body against the wall. He felt his stomach constrict and even in the cool room, he began to sweat. He couldn't breathe.

As Castillo was searching for more artifacts, Tucanil had entered a small room with three doors. A light was coming from the furthest door. As he walked past the first door, he held the lantern out into the doorway. It was an expansive area with some kind of large shapes standing on the floor. He couldn't make out what the shapes were. He entered the room and held up the lantern.

As he got into the room, he suddenly stopped. His heart was pounding because what he saw as large shapes were actually a number of men standing in a row, some with weapons in their arms ready to strike. He dropped the lantern, cowered, and waited for them to strike at him, but they didn't move.

He looked up warily, and his breath started to come back. He picked up the lantern, held it up, and saw the shapes were actually life size figures of Indian Warriors. They were carved from stone. He carefully reached out and touched the figures. The room was full of the figures, and one, which seemed slightly different, was standing in front. They were standing in rows of eight across and about ten deep. The one standing in the front of the group was a tall figure wearing an eagle mask. His body was incised with strange markings, and he was holding two scepters.

Tucanil backed out and went to the next doorway. He, again, held the lantern out into the door. There he saw a stairway which led down to another level. It was dark, and he couldn't see the bottom of the stairs. Suddenly, he heard a shuffling sound behind him. He quickly put out the lantern and pressed his body against the wall.

He waited what seemed like a number of minutes, and there was no further noise. He slid along the wall to the doorway of the lighted chamber and peered around the corner. There, in the light of torches, he saw what appeared to be a number of ancient Mayan priests standing around a table on which lay a body. He had seen this scene before in a picture, which was of the Ah Kin performing the ritual sacrifice of victims, whose hearts were offered to the Mayan gods.

He heard another scream, and one of the Mayans lifted his hand up in the air. There was an object in his hand and a liquid was dripping down. Tucanil froze with terror! He realized it was the heart from the body on the table. It was just as the ancient rite described to him by his father.

As he turned to run out of the building, a large figure, which was illuminated from the room behind him, was standing in his path. He dropped the lantern and put both arms up in protection and fear. The figure was a warrior, who stepped toward him and swung his weapon upward from the ground. At the same time, Tucanil stepped backward and hit his head painfully hard on the wall. Then, he felt as if a fire had penetrated his abdomen, as he saw the blade of the warrior go up past his face. He knew that he was bleeding from a wound from the warrior's weapon. Tucanil clutched his abdomen and ran out of the room.

Castillo saw Tucanil run out of the door holding his stomach with both hands. His eyes followed the Indian across the room and out of the entrance to the temple. Castillo turned back to the doorway from which Tucanil had come, expecting something to leap out at him. Castillo relit his lantern and held it up to see what Tucanil was running from.

A sound came from the doorway, and Castillo began to back away. At that moment, a huge figure stepped into the doorway. The warrior's form was illuminated by Castillo's lantern. His body almost filled the fifteen-foot doorway from side to side and top to bottom. Castillo was horror-stricken, and all he could do was stare at this colossal figure. The warrior wore a headdress, with white feathers which were tipped with black, that went from his forehead straight up to the top of his head. The feathers looked to be about four feet long with smaller ones going out from the side. The warrior's face was encircled like a picture frame with black feathers. His eyes were black and outlined in white. White stripes went down his nose to his cheeks, his neck, and the rest of his body. His body glistened in the light as if it was covered with oil. Castillo knew from pictures he had seen, this looked like an ancient warrior of the Maya. In fact, it was Jacatez, the warrior protector of the temple.

Jacatez was all muscle. He wore a loincloth, and his leg and arm muscles rippled in the light of the lantern. In his left hand, was a very ornate and brightly colored shield. In his right hand, he had what appeared to be a weapon with a wooden handle and a long steel blade that curved into a hook. The steel glistened in the light of the lantern, and Castillo could see it was dripping blood.

He stood there, frozen with fear, as Jacatez looked at him. Suddenly, a booming voice that seemed to come from the walls themselves said, "I am the protector of the temple. All those that enter this sacred place will die."

Castillo dropped the lantern and scrambled out of the room. As he ran out of the building and down to the trail, he looked back and could see no one following. When he reached the jungle, he turned to run down the trail and tripped over Tucanil. He was dead, and the smell of his body was overpowering. The Indian lay on his back, his eyes wide open with a look of horror, holding his groin. Castillo could see why. The Warrior in the temple must have cut open Tucanil's lower abdomen up to his ribs. Tucanil died while trying to hold in his intestines and organs. Castillo thoughts were not sympathy for this man. Instead, they were that he would not have to be concerned Tucanil would reveal the location of the temple to anyone else.

    He looked back toward the temple again and saw no one coming. He hid in the brush and waited for about thirty minutes. Still, he saw no sign of anyone coming from the temple. He went over to the body and took the money he had given Tucanil. He, then, dragged the corpse down the trail and into the jungle. He removed the clothing from Tucanil's body and buried it. He lightly covered the body with branches and leaves. In a few days, it would be no more than the bones of a human skeleton because mountain cats, vultures, and the insects of the jungle floor would strip the flesh down to the bones. Castillo put some marks on trees along the trail to ensure he could find the place again, if he could overcome his fear. He hurried back to where he had left his jeep.

    Castillo knew he had made a great discovery. He knew there were more artifacts he could sell, and they would be all his. He thought of Tucanil's wife and mother. When Tucanil didn't return, they might go looking for him or even tell the authorities. He was not sure if they knew where the temple was. He couldn't take any chances, so he drove back to Tucanil's barraca.

    Castillo's jeep pulled to a stop in front of Tucanil's home. He drew his pistol and walked into the barraca. The two women were sitting at the table, removing corn kernels from the husks. Without speaking a word, he shot both of them so quickly neither had a chance to respond. There was a huge pile of cornhusks in the corner, and he spread them all over the room, knowing they were dry and would burn quickly. Castillo, then, took the lanterns from the table and poured the oil over everything, including the women. He took a burning log from the fire and backed his way out the door. He threw the log inside, and, soon, the building was spewing flames. Castillo knew the killings would be blamed on banditos because it was the easiest solution for the local authorities. He got into his jeep and left.

    He drove back to his warehouse and examined the additional statue he had taken from the temple and the disk he had taken from Tucanil. He knew what he had was authentic and probably would be worth a lot of money. However, he didn't know anyone who could pay what he thought they could be worth. He had always dealt in well-worn and broken artifacts that were of questionable age or bogus provenance. Having the pieces and not being able to sell them was worse than not having them at all.

Then he thought of Jose Sucre, the curator for a small museum in Flores, Guatemala. Castillo had approached him before and offered pieces for sale. Sucre, however, always wanted to know from whom he had acquired the artifacts and where they were discovered. He would tell him he did not know, an Indian just came in and sold them to him. Sucre did buy a number of things from Castillo and always told him he would be interested in any pieces, which could be artifacts. He never tried to barter. He would tell Castillo what the pieces were worth, and when he paid him, he would make Castillo sign a receipt for the museum.

Castillo went to see Sucre and showed him the jade piece. Sucre examined the piece and told Castillo he was sure that is was an authentic Mayan artifact which was worth a great deal.

He smirked and told Sucre he wanted fifty thousand pesos for the figure, and Sucre told him he couldn't pay that much money for any artifacts. Then, Sucre said he did know someone who might be interested and could pay what he was asking. He told Castillo he knew a wealthy North American museum that might pay what he was asking. That was when Sucre contacted Edward.

Now, Castillo had sold his artifacts to Edward, but he did not get all of the money promised, he thought angrily. However, there was the opportunity to make much more money if he took Edward to the ruins. He wanted the money, but how could he face whatever killed Tucanil? He remembered the fear. No the risk was too great. However, he thought with a smile of greed, there were other ways to get the money from Edward and not risk going back to the temple.

CHAPTER TEN

The Aztecs founded the great city of Tenochtitlan in the thirteenth century, hundreds of years after the zenith of the great Olmec and Maya civilizations. Tenochtitlan is the site of today's Mexico City, the capital and largest city in Mexico. It is located in the Valley of Mexico, at an elevation of over 7000 feet. The city is bound by mountains on three sides and the climate is temperate all year round. Edward Amelot always liked Mexico City, but he didn't like the poverty that was prevalent there.

Edward had arranged with Renaldo Armando to visit him at the museum when he arrived in Mexico City from his meeting with Castillo. Renaldo was the Curator of Antiquities at the Museum of Anthropology. He had been educated in Mexico and Europe and was an authority on the ancient cultures of the region. His area of expertise was parallel to Edwards. They had a great deal in common and a great deal of respect for each other. Renaldo always enjoyed Edward's visits and their discussions of the ancient cultures of Mesoamerica. Over the years, they became close friends and knew each other's families. When Edward called and asked to use the museum's facilities, Renaldo assured him they would be at his disposal.

After Edward was settled in his hotel, he went to the Museum of Anthropology and was warmly greeted by Renaldo. They talked endlessly about their families and their interests, and Renaldo graciously made all the facilities of the museum available to him.

In the past, Edward had never fully disclosed his hypothesis to anyone, since his evidence was inadequate. Now, he thought he was very close to having sufficient confirmation of facts and decided to fully explain his theory to Renaldo.

"My friend," Edward began, "you know that for years I have toyed with a specific theory relating to the first cultures of Mesoamerica and their contact with other cultures. I recently acquired some artifacts from an undiscovered ruin, and with the information I have and can acquire, I could prove the people native to this area actually had visitors from the Far East, and their visits would have taken place hundreds of years before Christ."

"So, this is the theory you have always been so surreptitious about,"

Renaldo said in amazement. "I must say it is an extraordinary hypothesis. Do you have these artifacts with you?"

"Yes."

"And have you actually been to these ruins?"

"No," said Edward humbly. "But the man who sold me the artifacts says he can take me there."

"Edward, you know there are constant reports of newly discovered ruins which prove to be bogus," said Renaldo.

"I know this, Renaldo, I have examined the artifacts and have done some preliminary testing. I believe these artifacts are from the time of the ancient ones and that they are genuine. I would like to use your facilities to date the artifacts," Edward said.

"Certainly you may use any of the facilities of the museum," Renaldo said.

"These are the artifacts," said Edward, as he took them from his bag and handed them to Renaldo. "The animal figures are jade carvings, and the other I believe to be an azimuth circle."

Renaldo examined with great interest and said, "They certainly appear to be very old and this feline figure certainly looks to be Mayan or Olmec. The other is different. It does not look like it came from the same culture, but it is very worn, and it is hard to discern what the figure represents. Who did you get these from Edward?"

"I bought these from a man who lives in Chiapas. His name is Arno Castillo, and he runs an import/export business. I know buying these on the black market in Mexico is illegal, but I had to be sure that they would be available for me to use. It is my plan to donate these to your museum when I have finished my research," said Edward.

"That's very gracious of you, Edward," Renaldo said. "If you didn't buy them, they may have fallen into the wrong hands and would then be lost. I thank you, but I don't know how the police would react to this situation, so let's keep this to ourselves for now. I will personally order the tests from my most trusted technician and ask for his silence regarding the artifacts."

"Renaldo, I knew I could count on you. You are a good friend," said Edward gratefully.

"After you test the artifacts, will you go to the ruins?" asked Renaldo.

"Yes, I plan to get the man who sold these to me to take me to the ruin," Edward replied.

"What do you know of this man?"

"Actually, very little," Edward said. "Jose Sucre sent Castillo to me. Jose knew very little about him except he bought some minor pieces from him in the past. He says he is in the import/export business."

"That's not very much. It could be dangerous to go off alone with someone you know so little about."

"Yes, I have thought about that, but he said he will not work with me if there is anyone else along."

"That sounds rather ominous, but for now let's take things one step at a time and see what we can prove with the testing of the artifacts," said Renaldo.

When the testing was completed, it proved all of the artifacts could be dated B.C.E. In fact, they all came from the same period. Renaldo, again, studied the feline figure which didn't look like Olmec or Mayan art.

"So, Edward, you know your artifacts are real, but what is your explanation of this piece?" Renaldo asked.

"This piece is an integral part of unlocking my theory," Edward said, as he studied the figure. "I believe it came from the Far East. I can prove the jade came from another hemisphere by chemical analysis. However, then I will have to prove it has been in Mexico for hundreds of years. That would, of course, mean someone brought it here."

Edward turned to Renaldo and said, "So, the only thing I can do now is to go to the ruins where these artifacts were found and hope to find further proof. All I know is that they are somewhere in the general area of Chiapas. Castillo promised to take me to the ruin if I paid him more money."

"Edward, this may be a very risky venture," said Renaldo. "You know what some of these people are like."

"I know the man I bought the artifacts from has one goal in mind, to make money, and that's okay. I have dealt with men like him before. As long as you can feed their greed, you are in control. I know I have to be careful with him, but I must try to get to the ruins. I will be leaving shortly to go to Tapachula to see him," said Edward.

"Edward, you know, the Maya National Liberation Army in Chiapas has had some violent uprisings against local and national authorities. It has been quiet there for some time, but they could start up again any time. It is a dangerous place. You should not go into these areas with someone you don't know if you can trust." said Renaldo.

"I'm too close to give it up now," Edward replied.

"Well, if you have to go, then I would like you to contact Antonio Dega when you arrive. He's an old friend of mine. He is a retired professor of chemistry and a prominent person in the community. He knows the local people and the area."

"I certainly could use some help in a strange area," said Edward.

"Well, I think he could help you with more than his knowledge of the local area. Antonio helped me with some artifacts the museum had acquired, which we thought were from the Chiapas region. He also has a theory he has worked on for years. The first part of it is an accepted practice. By identifying the composite of the elements that make up an item, in most cases, he can identify the area the elements came from. Of course, some composites or even the individual elements may be indigenous to a number of different areas, which makes identifying the exact source of the object impossible. This is where the rest of Antonio's theory applies. His theory is the materials imbedded in the artifacts, such as microscopic fossils, animals, and vegetation can be aged and identified to specific locations. Then, the combination of the elements in the artifact and the residue may provide a specific location. This process could be useful in your project."

"Yes, I can see it could help. Do you think he would be interested in my work?" Edward asked excitedly.

"Antonio is constantly seeking more information about the Mayas. I am sure he would be most interested in your theory, that is, if you wish to share it with him. He's totally trustworthy, Edward," Renaldo said.

"Well, I will consider what you have said, and I will contact Dega when I arrive in Chiapas. But, first, I have some further research to do here on the piece which we could not identify," said Edward.

They shook hands warmly, and Renaldo said, "I will be leaving soon for a short trip to Europe, but please contact me when you return from Chiapas."

"I will, and I hope to provide you with a new page to the early history of Mesoamerica," Edward replied with a smile.

CHAPTER ELEVEN

Edward's journey to Tapachula was not very pleasant. He hired a small aircraft to take him to Tuxtla, which is the largest city in Chiapas, and from there, he hired a car and a driver to take him to Tapachula. The car left in the early afternoon, and he had never been so hot in his life. It was now the beginning of summer, so the temperature had to be near 100 degrees, and the humidity was stifling.

As he sat in the back seat of the Honda, he wished for air conditioning. All of the windows were down, but the breeze did little to cool him. He had taken off his jacket a long time ago, and the only area of his shirt that was dry was the front where the breeze from the window hit him. He was sure his back was soaked because he was sticking to the seat.

He tried to talk to the driver, but his Spanish didn't match the native dialect of the driver, so they could only communicate on a rudimentary level.

When they finally got to Tapachula, he went to a small hotel and checked in. He told the elderly man at the counter he needed a room which was equipped with a large table. He then arranged to rent the room by the week. He followed the old man upstairs to his room. He decided to shower, change, and then go to see Antonio Dega. The proprietor of the hotel knew Antonio Dega and where he lived. The old man got a taxi and told the driver where to take Edward. Dega lived in a large old home perched on the top of a hill on the edge of the town. Edward walked up to the door and knocked.

An elderly and stately looking man came to the door dressed in simple white cotton pants and shirt. He asked in Mexican, "Hola, lata yo ayuda ju?"

"Yes, I hope you can help me. I'm looking for Senore Dega," Edward replied in Spanish.

"Mi nombre es Senore Dega," the man said.

"How do you do, Senore Dega," Edward replied again in Spanish. We can speak in Spanish, but the dialects I have already run into here are unknown to me, so if you speak English it would be easier for both of us."

"Oh, yes," Antonio said as he smiled. "We can speak in English if that's easier for you."

"Thank you. Yes, it would be," said Edward.

"I'm Edward Amelot. Renaldo Armando directed me to you and gave me a letter to give to you. He said he would try to call you."

"So, Renaldo sent you to me," said Antonio. "I have not talked to him. We sometimes have problems with our phone system." He took the letter from Edward and read quickly. He turned to Edward, smiled and said, "Welcome to mi casa. Please call me Antonio. Anyone who is a friend of Renaldo is welcome here. Is Renaldo still the pompous character he always was?"

"Well, he's an old and dear friend of mine, so he probably would not want me to answer that question," Edward said smiling. "However, let me qualify my response by saying we are both probably equally grandiose given the opportunity."

Dega smiled and said, "I mention Renaldo's pomposity with affection. He's a close friend, a very learned man, and I have always admired him."

"Yes, he has a great deal of respect for you, also," Edward replied. "He said you were a tremendous help to him in his work."

"Renaldo, also, spoke highly of you in his note, Senore Amelot. He says you are the only Norte Americano who truly understands Mesoamerica. That you are like an 'alma campanero', which is high praise from Renaldo. My compliments to you Senore Amelot," Dega said.

Edward smiled and said, "Please call me Edward, and if we keep up all these compliments, we will all have reason to become conceited."

They both laughed as Edward extended his hand. Dega took it and shook it warmly.

"Please come into the library and let me offer you something to drink and, please, call me Antonio," Dega said.

"Thank you, Antonio, the drink would be most refreshing. After my drive here from Tuxtla, I could use one," said Edward.

After the exchange of pleasantries, Edward had a chance to get a good look at Antonio Dega. At first glance the man had the appearance of an elderly, but distinguished looking gentleman who spoke softly. At closer look, however, one could not help but notice his muscular arms and neck sloped down to strong looking shoulders. Dega, it seemed, was a man of contrasts.

"I apologize for our roads," Dega said. "They could be better, but the people of this area are very poor, and it seems all of the taxes they pay go to the politicians in Mexico City or to the tourist towns, in order to make things better for our visitors."

"Actually the roads are alright, but the worst part of the journey was the heat, I haven't adjusted to it yet. But it certainly is cool in here," said Edward.

"This old house was built over 150 years ago by my ancestors," Dega said, "and the walls are over twelve inches thick, which keeps the heat out and allows the air to flow through the house. Even when the humidity is high, the air flow decreases the moisture and cools the temperature in the house."

"It's too bad we don't take lessons from your ancestors. We would conserve a great deal of energy," said Edward.

"Is this your first visit to Chiapas?" Dega asked.

"Yes, it is. I had planned to come here with Renaldo in the past to visit the ruins at Plaenque with him, but there was always something more pressing at the time," said Edward.

"Well, maybe you can do that now," Dega replied.

"That would be very nice, but I'm afraid my time will be taken up with another project. Have you known Renaldo long?" asked Edward.

"We have been friends since we met at the University. We were both radicals in our youth, which was much longer ago than I wish to acknowledge," Dega said.

"Yes, he mentioned you have always been an activist for the poor and a defender of your heritage," said Edward.

"Well, that's kind of him. My activism today centers on preserving our heritage more than anything else. The people of this area are descendants of one of the oldest civilizations known to man. People think of Mexico as a backward country, but that's untrue," Dega said. "Our culture rivals those of any part of the world. But I am telling you something you already know."

"Yes, your ancestors were preeminent in many cultural developments. It is too bad the early visitors to this area did not take a greater interest in what they could learn from your culture, rather than the quick profit they could gain," said Edward sadly.

"Yes, they tried to be friends with the Europeans, but they just came to take the natural resources, the gold and silver, and then wanted to tell us how to run our country. We didn't want to mix our blood with theirs like the poor tribes in the north did, and we, like our ancestors, want no outside interference, especially from the Mexican government. However, I am telling you things you already know. I apologize, but I get very impassioned with our cause," said Dega.

"Is there a cause? I have heard of some insurrections in this area," Edward said.

Dega furrowed his brow and said, "Insurrections. How can there be insurrections? The government sent here by Mexico City should have no power over us; they are interlopers. I'm sorry for sounding like a misanthrope, but this is a subject that brings out feelings of indignation in me for my people. Please, let us talk about happier things. Tell me about your work and your visit here."

"I have been a student of Mesoamerica throughout my career. The culture and the people are fascinating, and there seems to be no end to the new and exciting discoveries about the societies that were indigenous to this area."

"You seem to have a passion for our history," said Dega.

"Yes, and I understand Renaldo got you to help him in his work," Edward replied.

"I certainly had some of the most exciting and interesting times of my life in helping Renaldo with his projects. You see, I was able to help Renaldo determine the age and, in some cases, the area of origin of some of the artifacts he acquired," Dega said.

"Renaldo told me that. Your process could be of interest to me for my project. Can you do this with just a small amount of material?" asked Edward.

"Yes," Dega said. "If the artifact came from this region, there is a good chance I can give a general provenance for the item. If it has microscopic fossils, animals, or vegetation embedded in it, these materials can further define the location of its origin or, at least, where it has been."

"That's most interesting, but it must be difficult to have to collect so much information on the chemical compositions and flora for different localities."

"Oh, I couldn't do this for just any area. You see, I have made a hobby of studying the composition of the earth and the fossils in this particular geographic area."

"That's most interesting," said Edward. "I have done some work in chemistry to determine age of artifacts, but it has always been with the assistance of experts in radioactive carbon dating. We could only arrive at very general estimates of the location from which the artifacts came, but, even then, our proof was usually based on the art and not the content of the artifact. If I understand the process you just described, it could be a great help in identifying the source of my artifacts. How much of a geographic area are you talking about in your work?"

"Well, Chiapas is bound southwest by the Gulf of Tehuantepec and the Pacific Ocean, east by Guatemala, north by Tabasco, and west by Vera Cruz

THE ANCIENT ONES

and Oaxaca."

"That may cover the area I'm interested in," Edward replied.

"It is interesting to talk to someone who understands the work I have done with Renaldo and how it can relate to the study of the ancient cultures," said Dega.

"Thank you. I am hopeful you can help me uncover some of the mysteries of your people. As one who is part of the culture, you must have heard wonderful stories about the people that are not in text books," said Edward.

"Yes, the people who live in this area tell many tales about their ancestors. They talk of their wealth, knowledge and mystery. The Indians who live here don't think of themselves as Mexicans, Guatemalans, or Belizeans, but rather as descendants of an ancient culture, a culture that developed before Christ and before the civilizations of Europe. Some of them still perform the ancient rites of the Ah Kin, the high priests in the temples of the ancient ones. They believe the Jaguar Lord, Jacatez, protects the temples and defends those who protect our culture. I have such a patronizing view of this because I am speaking of my own heritage."

"As you should," said Edward.

"I did not realize we have been talking for so long. I have been a poor host. Would you like some tea or coffee?" Dega asked.

"That would be very nice. Either one is fine with me," replied Edward.

"I'm sure Ixtanalia, my housekeeper, can also find some of her delicious pastries for us. I will return in a moment," Dega said as he left the room.

Edward sat there deep in his thoughts. From what he saw, he liked Antonio Dega and had a great interest in his process of identification.

Dega returned and said, "We will have tea shortly. For some reason, I have always been drawn toward the flavors of the teas from China. I hope you like them."

Edward smiled at that and said, "I am sure I will. Antonio, I need someone in whom I can confide, someone I can trust with a project that has been very dear to me. I have just met you, but I already feel a confidence in you. Besides, Renaldo has told me how much of a friend you are to him and that you are a man who can be trusted to keep his word."

"Thank you for the compliments. I, too, have a good feeling about you and our discussions," Dega replied.

"I would like to confide in you about some work I'm doing, related to your ancestors. But I must know you will keep it all in the strictest confidence," Edward said sincerely.

"I would love to hear about your work, but are you sure you want to confide in me?" Antonio asked.

"I have to have help from someone, and you are certainly the best candidate for my trust."

"I'm honored by your trust, and I assure you I will help you as much as I am able," said Dega.

"I have brought with me some artifacts that supposedly came from this area. I bought them illegally from a man by the name of Castillo," Edward said.

Dega responded with an obvious look of surprise and recognition, "Castillo, yes, he has a business in Tapachula."

"You recognize the name. Do you know him?" Edward asked.

"No, I don't personally know of him, but I do know of people who have done business with him. None of what I have heard of him is good. I understand that he is rather unprincipled and does this kind of thing. But you must know it is illegal for him to acquire and sell these artifacts," Dega said accusingly.

"Yes, I do," Edward, replied. He could sense that Dega had great disdain for Castillo. "But they seemed to be a direct tie to the theory I have had about the people in this area."

"Where exactly did these artifacts come from?" Dega demanded.

"I'm not sure. I was hoping to get more specific information from you about where they came from. Castillo said he bought them from an Indian who came to his place of business, but he does not know what his name is or how to contact him. He said he gets a lot of old pieces like these brought to him by the Indians."

"That may be true," Dega said. "Some of the old ones may have a treasured piece, which came from their Mayan ancestors," said Dega now sounding cold. "Some pieces may even be from a temple of the ancient ones that is known to only a few of the true believers. They sell them when they are in need of medicine or food to those that would take advantage of their plight. The government does not take very good care of our elderly."

"Yes, I know of this," said Edward.

"And when these temples are found, the unscrupulous ones rush to steal our heritage and sell it to anyone that will pay their price," Antonio looked at Edward with a scowl and said in an accusing manner. "But many have searched in the jungles and gotten lost, robbed by banditos, or arrested when they cross the border to remove the artifacts,"

"Antonio, I want to assure you, I never planned to take the artifacts out of Mexico. I have already told Renaldo they would go to his museum after my research was completed," Edward said trying to convince Antonio of his honesty.

"I am very happy to hear that," said Dega with relief in his voice. "You seem to be a man of honor, and I was sure you are not trying to steal from my people; however, if these artifacts do come from this area, I would like to see them placed in our museum here in Chiapas. Renaldo helped us to establish the museum here and even lets us acquire some artifacts from his museum to be placed in ours. From time to time, we call on him for help."

"Since I have promised them to Renaldo, I will consult with him, but I'm sure he would agree with placing them in your museum," Edward said.

"I thank you," said Dega. "They would certainly add immeasurably to our museum. Now, please continue with your theory."

"In my studies I have found many things about the Olmecs and the Mayas that could be related to another culture. I know that many cultures, even distant ones, have similarities, but there were too many that were too close to ignore. Then, a number of years ago in a paper from the Museum of Anthropology in Mexico City, I found some photographs of artifacts which were part of a private collection whose owner was unknown. The artifacts were supposedly found in a marketplace in Villahermosa. From the photos, I could see one had a resemblance to an Azimuth Circle. Are you familiar with its use?"

"Yes, it has something to do with location in Astronomy," Dega replied.

"Yes. The Azimuth Circle is an important auxiliary device used for indicating the bearing of an object, its direction measured from the north point. It is a graduated ring with sight vanes, which, when focused on the polestar, provides a means of taking bearings of both terrestrial objects and celestial bodies. What I saw at the museum could have been a forbearer of the Azimuth Circle."

"And you concluded this was used for navigation by the Olmecs?" Dega inquired.

"Not immediately. I researched how ancient seafarers traveled the oceans. My research was directed to astronomy, as it was used for navigation in that period. From this, I became interested in archaeoastronomy and discovered remains have been found, which link astronomy to the Olmecs and the Mayas. I believe these artifacts I saw and the ones I acquired may have been used for navigation as the Azimuth Circle was used."

"This is very interesting, but the Olmecs and the Mayas were never known to have been seafarers," Dega replied.

"Those were my thoughts, exactly, when I found the first photographs. In addition, I have never seen anything that related these cultures to ship building. I couldn't figure out why the Olmecs and the Mayas would have developed a tool for navigation without a need. Then, I thought the Olmecs might have used Azimuth Circle for calendaring, since the Olmecs were an agricultural society, and they would have a need to track seasons. This was a reasonable explanation; however, there were the other things that drew me to the conclusion that they had contact with another culture. So, I concluded that it could have been brought here by an ancient visitor to this area."

"Well," said Dega, "have you found anything to prove this theory?"

"Yes," said Edward, "new and quite revealing."

"How so?" Dega asked.

"Renaldo was able to determine, through his tests, that the artifact that I believed to be an Azimuth Circle was made hundreds of years B.C. In addition, the other artifacts that I acquired from Castillo came from the same period. They were jade figures of cats."

Edward took pictures of the artifacts from his pocket and handed them to Dega.

"It is difficult to tell with all of the soil encrusted on them, but they appear to be cat-like figures. I can understand your interest in the potential of the circle, but why the cats?" asked Dega. "The Olmecs and many of the other cultures of Mesoamerica worshiped feline deities."

"At first, I thought, like you, that they were just jade figures made by an ancient Olmec artisan. This in itself would be a most interesting find, but it would certainly be nothing revolutionary. However, it was difficult to exactly identify the exact form of the figures because they were so encrusted with soil. I did not want to remove the soil because I did not want to damage the exterior of the figure. Even so, as I began to study the two figures, I found each has a different feel to its surface, and when studied closely, the style of the art for each was different. One was what I have found to be indigenous to the Olmec artisans. The other, I concluded, comes from a completely different provenance."

"Yes, I can see one is in the art form of the Olmecs, but the other is not definable to me," said Dega.

"It is difficult with just a picture. I have studied the piece, and I feel I know where it came from. Jade art is found in Mexico and other parts of the western world as well as China and other countries of the Eastern Hemisphere. I know the jade found in Eastern Asia is a very different chemical composition from that found in other parts of the world," Edward qualified.

"That's very true," said Dega.

"This jade figure is identified as coming from the Olmecs and the other one, I believe, is Chinese. If my suppositions are true, the jade pieces would have a different chemical composition."

"Yes, you are right. You might say there are two kinds of jade. One is derived from jadeite, which is extremely difficult to break, and was used to make tools. It is vitreous when polished and is found almost exclusively in eastern Asia. Jade is also derived from nephrite, which has an oily luster. It is found primarily in Alaska and Mexico, but also emerges in some other countries. If the two specimens you have are different, we can find this out in my laboratory."

"Do you have a lab close by?" asked Edward.

"How about in my house? I still experiment from time to time. Do you have the jade figures with you?" Dega asked.

"Yes, they are at my hotel, but I can bring them to you. Could you also look at the clay circle and see if you can determine where it might have come from?" Edward asked.

"Certainly. Why don't you come and have dinner. We dine late here because of the heat, so it would be good if you came by at about six. That will give us enough time to test your artifacts before dinner," said Dega.

"That would be wonderful. I'll bring the jade figures, then," said Edward excitedly.

"I suggested to you that you might donate the artifacts upon the completion of your work. My good friend Camilo Reyes is the benefactor of our museum, and his family can be traced back to the ancient times. He has a great knowledge of the area and its history. I would like you to meet him, but more than that, I would like you to share your theory with him. Making his acquaintance might prove to be very beneficial to you."

I'm sure Senore Reyes is a good friend, but I have already talked to too many people about what I'm doing," Edward said. "I am mostly concerned the rumor of a lost ruin could bring many unscrupulous ones following me."

"I understand how you feel, but I can tell you Camilo would be of great help. In addition, I'm sure he would be willing to pay you whatever you paid for the artifacts when and if you are willing to give them to our museum," Dega said.

"Alright, if you think it would be helpful, then I would be glad to meet Camilo. Now, I would like to retire to my hotel and have a shower. Then, I will return at six o'clock with my artifacts."

"I will call for a taxi to take you to your hotel," said Dega.

"Thank you. I will look forward to seeing you later." As Edward left, he felt an exhilaration knowing that he might be so close to discovering proof of his theory.

CHAPTER TWELVE

As Edward left, Dega watched the taxi drive up the road and away from the front portico. He wanted to tell Edward that Castillo was an unscrupulous dealer in contraband and would sell anything to anyone for the right price. However, at this point he could not tell him any more without revealing information that was confidential to his cause.

Dega went into the house and told his housekeeper about the dinner guests. He, then, called Camilo Reyes and asked him to come see him.

Camilo Reyes was an old friend, who was also of pure Mayan blood. His father and his father's father were direct descendants of the high priests of the Mayas. They each had practiced their religious rites until they died and passed them on to their heirs. Camilo kept his heritage secret; although, he did still participate in rites of the temple. His passion, which he shared with Dega, was to have an independent Chiapas for the Mayas.

Chiapas was loosely tied to Guatemala in colonial days and involuntarily became a Mexican state in 1824. Since then, outsiders have been taking the resources and driving the Indians off the land. In 1994, there was an armed uprising by the impoverished Indians against the federal government that failed. Dega and Reyes had supported the uprising with the goal of an independent Chiapas. They knew if there was to be another attempt for independence, they had to provide a better plan and more support.

Reyes, like Dega, had all of the features of the Mayas. He was of a slight build and had dark hair that was beginning to turn gray. Reyes mother was born in Guatemala. Her family had been the owners of a number of large coffee plantations. After the sale of the plantations, the family invested the money, and the fortune multiplied itself many times over. Since he was the only child, he received all of the fortune when his father died. Now, he used his fortune to fund the causes of the Indians.

With Dega and other leaders, they formed a council to direct and provide support for their cause. The council consisted of a group of wealthy men from Mexico and other Central American countries that wanted a homeland for the Indians. A homeland where they could practice their old ways and not be dictated to by a government that didn't understand their life style and their traditions.

When Reyes arrived, Dega told him about Edward Amelot and the artifacts which were supposed to have come from Chiapas. He also informed Reyes of Edward's meeting with Arno Castillo.

"Castillo, he's the scum of the earth," said Reyes. "Do you think this has anything to do with the Indians who were found killed and burned near Anyxlatana?"

"I'm sure Amelot had nothing to do with this," said Dega. "The American Amelot is well known and is a good friend of Renaldo Armando. He would not send someone to me if he thought that that person had bad intentions. Besides, from what I have seen, I like him, and I think he's a good man. However, Castillo is another question."

"Does he know anything about our cause?" Reyes asked.

"No, I believe he is only here as a scientist in search of knowledge. He will join me here at six for us to work on his artifacts. I told him about you and our museum. I would like you to meet him, so would you join us for dinner at nine?"

"Do you want to question him about the source of these artifacts?" Reyes asked.

"Yes, but it must be subtle," Dega replied. "Earlier, I let my passion for our cause come out, and this might have made him a little hesitant to be open with me. From what he told me, he has some hypothesis about the Olmecs meeting with some ancient culture from across the oceans."

"Neither the Olmecs nor the Mayas traveled the seas; however, I do remember a legend about the ancestors being visited by some strangers from another world, but I always believed it was about spiritual visitors."

"Yes, I remember tales of men who came from the sun and were yellow like the color of the sun," said Dega.

"That's right, we were told they had come from the sun god. It would be interesting to pursue."

"Yes, there are many unexplained legends I would like to research, but we must now spend our time with our cause of freedom. Have you had further talks with Senore Brabant?"

"Yes, I visited Brabant a few weeks ago. He lives in Guatemala City and has major business holdings all over Central and South America. He still professes his sympathies to our cause and has offered to support us. I was overwhelmed by what he had to offer. He's one of the richest men in the world, but few know this because his business interests are so diversified.

He took me to a camp where he's developing a small army of mercenaries with all of the most modern weaponry. Not like we had when our people tried to rise up against the Federales."

"And we are now being pressured by the militant ones on the MYLN council to begin another offensive. How can we be expected to fight the whole Mexican Army?" Dega asked.

"Brabant is willing to provide us arms and training," Reyes said, "and he thinks we can accomplish our mission, but not just with military force. He proposes we begin a major publicity campaign, now, and increase the intensity of it as soon as the resurrection begins. We will let the world know how the Indians of Chiapas are being taken advantage of by the Mexican government. He believes that if we have a force sufficient to take over the government in Chiapas, we could close down the highways and railways and have a siege type of environment. We can keep the Mexican Army from using the highways, and at the same time, continue to build public opinion in our favor. At the same time, we petition the United Nations for a cease fire, holding the lines we form and asking them to assist us in gaining our independence."

"Yes, we have discussed this before. But tell me, why does Brabant have sympathies to our cause?" Dega asked. "I have been told that prior to World War II, his family was allied with Hitler. Is that true?"

"Where did you get this information?" Reyes demanded.

"Camilo, I spoke to each of the council members. Porfirio Arriaga said he also knew Brabant from the business world and told me it was common knowledge William Brabant's family supported Hitler and made great financial gains in Central America during the war."

Reyes replied, "In the past his family were the rulers of the country of Hesse, which is now part of Germany. The German government annexed Hesse long before Hitler. Before the war, they tried to regain their independence by forming various alliances. He likened his country's past struggle to gain independence from the Germans to our conflict with the Mexican government."

"So, he did support Hitler?" Dega asked.

"Let me explain. His family developed a huge industrial base in the early 1900's and tried to use this wealth to regain the independence of their country. When Hitler came into power, his family saw an opportunity to gain a powerful ally in the new German government," Reyes explained.

"They helped Hitler to gain power with their financial and political resources. In return, he promised to prosecute their cause. But after Hitler gained power, he nationalized many industries. When the Brabant's saw what Hitler was doing, they stopped their support and most of their family immigrated to South America before the end of World War II."

"After leaving Germany with as much of their wealth as possible, his family developed business interests in Central and South America. He now has homes in many places, including Guatemala City. Once the war ended, the family regained their German industries, and no one has brought up the subject of their support of Hitler since then," Reyes said.

"What is Brabant offering to our cause?" asked Dega.

"He offers to provide us with arms, supplies, and the use of his Hessian mercenaries for training. He would include surface to air missiles, and he has offered to have his men support our forces."

"Why does Brabant have an army?"

"No, Antonio, not an army," Reyes said. "He likens it to a large security force. He has industrial installations all over the world that had to be protected against internal conflicts and terrorism. So, he established a force of men and provided them with military training to guard his installations. He maintains a strike force in the event rebel groups attack any of his business interests. He has even helped governments train their armies."

"And for this assistance, what does Brabant ask?" Dega queried.

"He says in return for his assistance, he wants permission to set up his industrial base here, so he can control his industrial empire without interference from the government," Reyes replied.

"I wonder what 'without interference' means? How well do you really know this man, Camilo?" Dega asked.

"I have done business with him for many years. I have made a great deal of money from my association with Brabant. I have trusted him, and he has always lived up to his word," Reyes answered.

"Risking money and risking our homeland are two different things." Dega thought for a moment and asked, "Have you asked the council what they think of bringing outsiders in to help us in our cause?"

"No." Reyes said. "They are old men with little vision, and they take too long to make a decision. We should make this move ourselves and tell them what we did later."

"I don't like working like this," Dega said bluntly. "We are all in this together, and the council is supposed to be the directing force in our efforts. Where are you in your discussions with Brabant?"

"Brabant needed a response now, so he could begin to move some munitions into Chiapas," Reyes said. "I told him he could set up a camp in the mountains near the caverns with a training force only. The caves there are dry and will hold a great deal of supplies. What harm can it do to take his offer of arms?"

"My friend, no one gives anything for nothing, and I worry about the ambitions of powerful men like Brabant," said Dega.

"We can watch him closely," Reyes reasoned. "I can stop his movement if you think it is best."

"Not as long as it is only a limited force," said Dega. "We have to be very careful not to commit to anything we couldn't get the council to approve. I have already discussed Brabant with the council, so we can tell them we decided to allow Brabant to bring in a small training force under our control. However, I want to meet with Senore Brabant. I like to look a man in the eye if I'm going to trust him with my country."

"I will arrange that. Do you want him to come here?" asked Reyes.

"No, it might draw the attention of the government. Someone might recognize him and report it to the authorities." Dega said.

"All right. I will ask him to come to the camp they will establish in the mountains. He can fly his helicopter there from Guatemala, and we can see his progress," Reyes said.

"That will be fine, Camilo, but be careful. Tell Brabant only as much as he needs to know."

"Don't worry so much," said Reyes smiling.

"My dear friend," continued Dega. "You are always full of optimism, and I worry about someone taking advantage of your trusting nature. We should try to be cautious and not let our desire for freedom to cloud our good judgment. So, as I said, Senore Amelot will be here at six, and I would like you to arrive at nine."

"As you wish, Antonio, and I will contact Brabant about meeting with you."

CHAPTER THIRTEEN

For centuries, the Brabant family was one of the most prestigious and aristocratic families of Germany and was the landgrave of the state of Hesse. Despite efforts from the Brabant family, in 1918, Hesse became a republic. The family repeatedly petitioned the German government to regain control of those territories, unsuccessfully.

Gustav Brabant, the patriarch of the family, invested the family fortune successfully, and they became one of the richest families of Europe. In 1929, he decided to help finance Hitler's way to power. He believed Hitler would rule Germany, and the family could then fulfill their dream to regain control of Hesse.

Gustav's son, William, was a student of his father, and, even at a young age, he participated in his father's businesses and political maneuvers. At his father's direction, he became an insider in the Nazi party. The Chancellor fancied having blue bloods in his retinue, and William had the look of a true Aryan, over six feet tall, blonde, blue eyes, and physically robust.

As Hitler began his mad dash over Europe, Gustav saw each of Hitler's successes only whetted his appetite for more. He also realized Hitler's obscene quest for power would be his downfall. When Hitler invaded Russia, he was taking a great risk, but when he declared war on the United States, Gustav knew this was his final error. Being an astute businessman, he knew that industrial might and natural resources won wars, and he did not want his family to fall with the Third Reich. He decided in order to survive the destruction that would come to Germany, he had to move his financial base to other parts of the world.

The Brabant family had cultivated holdings in South America for many years, and Gustav wanted to expand further in that hemisphere. He decided to send William to oversee the expansion. As always in business, Gustav looked for an advantage. He talked to Hitler about building a network of industrial spies in the business world of the Americas, which could be used to Germany's advantage. Hitler liked the idea and gave his approval. Of course, Brabant's real objective was to give his son valuable information to build the family's business.

William proved to be a very astute businessman and an even smarter politician. He acquired significant sums of money from the Third Reich to build his spy network, and he bought industrial secrets and plans that ensured the growth of the Brabant businesses.

When the war began going badly, the Nazis began sending William great sums of money, so he could develop safe havens for them. He kept his ties with the Third Reich very secret and never had any direct contact with the Nazi war criminals. He even turned in some to ensure he would gain the cooperation of the local governments.

The war ended, and Gustav left Germany without realizing his dream to regain control of Hesse. After a few years, he died a broken man. William Brabant no longer considered the hope of regaining Hesse practical; however, having control of a government where he could conduct his business without worry about government regulation was a pragmatic endeavor.

He had found post war Central America had many weak governments. He began hiring his own expatriate countrymen, especially ex-military men of Hessian heritage, to build a mercenary army. Over the next three decades, Brabant financed and participated in revolutions all over Central America with the objective of gaining power from those who were at the head of the revolution.

To date, his attempts in places like the Dominican Republic, Nicaragua, El Salvador, and Panama had failed. Panama may have been the closest, but its future president proved to be too greedy and ignorant of how to deal politically with others. Brabant, however, had learned from each attempt and was now sure of his plan. Chiapas was a perfect target for Brabant.

Chiapas was a state in Mexico, but it had been independent and was still trying to secede. The local government was weak, the leaders of the revolutionaries were patriotic, and there was a great deal of sympathy in the world for the Indian's cause. Their first attempt had failed for many reasons, but Brabant, with his extensive resources of men, money, and influence, could address these problems.

The area was remote enough that, when an uprising began, it would take time for the government to respond. That was the advantage he needed. He learned this important lesson from his father who applied in business and all parts of life. He was confident that, with his planning and resources, the Indian leaders would follow his lead. Men like Reyes were not politically adroit and could be exploited in the name of revolution.

Brabant's plan was to give the Indians all the arms they needed and to send his army into Chiapas to support the uprising. The Indians would take over the local government forces, and his troops would operate any of the sophisticated weaponry.

When the Indians gained control of the state, he would launch a public relations campaign to tell the world about their plight. While the new country was being secured militarily, he would see that most of the Indian forces were sent to maintain control of the border. He would, then, have his army take over the central government and subordinate the revolutionaries.

Reyes was so eager to bring freedom to the Mayans that he was ready to accept Brabant's aid without the proper control over his forces. Brabant had talked to Reyes about setting up a camp in the mountains of Chiapas. He told Reyes he would bring in men and munitions to train the Indians. This would be the opening he needed to bring his mercenary force into Chiapas.

Brabant's army was currently in Guatemala, but they could cross the border into Mexico, in an area which was very isolated. The governments of Mexico and Guatemala did not have the forces to guard all of the mountain roads between the countries.

Reyes liked Brabant's plan but told him Antonio Dega, who was the head of the MLYN council, would have to agree. Brabant said he didn't like all of the delays. In order to placate Brabant, Reyes agreed that the mercenaries would begin to move a limited number of men while he went to talk to Dega. Brabant knew he, again, intimidated Reyes into accepting his plan. He was satisfied with this concession and would deal with Dega later.

CHAPTER FOURTEEN

Edward sat in his hotel room, thinking about the gravity of his situation and what he should do. He was in possession of artifacts illegally, and he was on his way to try to find an Indian ruin the government did not know about with Castillo, who is a known miscreant. What choices did he have? If he wanted to prove his theory, he had to keep the artifacts, he had to find the temple to gain further proof, and he needed Castillo to lead him there. This was not the best situation to be in, but, hell, he was so close to proving his theory he was ready to risk whatever he had to. He would just have to be careful with Castillo and not do anything to draw attention to him or what he was doing by the government. At least he had found help in Dega. He liked Dega, and he just might be able to help him with the artifacts.

He arrived at Antonio Dega's home just before six.

"Buenas noches, Senore. Welcome again to my home," said Dega.

"Thank you for having me here again. I have been looking forward to you examining the artifacts," Edward said.

"As have I," Dega said.

Edward took the figures out of his bag and said, "Here are the two jade figures and this disk."

Dega spoke as he examined the pieces. He rubbed the jade figures with his fingers. "I believe you were right about the jade. They do look and feel like a different composition. But to be sure, let's go into my lab and test them."

They walked through a hallway and down some stairs to an underground room which looked like a chemist's lab. In addition to various vessels, there were numerous pieces of what appeared to be relics of statues and other earthen pottery scattered on a long stone counter. There were also shelves along the walls stacked with many bottles of chemicals.

"You certainly have an impressive laboratory," said Edward.

"Yes, I have built it over the years," said Dega. "Actually, this room is only part of it. Through that door, I have computers and other electronic equipment to help in my work."

"I know you can test the jade for chemical composition, but do you think you could come up with any information on the disk?" Edward asked.

"We shall see. Let's do the easiest tests first. I'm going to examine each jade piece from their base to determine their chemical properties." Dega set about his work, while Edward looked at the relics in Dega's laboratory.

Edward walked around the lab looking at the pieces of pottery and the various chemicals Dega had in his laboratory.

After a short time, Dega looked up and said, "This piece is definitely jadeite from the western hemisphere. The other is definitely nephrite from Burma, Tibet, or China. "

"You have confirmed my suspicions," Edward said excitedly. "I know from age testing the pieces date from well before the birth of Christ and my belief was that the Nephrite piece is of Chinese origin. Now, can we do any further tests?" Edward asked.

"Certainly, what is it you wish to do?" asked Dega.

"We now know one of the jade figures is from this hemisphere and the other from the Far East. I was wondering if there is enough of the residue in the crevices of the artifacts for you to identify where the artifacts have been for the last two thousand years?"

"Hmm, there might be, but what further do you think you can learn?" asked Dega.

"The residue was also dated to approximately the same period as the jade. If the residue on the jadeite is from this area, and we have already dated it, then we can assume the jadeite piece from the Far East was brought here hundreds of years ago. The only mystery then will be how it got here," said Edward.

"Oh, I see," said Dega, whose interest was definitely peaked.

"Yes, and the Azimuth Circle could be the piece of the puzzle that will tell us how the jade piece got here. Can you also look at its composition?" Edward asked.

"Certainly, but I will need some time for this. You certainly have aroused my curiosity," said Dega. "I will do it for you first thing tomorrow if I may keep the pieces until then?"

"Of course. I cannot tell you how much I appreciate your help and interest," said Edward.

"That's perfectly alright. If you like, you can come by about noon tomorrow. I should be finished with the test by then, and we could have lunch and discuss my findings," Dega offered.

"That's more than generous of you. I want you to know, after some thought,

THE ANCIENT ONES

I have decided to donate these artifacts to your museum. I feel Renaldo would understand my decision, since he helped you with your museum. But, with the agreement that I would have access to them for my research," said Edward.

"Your gift is very kind. This is, without a doubt, the most significant contribution to our museum, and you will always have the opportunity to study anything in our museum. I would like to let Reyes know of this, but I will keep the details of your theory out of this wonderful news," Dega said.

"I'm sure that will be fine," said Edward.

"Well, let's go up and see if Reyes has arrived, so we can have dinner. My housekeeper, Ixtanalia, can cook wonderful meals, which she claims, are from ancient recipes. I told her we were going to put her in charge of the food preparation history section of our museum," said Dega as he laughed.

"I look forward to the chance to have such an authentic meal," said Edward.

"I warn you, according to Ixtanalia, Mayas lived on chili peppers, and they are always applied liberally in her cooking. She grows them, and they seem to have the fire from our volcanoes, so use them prudently. If all the Mayas ate them as liberally as Ixtanalia, then I have an idea why the culture is waning," said Dega with a hearty laugh.

"Duly noted," Edward said.

They went back up the stairs where they found Reyes already sitting at the dining table with a glass of wine in his hand.

"Hola, Camilo. I see you have a start on us," Dega said.

"Hola, Antonio. I brought you a new wine from Central America. It is outstanding. I couldn't wait to sample it," Reyes replied.

"Edward Amelot, I would like you to meet my dear friend, Camilo Reyes. Besides his attempts to be a wine connoisseur, he also has a significant knowledge of our culture and the ancient ones," Dega said as he introduced them.

"I have heard a great deal about you from Antonio, Senore Amelot," Reyes said as he shook Edward's hand. "He says you are a friend and a colleague of Renaldo. Renaldo has been a great help to us at starting our own museum. I hope you will have time to visit our humble beginning and see what we have to offer."

"Thank you for the kind words. I would love to see your museum," said Edward.

"Dinner is served," said Ixtanalia standing in the doorway.

During dinner, Dega told Reyes about Edward's artifacts, how significant they were, and his contribution to the museum.

"Senore Amelot, we will see your name is among the most prominent patrons of our museum. Thank you for myself and for our people," Reyes said.

After more talk and a great deal of wine, Edward excused himself and asked Dega to call a taxi to take him back to his hotel.

As Dega walked Edward out the front door, he said, "You have made Camilo and me very happy with your generous gift. Moreover, you have certainly raised my interest in your hypothesis. I will be ready for you tomorrow at noon. Buenas noches."

"I look forward to our meeting tomorrow, as well," said Edward, as he got into the taxi and drove away.

Dega returned to Reyes and said, "I'm very pleased with the gift from Senore Amelot. He has removed any misgivings I had previously about his intent."

"Yes, I'm also very pleased. Antonio, I must talk to you about something else. I have contacted Brabant."

"Did you tell him I would like to meet with him?" Dega asked. "Yes, and he agreed to meet with us at your convenience," replied Reyes.

"Please arrange this with him as soon as possible," Dega said.

"I will schedule the meeting. I have told him he can move enough men into Chiapas to handle the munitions and training. The rest of his troops can be moved after we have talked. That will give him some incentive to follow through on his desire to meet you."

"That's good. I would also like General Mixcóatl and some of his staff to be with these mercenary forces while they are in our country. Mixcóatl can keep us appraised of what Brabant's men are doing."

"I will inform the general and Brabant of this," Reyes said.

"Good, then you and I must bring this whole alliance to the council. We cannot proceed further without their approval," said Dega.

"I agree we should move cautiously, but as I said, the council is full of old men who will never agree to take the bold steps necessary to win our independence," said Reyes.

"Camilo, when our last attempt at a coup failed, we decided to move slowly and to take the counsel of the elders, as our ancestors did," Dega replied paternally.

"Yes," said Reyes; "however, you should remember our ancestors made their biggest gains when there was a strong leader to make decisions swiftly."

"And do you want to be that leader?" asked Dega.

"No, I know you are our leader, Antonio. I only want to get on with our plans. I will wait, and I think it is good that we meet with Brabant," Reyes replied.

CHAPTER FIFTEEN

William Brabant sat in his office in Guatemala City and thought about Chiapas. He was no longer the blonde, blue eyed, robust Aryan who had been associated with the Third Reich. His hair had turned white, but he still maintained a muscular body on his six-foot plus frame. He was also older and certainly wiser. As his telephone rang, he was thinking about the next steps to be taken in his planned coup in Chiapas. When he picked up the receiver, the voice on the line was Camilo Reyes.

"Hola, Senore Brabant. Senore Dega has agreed with bringing the men you will need to establish the munitions base and to train our men," Reyes said.

"Camilo, it is good to hear from you, but I thought we had discussed moving my entire group into your mountains in preparation for the revolution. We have already made plans to relocate completely," said Brabant.

"I know this is what we discussed," Reyes replied, "but we have to convince our elders this is the right step to take. Dega and I discussed this and we feel we must move slowly because of them. I'm sure that as soon as your men begin the training, we can move the rest of your forces into Chiapas. This is the only option we have at this time, William."

"All right," Brabant said, "My men are on their way."

"Just let me know when your men will arrive, and our commander, General Mixcóatl, will meet your men and help them to set up their camp," Reyes said.

"Fine. I will have General Von Papen contact you," Brabant said.

"One more thing, we would like to have a meeting with you, that is Senore Dega and I."

It was difficult to take William Brabant by surprise since he was used to facing the shrewdest business leaders in the world, but he was certainly taken back by the suggestion he would finally meet the leader of the MYLN. He thought Dega wanted to stay in the background and let others represent him. This was a common practice among some men of power, who did not like to give immediate answers when presented a problem or opportunity. He looked forward to meeting the leader of the MYLN face-to-face.

"I have always wanted to meet Senore Dega. Where and when would you like to have this meeting?" Brabant asked.

"I thought after the camp was set up, we could meet there," said Reyes. "That way you would both be out of the eye of the public and press. I know you are an important man, and you attract much attention in public places."

"That will work fine. I will be in touch Camilo," said Brabant as he hung up.

Brabant did not like this delay, but one thing he had learned was Indians moved at their own pace. He knew he could push Reyes, but he was not the leader of the Indian group. Dega was the one he had to control, and, now, they would finally meet. Maybe, he could also control Dega, but he doubted it. He called his assistant and told him to send Guenter Von Papen to his office.

Von Papen was a professional soldier. He wore a military uniform with five stars on his shoulders, and he looked fifty-two; although, he was actually seventy-two years old. He was six foot three, lean, robust-looking with a full head of white hair. In his earlier years, his face could have been on a poster for the typical German soldier. His eyes were still the same ice blue, and they seemed to pierce right through anyone who dared to look at him directly.

He had been a young officer during the last years of the Third Reich, and he was still totally dedicated to the cause. If Adolph Hitler rose from the grave, Guenter would have been his first follower. He had been commander of Brabant's private army for many years.

His mercenaries were primarily Germans, but there were other Europeans, South Americans, and Central Americans. Many of the South and Central Americans were half-German from the intermarriages of expatriates from the Third Reich. The core group of the men and the commanders were Hessian officers. These men loyal to Von Papen and Brabant and were steeped in the old traditions. New recruits went through extensive training and hazing that exceeded any of the military academies.

The men were equipped with and trained on the most modern military weapons Brabant's billions could buy. They were tough men who had no families with them. Some used Brabant's army to hide from the law just as other men did in the French Foreign Legion. Guenter screened each new recruit carefully and used their past to control them.

The men in the mercenary army were well paid and had all the luxuries that could be made available, but their term was for life. There was no resignation. If they wanted to leave the army, they had to desert, and if caught, they were executed.

Von Papen stood at attention before Brabant. "Guenter, I have an agreement from the rebels in Chiapas to let us send in enough of our men and equipment to establish a training facility and munitions base in order to supply the rebel forces," said Brabant.

"We have already begun to relocate the whole army. They are in the process of crossing the mountain. The Guatemalans are getting very emphatic about our leaving the country," said Guenter.

"I know," said Brabant, "but we need more time. We will get all of our men into Chiapas eventually, but we cannot push these Indians. I want you to send enough men to establish a camp for the arrival of the whole army under the guise of them being the training group. Move the rest of our forces near the border, so they can be ready to move quickly."

"We will need a significant number of men to build a camp large enough for all our men. It will be difficult to explain to the Indians," said Guenter.

"I know, but you can make some excuses about technicians for each weapon, strategy planners, and support staff to keep the camp. That will give you enough men to establish a foothold if we need it. As far as the building is concerned, tell them we are making room for their men."

"Yes sir, that deception will provide us with sufficient men to build the camps, but ammunition will be in short supply when we bring in the rest of our troops," said Guenter.

"Set up an ammunition depot in a controlled area to house the training stores. Once you have it established and the Indians see what you are doing send for more supplies. Just don't let the Indians near it again," said Brabant.

"Will we be going to the location we discussed?" asked Guenter.

"Yes," said Brabant, "and you can take the route through the jungle, which can handle the large trucks full of ammunition. The Indians will be sending a General Mixcóatl and probably others to meet you. I'm sure they just want someone in our camp. You can keep these Indians busy and out of the way."

"Yes, sir, that will be no problem."

"And, Guenter, make sure General Arriago keeps the Guatemalan army away from their northern border for the next few weeks."

"I will suggest he tell El Presidente there is a border dispute with El Salvador, and he's sending his men to the south to deal with it. He can keep their troops there for a few weeks, at least. But, General Arriago will not like us moving our forces around in his country without there being something in it for him," said Guenter.

"Just tell General Arriago we will double his payments until we leave the country," Brabant replied.

"That will make him very happy, and I'm sure he will find a way to let us to stay as long as you keep paying him. Arriago has accustomed himself to the good life. If it were up to him, we could stay as long as we wanted and with as many men as we needed; however, El Presidente cannot be bought. We already tried," said Guenter.

"I admire the president for his loyalty to his country," said Brabant. "He's a man of principles, and those are the most dangerous kind for us. When will you arrive?" asked Brabant.

"Since we have already begun the movement of the men, I'm sure we can be at the location in two days," Guenter replied.

"How long will it take you to set up camp?" Brabant asked.

"A permanent camp will take about four weeks," said Guenter.

"Good, then get started as soon as you can. I don't want to pay that damn Guatemalan whore, Arriago, any more than I have to," said Brabant with distain. "I want you to lead this operation personally," said Brabant.

"Certainly, sir," Guenter replied crisply.

"And one more thing. After the camp is established, we will have a meeting there with Reyes and Dega," Brabant added.

"Dega will be meeting with us!" Von Papen said with surprise.

"Yes, an interesting new development. The mysterious leader of the MYLN has decided to come out from behind his shield," Brabant answered.

"What do you make of it?" Guenter asked.

"I'm not sure, but whatever this Indian wants, we can handle him. I have dealt with much more intelligent and sophisticated men than him, and I have always prevailed. Now, get our preparations underway for our new homeland, Guenter."

"Yes, sir," he replied as he departed from the office.

Brabant looked out the window of his office and thought about his ability to buy men like General Arriago. Greed in some men could transcend all else, and the knowledge of this helped him to build the financial empire, which was probably the largest in the world.

His financial empire was never in the news because he was careful to avoid public recognition. He earned unfaltering loyalty of a few good men, and with them, he built his great conglomerations. Jointly, this collection of businesses controlled the supply of many of the products, which drove the world economy.

Energy sources were the most important investments he made. His plan was that when the oil fields in the Middle East started to dry up the price of crude oil would begin to skyrocket, and, then, he would tap into his oil fields in Central and South America. When oil becomes too expensive, other sources such as uranium will be needed. He, also, had acquired significant reserves of uranium. He would be able to set his own price for energy sources.

Brabant's dream was to build a country in which he could recreate the past glories of the State of Hesse. First, however, he needed a base from which to operate, so he would not have to answer to a local government and its archaic laws. He needed Chiapas and the government he would establish there. This might be his last chance, and he would pay any price.

CHAPTER SIXTEEN

Edward got up early the next day and went to the lobby of the hotel, which was actually only a small alcove near the front door. The proprietor, Senore Mandares, was an old man who dressed in a white shirt and tie, white pants, and no jacket. Edward had seen his wife bring his meals to the alcove, and Edward was not sure he ever left there.

"Hola, Senore," said Edward, "I would like to use the telephone, but the one in the hallway does not work."

"Buenos dias, Senore Amelot," Mandares said in broken English, "is your room alright? Since you are a friend of Senore Dega, we have given you our finest room."

Edward smiled. He knew all the rooms in the hotel were probably exactly alike. He also had checked in before anyone was aware he knew Dega. "Yes," he said, "my room is fine, but the telephone is not working. May I use your telephone?"

"Si, you could if it was working, but I think it has been two weeks since the telephones have been working. But, luckily, they did work last night," the old man said.

"They worked last night but not now?" asked Edward suspiciously.

"Si. Sometimes they are working, and we can make a call, and sometimes we finish the call before they stop working. I'm happy to say we did finish a call, but I am sorry to say that when I tried another, the telephone... it was not working."

"Then, how can I find a man and his business if it is located in Tapachula?" Edward asked exasperated.

"I can probably help you. I know most of the businessmen in Tapachula. What is his business, and what is his name?" asked Mandares.

"He's in the import business, and his name is Castillo. Do you know him?" asked Edward.

"Si, I know Castillo. You say he's in the import business. Is that what he calls it?" the old man said with a smirk.

"So you know him?" asked Edward.

"Si, his business is on the edge of the city. Would you like me to get a message to Castillo?" Mandares asked.

"No, I would like to go there. Would you get a taxi and tell the driver where to take me?"

"Si, but are you sure you want to go there by yourself? Castillo has a malo reputation," the old man warned.

"I'm sure I will be all right. I have met him before. Please, just tell the taxi driver to take me there," said Edward.

"As you wish," Mandares replied.

"You get the taxi, and I will return in a moment," Edward said.

Edward went back to his room to get his jacket and walked out the front door.

The taxi was waiting. Edward got in, and the driver drove away without a word. As they went through the business areas of the city, Tapachula looked like most mid-sized Mexican cities. Some new looking businesses, and some looked shabby. The taxi driver took him to a shabby building on the edge of the city. He asked the driver to wait, but he didn't understand, so he took a twenty-peso note and tore it in half. He held up both halves and gave one to the driver, who looked at him and grinned in recognition.

He walked up to the door of the business and knocked. An elderly woman with a broom in her hand came to the door.

"Hola, Senora, " said Edward, "I'm here to see Senore Castillo."

"Senore Castillo no aqui" said the elderly woman with a pained look on her face.

"Do you know where he is, Senora?" Edward asked.

"Senore Castillo…"

"May I help you?" a voice behind Edward asked in English.

As Edward turned, he saw a man in his early thirties, wearing shabby pants, and a dirty shirt walking up to him. "Yes, I'm looking for Senore Castillo." Edward explained.

"Who are you?" the man asked.

"I'm Edward Amelot. Senore Castillo and I have some business together."

"Si, Senore Amelot," he said with recognition in his voice. "I'm Jose Lopez. I work for Senore Castillo. He told me you would be coming here, but today he's at the plantation buildings."

"At the what?" asked Edward.

"Senore Castillo has a storage building on an old banana plantation a few miles away. Would you like me to take you there?" Jose asked.

"Well, how long will it take? I have an appointment at noon," Edward said questioningly.

"I can take you there, and you can be back for your appointment at noon," Jose offered.

"Alright," said Edward. He was apprehensive, but he had to see Castillo and make plans to go to the temple. "How will we get there?" asked Edward.

"I will drive us there."

"Then, I will dismiss the taxi that's waiting for me," Edward said.

Edward gave the taxi driver the other half of the twenty-peso note and said, "Gracias amigo. I will no longer need you to wait."

He turned as Lopez came around the corner of the building driving a truck whose color was unrecognizable under the dirt that covered it. It looked to be from the forties and sounded like every nut and bolt in it was loose and rattling.

"Please, get in," Jose directed his passenger.

The inside of the truck was no different than the outside. It was grimy, and the floor was covered with papers, cigarette butts, and ashes. Edward brushed some scraps of paper onto the floor and sat down on the bench seat next to Jose.

Lopez drove as if he was trying to catch the leader in the Grand Prix. The speed was bad enough, but it got worse as they started up the mountain. Lopez not only passed every car, but he had to do it even if it was on a curve.

At first, Edward thought there was some kind of way the driver knew he could pass, but it was absolutely impossible to see any oncoming traffic. Edward's heart was pumping, and his stomach was in one big knot. Finally, he just decided Lopez was totally nuts, but there was nothing he could do about it.

Edward concluded he couldn't look at where they were going and not have a heart attack, so, instead, he looked out the side window and tried to concentrate on where they were. They passed small adobe houses, which he knew were occupied by the poor. They would have one room in the front and one in the back. The front room acted as a living room, dining room, and kitchen, and the back room passed for sleeping quarters. If the back room was big enough and the family was small enough, they all slept in one room.

After Lopez drove for a while, he slowed down and turned onto a dirt road. As he drove further on, the road got narrower and bumpier, and the branches from the jungle plants brushed against the side of the truck. After being hit by a few branches, Edward had to shut the window. It was already stifling in the car, but his choices were sweat or be beaten by the underbrush.

Suddenly, they came to a clearing in which there stood a number of small buildings and one larger one. The only one that looked like it was safe to enter was the larger building. The truck came to a stop in front of the large building, and Lopez told Edward to wait. Edward got out of the truck to stretch his legs and watched Lopez walk up to the building.

Castillo was inside the building and heard the truck coming, and by the sound knew it was Lopez. He was checking a shipment of Czechoslovakian automatic weapons he had just received and left them and came to the door. "What are you doing here? Why did you leave the warehouse?" demanded Castillo.

"Hola, Senore Castillo," said Lopez with a big smile on his face. "I have brought your Senore Amelot to you."

"You did what? You idiot! I told you never to bring anyone here. This building is full of things no one should see."

"I'm sorry, patron, but you said you wanted to see this man as soon as he arrived," Jose said sheepishly.

"Yes, in Tapachula, but not here. Where is he, you fool?" Castillo thundered.

Lopez's smile left his face, and he looked down at the floor. "He's outside waiting in the truck."

"Stay in here, fool, and close up these cases. I have inspected them, and they are ready to be sent to their new owners. After I have gone, put them on the truck and deliver them. Do you know where to take them?" Castillo demanded.

"Si, they go to the old fishing village to Montaldo's boat," Jose replied.

"See that they get there today and stay off the main roads," barked Castillo.

"Si, Patron, I will see to it," Jose said.

As Castillo walked out of the building, he saw Edward Amelot standing next to the old truck with his jacket over his arm and wiping his forehead with a handkerchief.

"Hola, Senore Amelot," Castillo said as he waved to Edward with trepidation.

"Hello, Senore Castillo. This is quite a place you have here," Edward replied.

"Oh, it is just an old warehouse where we store useless things. My primary place of business is in Tapachula."

"I came to talk to you about going to the ruins where the artifacts came from. Have you been back there since we spoke?" Edward asked.

"No, I haven't. As I told you, it is very dangerous," said Castillo.
"Well, do we still have a deal?" Edward asked.
"Do you have the money?" Castillo countered.
"Yes," replied Edward.
"Then pay me as we agreed, and we will make plans to go to the ruins."
"Sorry, but I don't have the money with me. You will get it when you have taken me to the ruins," said Edward.
"When would you like to go?" Castillo asked slightly annoyed.
"I would like to go as soon as possible," said Edward.
"I can be ready to go in two days," said Castillo.
"Fine. How far will we be traveling, and how long will we be gone?" Edward asked.
"If we leave in the morning, we can be there the same day. We will drive as far as we can before noon, and, then, we will have to walk for about one-half a day," Castillo answered.
"Then, we will have to stay there overnight?" asked Edward.
"It is not good to try to find our way back in the dark," Castillo replied sarcastically.
"I was more concerned about staying long enough to study the temple. I don't have any camping gear," said Edward.
"I will take care of what we will need to set up a camp. We will leave the day after tomorrow at 7:00AM," Castillo answered.
"Good. Will you have your man take me back to Tapachula?" asked Edward. "I have an appointment at noon."
Castillo looked surprised. He didn't think Edward Amelot knew anyone in Tapachula. "I will take you back. Do you have acquaintances in Tapachula?"
"Yes, Senore Dega. I am meeting him. Do you know him?" Edward asked.
Castillo looked surprised. "Uh, no, I don't think so," he hedged. Castillo knew Dega was a powerful man who was reported to be the head of the MYLN. Castillo remembered he had sold weapons to the MYLN some time ago. The weapons were of poor quality, and some of them actually blew up when fired. Castillo had purchased them from a ship's captain who promised that although they came from Egypt, they were manufactured in Europe. Castillo did not believe this story, but the price had been so good he took a chance on them.
After the arms had failed, the MLYN's people came to Castillo and demanded their money back. Now, it was Castillo's policy never to give money back, so he offered them different arms in their place. Dega's people

would not be swayed, and they told Castillo if he did not return their money, he would no longer have a business in Tapachula. With this persuasion, Castillo finally agreed and returned their money. He had not done business with Dega's group since.

"Have you told anyone you were coming to see me?" Castillo asked.

"Yes, but only the hotel proprietor. I needed his help to find you," said Edward. He did not think it was necessary to tell Castillo he had confided in Renaldo and Antonio about Castillo. After all, he didn't want to scare Castillo away.

"It would be a good thing not to tell anyone about our business or that we are going to the ruins. Others would love to get to Tucanil's ruins before we do," said Castillo with a smile on his face.

"What, whose ruins?" asked Edward.

"Uh, Tucanil. He was the Indian who found the temple," said Castillo.

"So, you know it is a temple, and where it is located?" asked Edward.

"Si," Castillo replied.

"Will he come with us?" asked Edward.

"Uh, no, he is gone. These Indians come and go, and no one knows where they disappear to," Castillo stammered.

Castillo did want to go to the ruins to try to find more artifacts, but he didn't intend to take Edward there. His plan was to take the anthropologist into the jungle, relieve him of his money, and then dispose of his body. However, now others knew he had met with Edward and could tie him to the crime, if it were discovered. He decided, he would take Edward to the temple and figure out what to do later.

They got into Castillo's jeep and rode back to Tapachula in relative silence. When he dropped Edward off at his hotel, he said, "I will come here to get you the day after tomorrow at 7:00 A.M."

"Thank you. I will be ready at seven," said Edward.

CHAPTER SEVENTEEN

Edward went to his room, washed up, changed his clothes, and worked on his journal. Then, he took a taxi to meet with Dega at his home. He knocked on the door.

"Ah, Edward, welcome," said Dega.

"Antonio, thank you again for your hospitality," Edward replied.

"I have good news for you about the artifacts. I conducted some tests on them and found enough soil embedded in each of them to assure you they have been in this area for quite a long time. There is a particular type of clay in the residue which is only found in three locations in this hemisphere."

"If there are three places that have this type of clay, how can you say the clay came from Chiapas?" asked Edward.

"Well, as I told you yesterday, sometimes the flora particles embedded in the clay can help to identify the area from which the artifact came. The flora becomes trapped in the clay, which keeps it from decaying and enables us to identify its provenance. The flora particles embedded in the clay come from plants, which are indigenous to only a few areas. However, the combination of the two brings us to the conclusion they came from this area. This is as conclusive as I can get."

Edward was elated. He grabbed Antonio's hand in his and said, "Antonio, I don't know how to tell you what this means to me."

"I am so pleased I could help," said Antonio with a smile on his face.

"So," Edward said beaming. "What we know is one of the jade pieces was carved in the Olmec tradition and came from this hemisphere, and the other, carved in the style of China, came from the Far East. But, the soil samples embedded in both came from this area, and the radioactive carbon tests prove both pieces and the soil can be dated to hundreds of years B.C."

"This is a great discovery you have made," Dega replied.

"No, Antonio, not mine, ours. Without your tests, all of my findings would only be a theory, which the academicians would tear apart. You share greatly in this moment of discovery. Any paper I publish will give you credit and, if you agree, provide information on your process of identification, in order to confirm the results."

"Well, thank you, Edward. You are most kind in sharing your achievement with me. Of course I will provide you any information on my process you need. I cannot tell you how much it means to me to help to discover this fact about my ancestors. So, we are brothers in science," Antonio said with a big smile on his face.

"Yes, Antonio, and I can never repay you. I have been attempting to prove this theory for a long, long time, and now it is done." Edward took Antonio's hand in his and said, "Thank you, mi amigo."

Antonio Dega, a normally reserved man, had tears in his eyes. "Edward you have shown respect for our culture and have only worked to ameliorate our knowledge. You honor me with your friendship."

"I look forward to the day when I can donate these artifacts to your museum, Antonio."

"We should celebrate the denouement of your hypothesis," said Dega.

"That's very kind of you Antonio, but not yet. As I said, I still have to find exactly where the artifacts came from," said Edward.

"And how will you do that?" Dega asked.

"I met with Castillo this morning to see if he found the person who sold him the artifacts."

"Any luck?" asked Dega.

"No," Edward said. He hated to lie to Antonio, but he was afraid if he told him that he was going to attempt to find the ruin with Castillo, he might try to stop him. He knew that Dega did not trust Castillo. "However, Castillo said that he had some other sources he was contacting. I will see him again within a few days. At this point, I don't even know if the ruins are in Chiapas. As I'm told, the Indians travel across the border with Guatemala freely."

"That's very true, and many of those who cross the border do so because what they are doing is illegal," said Dega emphatically.

"So you think Castillo is unscrupulous?" Edward asked.

"What I know of Castillo is not good. Please be careful. This kind of man cannot be dealt with in good faith," said Dega caring.

"Thank you, Antonio, I will be careful," Edward said.

"Well then, let's have lunch. I am sure Ixtanalia has prepared us another wonderful meal. I will tell you about the artifacts we have in our museum, and after we eat, I will take you there," Dega warmly offered.

Edward did not like to lie to his friends, but because of Antonio's distrust of Castillo, he did not want to say he was going with Castillo in search of the temple. They ate and talked about Chiapas and the problems the Indians had with the Mexican government. When they finished, they walked into an old section of Tapachula. There, in an old Iglesia, stood the museum of which Dega was so proud. The two men spent hours looking at the artifacts and talking about them.

When they were through, Edward said, "Antonio, I don't know how to thank you again for the assistance you have given me."

"Edward, I'm glad Renaldo sent you to me," Dega said. "You honor me by being my friend. Edward, I want to share something with you that may seem strange at first for a man of science. I have spoken about the ancient ones, but this is not just an anachronism. They were the protectors of the temples and the gods and were left to spend eternity in the temples guarding the treasures and protectors of their culture. They were feared by the Indians in ancient times, and they are still to be feared," Dega said solemnly.

"Antonio, you really mean this. You want me to believe ancient warriors guard the temples today?" Edward asked.

"Yes, Edward," Dega replied. "I know it is hard for a man of science to believe in something you cannot see, but men here in Chiapas, including myself, have seen things that cannot be explained by any science. The common thread was the protection of the culture of the Ancient Ones."

"Yes, Antonio, it is hard to believe men or spirits of men from over two thousand years ago are still here guarding the past, but I have heard of other incorporeal spirits. I have not had such experiences, but I know learned men who totally believe in their existence. I respect you and what you believe, and I will keep it in mind," Edward said.

"I share this with you, amigo, because I worry about your welfare. Heed my words, the ancient ones do exist," Dega said.

"Antonio, I will be careful," Edward promised.

"And please be cautious with Castillo. Call me after you meet with him. Go with God, my friend," Dega said as they embraced and Edward left for his hotel.

As Edward got into the taxi, he said to the driver, "Please drive to the shopping district."

He sat in the taxi and thought about what Antonio had said. He was certainly taken back by what he had just heard from a man of science, but he couldn't be deterred. He had to go on. He looked up at the driver and said, "Will you please take me to a shop where I can purchase some clothing for hiking in the jungle?"

The taxi driver looked at him as if he was crazy and said, "You are going to hike in the jungle? Do you know this is the rainy season, and it gets very hot there?"

"Si," said Edward, "I do. But, please, I want to buy some clothes and boots. Do you know a place which will sell these things?" Edward asked.

"Si, I will take you there," the driver sighed.

They arrived at an open-air shop with a sign over it that said 'Zapato.' The taxi driver said, "Go in there, and you can get some bota. Then, there are three ropa shops as well."

"Thank you," said Edward. "Will you, please, wait for me?"

"Si," the driver replied.

Edward bought a pair of hiking boots, some cotton twill shorts and pants, and a rain parka for protection from the jungle showers. He also bought a hat, some insect repellant, a flashlight, a canteen, a pack, and a pocketknife. Finally, he found a wooden chest the size of a large jewelry box. Satisfied with his purchases, he had the taxi driver take him back to his hotel.

Edward spent the evening and the next day writing up his notes on the artifacts and, then, completed his journal of the events of the day. He had always kept daily journals when he traveled because it helped him to remember details when he wrote his reports later on. He wrote about his meeting with Castillo and the plan to go into the jungle, and he was doing the right thing.

Edward wrapped the Azimuth Circle in a towel and placed it in the chest he had purchased. He decided to take the statues with him to compare against any he might find. Finally, he wrote a note to Antonio, which read:

Dear Antonio,

I am leaving tomorrow to go exploring with Castillo. I know you think this is dangerous, but I have to find the temple. I understand the risk. I do ask you to please keep the Azimuth Circle for me until I return. Thank you for being my friend.

He placed the note in the chest. He would instruct the hotel proprietor to deliver the chest to Dega after he left.

He also wrote a note to Cara, letting her know about his success with his theory and about Dega, his new friend.

CHAPTER EIGHTEEN

It was early morning when Edward got his new clothing out and packed his things into his backpack. He wrapped the statues in his socks and placed them in his pack. He pulled on his new hiking boots and put his pocketknife inside one of them. A few minutes before seven, he got his backpack and his newly acquired chest and went downstairs where he found the hotel proprietor.

"Hola, Senore Amelot," said Mandares. "You look like you are going for a long trip."

"Buenos dias," said Edward. "Si, I will be gone for a few days, maybe a week. I would like to pay you for the next two weeks, so I can leave my things in my room."

"That will be fine. I hope you have a good journey," Mandares replied.

"One more thing, will you please mail this letter to my daughter and have someone deliver this chest to Senore Dega?" asked Edward.

"Si. I will have my grandson take it as soon as he arrives," said Mandares.

"Thank you. Tell him to give it to no one other than Dega. If, for any reason, he cannot give it to Dega, please return it to my room. And please, don't deliver the chest until this evening," Edward directed.

Edward walked out the door and saw Castillo sitting in front of the hotel in his jeep. It was loaded with supplies. "Hola," he said, as he saw Edward approaching.

"Buenos dias," replied Edward.

As Edward got into the jeep, Castillo asked, "Do you have the money we agreed on?"

"Not with me," Edward answered.

"But we agreed you would pay me today," Castillo reminded him.

"Yes, we did," said Edward, "and I already have."

"What do you mean?" Castillo asked.

"I had 10,000 U.S. dollars placed in an escrow account in both our names at the National Bank in Chiapas. Here is the account and the release for the funds. When we get to the temple, I will sign the release, and the money is yours." Edward said.

"This paper says the bank will pay me if you sign it. What will keep you from not signing it after I take you to the temple?" asked Castillo.

"As long as you make your best effort to find the temple, you will get the money. Are these terms acceptable to you?" asked Edward.

"I was planning to have the money today," said Castillo.

"Well, since it is 7:00 A.M., and we are leaving, there is nothing you can do with the money today. Don't worry. It will be here for you upon our return," Edward replied.

"What if we cannot find the temple?" asked Castillo.

"The money is yours either way. As long as I feel you have made an honest attempt, I will give you the money," said Edward.

Castillo scowled about this new development. His mind began to churn. He would go to the area of the temple and get Amelot to sign the release and then dispose of him. He would get the money and would not have to face whatever it was that killed Tucanil. "Well, I guess it is okay," Castillo said. "Let's leave before it gets too hot." They began to drive out of the city and soon were on remote country roads.

Edward asked, "Are you sure you know where temple is located?"

"Yes, I have been thinking about it, and I know the general area of the temple," Castillo replied.

"How long will it take to get there?" Edward inquired.

"We will drive for half a day and then walk for half a day. The drive could take longer if the roads are bad. When the summer rains come, the rivers flood, and bridges could be under water. We will have to see as we go," Castillo hedged.

"But it has not rained very much in all the time I have been here," Edward replied.

"Si, you are right, but when it rains in the mountains, the water flows out of the mountain streams into the rivers. When there is too much, there are floods everywhere."

They passed a village every few miles, but the buildings were all the same. They were all adobe, and their color matched the earth around them. They had either clay tile or flat roofs and very few windows. In each village, there were a few businesses, including, usually, a gas station, a general store, and some kind of eating and drinking establishment. The villages and the buildings became smaller and smaller, and the business establishments became all in one.

As they drove, the cool air of the morning became warmer and warmer. Around eleven o'clock, Castillo came into another village and stopped at a casa de comidas. They entered the dark interior of the restaurant, and Edward tried to look around the room as they made their way to an empty table. At first, all he could see were shadowy shapes and the white part of many eyes. When his eyes finally became adjusted, however, he could see there were two or three men sitting at each table who were all drinking beer. It certainly seemed like a good idea in the heat of the day. As they entered the room, the conversations of the men became muffled, and they were all looking at him and Castillo.

A lady came to take their order. Castillo ordered empanadillas, Edward ordered huevos con jamon, and they both had cerveza. He didn't really want beer with ham and eggs, but it was safer to drink than anything made with the water.

They ate slowly. As they looked around the room, the men still stared at them. Castillo certainly looked the part of the other men, but Edward, with his new hiking boots and clothing, looked very much the part of a gringo.

As they finished their food, one of the men at the table next to them looked at Edward and asked "Hola, usted Norte Americano?"

Edward was surprised and began to speak but Castillo blurted out, "No entender."

Edward looked at Castillo and said in English, "I understand him perfectly. What is your problem?"

"We don't want anyone to know where we are going," Castillo reminded him.

"The man was just being civil. He was not asking where we were going. Why are you so nervous?" Edward asked.

"I know these people. They just want to find a way to get money from you. They start with a question or a greeting, and soon they are in the middle of your business," said Castillo.

"You are the only one who has asked for money," Edward replied.

"Please don't use my name in here," Castillo warned.

"What are you hiding?" asked Edward.

"I'm not hiding anything," Castillo answered. "I just want to keep others from our business. If you are finished, we should be on our way or we will not get there before dark. I will get fuel for the jeep."

As Castillo left, Edward rose, turned to the man who had spoken to him, and said, "Yo disculparse por mi compnaero."

"So you do speak our language, and I speak yours," said the man in English.

Edward looked at him in surprise and said, "Again, I am sorry for my companion. He is a very suspicious man." Edward then smiled and said, " I'm sure he would be surprised by your English. Hasta luego."

The man smiled back and said, "Adios."

Edward then walked up to the bar and paid for the meal and the gasoline.

They got into the jeep and began to drive further down the road. After about a half-hour, Castillo turned sharply onto a road that appeared to be no more than two tracks into the jungle. They began to climb uphill and go deeper into the jungle. Edward could hear a low rumble, which became louder, until he finally identified it as the sound of swiftly running water. Suddenly, the road bent sharply to the right, and Castillo came to an abrupt stop.

"We must look at the bridge," Castillo explained.

Edward got out and saw a bridge extending over a canyon, which had been carved out by the swiftly running water. The bridge was about twenty feet across. At the middle, it looked to be about the same distance down to the water. The surface of the bridge was no more than a bunch of boards, which were laid across some beams. There were large gaps in the boards, which afforded a generous view of the river beneath.

"Are you planning to cross this thing?" Edward asked.

"Si. I will drive the jeep up to the bridge, and you will ensure the boards on top of the beams are lined up with the wheels. I will go slowly, so you can move any of the boards as needed. Here are some gloves for you to use. Please, let me know if you need me to stop," Castillo explained as he turned back to the jeep.

Edward put on the gloves and walked up to the edge of the bridge. He looked down and thought, "This is crazy. Why am I doing this? I'm too old for this shit." Then he reconsidered, "No, he thought, I started this, and I will finish it."

He backed out onto the bridge, making sure his feet were on the beams which were perpendicular to the end of the road. Castillo slowly drove up to the edge of the bridge and said, "Senore, be sure the boards are in front of the wheels."

Edward ensured the boards were positioned correctly, each about ten feet long, next to each other, and parallel to the end of the road.

"Alright, you can move forward slowly. But, stop when I tell you," Edward said nervously.

Castillo moved the jeep forward slowly.

After about eight feet he yelled, "Stop!"

Castillo stopped, and Edward lined up the next boards with the first and said, "Alright, you can proceed."

This process continued on until Edward began to line up the final boards of the bridge. Then, as he stepped to the side, his foot slipped off the edge of the beam, and he fell sideways. In a panic, he grabbed onto the beam with his right hand to keep from falling into the river. He swung his other arm up to seize the beam, the panic leaving him only slightly. He looked up and saw Castillo looking at him from the jeep. There was no emotion and no sense of urgency in his eyes. He simply looked coldly at him.

"Help me up, Castillo," yelled Edward.

Castillo just stared and thought to himself, I could be rid of this Gringo now. Then, just as quickly, he thought of the money he was to get from him. He got out of the jeep and knelt on the boards which were set for his tires. He reached down and grabbed Edward by the belt of his trousers. He lifted up and pulled.

As Edward climbed back up on the bridge, he looked at Castillo with a furrowed brow and said, "Thank you. I'm grateful for your help, but I hope if I am in danger again, you will move more swiftly."

"I'm sorry. I was momentarily frozen by the sudden events. I couldn't move," said Castillo sardonically.

Edward looked sideways at him. He knew Castillo was not the kind of man to panic. He always looked so cold and calculating. From now on, Edward would be very careful.

Castillo got back into the jeep and drove the rest of the way across the bridge. Edward got in, and they continued their journey.

After another half-hour of climbing, the road came to a sharp turn downward. Castillo, however, turned in the opposite direction and drove across the low growing vegetation until the road was out of sight and stopped. "From here, we will have to go on foot across the ridge and go down into the next valley," said Castillo.

"How are we going to carry all of this gear to our destination?" asked Edward.

"Please, wait one moment. I made arrangements with a local Indian to have a burro waiting for us. He's very familiar with this area," Castillo said, as he went down to what looked like a game trail. A few minutes later, Castillo came back with another man leading a burro.

Edward saw the man with Castillo was an old Indian. Castillo stopped and said to Edward, "The Indian's name is Keichi. He will help with the burro and keep our camp. Say nothing to him of why we are here."

Castillo then quickly turned to the Indian and said, "Load the burro with the supplies that are in the jeep."

The Indian went to the jeep and brought out a packsaddle. He put the harness on the burro and then proceeded to load all of the equipment onto the animal's back.

Edward watched Keichi as he packed the burro. He was short, slight of build, and his face had a certain stoic quality.

He said to the Indian, "My name is Edward Amelot, and I am pleased to meet you." Then, in his best rendition of the Mayan language, he added, "I assume you are descendant of Itzamná and the great Mayan nation."

Keichi looked up with surprise and said, "You speak my language."

"Yes, but very little," Edward said in English. "You must excuse my limited ability. I admire your people and your heritage. I have studied your people's culture for many years."

"Thank you, but we are no longer a great people. We just try to survive," said Keichi.

"I am sorry for that," said Edward. "Isn't this work hard for you?"

"I do what I must to earn a living," said Keichi.

Castillo looked at Edward and the Indian and was frustrated by the fact he could not understand everything they had said. He didn't like this collaboration, and he said to Keichi, "Let's get on with this packing. I want to leave quickly."

The Indian finished packing the burro. It seemed top heavy and unable to walk, yet when Keichi pulled on the reins, the burro stepped along briskly.

Castillo then drove the jeep into the underbrush. He got out, opened the hood, and took out the distributor cap. He walked over, put it in the pack on the burro and then covered the jeep with brush.

"What are you doing?" Edward asked.

"If we leave the jeep in the open, it may be stripped or stolen by banditos," he explained.

He then turned to Keichi and said, "Go and wait up the trail for us." Keichi went a short way up the trail.

He waited for the Indian to leave and then he turned to Edward and said, "We cannot let the Indian know where we are going. His people have very strong feelings about their past. Also, if we run into the Federales, we must tell them you are looking for Indian villages in order to talk to the old ones about their ancestors. They must believe this is your business. If they know anything about the temple or the artifacts, they will arrest us."

THE ANCIENT ONES

"That's no problem," said Edward. "As far as the Indian is concerned, he certainly will know what we are about when we reach the temple. I would tell him I'm not trying to steal his heritage, only to find out more about it."

"It is best he does not know anything," Castillo explained. "One can never know how these Indians will react to our expedition. When we get near the temple, I will make camp far enough away, so he will not see it. Now, let's be on our way," said Castillo.

Castillo walked up the trail, with Edward following behind him, until he came to Keichi and the burro.

They walked for almost an hour up the mountain to the top of the ridge. It was there Castillo stopped, and Keichi tied the burro to a scrub tree.

Edward and Castillo walked over to the edge of the mountain and looked out over the valley below. Edward asked, "Is the temple in this valley?"

"No," said Castillo. "We have to go down the valley, cross the river, and then go up the other side. After we cross the far ridge, we will come to the temple. We will let the burro rest here for awhile, and, then, we will proceed."

Edward sat down on a log to rest. He could hear the river's roar, but he couldn't see the water through the trees and underbrush.

"The river sounds very loud," said Edward. "Which one is this?"

"It is a tributary of the Usumacinta," Castillo replied.

"The Usumacinta is the border of Mexico and Guatemala. Are you sure, it is not the Usumacinta? If I'm going across the border, I want to know it," said Edward.

"Don't worry," Castillo said. "I would not take you across the border without telling you so. I have also been hearing the sound of the river. I'm afraid the heavy rains have swollen the waters."

"Will we be able to cross?" Edward asked.

"I don't know. There is no bridge across the river I know of, and there is only one place near here shallow enough to cross. If the water is too deep and swift, we must wait for the river to go down," said Castillo.

"How long will it take?" asked Edward.

"It depends on how high the waters are. Let's be on our way. I would like to cross before dark," Castillo said.

"I didn't realize it is only five o'clock," Edward replied.

"Yes, and it gets dark very early in the valley," Castillo explained.

Keichi took the burro, again, by the bridle and began walking down into the valley. Edward thought it would be much easier and faster going downhill, but he was wrong.

As they continued their decent, the trail began to be overgrown with foliage, like a low awning. The trail remained worn of vegetation from the local game and men who used this trail. There was not enough room for the burro with its pack, to pass under the canopy of foliage, so Castillo stopped and went into the supplies on the back of the burro. With a flourish, he suddenly withdrew a machete that gleamed in the light. He began whacking at the brush.

The progress was very slow going. Castillo said with all of the rain, the brush grew quickly over the trail, and a path had to be cut wide enough for the pack on the burro to pass through. Keichi, Edward, and Castillo took turns cutting the brush until they all felt exhausted. Suddenly, they broke into a clear, meadow area that led up to a rather large river.

"I'm glad we finally got to a clearing. This brush cutting is backbreaking work," said Edward breathing hard.

"Si, I agree," said Castillo.

Keichi tied the burro to a bush, and they all walked to the river. The water was extremely high and very swift. It certainly didn't look like anyone could cross it, and the waters didn't seem as if they were going to subside soon.

"This looks pretty bad," said Edward.

"Yes. It is too swift and deep to cross now, but it may not be long before it becomes passable. The storm clouds and the rain are gone, and so the water will withdraw quickly. We will have to spend the night here of course," Castillo said. He turned to Keichi and barked, "Old man, will we be able to cross the river in the morning?"

"It is possible. The rain ended in the mountains yesterday," said Keichi.

"You really believe this raging torrent will become passable any time soon?" asked Edward of the Indian.

"Si," Keichi answered. "I have seen change in this river in a matter of hours. You see, the runoff from all the mountain streams comes together in this river. We just have to wait until all that water has gone away before we can cross. It will be soon."

"I guess we have no choice," said Edward.

Castillo looked at Keichi and said, "You unload the supplies."

"What can I do?" Edward asked.

"You can collect some of the dried wood from the riverbank and set up a cooking fire. I will set up our tents," said Castillo.

They were busy for the next hour getting their camp ready for the night.

THE ANCIENT ONES

Edward noticed Castillo had a rifle stuck inside the rolled up tent. It was not unusual for someone camping in this part of the world to have a rifle, but this was an AK47. Edward also noticed he had a shoulder holster under his jacket. Suddenly, he began to wonder what exactly he was afraid of in this jungle.

CHAPTER NINETEEN

Castillo was cooking beans and rice over the fire. Edward noticed a string of hot peppers lying by the fire where he was cooking. After a time, he said, "The food is ready to eat now."

Edward went up to the fire and filled a plate and walked over to a dead tree, away from the fire, and sat down. He navigated his way through the peppers, with his spoon, as he scooped up the beans and rice.

When Keichi took a dish of the beans and rice, Edward motioned for him to come and sit on the dead tree as well. Castillo took his dish and sat by the fire.

Edward and Keichi ate in silence for a few minutes until Edward asked, "Do you have any children?"

"Yes, a son and a grandson," the Indian answered. "My son's name was Kinich. He was named after Kinich Ahau, the sun god, but he is no longer with us."

"What happened to him?" Edward asked gently.

"My son was killed by the Mejicano," Keichi replied sadly.

"Why did they kill him?"

"For being a Maya," the old man answered.

"What do you mean?" Edward asked.

"I have always lived a simple life, but my son wanted more. My son chose to follow the ways of his grandfather and his ancestors by practicing the rites of his religion. My wife's father was a Maya priest and my son became a priest, like his grandfather. For this, he was killed by the Federales," Keichi explained.

"I'm very sorry. Why would they do this?" asked Edward.

"The Mejicano's do not like the Maya's religion. They think our priests tell the people to rebel against the Federales. We do not do this. We just worship our gods. We have to hide our religion. My son was proud, and he would not hide. For this, he was killed."

"You and your wife must miss him," Edward said.

"Yes, I do miss him, but my wife died some time ago."

"I'm sorry. Was she ill long? Edward asked.

"No, when she became ill, I took her to a clinic. They said she had a virus, but they didn't have the medicine to cure her fever."

"What was the medicine she needed?"

"Penicillin," Keichi answered.

"That's such a common antibiotic. Why didn't the clinic have it?" Edward asked in astonishment.

"The people at the clinic said they couldn't afford to keep it in supply. They have little money to treat the Mayas who live in our valley. They said there was nothing they could do for her. I took my wife home to die with her family," explained Keichi.

Edward looked at the man with shock and dismay. He simply didn't know what else to say.

"It is sad my wife will not be with me to see our grandson grow into a man. It is also sad that my son is not with his wife and child. But he is now among the gods," Keichi said with sound of a defeated man.

"Is your home near here?" Edward asked.

"I live in a small house with my son's wife and her child. I'm her only means of support," Keichi explained.

Edward thought about his own family and the Indian's misfortune and said, "It must be very difficult for you."

"What is difficult?" Keichi asked. "Life is what is given to you. We learned long ago to accept all life places on us. My wife died because we couldn't get medicine for her illness. I miss her, but I had my son. When my son died, he left me with his wife and my grandson, who need my help. I do what I can. My people accept hardship and pain because we cannot do anything to change it. We look for the small things in our lives that bring joy. When my grandson was a baby and he discovered his hands, I loved watching him try to use them. When I come upon a lovely flower or bird in the jungle, I know life gives me a gift, and I cherish it."

"It would not be easy for most men to endure such losses and hardship without becoming bitter. It appears that you accept life no matter how bad it gets and still look for the good in what you have. That is a rare quality." Edward said, thinking of the loss of his own wife.

"We make do with what we have," said Keichi.

"It is sad since you come from such a proud heritage."

"Yes, I am a Maya. My ancestors had large cities with governments and rulers that helped the people. Then, the Spanish came and took our wealth, destroyed our cities, and gave our people sicknesses. They killed thousands with their diseases and their weapons. When they left, the Mexicans came. They wanted to rise from the bottom, so they looked for someone to dominate. They killed more of my people and kept the rest in poverty. We have grown used to being the dogs of their society," Keichi explained.

"Do you know where we are going?" Edward asked.

"I know Castillo expects to get a great deal of money from you for taking you to an ancient temple that only he seems to know about," the Indian replied.

"Do you know where it is?" Edward asked.

"No. There are always reports of temples in the jungle. They come from those who would sell the treasures of our people to outsiders," said Keichi.

"I'm an anthropologist, and I have been studying your people all my life," Edward explained. "I did buy some pieces from Castillo, and they were real."

"I saw the ancient pieces he sold, but I didn't know it was you he sold them to. We are used to having our ancient treasures taken away," Keichi replied.

"But I'm not taking them away," Edward explained. "I'm only keeping them to study. Afterwards, they will be given to Senore Dega and Reyes to be put in the Maya Museum."

"Si, I know of this place and these men. They are good men," Keichi said with a trace of a smile. "This is true? You won't take them with you to the Norte Americanos?"

"No, they will stay here for your people and others to see. I only want to learn more about your ancient cultures," said Edward.

Keichi looked hard at Edward and said, "I judged you unfairly. I thought because you were with Castillo that you were like him. I thought you were only looking for a way to take from the Maya. I did not know you are a friend to Senore Dega. He's a protector of our culture."

"Yes, I know," replied Edward. "We became good friends, and he asked me to help with the museum."

"Then, I warn you. Be careful if you do come to a temple. The Jacatez, the 'Jaguar Lords,' guard them. They are the warrior protectors of the Ahkin Mai, the high priest."

"You are not the first person to give me this warning," said Edward.

"It is said the Jacatez will rajar fuera entranas of any intruders," Keichi explained.

"Do you mean eviscerate? Uh… tear out the entrails?" Edward asked.

"Si. That is it," said Keichi.

"Do you believe this?" Edward asked.

"Yes, I do," the Indian answered quickly.

"I have heard some of this legend before. Do you think I could talk to your son's grandfather about the legend?"

"No, he is also gone," Keichi said. "But the legend comes from before the Mayas. It comes from the Olmecs. The legend is the supreme god, Itzamná, decreed the Sun god, Kinich Ahau, would descend in the form of the Jaguar Lord, Jacatez, to protect the temples of the ancient ones and those who protect our culture. It is also said he would take warriors from the Icono Ejercito to help him."

"Icono? Does that mean icon army?" Edward asked.

"Si, the stone army that comes to life," answered Keichi.

"What is the stone army?"

"I don't know. It is a legend told by my people, and I know no one who has seen it," Keichi said.

"That's an incredible story," said Edward.

Keichi reached over and touched Edward's hand, looked into his eyes, and said, "You appear to be a good man. Please, beware of the Jacatez." With that, the Indian rose and walked over to his blanket.

Edward sat and thought about what Keichi had told him and compared it to what Antonio had said. He walked over to where Castillo was sitting and asked him, "Can you tell me anything specific about the temple where the artifacts were found?"

"I told you, we would get there tomorrow. I will not give directions to get there," said Castillo.

"I'm not asking where it is. I am so lost in this jungle. I could never find my way back," said Edward. "I'm asking you what it was like. Is it a big building? Are there many rooms? Did you see anything like an altar or any other kind of strange things there?"

"Oh, I understand. Well, from what I remember, there was a large room with high ceilings when we, uh, I mean, I, entered. There were a number of carvings on the wall, which seemed to have something to do with the sun, the moon, the stars, and the sky," Castillo replied.

"Were they along the wall or high up?" Edward asked.

"They seemed to be on the ceiling, but I couldn't see the top of the wall when I looked up," answered Castillo.

"Could it be the walls were curved or rounded into the ceiling?"

"Si, that's what it was," exclaimed Castillo.

"What about other rooms?" Edward asked.

"There were many rooms. I didn't go into all of them. Just a few," said Castillo.

"Was there anything special in them?"

"Si." Castillo's voice now seemed very excited. "I went into one room and saw it was full of warriors made of stone."

"What?" asked Edward, with a voice full of excitement. "What did they look like? How many were there?" asked Edward.

"They were very large, taller than me. They all were warriors holding weapons. From what I could see with my lantern, there were at least fifty in this room. There was one standing alone in front that looked like he was half snake, half man. He was wearing an eagle mask and he was holding what looked like a weapon in each hand," Castillo explained.

"I don't believe it," said Edward. "The legend of the Olmecs is true."

"I don't know of this legend, but the Indians tell all kinds of stories. And most are just made up."

"But this is unbelievable. This could prove the Chinese connection," Edward said to no one in particular.

"What is this Chinese connection?" Castillo asked.

"The Terra-cotta army. It is just like the Emperor Shihuangdi of the Ch'in Dynasty."

"The what from where?" Castillo asked puzzled.

"There was a Chinese Emperor who lived around 200 B.C. He built a replica of his army, both men and horses. This army was life-sized and each of the statues had it's own unique face. They were made to guard the crypt the Emperor was to be buried in," said Edward.

"And you think this is the same thing?" Castillo asked.

"Maybe this army was carved to protect the temple," answered Edward.

"Yes, another Indian story," said Castillo.

"Is there anything else you remember that was different?" Edward asked.

"No. It was dark and hard for me to see. I didn't go into any other rooms. I will show them all to you when we arrive at the temple."

"Yes. I think I will go to sleep now. It has been a long day, and I would like to start early tomorrow, if possible," said Edward.

"Senore, I have been thinking. You said you would give me the money you promised even if we didn't find the temple."

"That's right, but only if I feel you have made an honest attempt," Edward replied.

"Si, of course, that's right. But what if something happens to you. Maybe you should sign the paper now just in case," Castillo hedged.

"No, it would be too much of a temptation for you, so I will wait," replied Edward with a smile.

"Oh, but I hope you don't think badly of me," Castillo said simperingly.

"Well, it doesn't matter. You see, the paper has to be signed by me in the presence of one of the bank officers. Buenas noches, it is time for me to go to sleep."

"Oh, yes, you should get a good night's sleep. Would you like some tequila to help you go to sleep?" asked Castillo, as he held out a bottle.

"No, thank you. I'll sleep soundly without any help. I will see you in the morning."

Edward crawled into his tent and lay down on the sleeping bag. He thought of what had transpired that day and grew concerned by some of it. He got out his journal and a small flashlight from his pack. He had left the journal he had been using in his room for safekeeping, and started a new one. In his notes about the day, he put in the time and place. Then, he tried to draw a map and to describe their route. He was not sure how accurate his readings would be, but he would try to be accurate.

He thought for a moment about the quiet dignity of Keichi and wondered how he could put the look of pain and sorrow that was in Keichi's eyes into words. He quickly made notes about the stone army and Keichi's legend. His eyes began to get heavy, so he would have to try to put in more detail in the morning. He laid the journal down next to him.

He looked outside the tent and saw Castillo sitting in front of the fire, drinking from the tequila bottle. It had only been twenty or thirty minutes since Edward came into the tent, yet the bottle was already half empty. Well, Castillo would have a sound night's sleep, at least. Edward put out his light, lay down, and soon fell asleep.

Castillo sipped at his tequila and thought about what Edward had just said. He had to sign the release at the banco. Now what would he do. Well, for now he would have another drink and worry about it in the morning.

CHAPTER TWENTY

Edward awoke to a strange noise. It didn't feel like he had been asleep very long. He sat up and looked outside the tent, and he saw Castillo, propped against the packsaddle, asleep next to the dying fire. The almost-empty bottle rested in his hand. He listened and heard some rustling sounds in the bushes behind his tent. Thinking it could be a big cat, he decided to wake Castillo and get his gun.

He put on his boots and began to crawl out of the tent when, suddenly, something hit him hard behind his ear. The world spun around and, then, everything went black. As he came out of the blackness, he realized he was on his back and being dragged toward the fire by his arms. When he began to struggle to get free, he was let go. He fell flat on his back and hit his head. He tried to rise, but, suddenly, there was a boot in the middle of his chest.

"Hablar Espanol," said an angry voice that definitely was not Mexican.

Edward couldn't speak because the boot on his chest was constricting his breathing. He opened his eyes, looked up, and saw a man in a jungle fatigue uniform. The man was pointing a rifle at his head. He couldn't make out the man's face because the light of the fire was behind him, and his head was still clouded from the blow he had received. When the man removed his foot from his chest, he rolled over on his side and wheezed and coughed. Then, he said, "Yo hablar Ingles."

"Oh, that's very good," said another voice from behind him in a very correct English with a definite Nordic accent.

Edward turned toward the voice.

"Let him up," said the voice. "I would move very slowly if I were you. What is your name, who is this man, and what are you doing here?" he asked as he pointed to Castillo.

Edward looked toward the source of the voice, and a man came into the light of the fire. The man also wore jungle fatigues, but he carried no rifle. He did have a belt and holster around his waist. The soldier was of average height and build and was pointing to Castillo, who seemed to be unconscious. Edward's mind was still a bit cloudy, but he tried to talk but, again, coughed.

"I will ask you again. What is your name, who is this man, and what are you doing here?" the soldier demanded angrily.

"I'm Edward Amelot, and this man is my guide. We were going to the Indian villages in the area to speak to the native Indians about their culture. Who are you?" Edward asked.

"I'm Colonel Wilfred Keitel. My men and I have been watching you since you began your march through the jungle, and we know you're not heading for any Indian villages. You passed up a village along your route. I ask again," he said in a very demanding tone, "Where were you going and for what reason, and who is this man?"

"He's Arno Castillo from Tapachula. I'm an American anthropologist, and I study the Indians in this country. We were going to some of the more remote villages, and that's why we passed the village on the way here. When we got to the river, it was too high to cross, so we decided to stay here tonight. What kind of uniform is that you have on? Who are these men? Have you done something to Castillo?" Edward asked.

"Mr. Amelot, I will ask the questions. We have done nothing to your guide. If you got close enough, you could tell by his smell, your Mr. Castillo is drunk. I could have driven a tank in here, and he would not have noticed. Now, go and sit over there by the fire," ordered the colonel. "Claus, get some water and throw it on this drunk."

The man, Colonel Keitel, had spoken to took the man next to the fire and went down to the river. Edward looked around, and there were at least ten men standing around the camp. They were wearing camouflage uniforms with camouflage paint on their faces, and each carried an assault rifle. They looked eerie in the light of the campfire. He could tell by the way they were dressed and acted that they were real military. He didn't see Keichi, and he decided not to ask the soldiers about him, in case he had evaded their capture.

The man called Claus came back and poured the pan of water on Castillo. It must have been very cold because Castillo jumped up to his knees immediately. When he saw the men in uniforms, he reached for his holster inside of his jacket.

"You looking for this?" Colonel Keitel said with a sadistic grin as he held out an automatic to the startled man.

Castillo looked up and shouted, "Who are you, and what are you doing in our camp? The Federales arrest banditos!"

Colonel Keitel responded, "There are no Federales in this area. Even if there were, they would be of no concern to me. Now tell me, what are you doing here? And be honest with me, or you will not leave this campsite alive."

Castillo's face went white with fear. He saw Edward by the fire and answered, "I was taking Senore Amelot to some of the more remote Indian villages. He's a scientist who is studying these people."

"Well, at least you have the same story," said Colonel Keitel sardonically.

"Will you tell me what you are going to do with us?" asked Edward.

"At this time, nothing. You will come with us to our camp and be our guests until I can decide what to do with you."

Castillo shook his head and stared ahead as if he was trying to take in the situation. "What about our things? If we leave them here, they will be taken by the banditos," said Castillo.

"Don't worry about your things. My men will take care of them. Sergeant, have some of your men get their supplies and bury them in the jungle. Take the burro into the jungle and shoot it. The scavengers will pick its body clean soon enough.

"Colonel Keitel, may I at least get my pack with my personal belongings?" asked Edward. "It is in my tent."

"Sergeant, get their backpacks and bring them along. Don't hand them over until I have a chance to look at them."

"Thank you, Colonel Keitel," said Edward.

"Where did you leave the vehicle you came here in?" asked Keitel.

"We didn't bring a vehicle," said Castillo.

Keitel signaled to one of his men who, then, hit Castillo on the back of the head with the butt of his rifle. He fell from his knees to the ground.

"Are you trying to tell me you came all this way on foot? I'm tired of your lying. Sergeant, take this man with you and kill him when you dispose of the burro."

The sergeant started to grab Castillo by the back of his jacket.

"Colonel, please wait," said Edward. "We came here in a jeep. It is hidden in the jungle at least 10 kilometers back from here. Castillo hid it so that no one could find us here."

"I believe you, Mr. Amelot. Oh, not all of it. I am sure your jeep is up the trail, but I am also sure someone will be looking for you. However, it won't do them any good. Okay, sergeant, let him go." The colonel pointed at Castillo and said, "You should be happy this man spoke up for you, or you would be dead right now. I will not ask questions twice. If you lie again, you will be shot!"

"Si," said a sheepish Castillo. Edward could see that under his cowering,

Castillo was controlling his anger.

"Alright. I want to leave this place as soon as possible, and I want it to look as if no one has ever been here. And if this man," he said, nonchalantly pointing at Castillo lying on the ground, "does not get up immediately, take him with the burro and shoot him."

Another uniformed man approached and addressed Colonel Keitel. "Oberst, there was another person here. We found a blanket over by that dead log. It's been slept on."

The colonel looked with anger at Castillo and asked, "Who else was with you here?"

Castillo looked at Edward for help.

"I want to know, now." And with that, he signaled to the sergeant behind Castillo who, then, grabbed Castillo's arm and twisted it behind his back. With his other hand, the sergeant held a knife, which was now pressed against Castillo's neck so tightly that small rivulet of blood began to flow down from the point of the incision.

Castillo said with a rasp in his voice, "It was my Indian helper. He must have run off when he heard you come in."

"Find him, now!" shouted Keitel.

At that moment, two men walked into the camp, each holding Keichi by an arm.

"Well, is this your Indian?" asked Keitel.

"Si, Si, Senore, that's him," Castillo stammered.

"Colonel, will you please tell the sergeant to take the knife away? The man is bleeding," said Edward.

"What else is there the two of you haven't told me?" Keitel asked.

"Nothing else. I swear," said Castillo.

"Alright, we've wasted enough time." He looked at the sergeant and said, "Get this place cleaned up and catch up to us when you're finished."

The sergeant removed the knife from Castillo's throat and nudged him in the back and pointed to the jungle. Castillo, Keichi, and Edward fell into line behind the uniformed men. Edward noticed one man moved out quickly from the ranks and disappeared into the jungle. Their point man no doubt. This enforced his earlier opinion that this was a group from a professional army.

They walked over very rough terrain for what seemed like an hour. They didn't cut a trail to follow because it would then be obvious that someone had passed this way.

However, Edward thought, if someone came looking for them, they would see the trail which he and Castillo had cut the day before. But whom was he kidding? He had kept his plans so secretive no one would come. He should have let someone know exactly what his plans were. He did leave the note for Dega, but even if Dega decided to check up on him, he would not know where they had gone.

At the instruction of the sergeant, the group stopped for a brief rest. Edward noticed the men moved into the jungle in different directions to drop their packs. They didn't bunch up, but automatically moved to set up a perimeter. The point man came back and talked to the sergeant and the colonel. They gave him some instruction, and he was off again.

After resting a few minutes, they continued their march for another hour. The men took particular pleasure in prodding Castillo along. Edward was trying to note the direction they were going, but it was too dark. He even had a hard time seeing the stars through the dense canopy the jungle foliage formed. Castillo moaned and groaned as they walked. The alcohol he had consumed and the rifle butt he took to the head was having an effect on him. Suddenly, he fell to his knees and the column stopped.

The sergeant stopped and shouted at Castillo. "Get up and move!"

"Please, Senore, I need rest, and I need water. I cannot go on. My legs don't work," said Castillo in a pleading voice.

As he pointed the assault rifle at Castillo, the sergeant said adamantly, "Get on your feet, pig, or you will die on your knees."

Meanwhile, Colonel Keitel halted the rest of the men and came back to where Castillo had fallen. "Okay, sergeant, let's give them another rest."

Edward sat at the base of a tree and leaned back against it. The walk through the jungle was difficult, but he knew he could at least keep up with the pace. Colonel Keitel came over and sat down with Edward.

When Keitel smiled, his teeth almost looked like an animals. His face was angular, and his skin was stretched tautly over his bones. His face could show no emotion, but his eyes were a different matter. Their ice blue color expressed a cold calculation, which matched his character perfectly.

"So, Mr. Amelot, you are an anthropologist. I have always been very interested in history. Many of our best leaders thought the present and the future were replays of a period or event in history. Avranches, for example, was conquered by the Romans, the Normans, and finally, by your country's greatest military leader, general Patton," said Colonel Keitel.

"That's very interesting, Colonel Keitel, but my interest in the past is in how civilizations developed, not how they were destroyed," said Edward haughtily.

Keitel looked at Edward with disdain and said, "On the contrary, civilizations like the Holy Roman Empire and the Chinese and Egyptian dynasties would not have developed without an army to conquer and hold the people together."

"Yes, and there was also the destruction by the Spanish of civilizations like the Aztec and Maya who lived where we are standing. Then, of course, there was the perdition of the Nazis. These were also accomplishments of the military," said Edward with disgust.

"I can see your knowledge of military history is lacking," said Colonel Keitel.

"On the contrary, I was part of the greatest military debacle of the twentieth century, Vietnam. It was supposed to help the downtrodden, but it ended up helping big government and big business," said Edward with disgust.

"So, you were a military man. I studied the Vietnam War. It was not lost by the military. It was lost because the politicians grew weak, and then the news media condemned the war and the actions of the military without cause."

"Well, that may be your assessment, but mine is we learned not to interfere in the politics of another country and not to let the military decide on the direction of our nation," said Edward.

"Your opinions are very interesting, Mr. Amelot. We will continue our discussions later, but for now, we must be on our way. Sergeant, let's get going. I want to get to our camp by dawn," commanded Colonel Keitel.

They all got up and continued their trek through the jungle. Edward knew they were not far from the mercenary's camp since dawn would be in another hour. They had been traveling for two to three hours, which meant the camp they were going to was about three or four hours from their camp on the river. At the rate they were walking through the dense under-growth, they would have traveled about five to ten kilometers. Not far. He looked back at Keichi, who kept pace easily with the others.

As the sun began to rise, the group left the trail at a ninety-degree angle and walked until they reached the top of a hill. The hill sloped steeply down into a valley, at the bottom of which was a camp. This was a perfect place to hide a small army. There were many tents and vehicles in the open meadow, and Edward could see a road that went toward two mountain peaks from the valley below. The jungle growth was thick on all sides of the valley, protecting it from intrusion. At first, he wondered why they left the trail, but then he considered that the trail was probably booby-trapped or strewn with mines.

As he stood there taking the scene in, Colonel Keitel walked up to him and said smugly, "A perfect location, Mr. Amelot, don't you think?"

"Yes, it is. You could hide an army in here," Edward said.

"Exactly. You have a keen eye, Mr. Amelot, but don't gather too much information," Colonel Keitel said suspiciously.

"Colonel, I have been lost since yesterday afternoon," Edward said with a forced laugh. Colonel Keitel didn't laugh.

The group made another sharp turn and made their way back to the original trail and then to the camp. Along the way, Edward saw several sentry posts hidden in the jungle. Any thoughts he had of escaping into the jungle were dampened by the thought of mines and men with rifles.

CHAPTER TWENTY-ONE

When they reached the camp, Colonel Keitel stopped the column. He gave some instructions to the sergeant and told Edward, Castillo, and Keichi to follow him. The colonel marched in front, and one man followed behind them, with his rifle pointing at their backs.

They reached a large tent with a guard posted outside. The colonel turned and said, "You will wait here." He entered the tent and closed the flap behind him.

A few minutes later, he re-emerged and said, "Please come in, gentlemen."

They walked into the tent. A distinguished looking man, also in a jungle fatigue uniform, was sitting behind the desk. He had five stars sewn onto his collar. Next to him stood a much younger man dressed in the uniform with the rank of lieutenant.

"Gentlemen, I would like to introduce you to General Von Papen and his aide Lieutenant Paulis. General, this is Mr. Edward Amelot, an American anthropologist; this is Castillo, his guide; and this Indian is their swamper."

"Gentlemen, welcome to our humble dwellings," Von Papen said. "I understand, Mr. Amelot, that you and your guide were going to some isolated Indian villages."

"Senore, I insist you release us immediately, or the Federales will hear of you and your banditos," interrupted Castillo.

"Do you think we are banditos, Mr. Amelot?" asked Von Papen.

"No, general, I don't," said Edward.

The general pointed at Castillo and said, "Oberst, get this idiot and his Indian out of my sight and secure them somewhere."

"I protest. You cannot do this!" shouted Castillo.

Colonel Keitel went to the tent flap and signaled the guard to enter. Then, he pointed at Castillo and Keichi and said, "Take these men away."

Castillo began to protest, but the guard jammed a rifle barrel into his stomach. Castillo coughed, and his face turned red as he backed out of the tent.

"Please, Mr. Amelot, sit down," the general said cordially.

"Thank you, General. Are you going to tell me what you are planning to do with us?" asked Edward.

"Well, your travel in this area is very inconvenient for us at this time. I cannot let you leave now, but you and your party will not be harmed if you follow orders."

"And what would those be General?" Edward asked.

"It is very simple, Mr. Amelot. You will be given a place to sleep, and you may have the run of our camp, but you must not attempt to leave. There are two trails in or out of this valley, and my men patrol both. Going through the jungle would also be unwise. There are mines planted all over the area, and if they don't stop you, the jungle, swamps, or quicksand will. Your stay here will only be for a short time," said Von Papen. "I suggest you accept my terms."

"And how long is a short time General?" Edward asked.

"I don't know exactly, but your ordeal will be over soon. If you will join me for dinner tonight, we can talk more about our mutual dilemma," Von Papen said.

"Certainly. You might say you'll have a captive audience at dinner," said Edward.

The general looked up with a smile and said, "Very good, Mr. Amelot. Until then."

Colonel Keitel signaled, and a guard reappeared, who ushered Edward out of the tent. In a few minutes, the colonel came out of the tent, as well, and they walked across the compound. As they did, Edward noticed the tents were camouflaged so that they would not be spotted by aircraft. Colonel Keitel stopped in front of a tent, looked at Edward, and said, "You will stay here, and you can have the freedom of the camp. However, if someone tells you not to go into an area, don't, and don't try to leave the camp. My men have orders to shoot to kill."

"Yes, I have already been told that by the general," said Edward.

Keitel pointed to another very large tent and said. "You can see the tent where my men are cooking. You can go there for food anytime it is available to the men."

"Thank you, Colonel Keitel. Now can I have my pack?" Edward asked.

"It is in your tent. Your straight razor was removed, as well as your flashlight. When you wish to shave, the sergeant will provide you with a razor. There are no lights here at night. If you light a fire or a match, my men will shoot first and put out the fire after. Any questions, Mr. Amelot?" the colonel asked.

THE ANCIENT ONES

"Just one. What have you done with Castillo and Keichi?" asked Edward.

"Castillo is under guard at the far end of the camp," said Keitel. "The Indian is with him. You can talk to them if you wish, but the guard will not leave you alone while you do so."

"So, I take it you feel I'm smart enough not to try to escape," said Edward.

"Well, I think you are smart enough to know if you try, you will die," Keitel said with a sardonic look. "Now, you must excuse me. I have work to do."

Edward went into the tent. There was a cot, upon which his pack and the contents were dumped out on the blanket. He went over his gear. The razor and flashlight might be gone, but his pocketknife was still in his boot. Apparently, they didn't think he would hide anything on his person. Wait, there were his socks but the artifacts were gone. He thought about running out to complain to Colonel Keitel, but he was sure it would not do any good. He would ask the general about them later. He took his toiletry kit and a towel and walked outside. He saw a canvas water bag hanging from a tree, so he took out some soap and washed his face and hands.

After he put his gear away, he walked over to the tent where the men were eating. He heard different languages being spoken. A number of men were speaking German, but the rest sounded as if they were speaking in some Slavic dialects he couldn't recognize. He went to the table where the food was laid out, and he helped himself to coffee, fruit and some bread.

He walked over to a table where three men were sitting and said, "Gentlemen, would you mind if I sit here?" he asked.

One of the men said, "Not at all. Help yourself."

As Edward sat, they all got up and left.

Sitting across the room was General Von Papen's aide, Lieutenant Paulis, and another man in an officer's uniform whom Edward had not seen before. They were deep in discussion in German, and they didn't notice Edward looking at them.

"So, Manfried," said Lieutenant Paulis. "I understand you have just been brought here from Argentina, and your family is friends of General Von Papen. He asked me to look out for you until you can meet with him. It is a very busy time here."

"Yes, General Von Papen and my grandfather are from Hesse and served together in the Third Reich. My grandfather saved Von Papen's life. When I came back from Germany after attending the University, I got into a bit of trouble with the government. My mother contacted Von Papen, who offered to get me out of jail if I would serve in his army. It is good to find others who have ties to Deutschland," Manfried said.

"You will find many like us in this army," Paulis said.

"Right now, I know nothing about what this army is doing or why it is here in Mexico," said Manfried. "I was just rushed off to Guatemala, given a uniform, and then sent here in a convoy of trucks that was bringing in munitions. I was told the general would see me later. When I asked about what we were doing here, no one would tell me anything."

"Well, since you will be seeing the general," said Paulis, "I guess it will do no harm to tell you about our army and this operation. The army you are in belongs to William Brabant, who is the richest man in the world. He is seeking a location where he can control the government, so he may have a favorable climate for his business operations and to bring back some of the values of our grandfathers. We will be helping the local Indians to revolt against the government of Mexico. There has already been one unsuccessful revolt in Chiapas by the Indians. They are struggling against government control. They have a leader by the name of Reyes who has been very cooperative with our leaders."

"As the general's aide, I'm privileged to sit in on all of the planning meetings for the operation we are to carry out here. Brabant's plan is to move our whole army into Chiapas under the guise of training the Indians. We will help the Indians take over the local government, but when the Indian forces disperse to guard the borders, we will take control of the central government."

"Will this work?" Manfried asked.

"If it doesn't, many of us will be dead, in jail, or looking for a new job," Paulis said.

Edward couldn't believe his ears. He knew Reyes and Dega had something to do with the Indian cause, but he didn't realize how much. In a state of shock, he finished his food and left the tent.

He walked down to where Castillo and Keichi were being held.

There was an armed guard standing outside the tent, and the flap was open. Keichi was sitting outside the tent, and Edward could see Castillo lying on the cot inside. As Edward approached, Castillo saw him and sat up on the cot. The guard looked at Edward but didn't stop him from going in.

Castillo looked at Edward with surprise and asked, "You are not kept under armed guard?"

Edward decided to appease Castillo and said, "No, apparently they think

THE ANCIENT ONES

I'm too scared to try to escape, but they believe you might try."

"Yes, I do know the jungles here, and I don't fear these men," Castillo said with bravado.

"I'm sure you don't," Edward said, "but it would be foolish to try to escape. They said they needed some time, so let's just wait for awhile and see what happens."

"You may wait, but I have a plan. I...."

Edward held up his hand for Castillo to stop and said, "This man outside the tent may be listening."

"I don't believe he speaks Englaise like you and me," Castillo said.

"The general said he needed a few days, and then he would turn us loose. I think we should just wait," Edward said.

"That may be well for you because you are a wealthy Norte Americano. They know this. I'm a poor Mexican, and they have no use for me. When given the opportunity, I'm going to leave," said Castillo.

"Don't do anything foolish," said Edward emphatically. "These men are professional soldiers. They have been ordered to shoot to kill, and they will. Just give it some time. I don't want to see you or Keichi killed." "Thank you, for your concern. When I go," Castillo replied, "I will not take the Indian with me. He would only slow me down."

"Well, consider what I said. I heard them say the area around the camp is mined. It would be better for you to wait."

"Maybe for you, but not me," Castillo said with disdain.

Edward left the tent, stopped in front of Keichi, and asked, "Are you alright?"

"Si, I'm fine. The man gave us some water," replied Keichi.

"Well, be careful. These men will kill you if you try to leave," Edward said.

"I heard you and Castillo talking," said Keichi. "When he tries to escape, they will be after him and it will be the time for me to go. If I can get into the jungle, the soldiers will not find me. Last night, they found me because I did not have enough time to get away. I will not be found again."

"Listen there are also men in the jungle watching, and there are mines out there," said Edward.

"Si, Senore, I saw the men in the trees. I will not be seen by them," said Keichi.

"I think you should wait. I believe they will let us go when it is time," Edward said.

"I am sorry, but for once, I agree with Castillo. You are a wealthy Norte Americano, but we mean nothing to these men. I have seen their kind before. They were in Guatemala when my home was there. They killed Indians just to see them die. When I have the chance, I will go."

"Please be careful. Don't try to leave unless you have to," Edward said with concern.

Edward walked slowly through the camp. He was very tired since he had only slept an hour the night before. He thought about what Castillo and Keichi said to him. If they tried to escape, he was sure they would be killed. He didn't want either of them to die. He needed Castillo to guide him to the temple, and he liked Keichi.

He went inside his tent and laid down on the cot. His mind was whirling around about their captivity and his lost chance to find the temple. Since Castillo seemed to be the type of man who would take chances, maybe, he should try to make a deal with Castillo now. If he could get a map to the temple, he would sign the release of the money.

He lay back on the cot and realized just how tired he really was. But now, he thought about Cara. He knew she would be worried, and he hoped he could get out of this mess soon, so he could call her. Well, for the moment, he would get some sleep, and then he would talk to Castillo. Yes, later he would explore the camp and try to assess what chance they really had to escape.

CHAPTER TWENTY-TWO

Alek rented a single engine plane in Puerto Vallarta to take Cara and him to Tapachula. He would have arranged a charter, but the charter service said the Indians in Chiapas had fired on their planes during the revolt, so they would only go to Tuxtla.

Cara was very nervous when they first took off. She had no way of knowing whether Alek was a good pilot and navigator. She began to relax when she realized she was in capable hands. She talked about her father most of the time.

He followed the coastline to Tapachula, rather than going over the mountains, which would have forced them to fly at higher altitudes. They made two stops for fuel and rest on the way and were now approaching the small airfield in Tapachula.

He looked at her and asked, "Didn't you think we would get here in one piece?"

She looked at him and smiled. "Well, I had my doubts in the beginning. Not about you, but I have never flown over the ocean for such long distances in such a small plane. But it became apparent you knew what you are doing."

"That was the reason I spent so much time checking out the plane on the ground and test flying it before we left. You never know how reliable the plane maintenance is in some countries. I also knew in order to gain time, I would have to take us quite a ways out over the ocean, especially in the final leg when we left Puerto Angel and flew over the Gulf of Tehuantepec," Alek explained.

The landing was smooth, and he taxied to the spot pointed out to him by a man in coveralls. He had radioed ahead to request a jeep to rent while they were there. After he guided the plane to the hangar, he got out, took their bags, and they walked to the airport office.

There was a large man in an official looking uniform sitting behind a desk and another man in coveralls sitting at a table when they walked in. The uniformed official said, "Hola Senore, Senorita, su pasaporte por favor."

"Hola Senore, usted hablar Ingles?" asked Alek.

"Si, I speak English well. May I see your passports please?"

"Si." Alek said as he handed the official their passports.

"What is your business here?" asked the official.

"We are here to visit some of the Mayan ruins," said Alek.

"That can be dangerous here. Do you know travel without a tour group is not advised?" the official added.

"Si, we are planning to find a tour group to join," said Alek.

"Senorita, how long will you stay?"

"Only a few days. We are on our honeymoon."

Alek turned his head sharply and looked at Cara with surprise. She was still looking at the official with a serious face.

"Oh, Senora, I apologize," said the official with a big smile. "I hope you have a nice visit in our country."

While they were talking, the man in the overalls left the office. Alek went outside and found him. "Senore, will you service our aircraft while we are away? I would like you to refuel it and check over the engine and the rest of the plane. By the way, is there a jeep for us here?" he asked.

"Si. The jeep is in the front of the building. I am told you have to sign the forms in it and leave them here. There is a map in the jeep with directions to the Hotel Sierra in Tapachula. While you are gone, I will take care of your plane. When will you return?" the mechanic asked.

"I'm not sure, but I probably will not be back for three or four days. I will call you as soon as I know. Can I use your phone to make a call to Tapachula?" asked Alek.

"I would be most happy to let you use the telephone, but it is not working. Our telephones only work on scheduled times," said the official.

"What is the schedule?" asked Alek.

"That's the problem. No one knows the schedule," said the maintenance man with a smile on his face. "I just tried to make a call, but I guess it is not a scheduled time," he said still smiling.

"Well, thank you anyway. We will just go to the hotel," said Alek.

Cara came out as Alek was loading the jeep with their luggage. As they sat in the jeep, Alek looked over the map, started the jeep up, and they left.

As they drove down the road, he looked over at Cara, and she said, "Before you say anything, I told the man we were married because I thought there would be less hassle if we were honeymooners. So, don't get the wrong idea. It was just to get that official off our case."

"Well, that's fine with me. I guess I should have booked the bridal suite at the hotel," said Alek smiling.

"No, two rooms are fine. Remember, we have to keep our relationship on a non-emotional basis. Finding my father has to be the most important thing to me and right now. My feelings toward you only complicate things, so I decided to suppress them," she said emphatically.

"Exactly what are they, now?" Alek teased.

"Please, I don't want to get into that now. Let's just keep our minds on the business at hand," said Cara seriously.

They arrived at the hotel and went inside to register.

"Hola, Senore, Senora, we are pleased to have you at our hotel. We have a beautiful room for you. Please sign the registry, and then I will show you to your room," said the old man at the desk.

"Pardone Senore," said Cara, "You said you have 'a' room for us."

"Si, Senora. We had thought you wanted two rooms, but then we did not know you are newly married. I had fresh flowers put in your room, and I hope you will like our hotel. Congratulations."

Cara began to speak, but Alek interrupted, "Thank you. I'm sure we will like 'our' room."

They followed the old man up the stairs to the room on the second floor. He opened the door and handed Alek the key. "I hope you and your beautiful novia will enjoy your stay here," he said.

As he left, Cara said, "Why didn't you let me tell him we wanted two rooms?"

"You started this at the airport. Apparently, the official called ahead and told them we are newlyweds. If we change our story now, everyone will be suspicious of what we are doing here," Alek replied.

"Oh sure, now we're supposed to play house," She said angrily. "Didn't we just agree to keep this relationship on a platonic basis," she demanded.

"Okay, okay, don't get upset," He said. "You take the bed, and I will sleep on the floor. There doesn't seem to be too many things crawling on it."

"Stop being such a martyr. I'll sleep on the floor, and you can have the bed. After all, you wouldn't even be here if it weren't for me," said Cara.

"What if I said 'okay'," quipped Alek.

"Well, I would take the floor," Cara replied haughtily.

"Oh, and how many times have you slept on a floor?" asked Alek.

"Well, I went to summer camp, and we slept on cots with just a thin mattress, and I have slept in a tent on the ground in a sleeping bag," said Cara.

"Sure, and when did you do this roughing it?" asked Alek.

"When I was twelve," she said defensively.

"Well, I'm sure you loved it, but I'll sleep on the floor, and we can take turns using the bathroom," said Alek.

"That's very nice of you," she said thankfully. "Actually, I did sleep in a sleeping bag one night. That is I tried to. I was up all night with my best friend, and we kept thinking about strange things crawling into our tent."

"I assume you meant insects," said Alek with a big smile. "Since we will have to take turns using the bathroom, would you like to be first?" asked Alek.

"Yes, I meant insects, and yes, I would like to wash up now."

"Fine. Before you go, let's decide what we are going to do about finding your father," said Alek.

"First, I would like to try to find Castillo. He's the man my father said he was going to go to the ruins with. Do you think it's the right place to start?" asked Cara.

"Yes. While you clean up, I will see if I can find where this Castillo can be located. I will be with our friendly desk clerk if you need me."

He went down to talk to the old man at the desk and asked him about Castillo. The old man looked at him with a puzzled look and said, "That is very strange. You are the second person who recently asked for Senore Castillo."

"Who was the first?" asked Alek.

"Senore Amelot," the old man replied.

What! Alek couldn't believe what he had just heard. He asked excitedly, "Edward Amelot is staying here now?"

"Si, yes and no," said the old man.

"What do you mean?" asked Alek. "Is he here or isn't he?"

"Well, I don't talk about my guests," the old man said proudly.

"Please, Senore. Mr. Amelot is the Senora's father, and we are looking for him." He said entreatingly. "If you know where he is, you should tell us. We would be very grateful for the help."

"Oh, so the beautiful Senora is Senore Amelot's daughter, eh? Aye, I should have seen the resemblance," said the old man.

"You said 'yes and no' when I asked if Senore Amelot was still here," said Alek impatiently. "What do you mean?"

"Well, he was here, but he left some time ago to go somewhere with Senore Castillo. He left a chest to give to Senore Dega after he left. He left his clothes in his room and said he would not be gone for more than a few days. He paid me to hold the room for two weeks, but that was a number of days ago," said the old man.

"You say he sent something to Dega?" asked Alek.

"Si. I sent it to him the same day Senore Amelot left."

"Where can we find Dega?" asked Alek.

"Dega lives not far from here. I can direct you. He's very well known, and he's what you call a simpatico person," the old man replied.

"You mean likeable?" asked Alek.

"Si, likeable."

"Fine. After we see Dega, I would like to go to Castillo's home or business. Can you tell me where it is?" asked Alek.

"Castillo lives on the edge of town," the old man answered.

"Thank you, again. You don't know how much you have done for the Senora," he said.

He bounded up the stairs with the good news for Cara.

He burst into the room with a big smile on his face. She was just putting on a clean blouse and turned away while she finished. Then, she turned with an angry look on her face and said, "you could knock and let me know you are coming, instead of busting in with that grin on your face."

"This grin is not for your state of undress. Well, it could be. I am grinning because I found out where your father is."

"What," she said with a look of shock on her face. "You did; where is he; is he okay?"

"Well, I mean I know where he was and where he went," said Alek sheepishly.

"Alek what do you mean? Please, tell me what you know," Cara said anxiously.

"Your father was staying in this hotel. Actually, his things are still here. He left a few days ago with Castillo, according to the hotel proprietor," Alek said excitedly.

"Where did they go?" Cara asked.

"That is what I don't know. However, the hotel proprietor, said your father left a chest, which he asked be delivered to Dega. So, I think we should go to see Dega first."

"You're right. Let's go to see Dega first," Cara replied.

"Okay, but let's be careful," he said.

"Careful about what?" asked Cara suspiciously. "Do you know something else about my father you are not telling me?"

"No, I just don't want you to be overanxious," Alek explained.

Cara pleaded with him, "I appreciate what you are saying, but if you know something about my father, you have to tell me."

"I have told you everything I know about your father. I'm just trying to conduct this investigation like I would any other," said Alek.

"This is not a government assignment, Alek. This is my father. I just want to find him and as soon as possible," said Cara almost in tears.

"I know. I'm just trying to keep emotion out of this in order to do my job. You have to let me help you the best way I know," said Alek emphatically.

"You're right, but it is hard not to be emotional when the situation involves someone you love. I'll let you lead the way," Cara replied.

They went down to the jeep, which was parked in front of the hotel and drove to the home of Dega.

CHAPTER TWENTY-THREE

As they walked to the door of Dega's home, Alek said to Cara, "Now, let's be careful what we say. We don't want divulge any more than we should."

"That won't be too hard, Alek. We don't know very much," Cara said sarcastically.

He shot a sideways glance at Cara, and they walked up to the door and knocked.

Antonio Dega answered the door and asked, "Can I help you, Senore?"

"Hola. I'm Alek Roman, and this is Cara Amelot."

Dega's eyes brightened when he heard Cara's name. He grabbed her hand and exclaimed, "Hola, Senorita. Are you the daughter of Edward Amelot?"

"Yes I am," Cara said, surprised with Dega's instant reaction.

"I'm so happy to meet you. Your father has told me all about you. You have his look, Senorita. Welcome into my casa, both of you. Please come in."

They entered and Dega said, "Please have a seat and let me get you some refreshments."

"Thank you," said Cara. "I came here looking for my father. He told me you did some work together, and I was hoping you could give me some information as to his whereabouts."

"Si, he was here, Senorita. We had some fine meals together. He's a most interesting man, and we talked and talked like I haven't done in a long time. Your father asked for my help with a theory he was trying to prove," Dega said.

"I got a note from my father," She said. "He told me he had come to see you, and you helped him a great deal. He also said he found a new friend."

"Yes, he's a very dedicated man," Dega said. "I admire his commitment to his work. He lets nothing stand in the way of his ideas. He and I worked together very well, and yes, we became fast friends."

"When was the last time you saw him?" asked Cara.

"Well, it was only a few days ago. He was here in Tapachula for a number of days while we worked on his hypothesis. He had some artifacts, and he wanted me to help him determine what area they came from."

"Do you know anything about where he went from here?" asked Cara.

"I got a note and one of his artifacts from him the day after he was here. The note said he was going with a Senore Castillo to find the ruins where the artifacts were found. I tried to warn your father that Castillo was an unscrupulous person, but I'm afraid I was not convincing enough. I called the hotel where he was staying, but they told me he had already left. I should have tried harder to convince him not to go. He didn't tell me he was going until after he left. He's a strong-willed man," said Dega.

"Yes," said Cara, "sometimes too much so."

"I tried to call Castillo a few times and, finally, went to his place of business. His man told me he didn't know where Castillo was, except that he had gone on a business trip with your father," said Dega.

Cara began to cry, and Alek moved to comfort her. Dega moved to Cara and took her hand. "Senorita, I haven't known your father for a long time, but in the time we spent together, I got a sense of a man who stays in control. We know he's an intelligent man and will know how to deal with a man like Castillo. I have already asked the local authorities to be on the lookout for your father. I, also, have many friends throughout Chiapas, who I will contact to be on the look out for him. They will let me know if they have seen or heard of him or Castillo."

"Thank you. My father was right about you. You are a good friend," said Cara.

"Would you like to refresh yourself, Senorita?" Dega asked.

"Yes, thank you. You are most kind," said Cara.

Dega took her by the arm and led her into a bathroom. When she closed the door, he returned.

Alek turned to Dega and said, "I would like to visit Castillo's business, so I may talk to his man. Would you help me find him?"

"I told the Senorita her father knows how to handle men like Castillo, but that was for her benefit only," Dega said with a somber tone. "From what I know about Castillo, he's as unscrupulous as a man can be."

"Did Mr. Amelot tell you where the ruins might be?" Alek asked.

"No, he did not, but that was because he did not know. Apparently, Castillo would not divulge the location of the temple," Dega explained.

"I don't mean this to sound disrespectful, Senore, but are you sure Mr. Amelot would have told you where the ruins are?" Alek asked.

"I understand your meaning. When Edward first came to see me, he was hesitant to tell me very much about what he was doing. In a very short time, however, we developed a great deal of respect for each other, and we became friends. He has even agreed to donate his artifacts to our museum of Olmec and Mayan culture we have here in Chiapas. I think Edward would have told me if he knew where he was going, even if it was in the note he sent me after he left." Dega said.

"So you haven't heard anything of him since he left?" Alek asked.

"I have tried to find out anything I can, but without knowing something about where they were going makes it very difficult. I will go with you to Castillo's place of business if you like."

Alek looked into Dega's eyes and with a cold look on his face said, "Thank you, Senore, but it might be better if I go by myself. If I find anyone there, I might be able to convince them to give me the help I need if there is no one else there."

Dega could see the conviction in Alek's statement and in his eyes. "Senore Roman, the type of people Castillo has working for him may not be easy to convince," Dega replied.

Alek shot Dega a cold hard look and said, "Senore, I have worked in this area for a number of years, and I'm familiar with men like Castillo and those who work for him. I know how to 'convince' them."

Dega looked at Alek and felt that he could be convincing if necessary. "I will give you directions, but please be careful with the Senorita. She should not be exposed to these people. I know how dear she is to Edward," said Dega.

"I promise you I will be careful with Cara. I don't expect to take her with me to see Castillo, and I won't expose her to danger. She's staying at the same hotel as her father. Perhaps, you would look in on her if I have to leave?" asked Alek.

"It will be my pleasure to look after the Senorita," Dega replied.

"Thank you," Alek said. "I will feel better knowing she has help if she needs it."

Dega walked over to the desk, took out a piece of paper, and wrote down Castillo's address and phone number and, on another, his phone number. He handed it to Alek and said, "Please, if you have to leave the Senorita, I would prefer she stay here if she wishes. I'm well known in this area. If it will help Edward, you may use my name, and if you need help, I have friends who might be useful to you as well."

"Thank you, Senore Dega. I will remember what you said. As far as Cara is concerned, she is a very strong-willed person, and I don't think she will stay with you while her father is missing. However, I will make your offer if I have to leave. At least, she will have you to call on," Alek said.

Cara entered the room and went over to Dega. Her eyes were red. "Thank you so much for being so kind and for being a friend to my father. I know he gets so involved in his work that sometimes he's not as careful as he should be," she said.

"Senorita, if there is anything further I can do, please let me know. As I told Senore Roman, you are welcome here anytime. And if you need a place to stay, my housekeeper can have a room ready for you in a few minutes," said Dega.

"I will remember that, and when my father returns, we must all get together to celebrate his discoveries, including finding such a good friend," Cara replied.

Dega took her hand, looked into her eyes, and said, "Vi con dios un caro."

They got into their jeep and drove away. "Well, what can we do now?" asked Cara.

"You told me you would follow my directions when necessary. I'm planning to go to Castillo's place of business, and I want to go alone," said Alek.

"Why can't I be there?" Cara exclaimed.

"I must have the freedom to do whatever is necessary to get the information we need. I can act more freely if you are not there. Also, I don't want to worry about you being in a bad situation," he said.

"But it is all right for you to be in a 'bad situation'. Alek, I don't know where my father is or if he's all right. Certainly, I don't want to add to my problems by putting you in a situation where you could be hurt," she said with a concerned look on her face.

"Cara, Senator McGruder told you I'm the best at what I do, and I am. You must let me do what I came here to do."

Cara looked caringly at him and said, "I don't want you hurt either. And if something happened to both of you, I couldn't live with myself."

He stopped the jeep turned to her and took her face in his hands and said, "As far as your father is concerned, believe me, I can handle whatever comes of that situation better than I could you that day on the beach."

Cara smiled through her concern and said, "You were very funny."

"So, let me do this my way. I will be there and back in no time at all, and

I will let you know everything I find out."

"Okay, I'll trust you. Just promise me you will be careful," said Cara.

"Don't worry about me. I know what I'm doing. By the way, Dega said if I had to leave you alone, you could stay with him," Alek said.

"That was very nice of him, and I'm sure he meant it, but I would like to stay in the hotel and get the proprietor to let me into my father's room. He always keeps a journal of everything he does, so I'll try to find any other clues I can," said Cara.

"Great idea."

Alek parked the jeep in front of the hotel, and they went in to talk to Mandares.

"Hola, Senore, Senora. Did you find Senore Dega?" the old man asked.

"Yes, thank you. The Senora wishes to look through her father's room and see if there is something there that might tell us where he went. Could we have his key?" asked Alek.

"Si. I'm sure this is alright." Mandares said.

He went to a box hanging on the wall, opened the door, and took out a key. "This was, ah... I am sorry, is your father's key. Take your time and return it to me when you are through."

"Gracias," said Cara. They walked up the stairs, and he took the key from her as they came to her father's room. He held her behind him as he inserted the key and slowly opened the door. He looked around the room to make sure it was safe and then allowed her to enter.

The room was neat and clean. Apparently, Mandares had the room dusted daily. There was a bed against the left wall, and a small sofa and end table were under the window directly across from the door. Against the right hand wall, there were a chest-of-drawers, a writing table, and a chair. The table was covered with papers neatly stacked, and there was a briefcase on the floor next to it. As he entered the room, he noticed the clothes hung on a rod, which was in the corner behind the door. There was a ceiling fan moving at a very slow speed.

Everything seemed in order, and Cara walked over to the table and began to look through the papers on it.

Alek said, "While you go through your father's papers, I'll check out Castillo's business. I'll be back as soon as possible."

"Alright, but please be careful. And come back as soon as you can. I'll be waiting for you," said Cara.

"Don't worry. I'm just going to talk to Castillo's help. I'll be back before you know I'm gone," said Alek.

She walked over to him, took his face in her hands, and kissed his lips. "I'm sorry, Alek," Cara said. "I know I was going to keep this purely business, but I do care. Please come back safe."

He just smiled. "Lock this door and the one in your room when you return there. Better yet, wait here if you want until I get back. See you soon," he said as he closed the door behind him.

CHAPTER TWENTY-FOUR

Alek went to the hotel proprietor, Senor Mandares, and asked, "I have to go to see Castillo's people. Can you tell me anything about his business?"

"Si, I know what he does. He says he sends Mexican products to other countries and brings in merchandise. However, everyone knows he truly deals in illegal merchandise, everything from American cigarettes to Russian rifles. He's constantly in trouble with the Federales. I tried to warn Senore Amelot about him, and you should be careful too," said Mandares.

"You are absolutely right. I will be very careful," Alek said.

Alek headed out in his rented jeep. After a short time, he arrived at Castillo's place of business. He walked up to the door and tried it, but it was locked. He knocked, waited, and no one answered. He looked around and saw no other entrance, so he pounded on the door. Soon, a man came to the door and opened it just a crack.

"I'm sorry, but we are not open for buying or selling anything today," said the man.

"I'm not here to buy or sell," said Alek. "I'm here to see Senore Castillo. Do you work for him?"

"Si," said the man, "I work for Senore Castillo, but he's not here today, so you cannot see him." He attempted to close the door, but Alek put his hand against it and held it open.

"I know he's not here now, but I wish to talk to you," Alek said.

The man at the door asked in a frightened voice, "I do not know anything to tell you. I just work for Senore Castillo and only do what I'm told. You should come back when he's here."

With that, he again attempted to shut the door, but Alek put his shoulder into it hard enough to knock the man back away from it. The man slumped down against the opposite wall and began to reach around his back, but Alek reacted too quickly for him. He moved forward, put his boot on the man's chest and held him down so he could not get his hand to the back of his waistband. He bent down and grabbed the man's right arm, and twisted it until he turned over. He took the automatic pistol that was stuck in his belt, lifted him up, and crushed him against the wall. Alek noticed the automatic pistol had no magazine and began to wonder if this man was stupid and didn't load it or what.

"Is there anyone else in the building?" asked Alek angrily. "And don't lie, or I will use the pistola on you, as you were going to use it on me."

The man answered in a pained voice, "Senore, please believe me. I would not shoot anyone or anything. The pistola has no bala, uh bullets. I couldn't do anything with the pistola except use it as a club. And there is no one else in the building."

"What is your name?" Alek asked.

"I am Jose Lopez, and I work for Senore Castillo."

"I hope you are telling the truth because I don't like to be lied to. Where is the magazine for the pistola?" asked Alek.

"It is here," he said as he reached in his pocket and handed it to Alek.

He let go of Lopez, put the magazine in the pistol, and pulled the slide back to load a shell into the firing chamber. "Okay, Lopez, now we're going to go into that office and talk about Castillo and where he might be."

Sounding forlorn Lopez said, "I don't know where Castillo is. I wish I did. Many people who have business with him have come here looking for him. Some are very angry that he is not here, like you. I don't know what to do. I'm all alone here."

"Surely, he must have told you something that might help me. Did you know if he had another man with him when he left?" asked Alek.

"Si, I met Senore Amelot. He was a very nice man. I took him to Senore Castillo's plantation warehouse," said Lopez.

Alek grabbed Lopez by the shirtfront, and pulled him toward him and said, "Did they say where they may be going?" When there was no immediate reply he said, "You had better come up with something fast because I'm becoming very angry. Angry enough to pull this trigger," Alek said as he jammed the end of the pistol barrel under Lopez's chin and pushed upward hard enough to force Lopez up on his tiptoes.

Lopez's eyes were like two large, white saucers, and they were watering so much it looked like he was crying. He tried to talk but couldn't because the gun kept him from opening his mouth. He gurgled and sputtered.

Alek saw Lopez was trying to speak; he lowered the pistol and shouted, "Speak."

Lopez took a deep breath and said, "All I know, is they were going to find the place where the jade figures came from. But I don't know where that is. If I did, I would tell you. I do not want to die."

"Do you know who Castillo bought the jade from?" Alek asked.

"Yes. He bought them from an Indian whose name was Tucanil. Tucanil brought one of the pieces here, and he and Castillo left together. Castillo was gone for the whole day and night, and when he came back, he had another jade figure and a disk. I remember he was very dirty when he returned. He said he had to sleep in the jungle, and he had almost been killed, but he would not say anymore," Jose explained.

Where does this Indian Tucanil live?" asked Alek.

"I don't know. Senore Castillo never mentioned where Tucanil lived."

Alek listened intently and believed Lopez was telling him the truth. But he had to be sure. He looked hard at Lopez.

"What is in the back room?" asked Alek.

"It is just a small kitchen. Castillo lives here in a room upstairs," Lopez replied.

"Okay. Let's go into the kitchen," Alek suggested.

With a look of fear in his eyes, Lopez walked into the kitchen but kept his head turned back enough to look at Alek.

As they came into the kitchen, Alek looked around and saw what he wanted. Along the right side of the room there was a table made of heavy wooden planks and a machete hanging on the wall over the table. He pushed Lopez toward the table, reached up, and took the machete.

"Alright, my friend. I want you to lay your hand flat on the table. Now!" he shouted.

Lopez pulled back with a look of terror in his eyes. "Please, I have told you everything. I would not keep anything from you," he said, his eyes pleading for mercy.

"Senore," He said in a quiet lethal voice, "you have more to say, and I will have it now. If you don't help me, one chop, and you will lose your left hand. If you still refuse, you will lose your manhood to," said Alek as he took the machete in his left hand and grabbed Lopez's shirtfront with his right. The cold look in his eyes brought fear to Lopez.

He began to shiver and grasped his hands together between his legs. "Please, I don't know anymore," he said as he bowed his head for further protection. Alek began to raise the machete when suddenly Lopez looked up and said, "Please, please, the only thing more I know is when Castillo came back from his trip with Tucanil, he had blood on his clothes. When I asked him what had happened, all he said is the world would be a better place without all the Indians. While he was gone, there was a report that two Indian women were killed and their bodies burned in their home."

He tightened his grip on Lopez. "Where did this happen?" Alek demanded.

"It was near a small village called Anyxlatana," said Lopez timidly.

"Where is that, and how do I get to it?" Alek asked.

"I have a map here, on the desk. I can show you the road to get there," said Lopez eagerly.

Alek released Lopez. They walked over to the desk, and Lopez showed him the road to the village. For a moment, he considered taking the Lopez with him in case he was lying, but then he thought better of the situation.

"I will need a few things," said Alek as he took the map, and they walked back into the warehouse.

"Anything," Lopez said.

"Where do you store the military goods?" Alek asked.

"What do you mean?" asked Lopez.

Alek took the pistol out of his belt and said coldly, "I will not ask you again. After you are dead, I will find them myself."

"Of course. They are in the back of the warehouse building behind a wall. I will lead the way," Lopez offered.

When they got to the back wall, Lopez moved a large packing case on wheels. There was a door in the wall that opened into a large room. When Lopez turned on a light, Alek saw a room with enough arms and munitions to supply an infantry company. There were automatic rifles, machine guns, rocket launchers, mortars, machine pistols, various kinds of grenades, anti personnel mines, and even a small field artillery piece.

"Well, you have quite a selection here," said Alek sardonically.

"I don't like the things in this room or the men who come to buy them. I don't do anything with these things. Only Castillo does," Lopez said meekly.

"Okay. Get one of those sacks and follow me," said Alek. He selected an American M-16 rifle, and he told Lopez to put twenty loaded M-16 ammunition clips in the sack. He, then, walked over and took six concussion grenades and six smoke grenades and placed them in the sack. He took a disposable rocket launcher and handed it to Lopez. He told Lopez to get him two boxes of nine-millimeter shells for the pistol, and as an afterthought, he took a pair of handcuffs and two blankets.

They walked out of the room, and he told Lopez to lock the door. Lopez then moved the packing crate back in front of the door, and Alek led the way back to the kitchen.

He looked around the room, and then back to Lopez. "Alright, I want you to move over to the sink," he said as he handed the handcuffs to Lopez. "Put one on your left wrist and the other around the pipe." When he was secured, Alek put the pistol in his belt and the machete in the sack.

"You will be fine," Alek said to Lopez. "You can reach the water and the refrigerator. I will lock the door and tell someone to come and let you out tomorrow. Don't tell anyone what you told me. If you do, or if you try to escape, I will return and finish what I started before," said Alek intently.

Lopez slumped down to the floor dejectedly and said, "I will do as you say."

Alek locked the kitchen door and then the outer door. He put the sack and the rifles in the back of the jeep and then covered them with the blankets. He looked at the map and plotted his route to the village. He drove along the edge of Tapachula until he reached the road he would take. He drove off into the jungle and hid his sack and rifles in the brush. He marked the tree near the sack with the machete and made a mental note of the location. He then drove back to the hotel.

CHAPTER TWENTY-FIVE

Alek pulled up to the hotel and walked up to the room. He knocked, and Cara came to the door with a book in her hand.

She looked at him with a smile and said, "Alek, you're alright. I was starting to worry. I found my father's journal, and it goes right up to the day before he left with Castillo."

She was standing there wearing a pair of white shorts and a blue silk shirt. Her tanned skin was alluring next to the pale color of her clothes. God, she was beautiful, he thought.

"Good," He said as he composed himself. " Does it give us any clues to where he might have gone?"

"Not so far; however, I haven't read it all, yet. Were you able to get any information on Castillo?" She asked.

"Not exactly. No one at his business seems to know exactly where he went; however, I have a lead on an area where they might have gone. Did your father mention an Indian by the name of Tucanil?" asked Alek.

"Yes," she said excitedly. "I began reading the entries of his journal for the week before he left, and he did mention Castillo had told him he got the artifacts from an Indian by the name of Tucanil. He was the one who found the ruins. Oh, Alek, that's good news isn't it?"

"Yes definitely. It confirms what I was told by Castillo's man. He also told me where this Indian might live. I have a map and a route to get there."

"Great! When do we go?" asked Cara.

"Cara, we've been through this before. I have to go alone."

"What are you, crazy?" She asked with look of incredulity on her face. "We're so close to finding my father. There is no way you can keep me from going with you to help find him."

"You can be most helpful by letting me do my job of finding your father rather than spending all my time worrying about you," said Alek.

Cara put her hands on her hips, looked at him angrily, and said, "Listen, I can take care of myself. I'm not some glitzy prom queen."

"I know you could deal with some of it, but you have to decide if you want to act noble and go with me to find your father or be practical and let me do what I know how to do," replied Alek.

"I can't just sit here and do nothing," she said with a feeling of helplessness.

"Look, Cara," he said with sincerity, "this lead may end up being nothing and then where will we be? You have to continue to review your father's journals and anything else he left that may give us a lead."

"Okay, but I don't like being left out. You're not just trying to humor me, are you?" Cara asked sorrowfully.

"No, absolutely not. I really don't know where this lead will go. If it doesn't pan out, we will have to begin again. However, if you look for other information while I follow this lead, we could save a lot of time later."

"Okay, you have convinced me," she said, yielding to his logic.

"One important thing. I don't know what your father looks like. Do you have a recent picture of him?" Alek asked.

"Of course," she said as she reached into her purse and handed a picture to Alek. "He seems tall, in the photograph, but he's of average height. He has dark hair that's mostly gray now, large dark eyes, and high cheekbones. He's physically fit. The picture of him and me was taken last Christmas."

"That's great. I get the bonus of having a picture of you, too," said Alek.

She looked into his eyes and said, "Okay, but please be careful."

He took her face in his hands and gently kissed her lips. She put her arms around his neck and pulled him close to her. "Please," she said, "come back with him. I want you both safe here with me."

"I will do my best," he said as he smiled at her. "With an incentive like that, how can I fail? I'm going to leave for the village now."

"Wouldn't it be better to wait for morning?" she asked.

"No. First, I would like to get started. And, secondly, I might find it very difficult to spend the night on the floor with you just over there in the bed," he said with a grin.

He left the room, and she walked over to the window and watched as he drove away in the jeep. She stood at the window starring out. So much had happened to her in such a short a time. She was so worried about her father, but now she also was worried about what could happen to Alek. She had never developed such deep feelings for anyone so quickly. All of her relationships with men had always been on her terms.

The truth was most men she met socially were not very interesting, and the artists she met in her work were more like children who constantly sought approval. Given her choices, she just drifted along from one relationship to another.

Now and then, her father would ask her if a certain man she brought around was someone serious. She knew he just wanted her to be happy and to share her life with someone, as he had with her mother.

She thought of her mother, and she wished she remembered more about her. All she could remember was a warm, loving person who was a refuge from all the bad things in the world.

She loved to hear her father tell of the wonderful times he and her mother had. His eyes glowed when he talked about Maria de la Cruz Amelot. The memories of dinners, dancing, shows, plays and concerts, or fun things like walking in the park, laughing, and just being alone. Special times like when he proposed to her on his knees in the middle of the Student Union, or when she took him away from work to go on a picnic to tell him she was pregnant. He had told her all of these stories lovingly so many times that she felt like she knew much more of her mother than she could remember as a five year old.

Cara wanted so much to have the same feelings about someone. Maybe, Alek could be the one. He was handsome, no doubt about that, and he was intelligent enough to keep up with her. He talked a great deal about his family on their way to Tapachula, so she could tell how close he was to them and how sad he was that they were no longer there to share their lives with him. And he certainly was sexy. Cara began to feel a blush in her face as she thought of their encounter.

She had strong feelings about him, and she was sure he felt the same. When they were together, he stayed close to her, physically close. He immediately took charge of seeing she was secure, in the plane, with Dega, and in the hotel. And she liked it. No, she loved it.

She sat down on the bed and sighed. She knew he would like her father, and she knew her father would like him, if for no other reason than because she liked him. Please, please, let them both come back safely she thought.

CHAPTER TWENTY-SIX

Alek stopped to see Mandares on his way out. He walked into the lobby ,and there he was sitting behind his desk.

"Ah, Senore, did you find Castillo's place?" Mandares asked.

"Si, thank you for your help," said Alek. "I would like to ask you to do something for me tomorrow."

"Certainly. What is it?" asked Mandares.

"Here is one hundred U.S. dollars. This job requires some contact with the Federales, and it also requires some tact."

"What is this 'tact', Senore?"

"That means ah… let me just tell you the job first," he said. "I had to lock up Castillo's assistant for awhile."

"Oh. You mean Lopez. I know him. He's a, a, a, what you call, I think, is a wham," said Mandares.

"You mean a wimp," Alek corrected.

"Si, that is him."

"Yes, that may be true. Anyway, I had to lock him up in the kitchen of the main building because I didn't want him to talk to anyone about me until tomorrow morning. So, I need you to get word to the Federales, without them knowing it is you. Tell them he's being held in the warehouse building, and they should go there to release him."

"Si, I could do this," Mandares replied.

"I know you can, but I don't want to make trouble for you. Can you make sure to do this without the Federales knowing it is you?" asked Alek.

"Oh, don't worry," said Mandares with a big grin on his face. "My wife's brother is in the Federales. He's not much good for anything, but I can use him for this."

"Good, but, please, be careful. I may be gone for a day or two. If the senora needs anything, please help her," said Alek.

"Si. I will look after the senora."

As he drove out of Tapachula, he stopped long enough to pick up the weapons he had hidden. He had a haversack he brought with him, which contained a high-powered infrared scope, and a few other goodies. He had planned to get rid of this stuff after he left his job with Uncle Sam, but never got around to it. "Oh hell, whom am I kidding" he said to himself. I wanted to keep this stuff. It's like a security blanket.

As he began driving down the highway, he thought it would be impossible to find Edward Amelot without help. He knew that either he had to get very lucky, or he had to find a way to get the local Indians to help him. He didn't tell Cara, but a few years ago when he was active in Guatemala, he had heard Dega was connected with the Indians in Chiapas. After their insurrection, he represented the Indians in the talks with the Mexican Government. At the very least, he knew the Indians trusted Dega, so he might get some help by using Dega's name. However, he was not ready to go that route yet.

He had not said anything to Dega about knowing his role with the Indians. Rule one, in his business: trust no one, especially if that someone was somewhat of a demagogue. So, he would follow the lead he had, and if it did not pan out and Cara got no other leads from the journals, he would use Dega.

He followed the road, which would take him to the Indian village. According to the map, he should be able to drive most of the way there. As he drove he passed a number of villages, each with a number of adobe buildings. Some were houses, but others were gas stations, general stores, or restaurants.

He stopped in each village and asked if they had seen a gringo traveling with a Mejicano. He offered to pay for the information, but he had no takers. He was not sure these people would tell him if they knew anything. At the next village he decided to go into the restaurant and, at the bar, ordered a bottle of Tecate. As he drank his beer, he began talking to the Indian sitting next to him. He asked him if the road ahead was okay to drive on, but the Indian ignored Alek. Finally, Alek said, "Sorry, amigo, I just wanted to ask a question."

The Indian looked up and said, "I tried to talk to the last gringo that was in here, but his Mejicano told me to leave them alone."

Alek jerked his head around to the Indian and said, "Sorry, amigo, I'm not like that. Can I buy you a beer or a tequila?"

"Okay, gringo, I will have a tequila," the man said with a smile.

Alek asked the man behind the bar to give them a bottle and some limes. He then went over to a table and motioned the man to follow.

"What is your name?" Alek asked.

"My name is Luis."

THE ANCIENT ONES

Alek poured a full glass for Luis and only a splash for himself. He held up his glass to the man, who promptly swallowed his whole drink. Alek merely wet his lips with his. The man then took a lime in his mouth while Alek refilled his glass.

"So, you saw a gringo here. I bet not many pass this way," Alek suggested.

"No," said Luis, as he downed the second glass. "You are the only other one in a long time. They also were driving a jeep."

He was sure he was talking about Edward Amelot and Castillo. He wanted to ask more specifics, but he was afraid he would scare him off. He thought a bit and then asked, "So, I guess the road going south must be okay if they drove on it."

"Si, the rains must not have done anything to the road to the south because the gringo and his Mejicano haven't come back this way," Luis replied.

He poured him another tequila and said, "Thank you for the information on the road. I will be getting on my way."

On his way out, he purchased some dried fruit, beef jerky, and a bottle of tequila. He now knew he was on the right track. His map showed a turn-off about 9 kilometers down the road from the village. He took the turn onto a road that was only two tracks. He drove for about ten minutes, and then he pulled off the road into the brush so he would not be seen.

He took the pistol from his sack, checked to see the clip was in, and pulled back on the slide to put a round in the chamber. He put the pistol on the seat and ate some of the dried beef and fruit. He then took out the bottle of tequila, took a long drink, and tried to relax. As he stretched out in the jeep, he laid the pistol at his side and tried to go to sleep.

As he lay there his mind started to drift to his past. In his adult life, he had seen the cruelty man could perpetuate on man, first in the Army, then as an operative for the government. When he was alone at night and all was quiet, his mind, involuntarily, would recall, with disturbing reality, these horrors. They never went away. They just repeated themselves over and over, and they usually came as he first fell asleep. In order to keep his mind from revisiting the horrors of his past, he became adept in controlling his mind's subliminal path. He would bring forth thoughts of anything pleasant so they would totally consume his mind. Tonight was no problem because he chose Cara.

He looked up at the night sky and saw her face. She was becoming an obsession with him. Lately, he couldn't think of anything else. She was beautiful, intelligent, had a great sense of humor, and her loyalty to her father only enhanced her character. He wondered if he was getting too serious about her. He couldn't let his feelings cloud his judgment at a time like this, when he should have a clear mind. With his thoughts of her and dawn closing in, he closed his eyes and went to asleep.

He awoke as the sky began to turn from darkness to gray. He got up, moved around, and tried to loosen up his body. He drank some water, got back in the jeep, returned to the road, and continued toward the next village.

As he drove along the road, he began to climb a hill. As he came down the other side, there was a sharp turn downward, which required that he had to slow down almost to a stop. He continued on the road, which only got worse and worse. The going was very slow, and it took him all morning to reach the next small village. He stopped at a building with a gas pump. It was a very hot and humid day, and an Indian emerged slowly from the building to see what Alek wanted. "Would you please fill the tank with gas?" he asked.

"Si," said the Indian, as he put the nozzle in the tank of the jeep.

"This is a very hot season here," said Alek.

The Indian said, "The rainy season will begin in three or four days."

"How do you know?" asked Alek.

"The plants and the animals tell us, if we pay attention to them," said the man.

"You sound very certain," Alek answered.

"Senore, I am Indian. My family has been predicting the weather for hundreds of years. It was a matter of survival for them."

"I understand," said Alek. "I'm looking for two men who would have passed this way in the last few days. One of them was Mexican, the other a Gringo. They were driving a jeep."

"No," the Indian replied.

"I will pay for any information you have," said Alek.

"I mean no, no Gringo's have passed here. I would be taking money for nothing. You are the first Gringo to come this way in months."

"Would it be possible they came through, and you didn't see them?" asked Alek.

"I'm here every day." The Indian pointed to the building and said, "This is where I live. I hear every one that drives by. If anyone, especially a Gringo, had passed this way, I would know. Believe me."

He paid for the gas, gave the Indian a large tip, and said to him, "Thank you."

He looked at his map for the distance to the next village. He figured it would take him four or five hours to reach the next village. Rather than drive that far just to ask if anyone they had seen Edward and Castillo he decided to take the word of the Indian that no one passed through here.

If he was right, it meant Edward and Castillo had to have turned off somewhere between here and the village where Alek had stopped yesterday. That spot would not be easy to find. As he drove back down the road, he stopped at every place, which looked suitable for a vehicle to pull off the road. After covering most of the road he had previously traveled, he came to the sharp turn he had navigated earlier in the day.

As he came into the turn, he looked closely and could see where a vehicle had left the road. He got out and could barely see tire tracks across the barren dirt at the side of the road that led into the jungle. It was good it had not rained yet because the tracks would have been obliterated. He followed the tracks and saw they led into the jungle to a trail.

He took out the sack with the weapons. He loaded one of the M-16's, and took two grenades and placed them in the open compartment in the dash. He put the rifle on the passenger's seat and, after having a drink of water and some dried fruit, began to drive down the trail.

He drove uphill and deeper into the jungle and began to hear the sound of running water. The road bent sharply to the right and he saw a bridge, which looked like a bunch of boards someone had thrown across some beams. He stopped and got out of the jeep. He rearranged some of the boards and then drove slowly and cautiously over them. He gave a long sigh of relief when he was in the clear.

After another half-hour of climbing, the road came to a sharp turn downward. He could see where the tire tracks left the trail and depressed the low growing vegetation. He stopped the jeep, picked up the M-16 and followed the tire tracks a short distance to where a jeep had been driven into some deep brush. Apparently, someone was trying to hide it and did a poor job. He looked in the vehicle to see if there was anything that might tell him who it belonged to. It was plain, and had no markings or license plates. There was nothing in the compartments, and when he opened the hood, he saw the distributor cap was gone.

He walked back to his jeep and thought about whether or not he should follow the trail. Then, he wondered who would leave a jeep in the middle of the jungle. He could tell from the vegetation that it had not been there long, so he judged it might have been Castillo. He went back to the hidden jeep and looked again in all the compartments. Nothing. Then, he saw something under the seat. It was an empty ammo clip from a Czechoslovakian AK47. Now that was something. He decided the ammo clip was just enough incentive for him to take the gamble and follow the trail.

He drove his jeep far enough off the trail so it couldn't be seen by anyone passing by. It was now almost dark, so he once again stretched out in the jeep and laid the pistol on his chest. His mind began to wander and he thought of Edward Amelot. He had to find him. He knew that Cara could not bear to lose him.

Losing people you care about was not an unfamiliar event to Alek. There was his mother and father, lost together in a tragic accident, other relatives, and military partners, including John Cody. Alek had seen men die in military operations and in covert operations, but John's death was a total waste. He thought of John quite often, but tonight, as he closed his eyes, his thoughts turned to the time he visited Cindy Cody, John's wife.

When Alek had cleared himself with the army, he thought about going to see Cindy Cody because he felt somewhat to blame for Cody's death, but he couldn't bear to face her. He did write her a letter and told her how much he liked Cody. He told her John talked about nothing but her and the farm they were going to have. She sent him a letter back, but he didn't get it until about six months later, after the beginning of his first assignment. Cindy Cody had thanked him and told him John had been buried in the local cemetery, and the Army sent men to officiate at his funeral. She said John had written to her about Alek, and she asked him to come to see her if he was ever in Iowa. She also said how difficult her life was without John. After a lot of deliberation, he finally had decided to visit Cindy.

He got in his car and drove west from Washington into Pennsylvania. It was early summer, and the mountains were green and cool. He enjoyed seeing the green mountains, which seemed to stretch up to the sky. It was peaceful, so peaceful that he almost forgot about the unpleasant visit he had to make.

As he left the Pennsylvania, it seemed as if the mountains ended abruptly, and the flat farmlands of Ohio went on forever. Next, came the rolling green hills of Indiana, the farm country of Illinois, and, then, the Iowa border. Keokuk was a town in Iowa. As he came into town, the sign read: Keokuk, population 12,017, but then some local had added three zeros at the end of the number as a joke.

About a half-mile past the sign, there was a motel called the Shady Rest. It was getting late in the afternoon, so he thought he would get a room. He got out of the car and walked toward a small house in front of the motel, on which hung a sign which said 'Office'.

He could hear the sounds of a family in the back, so he rang a bell on the counter. A man in an undershirt came out from the house. "Can I help you?" he asked.

"I'd like a room," said Alek.

"How long you staying?" asked the man.

"Just one night," said Alek.

"Okay, just sign in here," the man said.

He signed the registration card, and the man handed him a key. "That will be $36," the man said.

Alek paid the man and asked for directions to the address he had for Cindy's family. The man told him the way and then turned back to go into the house.

He decided he would bring his luggage to the room after he met Cindy, so he got back into the car and went to the address he had. The house was a typical colonial on a dusty, tree-lined street. The paint on the house was fresh, and there were flowers all along the front of the porch. There was an old metal fishing boat with an outboard motor sitting in the driveway. As he stepped onto the front porch, he noticed the name McGrath on the mailbox. He assumed this was Cindy's maiden name.

The front door was open, and the screen door was one of those with a wood frame. There was no doorbell, so he knocked, and the door rattled back and forth. He could see through to the living room and down a long hallway into the kitchen. He heard a female voice say, "I'll be right there."

A slightly stout, gray-haired lady came walking down the hallway. She had on a light blue, flowered cotton dress with a white apron over the top. Her hands were covered with flour.

"Hello, can I help you?" she asked with a smile and a mid-western country accent.

"Good afternoon," Alek said, "I'm looking for Cindy Cody. Does she live here?"

The expression on her face changed immediately. "Who are you?" the lady asked suspiciously.

"I'm Alek Roman. I was a friend of John."

"Well Cindy ain't here, Mr. Roman," she said defensively.

"Are you her mother?" Alek asked.

"Yes, I'm Cindy's mother, but she don't live here no more."

"If you could tell me where to find her, I would appreciate it. I came a long way to see her."

"What you want Cindy for?" her mother asked gruffly.

"As I said, I was a friend of her husband. I wrote her a letter about six months ago, and she asked me to stop and see her if I was ever in Iowa. I have been out of the country on business, and this was the first chance I had to get here," Alek explained.

"Well, I don't rightly know where she's staying these days. She had a room over in the hotel, but I heard tell they made her leave. Cindy is not the same girl that married John. I can't tell you anything else, mister. I have to go. My bread is ready for the oven," the woman replied.

"Well, would her father know? Could I come back to see him later?" asked Alek.

"Cindy's father don't have anything to do with her anymore, so it won't do you any good to talk to him," she said as she turned and walked away.

"Well, thank you, Mrs. McGrath," he said to her back.

He got back into his car and headed into the town.

There was a post office right on the corner, so he stopped and went inside. The clerk at the desk knew Cindy. "Yeah, I went to high school with Cindy and John. It sure was sad about the way she went to pieces after John died," said the clerk.

"Do you have a mailing address for her?" asked Alek.

"No," said the Clerk, "but the people at the Rainbow Grill might know how to find her. She used to wait tables there, and she hung out at the bar most of the time."

He asked for directions to the Rainbow Grill, thanked the clerk, and walked down the street.

The sunlight was fading now. He found the Rainbow Grill down a block on Main Street. He looked up at an old faded brick building, which according to the cornerstone was built in 1931. The front door was wooden, and it had a glass window near the top, covered with a metal grill. He entered and tried to look around the room. It was very dark inside, so he stood there and waited for his eyes adjust to the light. He looked around and saw a bar that ran the length of the room down the left-hand side.

There were four people sitting at the bar. An elderly man and woman were sitting near the door drinking beer and smoking. They were in a conversation with the bartender about whether the summers came earlier now than when they were kids. The other two at the bar looked like farmers with their bib overalls and tee shirts. Each wore a baseball cap. One was green and said 'It's a Deere,' and the other was an old Chicago Cubs blue cap with a gold 'Cubs' in the middle. There were some booths along the opposite wall, but they were all empty. There was a pool table in the middle of the room. Its green felt was faded, and the balls were scattered around the table.

He walked up to the bar and asked for a draft beer. The bartender poured the beer from a tap in front of him and, as he placed the beer on the bar, said, "you're not from around here."

"No," Alek said, "I'm just visiting. I am looking for someone. Maybe you could help."

"Who you looking for?" the bartender asked.

"I'm looking for Cindy Cody. I understand she used to work here."

"Yeah, Cindy still works here some. Why are you looking for her?" asked the bartender.

"I was a friend of her husband, and I said I would stop in to see her if I came this way," said Alek.

"Well, if that's the case, she's right over there in the last booth. She might be sleeping one off," the bartender replied.

Alek laid a five-dollar bill on the bar and thanked the bartender. He picked up his beer and walked over to the table in the corner.

The booths had high backs, and their seats were old and covered in a red vinyl. The tabletops were wood, which had been painted many times. The paint was chipped, warped, and had things carved into the surface. As he got to the last booth, he saw a woman sitting there with a glass in her hand. She was staring at the back of the booth.

He turned to face her and said, "Hi, are you Cindy Cody?"

"Yeah," she said looking up briefly, "who are you?"

"My name is Alek Roman. I was a friend of your husband's. May I sit down?" he asked.

"Sure, why not," she said.

Cindy Cody should have been about twenty-four, but she looked much older. Her hair was blonde, and it was long and stuck to the side of her head. Her skin was ashen colored and there were dark bags under her expressionless eyes. She had the vacant stare of the dead, no light, no reflection, just like faded glass. She had on a dirty tee shirt that had a designer name on it, like the ones you can buy in the streets of most cities for five bucks. She stared into the glass she held between her hands.

"So, who did you say you are?" she asked emphatically.

"As I said, I'm Alek Roman, and I was a friend of John. I wanted to come to see you after John died, but I was, well, it just didn't work out."

Suddenly, her expression changed and a light of recognition came into her eyes, and she looked up from the table.

"Wait, I know you. John wrote me about you. You're the one that was with him when he died. John said they kept him on that island because some officer was mad at you, but he also said you were good to him and helped him. He said being kept there was not your fault and you tried to get him off the island. Yeah, and I remember you wrote me a letter," Cindy said her speech slurring, at the end, as if she had run out of energy.

"Yes, I'm just sorry John got in the middle of all of it," said Alek.

Suddenly, the look of recognition on Cindy Cody's face turned to one of sorrow. Her head fell to the table, and she began to sob uncontrollably. Her sobbing turned into loud moans, and he reached out and touched her hand to comfort her.

The bartender came over and said, "Look, Cindy, if you are going to start carrying on again, like you've been doing, you are going to have to leave. I can't have you screaming, crying, and bothering my customers."

"It's all right," said Alek softly, "I'll take her home."

He got up and lifted Cindy from her seat. He thought if he could get her out into the fresh air, she might be better. He practically carried her out the door, but it was no hard task since she felt like skin and bones. They got outside, and it was almost dark. He told her to take a deep breath, and when she tried, her breathing came in gasps.

"Where do you live Cindy? I'll take you home," He said.

"I have a room upstairs," she said, as she pointed to a doorway at the far end of the building.

He got her to the door and opened it. There was a long stairway with a single light bulb hanging from the middle of the ceiling. The stairway was so narrow he had to get behind her and hold her waist to keep her from falling, as he boosted her up the stairs. When they got to the top, she leaned against the door on the right side. She got a key out of her pocket, but it dropped to the floor. He picked up the key, held her up with one hand, and opened the door with the other.

The windows in the room faced the main street, and the neon sign from the Rainbow Grill lighted the room in an eerie yellow glow. Alek felt around for a light switch and then saw a lamp on the other side of the room. Cindy leaned against the wall while he walked over and turned on the lamp. The room was a mess. A table and two chairs that didn't match were on the left side of the room, and behind the door to the right was a narrow bed, on which lay a sheet and blanket crumpled up in the middle. A pillow was on the floor. Cindy walked over and sat on the bed with her back against the wall.

"Are you okay?" Alek asked softly.

"I could use a drink," Cindy said.

"Do you think that's a good idea?"

"Yeah, it is," Cindy, said demandingly.

She got up and walked unsteadily over to the table, on which sat a bottle of cheap bourbon and some empty glasses. She picked up two of them and walked, teetering, over to a sink in the corner. She ran water into the glasses and poured it out. Then, she walked back to the table, sat down, poured some bourbon in each glass, and drank one straight down.

"Would you like some?" she asked.

"No, thanks," he said. "Why don't you let me get you something to eat?"

"Thanks, but I need this right now." She lifted the other glass with two hands and took a big swallow. "So, you were with John when he died. Did he tell you about me?" she asked.

"Yes, he talked about you all the time and kept your picture next to his bunk," he said.

Cindy put her hands up to her hair and then covered her face with them and said," I know I don't look like that anymore." She was sobbing and refilled her glass.

"What happened?" Alek asked.

"What happened," Cindy said angrily. "I'll tell you what happened. One day I was the happiest woman in the world, and the next day, my world came crashing down on me. John and I were in love just about our whole lives. We grew up together and began to talk about getting married when I was a little girl. We were together so much people used to think we were brother and sister. My girlfriends used to tell me I would never know what it was like to love anyone else, but I didn't care. John was my life, always.

After we got married, I was living in a dream world, and, then, John decided to join the Army. I was happy with what we had, but he wanted us to be on our own. He wanted a farm. When he went away, I stayed home, saved money, and waited for him to come home. I missed him every day he was gone. Then, one day a man in a uniform came to my door. We were just sitting down to dinner. He said, "I'm sorry, but your husband was killed in some hostile action." I fainted, and when I came to, hours later, the man was gone."

"My mother had the doctor come over, and he gave me a sedative. She said the man left some forms for me to fill out for John's insurance. I just looked at them and screamed. I ran out of the house, but my father found me and brought me home. I stayed in my room for two months, taking every form of sedative I could get. I didn't want to see anyone."

"The only thing I wanted was to be with John. When he said he wanted to join the Army, I cried for a week. He said it would be okay, and when he got back, we would have a great life. The one we wanted. I just wanted him," Cindy said as she sobbed. She poured more bourbon into the glass again and sipped at the brown liquid.

"I'm really sorry," Alek said. "I liked John and tried to help him."

"Oh yeah, everyone liked John, and now he's dead. Dead! Why? Can you tell me why? I tried everything to get past his death, but nothing worked. My father told me I had to get out and live my life. What he didn't understand was I had no life left. He forced me out into the world, so I started drinking. I found when I got drunk enough, I couldn't remember anything, not even John. Then, I would get sober and remember all over again, so I drank more and tried to stay drunk. The longer I stayed drunk, the less I cared about life. Then, I tried to replace John with other men. I had to get really drunk before I could be with them, and, then, I'd get sick over it afterward. After I stopped coming home some nights and word got around about me being with other men, my father threw me out of the house. He said I was no longer a good Christian woman."

"Isn't there someone who can help you?" asked Alek.

Cindy drank down the rest of the liquid, poured again from the bottle, and said, "Oh sure, my mother sent me to the minister of the church who found help groups and social workers. None of them could take away the hurt of losing John. I gave up the other men but not the drinking. Then, I found a new companion," she said with a childlike smile on her face. "It is the magic dust. It moves me into a world where there is no hurt and no pain." Then, she frowned and said, "My only problem now is getting the money to pay for it. Our savings and John's insurance ran out a long time ago." She looked up at Alek and said, "Maybe you could give me a loan."

"I'd be glad to help you out anyway I can, but I won't give you money for drugs. I am sure you know what you are doing will kill you," said Alek.

"So what," she said abruptly, "there isn't anyone who cares anymore whether I live or die. John is gone, and so, maybe, it is my time."

"You're wrong, John would not want you to do this. He would want you to go on with your life," Alek said.

"Well, mister, you're the one who's wrong," she said with a frown. The frown turned to a smile when she said, "when I get my magic dust, I talk to John for a little while, and I know he's waiting for me. The problem is I'm too much of a coward to join him," she said meekly.

"Please let me help you," Alek pleaded. "You are not talking to John. It's the drugs, not him."

She looked at him angrily and shouted, "Whatever it is, it takes me to John. And someday soon, I will be with him all the time." She looked down at the floor and said, "Thanks, but I know what I want, and right now it is to have another drink and to lie down." She turned the bottle up and emptied it into the glass. She drank down the bourbon in one gulp.

He looked at her with pity and said, "I'm going to leave you my name and phone number in case you decide you need my help. You may have to leave me a message since I travel quite a bit, but I will get back to you. Is there anything else I can do for you now?" he asked.

"No, right now I just want to go to bed," Cindy replied. "The room is spinning."

He helped her over to the bed, and she laid face down and said," I'm sorry you had to be here now. Maybe you can come…"

Cindy didn't finish the sentence. He covered her with the blanket and turned out the light. He walked over to the window and looked out at the neon sign and the lonely empty road going out of the town. He turned and looked at Cindy. He had listened to John Cody and his fears before he died, and now he had listened to his wife and her fears. Maybe the only way she would be released from her pain was to join him.

He started to walk out the door and stopped. He turned around and walked back to Cindy's bedside. He looked at her for a moment and thought of the great shame of shattering two lives because of one man's bigotry. He took five one hundred-dollar bills out of his wallet and then laid them on the table so Cindy would find them when she woke. Maybe this was not the right thing to do, but he didn't know anything else he could do.

He got into his car. It was now 10:00 PM, and he drove back out of town the way he had come in. He drove right past the motel where he had planned to spend the night. He had to get away from here, from Cindy, from the memories of John, and from impending death.

He drove all night listening to whatever talk shows he could find on the radio to keep him awake. He didn't want to think about where he had just come from and what he had just seen.

He shuddered as his reverie ended and he came back to the present once more. He had not thought about Cindy Cody for a long time, or the fact she died of a drug overdose about a year after he saw her.

Mercifully, sleep finally came.

CHAPTER TWENTY-SEVEN

When Alek awoke in the morning, he drove his jeep to the edge of the jungle just next to the jeep he had found the previous night. He looked for some trees that were covered with vines down to the ground and, then, found a large branch with a v-shape at one end. He used the branch to lift the vines from the ground until he had an opening large enough to drive the jeep through and propped up the vines with the branch. He drove the jeep under the cover, removed the rotor and put it in his pocket. He then took the rifle and the sack and walked out from under the foliage. He removed the prop and used some branches to remove his tire tracks and footprints. He went back to the other jeep and covered it with more brush. Again, he brushed the ground with a branch in order to cover the tracks.

He looked at the job he had just done and was satisfied that, without scrutiny, no one would know the vehicles were hidden in the brush. He took two concussion and two smoke grenades, some ammo clips, and the machete and put them into the haversack he had brought. He slung the M-16 and the rocket launcher over his shoulder and took the rest of the weapons and hid them in the underbrush next to a Mangrove tree. He marked the tree under a branch looked around, and picked out a couple of outstanding landmarks he could use to find his cache.

He then looked around and determined there were only two directions he could go from here. To the north was a road. If they went that way, they could have driven; he had just come from the west, so that left south or east. He looked at his map, which indicated there were a number of villages to the east. So, he chose south, which led to a more desolate area toward the Guatemalan border. There was a game trail in that direction, so he began his walk into the jungle.

As he continued down the trail the underbrush became thicker and thicker. He noticed someone had been cutting the underbrush to widen the path, and every now and then, he could distinguish a boot print. He came on to a large sandy area and saw very distinctly the boot prints of two men and moccasin prints of someone leading a burro. Perfect!

He could now hear the sound of a river. He looked on his map and saw it was an unnamed runoff from the mountains flowing into the Usumacinta River. If Castillo and Edward continued in this direction, they would cross the border into Guatemala. There was no bridge on Alek's map, so he knew he would have to find a place to cross the river. He hoped the tracks would lead him to the crossing they had taken.

He finally came out of the underbrush and into sight of the river, which was flowing very swiftly. He looked around and saw no one and no sign of anyone being there. He stopped and used his scope to check more carefully along the riverbank on both sides for any signs of life. After he was fully satisfied there was no one in the area, he made his way down to the riverbank. The ground here was covered with growth. It made it impossible to see footprints, especially in the dim light of the approaching evening. As he approached the river, he began looking for shallow areas where the party could have crossed.

He reached the river and began to walk along the shore, searching for signs of a campsite or of footprints entering the water. He followed the shoreline for about one quarter mile up and down the river, but found nothing. On his way back to where he had started, he paused and looked from the bank of the river up to the edge of the jungle. There was nothing to show anyone had been here, but he was convinced Edward had to come this way. The trail through the brush had been cut relatively recently because it had not had time to grow over. There were no footprints on the riverbank; apparently, someone had taken pains to hide the fact they had been here.

As he began to walk back up to the edge of the jungle, he noticed something strange. He walked over and picked up a piece of driftwood which was about two feet long and, then, noticed some other pieces even higher up the hill. How could these pieces of driftwood have gotten so far up from the river? You could tell by the line of bushes and trees that the water never reached this height, even when the river flooded. Someone had thrown this wood up the hill. Maybe it was wood that was collected for a campfire. On the other hand, maybe someone was trying to hide the fact someone had been here.

He turned back to the river and looked over the ground below him. He decided to give a closer look to the area along the river. As he walked down, he could see an area littered with dead vegetation. He didn't pay any attention to it before because, looking up from the riverbank, it just looked like a clump of grass. From the vantage point above, however, he could see the base of this clump of grass rose above the level of the ground around it.

THE ANCIENT ONES

He approached the spot and kicked the grass with his foot. It flew through the air, so the roots were not deep in the ground. The grass had been placed there over a cover of dead leaves. He knelt down and began to dig into the leaves with the butt of his M-16. Just below the surface, he began to uncover ashes and deduced someone had taken pains to hide the fire they had. He could tell the fire was not very old since the ashes were still in chunks. If it had rained on this spot, the ashes would have disintegrated from the water. The fire was not any older than the last rain, which was probably within the last few days or less.

He knew this had to be where Edward and Castillo made camp, but if that were so, why had they taken the time to hide their campfire, and where had they crossed the river? He now began a search. He picked a starting point at river opposite of the campfire and then selected a peak in line with his position and the campfire. He placed a marker 100 yards upstream and downstream to form a triangle. By walking the two sides of the triangle he would come across any trail which might have been made by Edward and Castillo leaving or coming to the river. If he did not find any tracks, then, he would conclude they crossed the river, and he would find a place to cross the river and begin his search on the other side.

It was late, but he knew he would have time to traverse the two sides of the triangle. He walked up toward the peak from the point he established about 100 yards up river from the peak. He kept the peak in sight as his target and began to walk up the hill. As he reached the peak, he was breathing hard, but he found nothing.

Now, he began to make his way down the other arm of the triangle back toward the water. As he walked along the path down to the river, he saw a cluster of brush to his right. It seemed to be flattened in the middle. He walked over to look in the brush, and lying there was the carcass of an animal, covered by army ants eating away the flesh left on the bones by the vultures.

The remains of the animal definitely belonged to a burro. It had been there for a short time, no more than three or four days. He looked at the head and saw the bridle was still over the skull. There was a hole in the skull. Apparently, someone had shot the burro. Alek made a quick search of the area around the dead burro and found some vegetation that had been trampled by a boot. As he looked further he found definite boot tracks. At the edge of the clearing, he found a number of empty shell casings. He picked them up and saw they were 7.62 millimeter and probably fired from an automatic rifle.

He continued down the slope to the river where he came across clusters of dead brush. He moved some of the brush away, dug with his rifle butt, and began to uncover what looked like the supplies. He found a tent, poles, and other camp supplies. He stopped when he found a book. He opened the cover and the first page, which had the date, three days ago, and under it were printed the words, 'Journal of Edward Amelot'! Unbelievable, he thought to himself.

He leafed through the pages and found where Edward had described his trek to this point with a map he had drawn. According to the journal, they were going to cross the river the next day and then go on to the site of the ruins. But why would they kill the burro and not to take all of their gear, especially Edward's journal. Cara had told him her father documented everything. This was a new journal, so why did he leave it. He put the book in his haversack and continued.

He covered the supplies and made the area look as it had before he came. He decided to finish his walk to the river. He came onto tracks where a number of people had walked into the jungle, many more than just Edward and Castillo.

He thought about what he had found. Edward Amelot and Castillo came to the river, made camp, buried their supplies, and went off into the jungle with a group of men. However, he believed the real scenario was probably that a group of men came across them either on purpose or by accident. These men then buried their supplies, shot the burro, and took them prisoner. Why? Were they banditos or drug runners? Why would they leave all of the supplies? Who were they? He would have to follow their trail tomorrow.

CHAPTER TWENTY-EIGHT

Edward awoke very refreshed. He had been extremely tired and had slept soundly. He looked at his watch, saw it was 6:30PM, and noted he had slept most of the day. He got up, put on his boots, and opened the tent flap. The camp was still very busy, and men were moving all around. He heard the sound of large vehicles, but it was coming from off in the distance. He walked over to a water bag hanging from a tree and turned the tap. He washed and then dried himself. He was hungry, but he wanted to find Castillo. He walked to the tent where Castillo had been earlier, but there was no guard and no one in the tent.

"Good evening, Mr. Amelot," said Colonel Keitel, as he approached Edward.

"Colonel, good evening. I'm happy to have run into you. There were some jade statues in my backpack. They are not there now. Do you know where they are?" Edward asked.

"Yes, Mr. Amelot, they are here in my bag," he said smugly as he patted the bag, which hung over his shoulder. "I was sure they were important to you. As long as you do as you are told, I will return them to you when you leave."

"Colonel, they are perfectly innocent Indian artifacts which have only academic value," Edward offered.

"Yes, Mr. Amelot, that is why I said they were important to you. They will be returned when you leave. Now, where are you going?"

"I was looking for Castillo. This is his tent isn't it?"

"He's no longer in the camp. He tried to overpower the guard earlier. So, we have him and the Indian moved to a safer place."

"Colonel, I have to talk to him. It is very important. Besides, he will listen to me, and I will convince him not to cause any more trouble," Edward said trying to be convincing.

"My dear, Mr. Amelot," Keitel said emphatically. "I'm afraid you don't understand. I'm not concerned with your Castillo. We will simply not put up with anyone, and I mean anyone, interfering with our plans."

"And what are your plans?"

In a very angry voice, Keitel said, "That, Mr. Amelot, is none of your business, and if you don't do exactly as you are told, you will also be sent to the caves."

He looked over Keitel's shoulder and saw Von Papen walking up to where they stood. "What is going on colonel?" he asked as he approached.

"This man," he said as he pointed at Edward, "keeps asking too many questions."

"Oberst, please wait for me at my tent. Mr. Amelot, I'm looking forward to having dinner with you this evening. Will you join me in my tent in, let's say, one half-hour?"

"Certainly. I was just asking about Castillo," said Edward.

"I know, Mr. Amelot. We will talk of him when we have dinner," said the general as he turned to walk away.

Edward walked back to his tent and looked for his journal in his pack, but it was not there. He remembered he had left it lying on the blanket in his tent the night before. He had made notes of the route he and Castillo took to get to the river; apparently, the mercenaries had taken it or left it at the campsite with the rest of their gear. Yes, if they left it at the campsite and someone finds it they could. He stopped short as he remembered that he had not completed his notes about crossing the river. Besides, this group of mercenaries was so good; he doubted if anyone would find what they had hidden.

He began to walk around the camp and recorded mentally where everything was. He tried to ascertain just how large of a force was in the camp. He stopped in the mess tent and saw there were tables in the middle and an urn of coffee on the serving tables in the back. He walked in, got a cup, and sat down. In a few minutes, a sergeant and a corporal came in and got some coffee. They looked at Edward and sat at another table.

They spoke in German. The sergeant said to the corporal, "This is one of the ones we took at the river. He's an American. The others were a Mexican and an Indian. The Mexican tried to escape, so Keitel sent him and the Indian to the caves."

"Wasn't he concerned they would see the munitions?" the corporal asked.

"You should not speak of these things here. This one may hear you," said the sergeant.

"He doesn't understand German," the corporal replied. He turned to Edward and said loudly, "Amerikanischer schwein—Du machts mir krank."

Edward forced himself to keep a stoic look on his face. He understood

German well enough to know the corporal had said 'American pig you make me sick.' Then, he turned to them with a puzzled look and said, "I'm sorry I don't understand."

The corporal smiled and said to the sergeant, "See, I told you. What do you think they are going to do with all the munitions that are being brought into the caves?"

"I don't know," said the sergeant, "but what bothers me more is having those Indians around who were sent by the MYLN. These are supposed to be their commanders. They never have any expression on their face. You never know what they are thinking."

Colonel Keitel walked in at that moment and looked at the two men sitting there and said, "Sergeant, both of you come outside."

The two men walked out of the tent and stood at attention in front of him.

"Sergeant, there are more trucks arriving, and we will need some of your men to help to unload the munitions. Get them over there at once," he ordered.

The two men left, and Keitel walked back into the tent. "Mr. Amelot, the General is waiting for you in his tent. I will show you the way."

They began walking through the camp, and Edward asked, "Have you been in Mexico very long, Colonel?"

Keitel looked at Edward with contempt and said, "Mr. Amelot, for some reason the general likes you. I will treat you in a civil manner only as long as you don't cause any trouble. When we arrived here or what we are doing is none of your business. Finding out too much could be a reason for you not to leave. Is that clear?"

"Certainly. I was just making conversation," Edward teased.

"Here you are. I hope you have an enjoyable dinner," Keitel said as he left.

Edward entered the tent and saw the general sitting at a table made up with linen, china, silver, and crystal. "This is very nice, General. I didn't expect to find anything like this in the middle of the jungle. You must be planning to be here for some time," Edward said.

"Mr. Amelot, I'm most happy to have someone of culture to share my dinner; however, though you present your questions innocently, I do not think they are innocent. Please, just endure your time here, and I promise you will be returned to your camp."

"Thank you, General. I will do as you wish," said Edward. "There is one thing. Colonel Keitel took some artifacts and a journal from my bag. Could I please have them returned? They are of no value to anyone except myself,"

Edward said.

"He told me of them. I assure you he will return them to you when you leave," he replied.

"When will that be?" Edward asked.

"In due time, Mr. Amelot, in due time. Now, I suggest we change the subject."

Edward realized further attempts to obtain information would be useless, so he said, "Whatever you wish, General."

"Good. Some wine?" Von Papen asked.

"Yes, this is also a surprise," Edward replied.

"I try to bring some amenities with me to camp. I understand you are an anthropologist, and you are studying the aboriginals of this part of the world. Is that correct?" he asked as he handed Edward a glass of wine.

Edward looked at him and decided to have some fun with his condescending manner. "Yes, I have been studying the Olmecs and the Mayas mostly. Their civilization dates back before those of Europe. When Europe was still in the Dark Ages, these people mapped the heavens, developed a writing system, and were masters of mathematics. They, also, invented a calendar. In fact, the cultural developments of these people parallel those of the early Egyptians and Chinese. Civilization was present in Mesoamerica when the Europeans could still be considered troglodytes," said Edward.

"What?" asked the general, with a strong question mark. "Europeans certainly passed being cave men long before these primitives. Your aborigines may have been roaming this God-forsaken country a long time, but as far as their civilization is concerned, you cannot compare it to the evolution of man in Europe."

"Yes, it is true the Indians of Mesoamerica reached a point in the development of their civilization when progress was retarded; however, of course, it was at the time when the civilized Europeans tried to enslave them and to annihilate their entire race. They were at peace in their world until they were part of a pogrom, officiated by a race of violent men who persecuted them. They were the targets of ethnic cleansing. Ah, but I'm sure you know about that kind of pogrom, General."

Von Papen looked hard at Edward. His face turned red and he said, "Peace and tranquility are words weak men use as an excuse for being indolent. I know the people you study are a race of primordials that do nothing to advance themselves. The world needs strong men and strong leaders to build the future."

At this point, Edward could see he had pushed as far he possibly could without retribution. In an attempt to divert the General's anger, Edward said, "Yes, it is true strong leaders take the world to the next level of civilization. I'm simply one who observes man's past. I do not judge the present or critique plans for the future. By the way, the wine is excellent, General."

General Von Papen was ready for another round, but Edward's remarks disarmed his anger entirely. "Thank you, Mr. Amelot. Yes, it is a nice wine. Let's have our dinner brought in now," he said, sliding down the hill of anger to a peaceful demeanor.

As they ate, they talked about the progress of man's technological achievements, art, and music. Von Papen was pleased to hear the fact that Edward's father was a renowned musician and said he had even heard some of his recordings.

When they finished eating, the General got up and walked over to his desk. He returned and placed a beautiful box on the table which, when opened revealed itself as a humidor. "Would you like a cigar Mr. Amelot? They are Cuban," he said.

"Thank you." Edward said as he selected a cigar and cut the end off it. The general lit Edward's cigar and then his own.

When he closed the humidor, Edward noticed that inlaid on top of the cover was a German Iron Cross with a Swastika, oak leaf, sword, and diamonds. Edward knew this was the Knight's Cross, which was commissioned by Hitler during World War II and awarded for an extreme act of bravery in battle for the Fatherland.

"Were you in the German Army during World War II?" asked Edward.

"I see you noticed my Iron Cross. Yes, I served the cause of the Fuhrer and the Fatherland," the General said.

The sight of this abominable medal and the thought of the horrors of World War II brought an instant detestation to Edward. He wanted to tell the General just what he thought about people who wanted to enslave others for their own benefit, but then he remembered how he had aroused his ire before. He thought it best to maintain a good relationship with him in order to find a way to extricate himself from his incarceration. So instead he said, "You must have been extremely brave to warrant such an honor as the Knight's Cross."

"So, Mr. Amelot, you know something about the German Army," he said.

"Yes, primarily from studies in history," Edward replied.

Suddenly, the cigar had begun to taste vile. Edward put it in the ashtray and said, "I guess I have stayed away from cigars too long. This just does not taste good to me. General, I wish to thank you for your hospitality, but I would like to ask one favor of you."

"I will try, Mr. Amelot. What is it?" the General asked.

"I would like to talk to, Castillo, the man who brought me out here," Edward replied.

"Castillo tried to escape and attacked one of my men. I will not tolerate disobedience of my orders. When you came here, I didn't incarcerate either of you. I tried to make this temporary stay acceptable to both of you, but that man broke his word."

"Yes sir, I understand. I'm not asking you to free him. I just want to talk to him about where we were going before we were captured," Edward said.

"Mr. Amelot, you are not going anywhere for a while," he answered.

"I know, sir, but I have the feeling Castillo will not want to continue our trip when you release him. I just need some information from him, and our conversation will not take long," said Edward.

"Alright, Mr. Amelot. You have been a pleasant dinner guest, and I will let you talk to Castillo. However, I will have him brought here, and you will have thirty minutes to talk. That's all," he replied.

"Thank you. I appreciate your goodwill," said Edward.

"As long as you are here, Mr. Amelot, and you follow the rules, you will be a welcome guest."

"Thank you. I hope I will not have to impose on you for very long," Edward said.

The general smiled at his repeated attempts to get more information. "That will be determined soon, Mr. Amelot. Thank you for the pleasant dinner conversation. I admire your work, and I know you will be able to return to it soon."

Edward left and returned to his tent. He waited for over an hour, when suddenly Keitel opened the tent flap and said, "Mr. Amelot, you have been granted ten minutes with Castillo. My men will stand guard."

Edward walked out from the tent and saw Castillo standing there with his hands tied behind his back. There were bruises on his face, and two men, the corporal Edward had seen in the mess tent and another man with no rank, stood behind Castillo. "Thank you, Colonel. I appreciate your bringing Castillo here. The general said I could have thirty minutes with him. Is that correct?" asked Edward as though he had not heard the colonel's statement of time.

Without answering, Keitel looked at Castillo and said, "And you, if you try to escape again, my men have orders to shoot you. They will not hesitate, especially after you attacked one of their own. Is that understood?" Castillo stood with his head bowed and nodded up and down in affirmation. Keitel walked away.

"Let's go to the mess tent and get you some coffee. Guard, please remove his bonds."

"I haven't been told to do any such thing," said the corporal.

"Corporal," said Edward in his most authoritative voice, "I wish to talk to this man while we have a cup of coffee. You may stand there with your rifles pointed at him for the duration if you wish. I'm sure you would not miss at that close range."

"I'm sorry sir, but," the corporal stammered.

Edward interrupted the soldier before he could continue. "Corporal, let's walk over to the general's tent and ask him whether or not the two of you can handle this man without shackles." He started to walk away in the direction of the general's quarters.

The corporal looked confused. While he wasn't entirely certain how to handle Edward, he was certain that seeing the general was not the right thing to do. "Wait. Sir, we can go to the mess tent. I will untie his hands there," the corporal replied.

They all walked to the mess tent, and Edward got two cups of coffee and some rolls from a large pan. He brought them to the table where Castillo was seated.

"Thank you, Corporal," said Edward. "You can wait outside, and I will call you when we are through," said Edward.

"No, sir. We will stay in the tent right over there," he said. As he pointed to a table in the corner, he added, "And we will watch your every move." The corporal glared at Castillo and poked him in the chest with his rifle barrel."

Edward was satisfied. At least the corporal and his compatriot were out of hearing range.

"Are you all right?" Edward asked when the soldier left. "Did they put Keichi with you?"

"I'm all right now, and so is Keichi. He's in the cave where they are keeping us. You do a good job in handling these men," Castillo said with admiration.

"Here, have some coffee and rolls. Have they fed you?" asked Edward.

"No, I have been sitting in the caves all day long," Castillo replied.

"What caves?" asked Edward.

"There are some caves not far from here," Castillo replied. "We walked along a ridge and past a valley to get there. In the valley, they are building a camp even larger than this one. At the cave, there were trucks arriving loaded with munitions from Guatemala. There are enough weapons there to supply a large army."

"What do you think is going on?" Edward asked.

"These soldiers, I think, are here to help the Indian rebels. Some Indians in uniform came into the cave, and I heard them talking," replied Castillo. "They were saying more Indians will be coming to this place so the soldiers can train them to use the weapons."

"I did not see many men since we have been here. Are there many more at the caves?" Edward asked.

Castillo was gulping down the rolls, "Not too many. The ones that come in the trucks leave when they empty the truck, but there will be many more soon," he said with a mouth full.

"How do you know that?" asked Edward.

"The men working in the caves talk about their army coming here," Castillo replied.

"Guatemala. Are you sure they are coming all that way?"

"It is not far. We are only a few miles from the border. There is an old road which leads through the mountains into Chiapas from Guatemala. I have used it to bring certain goods into the country, and I'm sure that's the road they are using," explained Castillo.

"What more do you know?" asked Edward.

"The camp I spoke of in the valley, the one you can see when you come from the caves, well, men are building many platforms there, the kind that will be used for tents. It is obvious there will be a large army here soon. What are we going to do?" Castillo asked.

"From what I can see, the camp is well guarded," Edward said.

"Yes," said Castillo, "and the trails we used are also protected."

"The general says we will be detained here until they accomplish whatever it is they came here to do," Edward said. "He says our captivity will only last for a short time."

"What is a short time? Do you trust what they say?" asked Castillo.

"At this time, I don't see any other choice. I think we just have to wait and see what happens," Edward replied.

"You will wait, but I will go again if I have the chance. If I can get into the jungle, they will not find Castillo."

"That's crazy. These men will kill you. They are professional soldiers. Even if you get into the jungle, they will hunt you down. Besides, they will tie your hands again. How do you expect to get loose?" Edward asked.

"While you were getting coffee, I took a knife from the table and put it in my boot. I'm smarter than you think," Castillo replied proudly.

"What about the ruins?" asked Edward?

"Is this your only concern? I'm concerned with my life," Castillo said angrily.

"As I am. However, I have an opportunity that may never come again. I must know, are the ruins in Mexico or Guatemala?" asked Edward.

"I will take you there when this is over," said Castillo. "If finding this temple is as important as you say, it will cost you more money. Now, I can only tell you we are very close."

Edward started to say something, but was silenced by the corporal coming over to the table.

"Alright, it is time to leave, Castillo. Stand up and put your hands behind your back," he said.

"Is this necessary, Corporal?" asked Edward.

"Yes, Mr. Amelot. Now don't interfere. Your time is up," said the Corporal.

Castillo stood and his hands were tied behind his back. The party left the tent and walked off down the trail. Edward watched them until they were out of sight and then sat down to think about what Castillo had said about the ruins. He thought about telling the corporal about the knife, then reconsidered when he imagined how they might react. Edward knew he would just have to wait and hope Castillo survived. In the meantime, he had to learn about the group of Indians in the camp.

CHAPTER TWENTY-NINE

Alek awoke and left at first light. He followed the trail for a mile and then stopped for a drink. The trampled leaves and broken branches made by the passing men indicated a significant number of men had traveled down the trail.

As he walked, his mind turned to thoughts of Cara. In the short time they had been together, she affected him in so many ways. Seeing her brought on a rush of emotion, touching her filled his senses, and holding her was his undoing. Even when he was angry with her for her deception with him, he couldn't deny his strong feelings for her. Now he had to return her father safely to her, then he could get on with what he was sure would be a new kind of relationship for him.

Reality suddenly snapped him back to his surroundings and he admonished himself. 'Look, fool, if you are going to get back safely, you better not think of anything but the work at hand.'

After walking for about two hours, he stopped to rest and have a drink. It was extremely hot already, and it was only nine o'clock in the morning. As he sat, he checked his weapons and the extra munitions in his haversack. From now on, he decided he would walk for fifteen minutes and then climb a tree to see what was ahead. He would also have to pay attention to the trail for freshly dug earth and trip wires which might be connected to anti-personnel mines. He looked around and found a tall tree he could use to see far ahead. From his perch, he could see he was coming to a high hill, and there were more hills beyond.

He walked at intervals for another hour and screened the trail carefully. As he approached the top of the next hill, he found a tall tree on the side of the trail that would be easy to climb. He laid down his rifle, the rocket launcher, and the haversack at the base of the tree and then reached up for the first handhold. As he began to lift himself, he suddenly stopped. He thought if he knew the tree was a good lookout point, so would anyone else. The tree might be booby-trapped.

He carefully walked around the tree and looked closely from the base to the highest point of the tree he could. Then, he saw it. As it passed through the branches the sunlight shone on a straight silver line. It was a wire. He went back to the front of the tree and carefully pulled himself up into the first crouch. From that position he could see the wire across the foothold in the tree. He followed it with his eye and saw it wrapped around the trunk and that, wedged in between the branches above, was a grenade. He was thankful for his instincts. If he had tripped the wire, it would have pulled the pin on the grenade, and it would have decapitated him.

He carefully pulled himself up, stepped over the wire, and looked in the branches above for more booby traps. He climbed as high as he could and looked out through his field glasses in a ninety-degree arc with his trail as the mid-point. There, off to the left about 30 degrees from the mid-point, he could barely see some smoke rising. He got out his compass and took a bearing on the smoke. Then, he carefully climbed down and checked the bearing with the direction of the trail. The trail headed in a slightly different direction, but that was probable because the jungle caused it to meander back and forth because of the terrain. However, just to be sure he resolved to stop every five minutes and check his bearings to insure he remained on course. He picked up his things and started down the trail.

He walked for another hour verifying his course frequently. He found another tree and checked it for booby traps. Then, he climbed as high as he could and saw, in a valley below, the smoke he had been tracking. The jungle brush and trees were still very thick, but off to his right there was a hilltop that was relatively bare of ground cover. He turned his focus back to the area where the smoke was and could make out some figures walking about. He took out his field glasses and saw men in camouflage uniforms.

Suddenly, as he swung the glasses along the line of the camp, he saw a slight movement in a tree. He swung the glasses back very slowly and there, in a tree off to his left, was a sentry sitting in the crotch of the tree with an AK47 rifle. He had what appeared to be night vision equipment hanging down on his chest.

Alek climbed back down and checked his rifle and pistol. He slung the rocket launcher and the haversack over his head, and then he began to walk down the trail. He calculated he could walk for another ten minutes and then head off through the underbrush to avoid the sentry. He didn't want to come up on the camp from the trail anyway. There probably would be mines planted in the brush along the trail. He would have to get well off the trail and walk through the jungle.

He looked again at his compass to determine the direction of the camp and set off through the jungle. Moving through the jungle bush was brutal. It was now so hot he was soaking wet. He could only walk for ten minutes at a time before he needed a rest. In that time, he could go a short distance because of the thick underbrush. He, also, was on the lookout for more sentries and booby traps. After two hours, when he began to smell smoke, he knew he was close to the camp.

As he got closer and closer, every muscle in his body began to tense up. Before each step, he had to insure there were no trip wires or flattened foliage. He stopped, took a drink, and told himself he had to relax. He took a deep breath, but the air was so thick it was hard to breathe.

As he began to move forward again, he saw a trip wire for an anti-personnel mine. He knew it was the kind of mine that exploded and shot out hundreds of pieces of shrapnel in a semi-circle, killing or maiming anything in its path. He carefully disarmed the mine, then turned it so it would fire the death charge toward the camp rather than away from it. This was just in case he needed some extra help when he left. He marked a tree where the AP mine was, so it would be easier to spot on his return. As he progressed further, he found two more AP mines and set them up for his exit.

As he came over a slight rise, he could hear voices. He moved up slowly and saw the camp. Based on the number of tents he could see, he figured there were somewhere between fifty and sixty men in the camp. He watched closely for about thirty minutes and only counted five men. Where were the others?

He slowly crept up to the edge of the camp where some of the men were constructing more floors for tents. He stopped and listened.

They were speaking German, and he understood them perfectly. The men were griping about having to build the tent floors, and the sergeant in charge said, "We only have to build five more floors. You ought to be happy you are not at the caves. Unloading the munitions trucks in this heat would be much worse than this detail, so get on with your work. The rest of the men are scheduled to be here soon." Caves, munitions, more men. Alek wondered what was going on here.

Five more floors to go, and then they were finished. Based on the size of the floors the men were building, there would be room enough for about sixty more men than he originally calculated. He decided to see what else was in this camp and if he could get to the caves the men were talking about. He moved around the perimeter of the camp until he saw a tent that was off by itself. This was probably the command post of the unit since it was much larger than the others were. He got within about ten feet of the tent, still staying in the underbrush, when he saw two men about to enter the tent. They both had on jungle fatigues like the other men, but one had a bird colonel's insignia, and the other wore five stars.

The general was making some furious hand gestures while the colonel held open the tent flap as if to invite the general in. He wanted to hear their conversation. He cut some large palm branches and covered his body with them, and he crawled to the back of the tent. When he got to the back wall of the tent, he listened to the dialogue between the two men.

"Oberst, I will not let some aborigine tell me what I can or cannot do with my army," shouted the general. "Who does he think he is?

"You are right, General."

"Well, why did you bring him to the caves?" demanded the general.

"I had no choice but to bring him to the caves when he insisted on seeing the types of munitions we were bringing in," Keitel said sheepishly. "We thought he would accept our story about needing more munitions, but he suspects we are not telling him the truth, and now he's threatening to tell the MYLN leaders we are violating our agreement. He has asked to use our radio to call the MYLN," said Colonel Keitel.

"Who is with him?" demanded General Von Papen.

"He came with two other commanders. They are all in the mess tent having coffee," the colonel replied.

"Oberst, listen carefully. These Indians are not to use the radio, and they must not leave this camp. I will not have them upsetting our plans. Do you understand?" the general demanded.

"But, General, they will eventually want to leave, and certainly someone from the MYLN will be looking for them," the Colonel reasoned.

"We can take care of whoever looks for them later. First, I want you to take these Indians and secure them in the caves."

"They will not like that, General," the Colonel replied.

"That is of no consequence. Take them in restraints if you have to. They are now prisoners, not guests. Then, I want you to contact Reyes and tell him his men agreed to help you define the defensive positions at the border of Guatemala, and they will be in the jungle for a few days. That will buy us some time."

"It will be my pleasure to put those aborigines in their place, and I'm sure your idea will work with Reyes," said Keitel. "He will be thrilled that we think they know something about armies and warfare."

"Don't underestimate this man, Keitel. I understand that he and his men held the Mexican Army at bay for weeks, then escaped into the jungle."

At that moment, an orderly brought in a message, which General Von Papen promptly read. He turned to Keitel and said, "The meeting I told you about is on. Brabant is coming here to meet with the Dega, the leader of the MYLN."

Alek felt like his heart jumped up to his throat when he heard Dega's name. 'Dega! So he's the leader of the Indian group.'

"What should we do about the camp we are preparing for the entire army?" Keitel asked. "If Dega sees both camps, he will know we are preparing for more than just training his men."

As Von Papen turned to a table to pour a drink he said, "Oberst do you think Herr Brabant is not aware of this. He will expect us to keep our work here hidden from Dega."

Dega and Brabant. Alek knew who William Brabant was. He had first heard his name a number of years ago when he was on an assignment in Panama. Brabant had put the country in chaos. He had brought together the leaders of the radical opposition to the government and financed a plot to assassinate the president and several members of his cabinet. The plot was a failure, and the opposition leaders were killed in the coup attempt. The investigation to implicate Brabant in the alleged plot was never completed, supposedly owing to lack of evidence. In fact, it failed because he had bought off the investigators and the judges.

Brabant was ruthless and very wealthy. A combination that could be trouble to any government he chose to attempt to subvert.

As Von Papen turned back to face Keitel he said, "a helicopter will pick up Dega and Reyes at Tapachula and bring them here. Brabant will arrive in another helicopter. All of them will arrive by ten o'clock tomorrow morning, so we will radio our men in Guatemala and tell them to stop moving munitions. Have our men camouflage the work they are doing on the big camp in the valley. I will signal the pilot bringing Dega, to approach the camp only from the north so he will not fly over the caves or the valley, but just in case, I want the work there camouflaged. Now, go and get these things started."

"I will take care of our Indian guests first," said Keitel with a grin.

"Remove them quietly. I don't want Amelot to see this happen," the general said.

Alek's heart almost stopped beating, again, as he gasped involuntarily. He couldn't believe what he had heard; Cara's father was here.

THE ANCIENT ONES

"General, why must we put up with this man? He's a potential danger to us. If we did away with him, no one would be the wiser," said Keitel.

"Oberst, there may be people who know he came into this area. He claims to have left letters telling his associates where he was going. We do not want to involve the United States in our dealings by killing one of its prominent scholars. No, he must stay unharmed, and he must not know about the Indians." He looked coldly at Keitel. "Is that clear?" he demanded.

"Yes, General, it will be as you say. I understand the implications. I just don't like the man."

"Take care of these Indians, Oberst."

Keitel left the tent, and Alek slowly crawled back into the brush, dragging his palm fronds behind him. When he reached his cover, he knelt down and began to think about his plan of action. He now knew Edward Amelot was in the camp, but he did not know where. He also knew an army was being assembled, and some significant action was about to begin. The first thing he decided to do was to have a look at the caves so that he would know just what he was up against.

He set out around the perimeter of the camp until he saw a trail into the jungle wide enough to drive a small truck through. He followed the trail until he came to the edge of a valley. He could see a clearing at the bottom of the hill, so he stopped to look with his field glasses. There were twenty men working in the valley building on what appeared to be tent floors. There were at least thirty floors, and it looked like there were another fifty floors laid out for construction. Alek calculated there could be almost one thousand men to be housed there. With that many professional soldiers, anything could happen.

Brabant must have designs on Chiapas. That's why he is working with the Indians. He must be helping them with their revolution like he did in Panama, and he surely was planning to double cross Dega if the revolution succeeded. Alek knew a plan like this could work. After all, it had happened a number of times in Africa, so it probably could happen here.

Chiapas was so isolated from the rest of Mexico that an army could set itself up quickly and take command of its borders. The western and northern borders would be difficult for the Mexican army to traverse and easy for the mercenaries and the Indians to defend. To the south was Guatemala and to the east was Belize. These governments were not the best friends with Mexico, besides they had their own problems. They would not be too concerned about what was happening in Mexico, as long as it did not cross their borders.

Alek went down the trail and found the caves. From his vantage point, he watched as trucks pulled up to the caves and unloaded their cargo. With his binoculars, he could see into the caves. There were arms, ammunition, artillery pieces, rocket launcher pads, and many other cases of military goods.

He now began to think about his options and about finding Amelot. If he could only reach him at night and sneak him out of camp... well, it might be a viable option. With all that was going on and would be happening, it might work. Of course, the mercenaries would be on their trail as soon as they knew he and Amelot were gone, and he would have to deal with that, but first he would have to find Edward Amelot.

His only other option was to get the government to send troops in here. However, by the time he could convince the military officials to send a sufficient force here, they might be facing a professional army of mercenaries. More importantly, if there were a battle, Edward Amelot might be wounded or killed. In the end, he decided the best plan would be to get Amelot out himself.

He made his way back to the camp area. He went back into the brush, worked his way around the perimeter, and checked each tent for signs of Edward Amelot. After circling three quarters of the camp, he finally saw an armed guard watching a tent. He waited in the brush until a man came out of the tent. It was Edward Amelot; he definitely matched the picture Cara had given him.

Edward Amelot walked over to another tent, which looked like it could be the mess tent. His guard followed at an acceptable distance. Therefore, he had the run of the camp, with his escort. That was good because if he and the guard were gone from the tent, no one would suspect anything for a while. Alek decided for now he would hideout near the general's tent and keep watch. This is where he would get information on what was going to happen.

He made his way back and found a place in the crook of a tree, which kept the ground insects off and offered an adequate vantage point to observe any activity. It was now about six o'clock, and he set his wristwatch to wake him at eleven. It would be dark by then, and he would be able to get his haversack and begin to work his way back to Edward's tent. Exhausted from his activities, he quickly fell asleep.

He awoke with a start when he heard shouting coming from an area to his right. Men were shining hand held searchlights everywhere, and he heard someone yelling orders to the men. Apparently, they were looking for an escaped prisoner. Oh shit! Did Edward Amelot try to escape?

He immediately turned to focus on the direction of Amelot's tent. He saw the guard was at his post but closer to the edge of the jungle looking out toward the lights. Then, he relaxed when he saw Edward Amelot come out. The soldier who was standing guard tried to push him back into the tent. Edward resisted, and the soldier shoved him forcibly back into the tent. The soldier then turned toward the noise of the men and the sergeant who was shouting orders.

Suddenly there was an explosion, which came from the same direction as the lights. Some soldiers approached his hiding spot, and he had to duck behind the trunk of the tree to avoid their flashlights.

Colonel Keitel came running with an automatic pistol in his hand and some of his men trailing behind. He started giving the men orders and they focused their lights in the area of the explosion. Alek could see a man lying on the ground. The sergeant called for the men to stop as he walked up and poked at the body with the barrel of his rifle. The man didn't move. Apparently, he had set off one of the anti-personnel mines which ringed the perimeter. He wondered if the dead man was one of the Indians the general had been referring to earlier.

He then heard Edward Amelot arguing with the guard. Colonel Keitel told the guard to let him through. He walked up to the lighted area and looked down at the body.

"Is it Castillo?" Edward asked.

"Yes," Keitel said. "I understand he cut his bonds with a knife. He killed one of my men and tried to run, but the fool ran straight from the caves into the camp. If he had run into the jungle from the caves, he would have made it. We haven't had time to mine that perimeter."

"Is he dead?" Edward asked.

"Of course, he's dead," the colonel replied indignantly.

"What about the Indian that was with him?" Edward asked.

"He too tried to run, but my men captured him before he could get into the jungle. They are bringing him here, now."

At that moment, two men walked into the clearing, holding Keichi by his arms. The front of his shirt was covered with blood, and it was obvious he had been hit in the face. He looked up at Edward and started to say something, but one of the mercenaries hit him on the side of his head to silence him. He fell to the ground.

Edward knelt down and glared at Colonel Keitel, "that was not called for. This man needs medical attention."

"These men disobeyed our orders," said the colonel. "I will not give this Indian comfort so he can defy me again."

Edward tried to keep his composure and said, "this man did nothing to harm you, and if he did escape, all he would do is go home. He needs help now!"

"Don't tell me what to do. I'm sick of listening to you."

"You cannot treat people like this."

Keichi started to get up, and Keitel shouted to him in German, "Kene falsche bewegung."

Keichi looked at Keitel and then to Edward who said, "Keichi, he said don't move. Please don't."

Keichi began to speak to Edward, and Keitel shouted again in German, "Nicht handeln."

Before Edward could tell Keichi not to speak, the Indian rose up and said to Edward, "I have done nothing wrong. Why am I treated like this?"

Before Edward could respond, Keitel lifted his arm, and shot Keichi in the chest. Keichi fell to the ground, and Edward was frozen in place and stunned into silence. He looked at Keichi and then at Keitel, who was flushed as the result of his actions. Never, even in war, had Edward seen such a cold-blooded violence.

Edward could see Keichi tried again to speak, so he stepped between him and Keitel. Keitel now pointed the pistol at Edward and glared at him. He ignored the action and bent over Keichi who was trying to say something. He put his ear close to Keichi's mouth, and he heard a soft raspy voice say, "You have been kind, and I ask you to tell my daughter that I'm gone. And thank you for treating me like a man." With that, he stopped breathing.

Edward rose slowly, took a step toward Keitel, and said with a cold glare, "You son-of-a-bitch. That Indian didn't do anything wrong. He was an old man and meant no harm, but you just put a bullet in him anyway, like he was nothing."

"He was nothing, Mr. Amelot!. Now, I ask you; where did Castillo get the knife? You were the only one Castillo came into contact with besides my men." Keitel's face turned red. He pulled back the hammer of his pistol an pointed it at Edward, and said, "You will answer me, now, or you will join these two."

Edward stared at him defiantly and braced himself, but at that moment, General Von Papen walked up and said to Keitel, "Lower your pistol." Keitel looked at Von Papen and then at Edward, but he did not move.

Then, in a thundering voice Von Papen said, "Oberst, I am not going to tell you again, lower that pistol, now!"

As Keitel lowered his arm, Von Papen turned to Edward and asked, "Did you give him the knife, Mr. Amelot?"

"No, General, I didn't. He took it when we were in the mess tent," said Edward.

"Mr. Amelot, you knew about this theft, but said nothing," said the general. "I trusted you, and you abused my trust."

Edward finally became incensed and exploded, "What the hell are you talking about? Trust. You are holding me here against my will, and you want my trust? Do you think I should be grateful to you? You forced Castillo to run, and then you killed him." Edward then pointed at Keitel and said, "Then, this butcher of yours gunned down an unarmed, innocent old man. Now, are you planning to kill more? How many more, General? What is your goal? Who are you going to try to dominate now?" Edward shouted.

Keitel raised his pistol and took a threatening step toward Edward. The general replied in a booming voice, "Stop," looking at Keitel. He, then, turned to Edward and with a stern and strong voice said, "The world needs strong men, not indolent lice like this man" he said, pointing at Castillo, "or weak ones like this one!" he said, pointing at Keichi.

Edward tried to restrain himself because he knew if he said anything, he would probably be killed. He turned away from Keitel and Von Papen and took a deep breath, but when he looked down at Keichi, he could no longer control himself. He turned back to Von Papen and said, "So, Castillo died, not because he was a criminal, but because he stood up to you. And what about the Indian? Was he like the Jews, the Gypsy's, the Poles, and all the others that were massacred as indolents under the Nazi's?"

"What are you saying Mr. Amelot?"

"Your Hitler had killers that were just like this man," he said, again pointing at Keitel.

"Our Chancellor was trying to develop a better world by ridding it of the degenerates and the anarchists. Sometimes, in order to improve, we first have to destroy. You cannot build a new building over an old one. You must first bring down the old," said the general.

"A poor analogy, General. Mine would be that in order to build a fascist state, like the Third Reich, you must first extirpate anyone that can think for themselves, while worshiping a demagogue."

"The Fuhrer was our savior and our guide to the future of Germany."

In a strong and angry voice Edward said, "No, General, I would not call Adolph Hitler a savior. I would label him as the antichrist, the iconoclast of what man had developed as a society."

Von Papen stuck his finger in Edward's face and said, "That's enough, Mr. Amelot. You cannot defame Germany's greatest leader."

"General, you cannot defame a despot," shouted Edward.

The general's face turned a bright red, and he slapped Edward across the face with the back of his hand and said, "Mr. Amelot, you are through here. There will be no more trust. My men will have the same orders for you they had for Castillo. If you try to do anything to escape, they will shoot to kill. From now on, you will restrict yourself to your tent." He turned to face the colonel and said, "Do you understand these orders, Oberst?"

"Absolutely," said Keitel with a smile on his face, "Sergeant, take this man to his tent and post a guard on him. You heard the general's order."

The sergeant lifted his rifle, poked Edward Amelot in the back, and pointed toward Edward's tent. Edward walked away with the sergeant. He did not look back. Wow! Alek thought to himself. What a show.

The general turned to the colonel and said, "Get rid of these bodies and hide all evidence of the explosion. When our guests get here, I don't want them to see any of this. Do as I have said about Edward Amelot, but remember, Oberst," Von Papen said with a glare, "I will decide his future, not you."

"Yes, General," said Keitel.

CHAPTER THIRTY

The guard forced Edward Amelot into his tent. He was furious at the manner in which he was being treated and the way Von Papen dealt with the murders of Castillo and Keichi. He couldn't help thinking that if he had not insisted on going to the temple, then they would still be alive.

As he sat on the cot thinking about the events, he reminded himself about who was really at fault here. Von Papen and Keitel were the men to blame for the murders. It was their mission, which brought about the capture and the murder of Castillo and Keichi.

He thought for a moment about the dangerous situation he was in, how he could no longer be assured of his release or his safety. He decided to look for an opportunity to escape. He would have to find his way out of the camp and into the jungle without running into the camp's deadly defenses. If he could slip away unnoticed during the night, he might have some time to run. He knew he could no longer just sit there and wait for his fate to be decided by Von Papen or, worse, Keitel. He looked out of the tent and saw the guard. He would have to wait for the right moment.

He lay back on his cot and thought about his conversation with Castillo. The revelation about the stone guard in the temple was so similar to the Chinese terra cotta army of the Ch'in dynasty that it just lent more credence to his theory. If he could only find the temple, he was certain he could prove his theory. However, finding the temple without Castillo was not very likely. It was very frustrating for him to be this close after so many years, and, now, what could he do?

Then, of course, he no longer had his artifacts. They were in the possession of his worst enemy. If Keitel knew how much the artifacts meant to Edward, he probably would destroy them. His outburst had probably ensured he would never see them again. He took a deep breath and thought to himself, 'Edward some day you will learn to control your temper.' However, right now he had the small problem of being a prisoner. Somehow, he had to get word to the government about this mercenary army before it moved on their plans and before Von Papen considered getting rid of him, too.

As Edward was pondering his situation, Alek decided to go to the general's tent, and try to hear what the plans were for this armed force and for Edward. It would certainly help if he knew what was going to transpire.

When he got there, the general had stalked back to his tent. He was disturbed at how Edward Amelot had baited him and how he lost control in front of his men. As he reached his tent, his orderly came out. "Lieutenant," he said, "get Oberst Keitel for me right away."

Von Papen sat down and began to think about how they would deal with Dega. He knew Reyes was so anxious he wanted to believe everything they told him, but from what they knew, Dega would not be as easy to delude. The lieutenant came back into the tent and said, "Oberst Keitel is here."

"Send him in," said Von Papen.

"You sent for me, sir?" asked Keitel.

"Yes, I have been thinking about our guest, Mr. Amelot. I have decided I don't want him here when the head of the MYLN arrives. If something happened, and Dega saw him, we would have a difficult time explaining his presence. Have him taken, under guard, to the caves and keep him there until we are through with our meeting."

Keitel smiled and said, "with pleasure, General."

"Keitel, remember what I told you about Amelot, and, also, remember that we have to remain on good terms with the MYLN and Mr. Dega."

Alek heard this and realized something he had not thought about before; Von Papen did not know Edward and Dega were friends.

"Have you stopped the munitions trucks?" asked Von Papen.

"Yes, they are being held at the border until you say otherwise," Keitel replied.

"Are they in a safe area?"

"They can stay where they are as long as you like. General Arriago agreed to take the most of the Guatemalan Army to the southern border of Guatemala in the guise of military maneuvers," Keitel explained.

"Good. Now, I want Amelot taken to the caves. I still intend to release him unharmed, so see to it he is not abused. Is that clear?" asked Von Papen emphatically.

"I understand, General. If you decide not to release him, I will take great pleasure in eliminating this libertarian annoyance personally," Keitel seethed.

"Oberst, you will do nothing to this man until I decide what I will do with him. Mr. Brabant would be most unhappy if his efforts were undermined by a foolish move like killing a prominent American citizen. Our plan is more important than this one man."

"Yes, sir. I will see he's moved at once," said Keitel.

The aide came into the tent holding a message in his hand and said, "I have a message from Mr. Brabant."

Von Papen read the message, and turned to Keitel, and said sternly, "Mr. Brabant is on his way here right now, and his helicopter will be landing at any time. I will go and meet him. You make sure we have a place prepared for him immediately."

"Yes, sir. I will see to both matters," said Keitel.

After hearing this, Alek began to make his way around the perimeter of the camp to get back to Edward's tent. Dega's arrival could be the perfect time to get Edward out of the camp. As he approached the tent, he heard some loud voices. As he got closer, he could hear Edward's voice and see Keitel, a sergeant, and a corporal standing outside of the tent.

"I demand to know where you are taking me," said Edward boldly.

"Mr. Amelot, you are not in a position to demand anything. You are going to another location for now, but you will return soon."

"Are you hiding me, Keitel?" asked Edward.

"I have told you before, Mr. Amelot, you are to ask no questions. Now, you will go with these men peaceably. If you cause trouble, they will not hesitate to use force. Do you understand?" demanded Keitel.

"I understand you are hiding me from someone or hiding something from me. Therefore, it probably is as illegal as having an alien armed force in this country."

"That's enough, Mr. Amelot. You are to leave, now. Sergeant, take this man to the caves and report to the lieutenant at the construction site," Keitel said as he turned and walked away brusquely.

Edward took his backpack and followed the sergeant. Alek watched them as they made their way out of the camp.

After a quick assessment of the situation, he decided this might have been the best thing that could have happened. After all, Keitel said they had not had time to set mines out in the area surrounding the caves.

The men led Edward to the trail and motioned him to proceed. As they walked, they spoke in German. "Why are we bringing this one to the caves?" the corporal asked in German.

"I understand Brabant will be here any time. He is going to meet with the leader of the MYLN, who is due to arrive early tomorrow. They don't want anyone to see this man," the sergeant said as he pointed at Edward.

"Another Indian?" asked the corporal.

"Yes, I heard the Oberst say he's coming from Tapachula," said the sergeant. "His name is Dega."

At hearing Dega's name, Edward stopped dead in his tracks.

"What is wrong with you?" demanded the sergeant in English.

Edward had to think of an excuse quickly, or they might think he recognized Dega's name. "Sorry. I think I have a stone in my boot."

"Alright, remove it quickly," the Sergeant said.

Edward sat on the ground and began unlacing his boot. So, Dega was coming here. He couldn't help but wonder why he would have anything to do with men like this? He couldn't be wrong about Dega, could he?

The men continued in German. "So, all of the big ones are coming here. I guess something will happen now. Is that why we are preparing a camp for so many of the Indians?" asked the corporal.

"Not the Indians, fool, our men. Keitel said all of our men are at the border waiting to move into Chiapas. The MYLN think we are here merely to train their men."

"Won't this Dega realize what is going on when he sees the camp and all the munitions?" asked the corporal.

"He'll never see them. And besides, if he does, Keitel will take care of him like he did the other three Indians," the sergeant said.

"You mean the Indian General from the MYLN?" asked the corporal.

"Yes," said the sergeant, "and his men."

"I thought they were being kept in the caves so they wouldn't see what was going on," said the corporal.

"They were, but they kept complaining about being kept there, so Keitel went to talk to them. The Indian General didn't like being treated as a prisoner, and he demanded to be allowed to use the radio and to move about the camp freely. Keitel tried talking to him, but the Indian told Keitel he knew what was going on, and he would report this to the MYLN. He shoved Keitel to the side and started to walk away. I never saw Keitel so angry. He shot the Indian in the head. The other two Indians started for him and the guards cut them down."

"I know Keitel doesn't like this one," said the corporal pointing at Edward. "He'd probably like to blow his head off, too."

"Yes, I'm sure he would. Keitel is definitely not the type to cross. I just do whatever he says and 'yes sir' him to death," said the sergeant. Then, in English he said, "Alright, let's get going," he said to Edward.

Edward rose and began to make his way down the trail. As they passed the valley floor where the tent platforms were being built, he took in all the activity. He could still see some of the floors and the men scurrying around cutting vegetation and covering the wooden platforms. Surely, he thought, they were hiding the construction from Dega.

When they reached the caves, he was shocked to see the enormous amounts of munitions. They entered the cave, and the sergeant called two men over.

He said, "Mueller, take this man and secure him in the cave. You, Schmidt, and Kraus will stay here. The rest of the men will leave on the trucks. One of you will monitor the radio, one will guard the prisoner, and the other will stand guard outside the cave. See to it you rotate duties because you will have no relief. Take these shackles and secure the prisoner away from the opening. Keep watch over him, but do him no harm."

"Yes, Sergeant," said Mueller.

The sergeant and the corporal walked down the trail toward the camp construction site as Edward was led into the recesses of the caves. The corporal put the manacle on his left wrist and attached the other end to a bar on the side of a forklift. In English he said, "You may as well sit. Here is a canteen of water. I will return in a minute, so don't do anything foolish."

At the same time Alek had made his way to the trail leading to the caves. By the time he made his way to the construction site, the sergeant and the corporal who led Edward Amelot away, were approaching an officer. He could see the men were spreading jungle foliage over the floors which were being constructed for the tents. The officer was yelling at the men to hurry with their work.

"Lieutenant, we were told to report to you," said the sergeant.

"We are just about done here, Sergeant. You take over, and when the men are done, take the remaining trucks up into the mountain pass with the rest. Tell the men to make no fires. I don't want any smoke to be seen. I am going to report to the general as soon as I have one last inspection of the area," said the lieutenant.

"Yes, sir."

Perfect, thought Alek. Most of the men will be gone from the caves and that would be his opportunity to free Edward Amelot. Alek decided to wait in the jungle and decide how he would make his rescue attempt.

CHAPTER THIRTY-ONE

Von Papen and his aide made their way to the landing zone and awaited Brabant's arrival.

He turned to his aide and asked, "Did you talk to the cook about preparing a dinner for Herr Brabant?"

"Yes, sir. As you requested, he's preparing a special vegetarian meal."

"Good. In addition, Herr Brabant does not approve of drinking tea, coffee, or alcohol, so be sure we have mineral water for him. And no one is to drink or smoke in his presence."

"Yes, sir," the aide replied.

Suddenly the aircraft came into view. It was not Brabant's usual business helicopter. It was a RAH-66 Comanche armed reconnaissance helicopter, which would be used in the upcoming insurrection. The helicopter landed, and Brabant came down the stairway.

"Welcome, Herr Brabant."

"General, thank you. I brought you one of the latest weapons to add to your arsenal."

"Thank you for the additional fire power. We will put it to good use in our upcoming campaign," said Von Papen.

"I'm sure you will. I do not like the reports I have received regarding the way you have been dealing with the Indians and taking an American prisoner."

"Yes, sir, it is very distressing to have these complications arise now. If you like, I have arranged quarters and a meal for you. We can talk further about these things there."

"Yes, very good. Let's be on our way," Brabant said.

When they arrived at the tent, Von Papen asked, "Would you like me to send for your dinner, sir?"

"No, I don't like to discuss difficult matters while I'm eating," Brabant replied. "It makes for poor digestion. But something to drink, perhaps, would be suitable."

"Yes, sir, there is some mineral water here for you."

"I hope this is not something bottled by these local cretins," Brabant said.

THE ANCIENT ONES

"No, sir, this is the brand you have imported from the Alps," Von Papen assured him.

"Good. Now tell me about what has happened here. First, tell me about Dega's men."

"The Indians were treated well as you directed. Oberst Keitel talked to them about training and showed them the weapons you would be supplying them. The problem was their leader, General Mixcóatl, was much more sophisticated than the others were. It seems he knew much more about military operations than we thought. He asked too many questions of the men, and they didn't respond to some of them."

"Why wasn't Keitel with the Indians?" Brabant demanded.

"Keitel was busy and thought it would do no harm if the Indians were left with the trainers. He believed the Indians to be ignorant of military matters."

"Then, what happened?" asked Brabant.

"General Mixcóatl saw the amount of munitions. He deduced they were not only for the MYLN training. Keitel came to talk to him, and he told Keitel he believed we were going to do much more than train their men. He said he was going to tell Dega of his suspicions. When he tried to leave, Keitel tried to stop him, and he hit Keitel. Keitel lost his head and shot him. The other Indians went after Keitel, but they were shot down in the attempt by the other men."

"Keitel is a fool. You and I both know we cannot underestimate our enemies or our allies," Brabant said.

"Keitel has been under a great deal of strain getting ready for our campaign," Von Papen explained.

"And what of the American and the others you have in camp?" Brabant asked.

"When Keitel was doing an initial reconnaissance of the area around the camp, he came across a party of three within the safety perimeter of the camp. He felt it was necessary to take them captive before they stumbled onto our camp. There was a Mexican, Castillo, who was supposed to be an importer. Later, we found out from Dega's men that he was a gunrunner. The man with him was an old Indian named Keichi. As far as we know he had no relatives, except a daughter somewhere in the border area of Chiapas and Guatemala."

"And the American?" asked Brabant.

"Edward Amelot is an anthropologist from a museum in Washington,

D.C. He apparently bought some artifacts from Castillo and claimed they were going to some of the outlying Indian villages to talk to the natives about their culture. We think, however, they were going to find a ruin where the artifacts were found."

"And what happened to the Mexican and the Indian? Brabant asked.

"They were held separately from the American. Castillo somehow got a knife, killed one of our men, and tried to escape. He ran into one of our mines, and it killed him. The Indian was then shot by Keitel."

"Keitel again. This is very shoddy work, general. An ignorant hustler outwits your men and causes chaos in your camp. Is this what I can expect from you and your men in the important upcoming campaign?" demanded Brabant.

"I can assure you, Herr Brabant, my men and I will perform above and beyond your high standards. All I can say on behalf of my men is Castillo and the Indian didn't escape, and this kind of incident will not happen again."

"And what of the American? Is he aware of what happened to his traveling companions?" Brabant asked.

"Yes. He was in the camp when the mine exploded. I have had him removed to the caves, and he's under continuous guard."

"He cannot leave this camp to tell his story. Even after we have achieved a victory, we will need public sentiment on our side. If he were to tell what he has seen, we would be condemned by the world, especially by the Americans. We cannot afford to alienate them. Therefore, we must make the deaths of Mr. Amelot and his companions look like the work of the bandits. It is known that they prowl the border and prey on the travelers in this area."

"I will call my men back from the border and see that Amelot is taken care of immediately."

"No, we will wait until after our meeting with Dega," Brabant said. "I don't want anything to interfere with the matters we have to discuss. We don't need any more distractions. For now, I must gain Dega's confidence and bring him into the fold, so to speak. He cannot be bought with anything less than an independent country for his beloved Indians."

"What about his men?" Von Papen asked.

"Your story about sending them to the border to plan with our leaders will suffice for now. Later, we can come up with an unfortunate incident that caused their deaths."

"Yes, sir. Do you know the purpose of Dega's visit?" Von Papen asked.

"All I know is Dega wants to meet face-to-face with me to discuss our plans. Dega is the power, so we must impress him with our organization. I would much rather deal with a radical like Reyes, who I can always incite him with promises of independence, but we cannot always have things the way we want them."

"Yes, he's like an excitable child," Von Papen replied.

"Well, just be careful what you say to Dega because he's not a child or an aboriginal idiot."

"Yes, sir."

"What is the status of our preparations and the men?" Brabant inquired.

"All of the platforms for the tents are completed, and they have been camouflaged so they cannot be seen from the air. There is still the need to build some support buildings, but we didn't want to do this until all of the men arrive. Most of the men who were in the camp have left in the trucks and will remain in the mountain pass until we give them word to return," Von Papen replied.

"How soon can we have our men and equipment in the country and ready for action?"

The general thought for a moment. "It will take another two weeks to finish the camps. The men and equipment are ready now," he said.

Brabant stepped towards Von Papen, placed a hand on his shoulder, and said, "General, I want you to see to the preparations personally. There can be no more mishaps or accidents. This is our golden opportunity. Our chance to begin a new nation as our forbearers envisioned."

"Yes sir. There will be no failures. My code still is as it was in the S.S. 'Thy Honour is Thy Loyalty'. My men will follow."

CHAPTER THIRTY-TWO

In order to get a better look at the caves, Alek went further into the jungle and found a tree in which he could watch and wait for the right opportunity. There was a sentry on duty at the opening of the caves, and he paced back and forth while never getting too close to the jungle. He could see no other men or activity, but he knew there were two more men inside.

While he was waiting, he was trying to come up with a plan to disable the guard at the entrance to the caves. He couldn't get close enough to the guard to surprise him, so he needed a way to take him out. If he had a silencer for the pistol there would be no problem. He finally hit upon a solution, something which he remembered from an assignment in Argentina. The Gauchos used a bolas, to disable an animal or a man from a distance. It was a device made of leather cords and three iron balls or stones. He knew if it were thrown at the victim's legs, he would trip and be immobilize briefly. He decided he could make a bolas using rocks and strips of leather, which he cut from his bag. His plan was to hit the guard in the legs, bring him down, and then quickly jump him. When he finished the bolas, he placed his bag in the undergrowth and waited in the tree.

There had been no traffic in or out of the caves for some time, so now was the time to make his move. He made his way out of the tree to a spot where he could watch the guard undetected. As the guard turned to walk away from him, he stepped out raised the leather thong over his head, and began to twirl it. When the guard heard the whirring of the bolas he turned back and looked at Alek in total surprise. Alek gave a couple of last twirls with the thong to build up speed, and then let go. The bolas hit the guard just below the knees, and he fell to the ground face-first.

Alek ran up to the guard immediately after the bolas hit the guard. He had fallen face-down, and Alek jumped on his back, grabbed his chin with his left hand, and pulled his head back. At the same time with his other hand, he reached around to bring his knife to the guard's throat. It was then he realized that there was no resistance from the guard. In fact, he was not moving or breathing. As he pulled back on the guard's head, he knew the man had broken his neck in the fall.

He quickly pulled the body and the man's weapon into the undergrowth and, then, crept back slowly to the cave entrance. He looked inside to try to locate Edward but was immediately transfixed by what he saw. The ceiling was forty feet high, and from what he could see, it went back for a great distance. There were rows of munitions boxes stacked six feet high. He crept in behind them and moved from row to row to see if Edward or anyone else was there. He finally came to the end of the rows of munitions, and there he could see the openings to three more caverns.

He could hear voices, so he moved along the wall until he came to the first opening. He peered around the corner and saw two men sitting at a table playing cards and talking. One of them had a rifle leaning against the table next to him.

He could hear him say, "Don't worry about it, Deiter. Schmidt is on guard outside, and the American is locked up in the next cave. As long as we have to stay awake, we may as well have a game of cards."

"Alright, let's play." Kraus began to deal, and they both focused on the cards.

Alek waited patiently until they were very engrossed in the game. He then took the opportunity to slip across the opening and get into the next cavern. He looked inside and along the right wall saw stacks of crates marked 'AK47'. Along the opposite wall, there were fewer boxes which were labeled 'Hand Held Rocket Launcher'. Along the back of the wall, he could see a forklift but nothing else. Where was Edward Amelot?

He made his way along the row of AK47 crates and, finally, reached the forklift. He began to walk around the right side when he heard a noise. He turned with his M-16 pointing forward and saw a man whose left hand was manacled to the forklift. In his right hand was a crow bar raised and ready to strike. The man swung down with the crowbar, but Alek easily caught it with the stock of his rifle. He swung the rifle butt upward against the crowbar, which caused the man to lose control of his weapon. It went flying against the boxes and fell to the ground with a loud clanging noise.

He pointed his rifle at the man and ordered, "Hold it," as quietly as he could. He was afraid the men in the other cave might have heard the noise, so he stood there listening for any movement.

The man lowered his arm and said, "Alright, alright, it's over. You can't blame me for trying. You left the damn crowbar right on top of the forklift."

"Please, speak quietly. Are you Edward Amelot?" Alek inquired.

"Who the hell do you think I am? And who the hell are you? Don't you people know what's going on in your own place?" Then Edward saw the man was not wearing combat fatigues. He had on jeans and hiking boots. He now looked puzzled and asked, "Who are you?"

Alek looked into Edward Amelot's eyes and said softly, "Mr. Amelot, I'm not one of the mercenaries. I'm a friend of Cara's. Please... we have to be very quiet."

Edward's eyes popped wide open at the sound of his daughter's name. "What? You are what?"

"My name is Alek Roman, and I'm a friend of Cara's. Right now, we have to get out of here, and then we can talk."

"Cara?" Edward asked.

"Yes, sir. Please, let's get out of here," Alek said as he grabbed Edward by the arm.

"I have a slight problem," Edward said sardonically. "I can't drag this forklift with me, and the guy who has the key just left. I thought you were him coming back."

"I don't think he will be back for awhile," Alek said. "Let me see the lock on the cuffs."

He examined the lock and then twisted the manacle around to look at where it was joined. He reached into his pocket, took out a knife, and then he opened up a small blade which resembled a pick. To Edward's surprise, Alek didn't try to pick the lock; instead, he inserted the pick where the handcuffs joined together, twisted the pick once, and then pulled the handcuffs open.

"Wow," said Edward with an amazed look, "are you a professional something or other?"

Alek smiled and said, "Yeah, something or other. Do you know how many men are in here?"

"There were about twenty or so awhile ago, but suddenly, they all packed up and left. Besides the guy that was left to guard me, I saw two others. They are under command to kill me if I'm not well behaved. You know I have two years left on the warranty on my car, and I'd hate to see it go to waste," Edward said as he laughed quietly and nervously.

Alek smiled at Edward's attempt to lighten the mood and said, "These men are professional killers, and we must be careful. I saw the two men you are speaking of, and they're playing cards in the first cave. The third one was guarding the outside of the cave will not cause us any problem. Let's hope that's all we have to worry about."

"Good. I don't know how you got rid of the guard outside the cave, but I hope you have some more moves left in you in case we meet others." Edward said.

"Now," Alek advised, "we have to get out of here quietly and quickly, so follow me, stay low, and be quiet," Alek advised.

"Quiet, I can be. Low, however, is getting more difficult at my age."

They made their way out of the cavern they were in and came to where the two mercenaries were playing cards. There was a recession in the wall between the first and second cavern, and Alek motioned Edward to stop and move back into it to keep from being seen.

Alek inched his way up to the opening and saw one man had his back to the opening and the other was sitting sideways in his chair. He watched the pair for a few minutes to observe their movements. He noticed the man at the far end of the table, who was sitting sideways, would draw a card and then look up at the top of the cave for a few seconds deciding on his next move. He figured the time he took to look up could be sufficient for him and Edward to cross the opening.

Just as he was about to tell Edward to go, the men finished a hand and the guard said, "Deiter, I really should go and see what that noise was, and I better check on my prisoner. Don't deal until I get back."

Oh shit, thought Alek. There was no time to get back or to explain to Edward what was happening. He would have to take out the guard here, as quietly as possible, and hope the other one didn't hear anything. He turned and saw Edward was right beside him. He quickly pushed Edward back into the recession of the wall and whispered. "Stay back, one of them is coming out!" He then pressed himself into the wall next to Edward. The guard walked to the cavern opening and turned to his right in front of the recession. As he passed, Alek swung his rifle at the back of the man's knees, which made them buckle. The guard fell forward, and before he could do anything else, Edward stepped forward and hit the man on the back of the head with the crowbar. Alek didn't even know he had it with him. The guard was out.

The other guard heard the scuffle and called out in German, "Kraus, are you okay?"

Alek thought for a moment and responded in a muffled German, "Damn rocks! Come here for a moment, Deiter."

He once again pushed Edward back into the recession and then stood pressed against the wall next to the cavern opening. He set his rifle down and took his knife from its sheath. When the guard stepped out from the opening of the cavern, Alek stepped forward and delivered a karate kick to the man's midsection. The guard doubled over and gave a loud grunting sound. He quickly grabbed his hair on the top of his head, pulled back, and thrust his knife upwards, through his ribs and into his heart. There was a muffled grunt and then a gurgling sound as the guard slumped over. Well, so much for getting away unnoticed. He turned to Edward and said, "Let's get the hell out of here. Now!"

CHAPTER THIRTY-THREE

They sprinted for the opening of the cave. Alek quickly checked the area outside of the cave and proceeded into the jungle with Edward close behind. He stopped to get his bag and then continued to move deeper into the jungle. He finally stopped and crouched down with Edward in some jungle growth. They were both breathing hard.

"You were very good in there," said Edward.

"You weren't so bad yourself. I didn't know you brought the crowbar," Alek said.

"I thought I might need it," Edward said as he smiled.

"Thanks, Mr. Amelot. We should be leaving now."

Edward hesitated. "Do you think it is safe to stay here and talk for a moment?"

"Sure, Mr. Amelot, but not for long," Alek warned.

"First, Alek, since you probably saved my life, you should call me Edward. Next, before we go any further, you said you know my daughter. How do you know her, and why are you here?"

Alek smiled. "It seems we have a mutual friend in Senator McGruder. He sent Cara to see me when she couldn't find you on her own."

"So, Alek, is it your work to find missing fathers?"

"No, actually I came here with Cara to find you as a favor to Senator McGruder. He was a very close friend to me and my father," Alek explained.

"McGruder. You know McGruder. He's a most tyrannical, quixotic idealist. But then, he's also a friend without equal," Edward said as he smiled.

"Well, I never heard him described quite that way, but I'm sure you're right."

"You said you came here with Cara. You didn't bring her here, I hope?" Edward asked.

"No, she's in Tapachula at the same hotel where you were staying. I'm sure she's waiting for us, but not too patiently," Alek said.

Edward chuckled. "I see you know something about my daughter. She could never be accused of being patient."

"I'd like to keep this conversation up," Alek said as he looked around nervously, "but it will soon be light, and they'll discover you are gone. We have to get going."

"Alek, I can't leave," Edward said.

His eyes flew open wide. "What? Are you crazy! In a short time this whole camp will be swarming with men looking for you. They won't try to capture you. They'll just kill you. Those are their orders, remember."

"I know, but a Dega is coming here, and I have to warn him that Brabant is planning to deceive him and maybe kill him. These men were supposed to be here to help the Indians, but that was just a ruse so they could get into the country. Colonel Keitel has already killed the three men the MYLN sent here because they discovered this plot. From what I understood, one was the General of the Indian forces. Dega is a very important man to the Indians in Chiapas and has been a good friend to me. I cannot leave him to this fate."

Alek sighed. "I know who he is. Cara and I went to see him before we came here, and I also know he's the head of the MYLN."

"Yes," Edward said. "I didn't know that before; although, I suspected he had something to do with the Indian sedition. I know there is danger in staying, but I cannot run from a friend who needs my help."

"So you want to stay and help him when we are right in the middle of, shall we say, the lion's den," said Alek.

Edward stiffened with resolve. "Yes, I have to. He's a good friend."

"You certainly are your daughter's father. She also gets fixated on a problem," Alek said.

"Alek, I'm grateful for your help," Edward said with sincerity, "but you should get away now before anything happens. Besides, I need you to look out for Cara. I don't want her in harm's way if there is a rebellion in Chiapas."

"Mr. Amelot, I don't want to see Cara in danger either, but I'm sure she's all right for now," Alek replied. "It would just be better if you come with me now. Then, the three of us can leave Chiapas."

"I know you are right, but I cannot leave a friend in danger. I'm not sure Dega knows what kind of people he's dealing with, and I am certain he doesn't know what he's getting into. I have to warn him. I don't know what words could tell you how grateful I am to you for freeing me, and now I have to ask you to help me again. Please, go and take care of Cara."

"Mr. Amelot, there are three very good reasons I cannot leave you here. The first is Senator McGruder asked me to help you, and I cannot let him down. Then, there is this group of mercenaries that resemble the second coming of the Third Reich. The final reason is I promised your daughter to bring you back, and I could not face her, unless you were with me. So, let's just say I'm staying in the game." Hmm, Alek thought to himself, it seems like I have heard that before.

"Alright, Alek, I won't argue with your staying because I know I could use your help. We have to get to Dega somehow," said Edward.

"I heard them say he's coming by helicopter first thing this morning. The LZ, eh, the landing zone for the helicopter, is on the other side of the camp. I don't know how many men will be there when he arrives, but they will have to take the trail back to the camp. If we could overpower them quickly and quietly it might be possible to get to him, but it will have to be before they get into the camp."

"I heard most of the men left with the munitions trucks. Von Papen sent them away so Dega wouldn't see how many men he brought into the country. He, also, has hidden the camp he is building for the army that's coming from Guatemala. And I know what an LZ is. I was in Vietnam."

Alek smiled. "That's true about the men and the trucks. There are about a dozen men left," he said.

"That's not very good odds for our side," Edward replied.

"It may not be so bad. When they discover you are missing, they will take some of the men to search for you. That drops the odds. I just wish there was a way to get them to search the jungle where their mines are located. I reset them to get anyone coming out of the camp."

"Well, how could we do that?" asked Edward.

"If I had taken something from one of the guards, I could have planted it on the trail back to the camp. Damn, I should have taken their rifles."

Edward was holding a pistol in his hand and said, "Would this do? I took it from the first guard while you were doing in the second one."

Alek grinned. "Mr. Amelot, you are really something. Yes, that'll be great. Let me have it, and I'll go and leave it on the trail. I'll be right back."

He went off into the jungle and left Edward sitting by a tree. Edward took the canteen Alek had attached to his rucksack, took a long drink, and thought it is good to be free of those people. Alek was probably right when he said they should leave, but he could not desert Dega. Edward leaned back against the tree and closed his eyes. Thoughts of Cara came to him. He hoped she was all right and would understand what he was doing. This man, Alek, seemed to care for his daughter a great deal.

Suddenly, Edward heard someone coming through the brush. He jumped up quickly, looked around for a weapon, and saw there was a rocket launcher lying on the ground next to the rucksack. He couldn't fire it at someone, but he certainly could use it as a club. He crouched behind the tree and waited. Alek came into the clearing holding his rifle at ready and looked for Edward.

Edward said, "Don't shoot! It's me coming out from behind the tree."

Edward walked out holding the rocket launcher, and Alek lowered his rifle with a grin. "You seem to find a weapon anywhere you are. However, it would have been very difficult to shoot me with a rocket launcher," he said.

"Oh, I'm familiar with rocket launchers. I wasn't going to shoot you with it. I was just going to club you to death," Edward said with a smile.

"I put the pistol on the trail where it will be found if a search takes place. I made it look like you went into the jungle there. When they follow the trail I left, we should hear some fireworks," Alek said.

"It's will be getting light soon. Can we get to the LZ while it's still dark?" asked Edward.

"Yes. Follow me very closely. It will take us about thirty minutes to get there, and that should give us some time to think about how we are going to go about rescuing Dega," said Alek.

"It seems like we Amelots keep asking you to rescue people. You know, I wouldn't ask for your help, unless I thought it was extremely important," Edward said.

"I know," Alek said. "It's just I would like to see this 'mission' end with both of us getting out of here, and I know there are a lot of people out here who would rather put an end to us instead."

They made their way through the jungle. Edward tried to emulate Alek's movement as he carefully walked through the undergrowth. There was absolutely no air circulation, so the humidity was stifling. They stopped twice for a drink and a rest, for which Edward was thankful.

Alek was impressed with the way Edward kept up with him. He knew he was not a professional, but if there was no other choice, he was relatively sure he could count on him.

When they reached the LZ, he looked for a tree he could use for observation. There was a tall tree a few meters away, which appeared easy to climb, so he told Edward to get under cover and rest up. He went to the tree and checked it for booby traps. As he climbed the tree, he thought he heard voices and, then, saw a light. When he got to a level at which he could see clearly, a sergeant holding a light while two of the mercenaries cut back some brush in the LZ.

He climbed down the tree and went back to the place where Edward was hiding. He approached cautiously since he now knew Edward had probably found some kind of a weapon to use against him.

Edward saw him coming and asked, "Did you see anything?"

"Yes, there are two men clearing the LZ. It is now 5:00, and it won't be full daylight until 6:00. Let's assume the helicopter that's picking up Dega will leave at dawn and take an hour to get to Tapachula. Then, it will take them at least another hour to get here. That means Dega will probably be here between 8:00 and 9:00. We should take advantage of this gap and get a couple of hours sleep. I'll set my watch to wake us in two hours."

"I hope your alarm isn't too loud," Edward said smiling, as Alek was setting his watch.

"No alarm, just a vibration," Alek explained.

"Okay, let's get some sleep. We'll talk about our plan when we get up," Edward said.

"Oh, do you have a plan?" Alek said questioningly.

"No, but I get some of my best ideas when I sleep," said Edward with a smile on his face.

They both leaned back against the tree and closed their eyes, each deep into their own thoughts about the same person, Cara.

CHAPTER THIRTY-FOUR

At the same time in Tapachula, Cara could not sleep. She tossed and turned, thinking about her father and Alek. What could she do? She had read and reread her father's journals, and they didn't seem to provide her with any more information about where he might have gone with Castillo.

In the journal, her father said he was warned about the kind of man Castillo was, and he knew Castillo couldn't be trusted, but he had to take this chance to prove his theory. She went through all of his other papers, and there was nothing to give her a lead as to where they might have gone.

Dega had called her everyday and invited her to dinner or to stay with him. She thanked him but told him she didn't want to be away, even for a minute, in case Alek called. He said he had given Edward's name and description to everyone that he could think of that might have encountered him, but so far, there was no response. He always asked if she was all right and if she needed anything. He seemed like a good man who truly cared about her father. She understood why her father had become such good friends with him in such a short period of time.

As she waited and waited, she kept going over things, and Alek kept coming to her mind. She thought about how funny he was when they met on the beach. He had reminded her of a teenage boy trying to meet a girl for the first time. He had been clumsy, but charming in his own way. Now, he was giving the direction in how to find her father, and she didn't mind. This was not like her. She was a strong- minded person and always led the way in her business and personal life.

She hadn't been with Alek long enough to learn too much about him. She did know Senator McGruder had total confidence in him. In the short time they had been together, she had been captivated by him. Now, all she could do is pray that they both would come back safely to her. She could not think about any other eventuality.

It was now three a.m., and she still couldn't sleep. She felt so helpless. Whenever she had problems to face, she would form a plan of action. Yes, that's it. She would begin by going to see Dega in the morning to see if he had heard anything. If not, then she had to find a way to get her own information. She was always very persuasive and resourceful when she had to be. She had to do maintain control of the situation. It was not like her to flounder. Well, in the morning she would begin her new direction, as soon as she figured out what it would be.

CHAPTER THIRTY-FIVE

It was the end of the day, and Antonio Dega sat in his favorite chair on the patio of his home and reviewed in his mind the problems he would soon be dealing with. He tried to remain focused, but his mind wandering to thoughts of his wife, Inés. He could always discuss his problems with her. Sometimes she didn't understand his problems, but she always listened and tried to get him to think his was out. He always felt better after their discussions. Their time together was the happiest of his life, but it was much too short.

He had met her when he was a student at the university. She was just seventeen when he first saw her in her father's bookstore. She was the most beautiful thing he had ever seen. He always thought of her as a work of art he could look at but never touch. However, fate had been kind to him, and they fell in love and got married.

After being married for a number of years, Inés became pregnant. They were both so happy and began to plan their new future. When the time came, however, there were complications with the birth, and in an instant, Inés and the baby were gone. Antonio was in total anguish, and in looking for a substitute for his passions, he took up the cause of the Mayas.

Now, he had to face one of the most difficult problems in his life without the sympathetic ear of Inés. He would soon be meeting with William Brabant, one of the richest men in the world. He could find very little information about Brabant through the normal sources. He did, however, receive a most disturbing report from the United States State Department, through his friend the Counsel General of Mexico. The report was classified, but the Counsel General provided excerpts as follows:

> Dear Antonio,
> The following information in this report is for you only. Please do not share it with anyone else. I hope to see you again soon.
> Your Friend.

Dega read the account of William Brabant's life, from the spy network he arranged in World War II, to the coup attempts he financed in Central America, including his attempted takeover of the Panamanian government.

Therefore, he was much more than a businessman with a large security force, and Dega was sure he was seeking more than a favorable climate for doing business.

Dega had discussions with the council of the MYLN about the pending plans with Brabant. The council decided to leave the final critical analysis and decision to him and Monzial, who was the elder statesman of the MYLN and his mentor.

They talked about Brabant and the views of the council. They knew they would be taking a great risk in working with someone like Brabant. On the other hand, it would be most difficult to achieve their goals without his help. When their discussions ended, Monzial said he would support whatever decision Dega made.

Dega agreed to let a training cadre of Brabant's men into Chiapas. He sent General Mixcóatl, the military commander of the MYLN, to meet with Brabant's men under the guise of planning for the upcoming coup. The general's real mission was to find out as much as he could about the mercenary army and what they were up to.

Dega began receiving secret radio transmissions from General Mixcóatl about the forces and supplies moved into Chiapas by the mercenaries. Mixcóatl said he now suspected treachery, based on the amount of munitions they were moving in and the preparations they were making for more of their men. He said that he felt Brabant's forces would not remain in Guatemala to protect the flank of the Indian army as planned. They would move their entire force into Chiapas as soon as the insurrection began. This could only be in preparation for a move to take over the government.

Dega was horrified that he had allowed someone like Brabant and his army into Chiapas under the guise of assistance. Reyes was the catalyst in this joint venture, but Dega couldn't blame him for the dilemma. His intentions were always good, if not his judgment. So now, it appeared the cure they had selected for the plight of the Indians of Chiapas was worse than the affliction.

With the knowledge of the deception, Dega developed a plan to deal with Brabant and his army. He had made the necessary contacts and had written a letter to Monzial detailing his plan.

In a similar letter, he told his friend Camilo Reyes of the information he had received about Brabant from the government and from General Mixcóatl.

He also told him of his plan to deal with Brabant. His plan would be bold, but the situation called for definitive action. He would give the letter to Reyes when he told him he was going alone to see Brabant. As he prepared to leave, he gave instructions to his housekeeper to take the other letter to Senore Monzial. He also told her if he didn't return, there was a letter in his desk that would direct the proceeds of his estate.

The housekeeper looked at Dega and said, "The Senora asked me before she passed away," she looked down and made the sign-of-the-cross, "she asked me to look after you but to stay out of your way. I have tried to do this. Now, I must say, I couldn't live here and keep your house without knowing what you are doing. Let someone else go to do this thing you are going to do. Your Inés was my friend, and I say this for her sake."

Dega looked at Ixtanalia warmly and said, "You have made my life without Inés more bearable. I was deeply depressed when she died, and I probably would have fallen into utter despair without you pushing me out the door every day. You were a good friend to Inés and a good friend to me." And as he touched her face he smiled, he said, "Now, do this one last thing for me, for I must go."

When he arrived at the airport, Reyes was waiting for him.

"Antonio, the pilot of Brabant's helicopter has been waiting for us. He says he must leave immediately to avoid being observed. Are you ready to go?" asked Reyes.

Dega put his hand on Reyes' shoulder and said, "Yes, old friend, I'm ready to go, but you must stay here."

Reyes was shocked. He looked at Dega and said, "What are you saying?"

"You must stay here to carry out the course of action we have developed to deal with Brabant," Dega said.

Reyes was flustered. "What are you talking about? What plan? We are both supposed to meet with him to review the plans for the coming campaign. Our men will be ready soon."

"I know, my friend. Just trust me. Take this letter. It will explain everything. I will leave now, but first, I will tell you that you have been as a brother to me. We have done our best to help our people. Someday, maybe soon, you will be their protector. Now, go and read my letter. Our course of action will work if you believe in it and do as I have ordered. All the others involved have been informed."

"Antonio, what are you saying? We must talk," pleaded Reyes.

The pilot of the helicopter leaned out the window and said, "Senores, we have to leave now." Dega got onto the helicopter and turned to wave goodbye to Reyes, who stood there holding the envelope with a puzzled look on his face.

As he boarded the helicopter, he turned to the pilot and said, "I'm Senore Dega. We may leave now."

The pilot replied, "I'm supposed to bring you and Senore Reyes."

He turned to look at Reyes. "He will not be coming. We should leave now, or as you have said, we will be detected."

The pilot shrugged his shoulders and began his ascent. When he was clear of the city, he radioed ahead to let Brabant know he was only bringing Dega with him. As the helicopter made its way to Brabant's camp, Dega looked out at the beauty of his country. The mountains looked as if they were cutting into the sky. The jungle was emerald green with rivers like ribbons of blue, and it was all being enhanced by the golden sunrise.

It took about one hour for the helicopter to arrive at the landing zone. As soon as they landed, a man in a uniform walked up to the helicopter.

"Good morning, Mr. Dega. I am Colonel Keitel. I will take you to Mr. Brabant. He had a call about one of his business interests, and he sends his apologies for not being here to meet you. If you will please follow me."

Dega didn't know who this man was, but he could sense his condescension and hostility. As they walked away from the helicopter, Keitel took a path through the jungle to the camp. As they walked, he began to comprehend fully where he was and how truly alone he was. He had to deal with a leader who, by the reports, could be as sanguinary as the mercenaries he hired. He realized just how precarious his situation was, and he knew the next few hours would be the most difficult of his life.

As they approached a clearing, Keitel waited for him to come alongside and said, "We are sorry Mr. Reyes couldn't accompany you."

Dega deliberated about what he should say. Then, he looked at Keitel and said, "He also expresses his regrets. Last minute affairs in Tapachula required his immediate attention."

"Oh, I'm sorry other matters have detracted your attention. We have approached this operation with absolute dedication. We naturally assumed you would too," said Colonel Keitel haughtily.

Dega glared at him and said, "Colonel, thank you for your concern, but we can make our own judgments regarding what matters are vital for our cause."

Keitel did not expect such a curt reply and thought it best to change his tone, "Certainly, sir."

They walked out of the jungle into the camp. As they reached a large tent, a man walked out and said with a businessman's smile, "Senore Dega, welcome. I am William Brabant, and I apologize for not being at the helicopter to greet you." He held his hand out, and Dega took it in a firm grip. "I was sorry to hear Senore Reyes couldn't meet with us today."

Dega held his ground. "Thank you for meeting with me, Senore Brabant. Yes, your colonel has already reminded me of how important this meeting is to our cause. I, too, am sorry Camilo couldn't be here."

Brabant cast a look at Colonel Keitel with a sidelong expression. He knew Keitel was anything but diplomatic, and his racism came through to others all too often. Brabant thought it best to dismiss him before he did any more damage. "Thank you, Colonel, that will be all," he said. Keitel looked sheepishly at Brabant and withdrew quietly. "Please, have a seat and let me get you some refreshment," Brabant offered.

"Thank you. Nothing for now," Dega replied.

"I'm pleased to meet the leader and decision maker of the MYLN. Camilo has told me about you and your dedication to the cause."

"Thank you, but we have a council that leads our cause and makes the decisions on our course of action," Dega said.

Brabant could clearly see his tactic. If he needed time to consider any offer, it would be best to say he would have to consult with a council of elders before deciding; however, Brabant knew Dega was the real power of the MYLN. "Certainly. I hope you have consulted with them on our alliance," Brabant said.

"Yes, we have talked about the offers you have made to us through Camilo. Now, I would like to discuss our relationship in more detail before moving ahead," Dega suggested.

Brabant hedged a response, "I'm not sure what you mean."

Dega made a point of looking directly into Brabant's eyes and said, "Let me be blunt, Mr. Brabant. I know you and Camilo have established a good business relationship, and according to him, it has been very lucrative. You have definitely won his trust. I have heard from Camilo that you could bring a great deal of sophisticated weaponry to our army. But I'm curious, Mr. Brabant, as to why you want to take such risks to help a group of Indians."

"I thought my reasoning was clear to Camilo, but I would be glad to define it for you as well. I have sympathy for your cause because it is very similar to our struggles to gain independence for our own country, Hesse, from the German government. Both of our peoples have struggled under autocratic rule, even if it is under the guise of democracy.

However, I will confess I have my own selfish interests, also. I would like to relocate my business headquarters to Chiapas because it would provide me with a sympathetic government. I'm not asking for corruption or unethical advantages. I only seek a sympathetic ear for my business causes. Simply put, today's governments hinder their own national businesses with archaic laws. In today's fast-paced world of enterprise, entrepreneurs must have the ability to create new revenue without concern that some low-level bureaucrat will put unnecessary regulations on them."

Dega smiled. "That's very well stated. How could anyone argue with your reasoning? I think it would be advantageous for us to move forward, then, and develop a plan that I can bring to our council."

"Senore, we had developed a plan with Camilo for Chiapas to become a sovereign nation with political liberty. We devised the political and military tactics that would bring this about. It was my hope that today we could come to an agreement on these decisions as well. Then, we could begin to move on our objectives. Is that possible?" Brabant asked.

Dega thought for a moment. Then, he looked at Brabant and said, "I will be most happy to discuss your plan with you, but then I must review these plans with our council. Then, we can move forward. I thought, as a first step, we should talk about training our men."

Brabant sensed that he couldn't push Dega like he could Reyes. He knew he would have to take a different course of persuasion with Dega. "Yes, you are right. We will take things in order," he said.

"When can our troops begin the training?"

"We have built the camp for quartering groups of your men as they are trained. In addition, we have stored the munitions needed for their training, close by."

"Have your men reviewed their training plan with General Mixcóatl and his aides?" Dega asked.

"Yes, this has been done," said Brabant.

"I would like to discuss the training plans and the battle plans with General Mixcóatl and his aides. Will you please send for the general and his advisors?"

Brabant shifted uneasily in his seat. "I believe they went with some of my men to review a defense plan for the border with Guatemala. We had an agreement with Senore Reyes that this would be a proper role for my men. General Mixcóatl also agreed," he said.

"When will they return?" Dega countered.

"Oh, it will not be until tomorrow," Brabant hedged, "but I will ask General Von Papen to try to contact them by radio and ask them to hurry back. It may be difficult since radio transmissions in the jungle and the mountains are difficult. We can prepare a place for you to stay tonight if you like. As a matter of fact, the wait would allow us more time to discuss our plans."

"That would be very good," Dega replied.

Brabant walked over to the table and picked up a large binder. He set it in the middle of the table and said, "In the meantime, this is the plan for training your troops and subsequent action against the government in Chiapas. General Mixcóatl has reviewed it and given his approval."

"Then, I would also like to review it. When General Mixcóatl returns, we may all discuss these plans together," Dega said with a smile.

Brabant grew uneasy. "Of course. As I said, I will try to contact General Mixcóatl while you review these plans. Please, help yourself to some refreshments in the meantime. I will leave a man outside in case you want anything. Just have him call me when you are through, and I will return with General Von Papen to answer any tactical questions you may have."

"Fine, I will let you know when I'm done. Please notify me if General Mixcóatl returns," Dega answered.

Brabant was relieved to go. "Very good," he said. "Let's say I will return in two hours, and we can have lunch."

Dega watched Brabant leave. He knew immediately Brabant was lying because Mixcóatl would never agree to let anyone guard the rear of his army. During the last revolt, the army had agreed to let a group of dissident mestizos protect one of its flanks, and this was the weak point the Mexican army exploited. Dega walked over to the opening in the tent and saw the armed guard standing there. He was sure the guard was there to watch him and not to act as a messenger. In his resignation, Dega sat at the table and began to read the plans which Brabant had left with him. He would simply have to stall until he could meet with Mixcóatl.

CHAPTER THIRTY-SIX

Edward slept fitfully for about an hour and then opened his eyes and saw Alek disassembling his M-16 and wiping the parts with a cloth.

Alek looked up as Edward stirred and said, "We still have time, Mr. Amelot, if you want to sleep."

"I really haven't been able to sleep," Edward said. "I have been thinking about Cara. She should never have come here to look for me. How is she? I am really worried about her."

"She is safe in your hotel. Senore Mandares took a liking to her, so he will watch out for her. However, I did have a difficult time convincing her not to come with me. She's very strong-minded," Alek said again.

Edward smiled, "Yes, when that girl became a teenager, she discovered she had a mind of her own. From that point on, she was never led by anyone, not even her father," he said.

"Well, I was not sure the information I had would lead me to you, so I convinced her she would be doing more to help if she went through your journals and papers to see if there were any leads to follow."

"Very smart," Edward said. "Give her something useful to do and keep her out of trouble. Hmm, maybe I can learn something from you."

"Thank you, Mr. Amelot, but I just did what seemed expedient at the time."

Edward paused and said, "Please call me Edward. Just what do you do, Alek?"

Alek smiled, "I'm in between careers. I worked for the government and spent a great deal of my time in Central America. The profession I was in was getting to me, so I decided it was time to quit. I was in the process of choosing a new profession when Cara brought the request to help find you from Senator McGruder."

"Was your 'work for the government' as nefarious as it sounds?" Edward asked.

Alek paused. "Well, I guess it does no harm to tell you. I was a government operative. I usually worked alone and, well, let's just say if I could talk about my job, most nice people would not want to hear about it."

"Well, do they let you just quit that kind of job?" Edward asked.

"No, not really," Alek said sheepishly. "With Senator McGruder's help, I was able to be put on what they called an inactive status."

"Well, I'm sorry if we had to reactivate you," Edward said with a smile. "I would like to inactivate you again, if that's the right term, as soon as possible."

"Whatever way you want to say it is fine with me, as long as we both get out of here as soon as possible. I'm surprised the mercenaries haven't discovered you missing or the guards dead. Apparently, they intended to leave you out of sight until this meeting is over," Alek said.

"I didn't ask, but how did you find me?" Edward asked. "I didn't tell anyone where we were going. Hell, I didn't even know where we were going."

"I talked to Castillo's man and got some information from him that led me to a general direction of where you might be going. From there, I guess I was just lucky," said Alek with a smile.

"From what I have seen of you, you seem to have each situation under control. I'm sure your efforts had much more to do with finding me than luck did. Do you have any ideas of how we might get to Dega without the whole camp coming down on us?" Edward asked.

"I have been thinking about that since you decided to stay, and I have not come up with anything conclusive yet. About all we can do is wait for the right chance," Alek replied.

"When we do get him," Edward said optimistically, "do you have any ideas of how to get out of here?" he asked.

"From here, only on foot. But I have a jeep hidden in the same place where you and Castillo hid yours," he said with a smile. "If we can get to the jeep we can make our way back to Tapachula. I have a chartered plane there."

"So you found our jeep," Edward said smiling. "It almost daylight, should we go to the LZ?"

"Well, as I said, I have been thinking about what we might do, and my conclusion is that the LZ may not be the right place to try to get to him. We would probably get into a firefight with those coming to meet him, and I'm not sure how we can protect him as well as ourselves. Then, the gunfire would bring the remainder of the mercenary force down on us. Those are not good odds. I think we should go to the camp and wait for a chance to try to get to him without being detected."

"You're sure we don't have a better chance to get to him at the LZ?" Edward asked.

"If we can contact Dega without risking exposure, it would be better for all of us. As I said, I would prefer not to get into an armed conflict with these men. They are professional soldiers," Alek said.

Edward thought for a moment and said, "That makes sense. There's a command tent where they probably will meet. I noticed it is very close to the jungle growth, actually closer than any of the others. It must have been put up as an afterthought when they cleared the brush for the camp."

"Good observation, Mr. Amelot," Alek said. "I have seen it, and I know we can get close enough to the tent to hear what is going on. I did it earlier. So let's get going, and, please, be careful where you step."

"I will, and, please, call me Edward, Alek."

They made their way carefully through the jungle until they came to the camp and the command tent. As they settled into their position, they heard a helicopter approaching.

"That's probably Dega," Alek said.

As they sat in the brush waiting, Edward thought about how Dega had helped him when they barely knew each other and how he instinctively trusted Dega with information that he was reluctant to share with anyone. They had both made quick judgments about the other, and in his case, Dega had turned out to be a good friend. Now, Dega was in real trouble. He couldn't help but smile at the irony of his thought. Dega wasn't the only one in real trouble. Here they were in the middle of a Mexican jungle, with an army of mercenary soldiers near by, and with an officer who would like nothing better than to give him a lobotomy with an M-16. Edward smiled and looked at Alek.

"Well, Mr. Amelot, I always liked people who could smile at adversity," Alek said.

"So, you think I'm smiling at adversity. It could be I'm a lunatic," said Edward grinning.

They waited for what seemed like an eternity to Edward. When he saw Dega walking up to the tent with Colonel Keitel, he involuntarily let out a small gasping sound.

Alek whispered to him that he was going to get closer in order to hear what was going on. Edward saw him approach a tree that overhung the tent. As Alek began to climb, it seemed he was feeling his way up the tree. Strange, thought Edward. A few minutes passed and another man in plain khaki clothing walked into the tent. Keitel left then, and Edward could only hear a rumble of voices. After a short time, the civilian left, and moments later, Alek came down from the tree and returned to where he was waiting.

"Mr. Amelot, I'm afraid your friend may be in a great deal of trouble. The man who went in there was William Brabant. He's an extremely wealthy and ruthless man who will stop at nothing to get what he wants."

"Oh yes, I heard some of his men talk about him. It seems he has been going around financing insurrections all over Central America. Now, he wants Chiapas," Edward said.

Alek shook his head. "I wish that were all. From what I understand, your friend is here to discuss an insurrection, which will be aided by Brabant's mercenaries. The goal is to take Chiapas from Mexico.

Brabant wanted to get approval for the plans they have made with the MYLN. Dega told Brabant he wanted to talk to his men first. What he doesn't know is they are dead. Brabant told him his men were out of the camp, and he would send for them. I don't know what he's up to now, but I do know it will not be anything good for your friend. Brabant left Dega with some military plans to review and said he would be back in two hours."

"Is there a way for me to get into the tent unobserved?" Edward asked.

"That's pretty dangerous, Mr. Amelot," he replied.

Edward sighed. "Perhaps, but it's the best way to get to Dega and warn him."

"Are you sure you want to take this risk? I could go in there and talk to him," Alek suggested.

"No, I'm not sure he would trust what you have to say," Edward replied.

"Okay," Alek said. "What are you going to do when you get in there?"

"I intend to tell him what has happened and get him to leave with me. Then, I assume, the three of us will get the hell out of here," he said.

"Your meeting will have to be fast," Alek said.

"One last thing," Edward said. "I want you to make me a solemn promise."

"A what?" Alek asked.

Edward looked at him intently. "You said you could never go back on your word to McGruder. Can you make me that same promise?"

"Sure, I guess, depending on what it is," Alek said uneasily.

"You have to promise that if anything happens to me, you will leave and get Cara out of harm's way. Take her back to the States or anywhere else, but get her out of here."

"Mr. Amelot, I couldn't leave you here," said Alek.

He put his hand on Alek's shoulder and said, "If doing something to help me would prevent you from getting Cara to safety, you have to leave me and go to her," Edward said emphatically. "I'm not doing this because I'm noble or brave. Right now, I'm scared to death. However, the most important things in my life were my wife and my daughter, and, now, there is just Cara. Whatever happens, I want her to be safe. Please, promise me that."

"Alright, Mr. Amelot," Alek agreed with a sigh.

Edward smiled. "Good. Now, how do I get into the tent?" he asked.

"The guard is stationed in front of the tent. His only duty is to know when Dega leaves the tent. There are some AP mines set up in the rear of the tent, and I will show you where they are. You'll have to loosen one of the tent pegs, so you can slip under the tent. I don't think there is anyone else with Dega, but I'm not sure. Take my pistol with you just in case."

Edward paused and smiled. "By the way, I'm curious. I noticed both times you climbed a tree, you looked like you were feeling your way up the bark. What were you doing?" he asked.

Alek shrugged. "Well, I was checking for booby traps. I found the first one on the trail into the camp," he said nonchalantly.

"You really are a professional, aren't you?" Edward said with admiration.

"I hope so, for both of our benefits," Alek replied.

Edward braced himself and said, "Let's get going, Alek."

"One last thing. When you come out with Dega, we are going to have to move fast, so both of you be ready," Alek warned.

They slowly made their way to the edge of the jungle.

Alek whispered to Edward, "Stay low and crawl under the tent in the middle. I'm going to the left to watch the guard. Don't stay in there too long." Edward waited for Alek's signal and crawled to the back of the tent. Then, he pushed on the tent peg that was holding the middle section of the tent with his boot. He listened for a minute to see if he heard any voices, but there were none. He lifted the tent and crawled under. As he cleared the tent wall, he could see Dega sitting at a table reading. He hissed at Dega, who finally turned to see what this noise was.

Dega's eyes opened wide in surprise, and Edward put his finger up to his lips as he crawled the rest of the way into the tent. Dega jumped up and went quickly to lift the tent flap.

Edward's heart paused, and his breath stopped as he thought Dega was going to call the guard. He reached for the pistol in the back of his belt and aimed it at the opening to the tent. Just as quickly, Dega pulled the tent flap closed and turned to him. Dega started to walk over to him and then stopped in mid stride, as he saw the gun in Edward's hand. He quickly lowered the hammer and put the gun back in his belt.

Dega continued over to Edward and grasped his hand in both of his. "Edward, what are you doing here?" he whispered. "Do you know the danger you are in?"

"Yes, I came to warn you, Antonio," Edward said.

"Warn me of what?" asked Dega.

"Please, let me explain. I left Tapachula with Castillo to look for the temple where the artifacts came from," Edward replied.

"Yes, I know. I got your letter. That was a very dangerous thing to do."

Edward smiled. "Yes, you were very right. Since we left, things have been in an upheaval. After driving for a day, we left the jeep and began walking. We made camp and, in the middle of the night, Colonel Keitel and some of his men took us prisoners. They brought us here, and we have been here ever since," he said.

"And now they have let you all go?" Dega asked.

"No, not at all. They killed Castillo and an old man who was with us. They were holding me in a cave. The man you met who was with my daughter, Alek Roman, came and freed me," Edward said.

"Yes, they came to my home looking for you some time ago, but I didn't think it would have anything to do with these people. Is your daughter alright?" Dega asked.

"Cara is not here. Just Alek. She's in Tapachula."

"Well, that's good, Edward," Antonio said with a sigh of relief.

"As I said, I was being held in a group of caves where Brabant's men have a large store of munitions. I'm not a military expert, but I can see there are enough munitions in these caves to supply a sizeable army," Edward said.

"Are you sure about the amount of munitions that were there?" he asked firmly.

Edward stared intently at his friend. "Yes. I heard the men in the caves remarking the munitions were to supply Brabant's whole army. Alek had to kill the guards at the caves. I am surprised they have not been discovered yet. When they are discovered, Brabant's men will begin searching for us."

"This is a terrible thing for you to go through, Edward," Antonio said with indignation. "I will insist Mr. Brabant escort you out of here immediately."

"No, you cannot do that," Edward begged. "When I overheard them say you were coming here, I had to warn you. These people don't intend to help you, Antonio. They are only using you."

"I know, amigo," Dega said with a smile.

"You know this," Edward exclaimed, "and you still met with them."

"I have come to warn my men and to get them out of here," Dega said.

"General Mixcóatl?" Edward asked.

"Si. You have seen him?" Dega asked.

Edward lowered his eyes and said in a soft voice, "No, but apparently General Mixcóatl could see through Brabant's plan. I'm sorry to tell you this, Antonio, but Colonel Keitel killed him and the men you sent here." Edward then turned his eyes to Dega with a look of detestation. "Keitel is a cold-blooded butcher who kills without compunction. He's the incarnation of evil."

Dega stood there staring at Edward. His eyes were vacant, but his voice held raw emotion. "They killed Mixcóatl! No, it cannot be. He's one of my oldest and dearest friends. What will I tell his family?" He said sadly.

"Antonio, I'm very sorry," Edward said with compassion. "But we have to get out of here right now. I don't know where Brabant went, but he could be back at any minute."

"Don't worry, Edward, he will not return for a while," said Dega.

Antonio Dega stood there, his eyes fixated on a point somewhere straight ahead of him. He was seeing his old friend with his wife and children, and, suddenly, tears began to fall down his face.

"I knew they were evil. I knew this was wrong. I should have removed our men from here sooner, but I was afraid we would give away our plan. I came here to warn them." As he continued to speak, his voice got more deliberate and was growing with anger. "I was too late to save my friend and his men, but others will not suffer for these evil ones. No more! No one!" he said with a cold look in his eyes.

Edward looked at Dega with compassion and said, "Antonio, I'm sorry for the loss of your men, but we can see that Brabant and his men are punished after we leave. They will not let you leave here alive. We have to go, now, before they return."

Dega looked up at Edward with a sudden recognition of the events at hand and said, "Yes, you are right. You have to leave this place as quickly as possible."

Edward's eyes flew open, "What? Not just me. I waited to tell you of this so you would come with us. Antonio, let's leave this place and report what is going on to the authorities," he said.

Dega turned and looked at Edward. Now, his eyes were warm as he looked at his friend who had risked his life to save him. "Edward, you are truly a good friend to risk your own welfare to warn me. I'm sorry you got into this, but I must stay here, and you must go quickly," he said.

"Antonio, you cannot be serious. Your life is in danger. You have to leave with us," he begged.

"No," Dega said calmly. "We cannot leave together. If we do, all I have planned will be for nothing."

Dega, looking like he was taking charge, held his finger to his lips to signal Edward to be quiet. He turned, walked to the tent flap, and looked out. He returned to Edward and said, "It is alright. The guard has not heard us. My plan is in place to take care of these ruthless barbarians. Listen carefully. I have learned from political sources about Brabant's past and his repeated attempts to finance the takeover of governments in Central America."

"I have also been receiving secret radio transmissions from General Mixcóatl since he has been in this camp. He had always been suspicious about the activities of Brabant's mercenary army. We know about the munitions they brought in and all of his trucks and men in the mountain pass. We also know the rest of his army is now at the border of Guatemala waiting to enter Chiapas."

"I have contacted the Mexican Government; apparently, they and the Guatemalan Government had been aware of the movements of Brabant's army around the border. A United States reconnaissance satellite detected their movements in Guatemala and warned both governments. I went to the government and told them why this large force was crossing the border. This camp will be invaded by Mexican commandos, from the air, tomorrow at dawn. At the same time, the Guatemalan army will come into the mountain passes and trap Brabant's men and trucks. Between the two armies, Brabant's forces will be totally surrounded," Dega said.

"Good. Now, we can both leave," said Edward.

"No, Edward, dear friend. I must stay or these mercenaries will become suspicious and be alerted to our action. Then, there would be more casualties, and I cannot be responsible for one more unnecessary death," he said emphatically. "I had planned to leave with Mixcóatl and his men. Now, I will slip away as soon as the attack is started. Now, please, go with all of my good wishes, amigo," he pleaded.

Edward looked into Dega's eyes and said, "You are very brave, but, please, be careful. These people don't hesitate to kill." Edward took Dega's hand and said, "Friends are cherished by me, especially those who have meant so much in such a short period of time. Take care of yourself. I will wait for you in Tapachula."

Dega smiled at him and said, "We will meet again shortly and join your beautiful la hija for one of Ixtanalia's wonderful meals. Vi con dios, mi amigo."

"I look forward to seeing you again, soon," Edward said as he raised the back of the tent, looked around, and slid back into the jungle.

CHAPTER THIRTY-SEVEN

William Brabant stormed into General Von Papen's tent and said, "We have a problem with Dega. He wants to see General Mixcóatl. I have stalled him for a few hours, but that's all. When can we be ready to launch our offensive?"

"Sir, the camp isn't finished, and the men don't have all of their equipment," Von Papen said.

"Camp, hell," Brabant shouted. "General, we are about to begin a war. The men must be called on, now. They can bring the equipment they need with them."

"I will have to contact the trucks in the mountains and tell them to go to get the rest of our men. They may be able to get a significant force here by the day after tomorrow." Von Papen said.

"Why will it take so long?" asked Brabant.

The general shrugged. "We don't have the satellite transmission radios, so I cannot reach them because of the mountains. I will have to send someone there with our orders, and they need time to move," he said.

"Do it now." Brabant thundered. "I don't think we have much time. We cannot hold Dega too long before he becomes suspicious. On the other hand, we cannot let him leave here before we launch. It will be too risky. If we don't attack quickly, we will have lost the opportunity, and we will have to withdraw. We will have to get the MYLN to move now."

"And if we have to withdraw, we will have trouble with the Guatemalans," said Von Papen.

"To hell with the Guatemalan army!" Brabant seethed. "They are a joke like General Cortez. Besides, I don't plan to fail here. We just have to move up our plans. I will explain to Reyes our forces have been detected, and Dega and I have decided to act now. He will have to gather the Indian forces together as soon as possible. We can send the message from Dega. He will order Reyes to have his Indians to attack as soon as we have our men in place. Reyes is so anxious, he will act, especially if he thinks Dega is in with us."

Colonel Keitel came into the tent looking rather embarrassed. In a low tone he said, "I'm sorry to interrupt, but Edward Amelot has escaped."

"What? When?" Brabant demanded angrily.

Keitel visibly cowered. "I don't know, Herr Brabant. He was taken to the caves last night. This morning, when I sent some men to the caves, they discovered our guards dead."

"How could you have been so stupid as to leave him for such a long period of time without checking on him?" thundered Von Papen.

"General, we have been so busy, and I have very few men left in the camp. Most are in the mountains. I thought three men would be able to handle him through the night," Keitel explained.

"Does this man Amelot have such skills as to overpower three of our men? Have you considered he had an accomplice?" asked Brabant sarcastically.

"Herr Brabant, it would be impossible for anyone to have followed him and gotten so close to our camp. We would have seen him."

"Didn't you say last night the cave approaches are not yet mined?" Von Papen demanded.

"Yes, Herr General, that's true," said Keitel.

Von Papen dropped his head into his hands. "Get some men and find him quickly. He couldn't have gotten very far in the jungle. Find him fast. Go and see it is done and do this yourself," he said.

Keitel stood at attention, clicked his heels, and said smartly, "Jawhol, Herr General," and left the tent.

"Now, quickly send a man to contact our men with the trucks," said Brabant.

"Yes, sir," Von Papen said as he left hurriedly.

Brabant sat in a chair, leaned back, and stared at the top of the tent. Things were now moving quickly. He knew there was an opportunity here. He was used to seizing the moment during chaos and turning it into his favor.

Now, in order to carry out his plan for Chiapas, he would have to have someone in charge of the Indian insurgents to act when he needed them. He knew he would not be able to count on Dega to execute his plan. Therefore, he had to be removed. Suddenly, his eyes popped wide open. He knew exactly how he would get rid of Dega and solve the other problem he had too. After a few minutes, he left the tent and went looking for General Von Papen.

CHAPTER THIRTY-EIGHT

As Edward crawled out of the back of the tent, he looked around to make sure he would not be seen. When he could get to his feet, he began to look for Alek. Suddenly, a hand reached out and touched his shoulder. He turned paralyzed with fear, until he saw it was Alek standing there with his fingers touching his lips. They went into the jungle and around the edge of the camp. They stopped and crouched down behind some trees.

"I thought you were never coming out. I was about to go in and get you," said Alek.

"Sorry I took so long, but we had a lot to say," Edward said apologetically.

"Where is Dega? We have to move quickly."

Edward looked down and said, "He's not coming."

"What? Are all of you crazy!" exclaimed Alek. "Did you tell him they killed his men and Brabant plans to take over Chiapas?"

"He knew about Brabant, but he didn't know about his men. He was very sad when he heard about them," Edward said.

"What? He knew about Brabant's plans, and he still came here. What's going on here? Do you all have a death wish?" Alek demanded.

"Listen, Dega has known for some time about Brabant's plans. He has joined forces with the Mexican and the Guatemalan governments. Mexican commandos will be arriving here by helicopter around sunrise tomorrow. At the same time, the Guatemalan army will attack Brabant's men in the mountains. Brabant's army is surrounded," Edward explained.

Alek paused to take all this in. "Well, if all this is true, what the hell is Dega doing here?" he asked.

"He came to warn his men and to get them out."

"That's pretty damned courageous. Not many leaders are willing to put their life on the line for a few men," Alek said with a tone of respect in his voice.

"Yes, he's quite a man," Edward nodded.

"Well, one good thing is this camp is not heavily manned, so the Mexican forces will not face much opposition. However, as I told you, the area around the camp is heavily mined."

Edward thought a moment and asked. "How can we help them?"

"Well, we have some time before the attack. I guess I can disable all of the mines I know."

"Good! Let's go," Edward said excitedly.

"Mr. Amelot, we've gone through this before," said Alek almost parentally. "I'll do the disarming, and you wait here."

"No, not this time," Edward, said shaking his head. "I will come with you. While you are working on the mines, I will stand guard, and I promise not to shoot at shadows. Let's go. We don't have time to argue."

He stared at Edward. "You are very stubborn. Now I know where Cara gets it. Just stay close. I'm still worried about being discovered."

The pair made their way around the perimeter of the camp, and Alek disabled the mines as they went. Suddenly, they heard a commotion. Alek motioned Edward to be quiet and stay low to the ground. They made their way up to the edge of the jungle behind some large-leafed bushes. There he saw Keitel, stomping his way across the compound with his arm pointing at a man on the other side.

"Lieutenant, where have you been?" he demanded.

The soldier stood at attention and saluted. "I was checking on the perimeter of the camp to ensure the area is secured. We don't have many men left for guard duty, sir."

"Well get me three men and Achman the tracker and form them up here immediately," barked Keitel. "Amelot has escaped."

"Yes, sir," the lieutenant said as he hurried away.

Alek looked at Edward dejectedly and said, "Well, our good luck just ran out. In a few minutes, Keitel's men will be looking for us."

Edward smiled at him and said, "I have an idea."

"Mr. Amelot, you seem to have a great many ideas and each of them so far has pulled us closer to the fire," Alek replied.

"Exactly, closer to the fire. I propose we make our way into one of the empty tents and wait for the colonel and his men to leave the camp. Then, we can have enough time to decide what course we can take to get out of here, and there is still the matter of the mines. I would hate to leave the job undone," Edward said.

"I really have to hand it to you. Going into the lair while the lions run into the jungle may be pure genius. I approve. Let's wait for Keitel to deploy his men. And now, as far as the mines are concerned, we really have done as many as we can," Alek reasoned.

Edward looked at Alek and said, "We have to do all of them. I have seen what an anti-personnel mine can do."

Alek just looked at Edward in amazement. "There will be armed men scouring the jungle, and you want to wander around and fix mines," he said.

"Look, we can wait until the soldiers move far from the perimeter of the camp and, then, go out and disable the mines. There will be less risk then," Edward reasoned.

"Okay, Mr. Amelot, I will do as you ask."

Edward smiled. "Thank you, Alek, and, please, call me Edward."

They made their way to the tents where the men in the camp were quartered. They observed from a safe distance until they knew which tents were empty, and then they quickly made their way into one of them. Alek went to the front flap and looked around the camp. Just as he was about to close the tent flap, he saw Brabant and General Von Papen approaching him from opposite directions. He motioned to Edward to be quiet. Edward peeked out and saw the two men stop a few feet away. Alek and he just stood there and listened.

Brabant was agitated, "General, I have decided we cannot let Dega leave this camp. He's suspicious of everything, and who knows what he will do when we get the Indians to begin our attack plan? So, we must eliminate him. If Dega is gone, Reyes will become their leader, and we will need his help if we are to take over Chiapas," he said.

"Do you want me to have him executed and buried with the other Indians?" asked Von Papen.

Brabant smiled, "Not exactly. But I do want them to die together."

"Sir, I don't understand. The other Indians are already dead," Von Papen replied.

"That is correct, but I have a plan. I will tell Dega, Colonel Keitel is going to take him to meet with General Mixcóatl. Before they leave the camp, you will put the bodies of the dead Indians in the back of their truck along with an explosive charge, which will be set to go off, let's say thirty minutes after they leave the camp. The bodies of Dega, Keitel, General Mixcóatl and the other Indians will be shown to Reyes, who will assume they were killed by a mine which was placed by the Mexicans. Having one of our own men die with them will make the story believable."

"But sir, Oberst Keitel?" Von Papen asked in disbelief.

"Exactly. I'm tired of his incompetence and his uncontrollable temper. It's time we did something about him," Brabant said emphatically. "We cannot just let him go, so his death will be used to help us execute our battle plans."

Von Papen stared blankly at Brabant. "Yes, sir. What will I tell Keitel?"

"Tell him he's to take Dega and the bodies of the other Indians into the mountains where the trucks are waiting. Tell him, when he gets to the border, he's to kill Dega and bury all of the Indians in the jungle. He will enjoy that," Brabant said.

"Yes, sir," Von Papen said.

"Now, you must make sure the truck explodes at a safe distance from the camp."

"Yes, sir. I have a man who is a genius with explosives, and he can have the charges set to detonate whenever we wish. He can set a timer which will activate when the vehicle is started and then ignites the charges thirty minutes later," Von Papen said.

"Good," Brabant said with a sardonic smile. "Have the bodies of the Indians placed in the back of the truck and covered from view. How much time will you need to set the explosives and get the vehicle here?" he asked.

"Well, we'll have to put the charges under the hood. This will insure that, after the explosion, there will be enough of the bodies left for Reyes to identify. It won't take long," the general said.

Brabant smiled as he always did when his plans were coming to fruition and said, "Very good, General. I will go to see Dega and tell him about this meeting with his General Mixcóatl. Then, after this is over, I will call Reyes and tell him Dega wants him to join us. I will send the helicopter for him."

Brabant and General Von Papen left in different directions but each had the same goal in mind.

CHAPTER THIRTY-NINE

When Alek closed the tent flap, Edward turned to him in disbelief. He motioned Edward to follow him. They left the tent from the back and never stopped until they were deep into the jungle.

"Alek, we cannot let this happen," said Edward.

"Look, Mr. Amelot, I told you these men would stop at nothing to carry out their plans."

"I certainly believe that, but I am shocked to think they would kill one of their own officers deliberately. We have to protect Antonio. What can we do?" Edward asked.

"To try and stop them would be very dangerous. The sensible thing to do is to get out of here, now," Alek explained.

Edward nodded. "You're right. The prudent thing to do would be to get out now before things get hotter; however, I simply can't leave Dega to die. You go now, and I will get Antonio, and we will make a run for it."

Alek held up his hand, like a policeman stopping traffic, and said, "Look, let's not get into this discussion again."

Edward put his hand on Alek's shoulder and said, "I understand your commitment to your word, but I cannot leave without helping Dega. Look at it this way. When you get far enough away, you can set off some of the mines for a diversion, and we can just slip away."

"You will not get to Dega before they take him," Alek said. "Brabant is on his way to tell him about the meeting, remember? They will watch him very closely, and you will not get anywhere near him now," Alek warned.

"Then, I must find another way."

Alek shook his head in frustration. "Mr. Amelot, you forget there are men in the jungle looking for you. They could easily pick up some of the tracks we have been leaving. Getting to Dega is not a practical plan."

"Edward said vehemently, "Alek, this man is my friend. I cannot leave him!"

"Fine, then, I will stay with you, and we'll both go in," Alek said.

"Alright, if I can't talk you into leaving, then I certainly can use your help. You're the professional. What can we do?"

He looked at Edward shook his head and sighed. "Our only chance may be to stop the truck after it leaves the camp and overpower the driver and Keitel," he said dejectedly.

"Can we do it?" Edward asked.

Alek shrugged. "I don't know. We will have to see where the road out of the camp leads and, then, see if there is an opportune place to stop the truck. What we do after that is the next question," he said.

They cautiously went around the camp and then out to the road to the mountains. After ten minutes, they came to a place where the road made a U-turn to the right and, at the same time, climbed up at a severe angle. This would be the ideal place to set the ambush of the truck. The truck would have to slow down for the turn and would not be able to accelerate very quickly up the steep grade. "This will be an best place to stop the truck. We can drag some of those dead trees onto the road so the driver won't see them until he makes the turn. He'll have to slow down when he reaches the turn. When he sees the trees, he will have his hands full trying to stop the truck and keep it from rolling back down the road. I don't think they will send more than one man with Keitel, but we will still have to act quickly," Alek explained.

They dragged three dead trees to block the roadway. After this strenuous work, he turned to Edward and said, "They will be coming soon. The only trucks they have left are the Humvees with two rows of seats. As soon as the truck slows enough, I will jump on the running board and get the drop on whoever is in the front passenger seat. It should be Keitel. You cover the driver. He should have his hands full, but don't take any chances with him. You have my pistol, use it if you have to, and, remember, the truck is set to explode thirty minutes after it starts. I figure the truck will run a few minutes in camp, and then, it will take about ten minutes for it to get here. That gives us some time to act, but let's not count on using too much of it," Alek said.

"I don't know what to say to you, except I'm grateful for your help," Edward said.

"Quiet! I hear the truck coming. Get off the road and into the brush. Don't come out until you see me jump on the truck," Alek ordered.

They both left the road and hid in the brush. Edward was sweating profusely. His mind seemed to be whirling around and not focusing on any one thing.

He saw the truck coming around the curve and prepared to leap out of the bush. The driver made the turn and, when he saw the trees in the road, came to a screeching halt and struggled to keep the truck from rolling down the hill into the jungle. When Edward saw Alek jump out of the bush, he did the same.

As Alek jumped on the running board, he saw Keitel reaching for his pistol. He put the muzzle of the M-16 into Colonel Keitel's ear and said, "Leave it in the holster, Colonel, and tell the driver to put on the emergency brake. And if you give me that 'I don't understand look,' you and your driver will be dead right here. I would just as soon get rid of you, now, but that's up to you."

Keitel looked at him and said to the driver in German, "Stop here and put on the brake." Then, he looked past the driver and saw Edward on the other side. The color of Keitel's face changed to a bright red as he sputtered, "You! I should have killed you back at the river."

"Colonel, you don't look very happy to see me," Edward said with a smile on his face. "Well, if you knew what I know, you would be very happy to see us," he teased.

Dega had been tossed to one side when the truck stopped so suddenly. As he pushed himself up, he saw Edward on one side and Alek on the other each pointing weapons at their respective targets.

Before Edward could say anymore, Alek said, "Alright, Colonel, clasp your hands behind your neck. Have your man roll this truck slowly back down the hill and stop it at the bottom where it is level. Tell him if he tries anything, you will die. And if you move, I will not hesitate to kill both of you. Now, tell him, Colonel," Alek shouted.

Keitel turned to the driver and said in German. "Klaus, back the truck to the bottom of the hill, slowly."

The driver obeyed the order and then came to a stop.

Alek said, "Mr. Amelot, step down and to the side, out of the line of fire, but keep your pistol on them. When I get down, Colonel, I want you and your driver to come out of this door slowly. You tell him to put his hands behind his neck, also. If either of you lower them before you get out, you are both dead. Is that understood?"

Alek stepped down and opened the door. Keitel turned to the driver and said in German, "Klaus, put your hands behind your head. When I step down out of the vehicle, shoot the one with the rifle, and I will get the other one." Then, he turned to Alek and said, "Alright, we are coming."

As Keitel began to step out of the vehicle, he dove to the ground and heard a shot fired. He rolled over, and with his pistol in his hands got to his knees. He saw Alek standing and pointing his smoking rifle barrel at him. Then, he saw the driver lying dead on the front seat.

"You bastard. That man didn't have to die," Alek said, "I speak German fluently. Now, you will now put your hands behind your head and stay where you are. Senore Dega, please get out on the other side."

Alek walked to the back of the vehicle where he could see Edward and Dega on the one side of the vehicle and Keitel on the other.

Dega got out of the truck, walked to the back and said, "Edward, I thought you were well away from here by now. I don't understand what is going on. We are on our way to find General Mixcóatl."

"Antonio, we were about to leave the camp when we overheard Brabant and General Von Papen plan to kill you," explained Edward.

Dega shrugged. "Why would they do this, now? They had no reason to suspect me," he said.

"Brabant couldn't produce General Mixcóatl, and he knew, eventually, he would have to answer to you. He was sure you didn't trust him and you would not want to cooperate with him, so he planned to blame your deaths on the Mexicans. He thought this would bring Reyes and your men even closer under his control."

"How would he explain the disappearance of the others?" Dega asked.

"I'm sorry, Antonio, but their bodies are in the back of this vehicle. There are charges set in the truck to go off in a few minutes. They were going to blow up the truck and then show all your bodies to Reyes to make him think the Mexicans did this."

"Diablos," Dega said.

Colonel Keitel strained to hear what Amelot and Dega were saying, but he could only hear their mumbles.

Alek saw Keitel trying to hear and said, "What is it, Colonel? They didn't let you in on their plan, did they? You are in deep shit, my friend. No one seems to want you."

Keitel stood up, brushed off his uniform, and stood very erect. He said, "What are you talking about? And who are you anyway? I have many men scouring this jungle, and they will be here soon. I order you to release me immediately. If you follow my instructions, I will not have you shot," he said haughtily.

"Colonel you sure are an arrogant SOB. If you know what's good for you, you'll stand there and be quiet until I decide what to do with you." Then, turning to Edward, Alek said, "Mr. Amelot, what this pompous ass said could be right about his men. Besides, we have to get away from this vehicle. We only have minutes."

"I have to get the colonel's bag out of the truck. My artifacts are in there," Edward said.

"Okay, but hurry because either his men will be here or the truck will…"

Before he could continue, he heard a noise behind him. He turned in time to be hit on the side of the head with a rifle butt by one of the mercenaries who had been sent to look for Edward. He fell to the ground out cold.

At the same moment, another mercenary stepped out from the other side of the foliage, put his rifle in Edward's back, and took the pistol from his hand. Two more men stepped from the jungle with weapons pointed at Edward and Dega. They motioned for them both to raise their hands.

The sergeant said in German, "Oberst, what would you have us do with these men?"

Keitel walked slowly toward the back of the truck. As he passed Alek, he looked down, kicked him hard in the ribs, and said, "Who's in deep shit now, asshole?"

Edward and Dega were facing the back of the truck, and the three mercenaries were standing, facing them with their weapons pointed at Edward and Dega. The fourth man stayed on the other side of the truck with Alek.

Keitel looked with deep hatred at Edward and said, "Finally, Amelot. You now belong to me. First, you will tell me, who is this man with you? And what plan was he talking about?"

Edward looked at Keitel and said, "Why would I want to help you? You're going to kill us anyway."

"If you cooperate, Amelot, I will not kill you," Keitel said.

"Ha, you expect us to trust you?" Dega scoffed.

"I only said, you, Amelot. For some reason, the General and Mr. Brabant want you alive." Then, he turned to Dega and, with a look of contempt, said, "But this aborigine will die with the others."

Moved by hatred, Dega looked at Keitel and said, "You are a demented creature that kills for pleasure."

"Dega, you will die squealing for mercy as your men did," Keitel sneered.

Dega dropped his arms and began to move toward Keitel. One of the mercenaries stepped forward with his rifle and pointed it at Dega's heart. Dega withdrew and raised his hands again.

"Colonel, there is nothing I can tell you," said Edward.

"Sergeant," Keitel said, "try to get General Von Papen on the radio before

I kill these two."

Edward looked at his watch, "Well, Antonio, I guess in 60 seconds we will be dead," he said emphasizing the 60 seconds as he looked deliberately toward the truck.

Dega looked at Edward with a slight nod of recognition and said, "Si, amigo."

Edward and Dega dove away from the truck just as it exploded. They were thrown hard to the ground by the blast. The three men standing on their side of the truck were blown off their feet. The fourth man, who was in the truck, was killed when the bomb exploded. When Edward hit the ground, he rolled to his right and saw Keitel at the back of the truck scrambling on all fours into the jungle. He had been somewhat protected from the blast.

He looked over at Dega, who rose from the ground, picked up one of the mercenary's rifles, and ran into the jungle after Keitel. Edward got up slowly, groggy from being thrown to the ground. He looked at the mercenaries who had been standing by the truck. They were all dead. He staggered around the truck to see if Alek was okay. As Edward bent over him, he began to stir.

"Are you alright, Alek?" Edward asked.

"Yes. When I was hit on the head, I went out for a minute. But as I was coming to, I started to look around to see how I could get at the guy who was covering me. That's when the truck blew. Are you alright, Mr. Amelot?"

"Yes, I think I am." Edward said. "I dove to the ground as the truck exploded."

"What about the others?" Alek asked.

"The men who were guarding us are dead except for Keitel. He took off into the jungle and Dega followed him. I have to go and help him," Edward said.

"Wait!" yelled Alek. "Help me up, and I will go with you."

Edward got Alek to his feet and started to let go of his arm, but then, he slumped back down to the ground.

"Alek, you probably have a concussion," Edward said. "Stay here. I'll come back as soon as I can."

"Mr. Amelot," Alek started to say as he tried again to rise, "don't go off in the jungle. Keitel is a professional. You don't know how to..." Alek slumped back down to the ground before he could finish his thought.

"Sorry, Alek, I have to go," Edward said urgently. "I'll be back."

Edward picked up a rifle, turned, and went off into the jungle. He could easily spot the trail by the trampled vegetation. He quickly picked his way through the bush and looked ahead for the two men.

Dega ran after Keitel as fast as his feet could carry him. As he ran, he was holding the rifle in front of him to help deflect the branches from his face. Suddenly, his body continued through the air and his feet were no longer on the ground. He had tripped over something. As he hit the ground, he remembered his military training. He held his weapon close to his chest, tucked his head and shoulder, and hit the ground rolling.

He came to a stop by digging his rifle butt into the ground. He was in a sitting position when he looked up and saw Keitel coming toward him with both hands extended. As Keitel lunged toward him, Dega rolled over to his side and Keitel went sprawling to the jungle floor. Dega then pointed his rifle at Keitel who was lying face down.

"Don't move, Colonel," Dega seethed.

"Well, sir, you have the advantage," Keitel said in a tone of capitulation. "Surely, you will allow me to face my adversary. After all, I am unarmed," he said.

"Turn over slowly," Dega replied. "I will not hesitate to shoot if you try anything."

As Keitel began to turn over, he said, "Surely, Senore Dega, you can understand a soldier has duties to his country. You are fighting a similar battle with your army," he tried to reason.

Dega looked at Keitel with pure hatred and said, "Don't you dare compare our cause to your cowardly pursuit of power and money. Brabant is the personification of evil and you and Von Papen are his minions. Not even a wild animal takes the pleasure of killing as you do."

"Then, what now?" Keitel questioned. "Are you to be my executioner?"

"No, I will take you back so you may stand trial for your carnage. You will have to answer to the people, especially those whose lives you have devastated by killing their loved ones," Dega replied.

As Edward made his way through the jungle, he suddenly heard Dega talking to Keitel. As he approached them, he saw Keitel lying on the ground but rising to his knees. From the position he was in, he saw Keitel reach out with one hand as a diversion while he reached into his belt for a knife. He knew Dega could not see the knife. As he yelled, Keitel whipped around and threw the knife, which hit Dega in the chest. Edward gasped and froze for a moment. Then, he ran forward firing his rifle at Keitel as he ran. After three or four shots, the rifle jammed. Keitel had dropped down and rolled to elude the shots, but as Edward got to him, he rolled towards Edward and knocked his legs from him. Edward fell to the ground dropping the rifle.

Keitel picked up Dega's rifle, cleared the jam and fired a shot in the ground near Edward and laughed. "You are not very good with a weapon, Amelot, but that does not surprise me. Now, you are going to die by my hand, but first you will tell me what you know about the bomb in the truck."

"If you are going to kill me, why should I answer you?" asked Edward.

"If you tell me what you know, you will die quickly. You see the bullet I'm putting into the chamber of the rifle? It is an incendiary round, which means the slug enters the body burning. It also has less powder, so it will penetrate but not go through the body. If you don't tell me what I want to know, I will simply shoot you in the stomach and tie you to a tree to die. Dying from a shot in the stomach, especially with this bullet, will be excruciatingly painful. It will feel like someone has stuck a hot poker inside of you. And if you are lucky, you will die in only a few hours," Keitel said with a sneer.

Edward looked over at Antonio, then back to Keitel, and said with all the anger he could muster, "You are the lowest form of life on earth. You should be eradicated like the loathsome vermin you are."

"That's enough, Amelot," Keitel shouted back. "We'll see who is going to be eradicated." As he began to raise the rifle, there was a loud rumbling sound and the sky suddenly became very dark. He turned to look at where the sound had come from, and he saw a huge Indian who appeared at the edge of the bush. Keitel was paralyzed with fear.

The Indian wore a headdress with feathers extending straight up from the top of his head. The feathers were almost four feet long. His face was encircled with small black feathers that curved out around his head. His forehead and his temples were painted black. His eyes were outlined in white. His body was covered in oil. He wore a loincloth, and his leg and arm muscles rippled. In his left hand was a very ornate, brightly colored shield. In his right hand, he had a wooden handle with a long steel blade attached, which curved into a hook.

Keitel stood looking in disbelief at this figure that looked ten feet tall. A voice like rolling thunder came from the warrior who said, "You are the evil one who has taken the lives of those who protect and believe in the Ahkin Mai. Because of you, they roam the spirit world looking for their resting place. They will get there when they are avenged. You will be their sacrifice."

With those words, the Indian stepped forward and swiftly swung his weapon upwards into the abdomen of Keitel before he could move. Keitel screamed savagely, and dropped the rifle. He clasped both hands to his abdomen, and tried to keep his insides from spilling out. He dropped to his knees and tried to say something, but only blood poured from his mouth. He died as he fell to the ground.

Edward looked at the warrior with disbelief. Then, there was another loud crash of thunder, and a flash of sunlight light blinded Edward. He shaded his eyes and looked for the warrior, but he was gone.

Edward heard a muffled voice and turned. It was Antonio, and he was still alive. Edward quickly crawled over to him and lifted his head onto his lap. He could see the death's head SS dagger on the ground. Apparently, it had fallen out when Antonio fell to the ground. He was bleeding profusely, and Edward put his hand on his chest to stop the flow of blood.

Antonio whispered, "Is he dead?"

"Yes, Antonio," Edward said. "Did you see the Indian warrior? He was huge, and he moved like a cat."

"He is Jacatez. He came from the ancient ones to seek revenge, as I told you," said Antonio excitedly.

"Antonio, please, lie quiet and let me get some help for you," Edward said.

"No, mi amigo. There is no time for that. However, you must understand the ancient ones will protect the culture of my people. You must be careful where you go."

"I will, but please let me get help," Edward begged.

"No, please listen to me. There is little time left," Antonio urged. "Tell Camilo I died in the cause of our heritage and that the ancient ones are still here to protect our culture. Tell him he must never, in his attempt to gain independence from Mexico, sell his soul to a despot. He must not let men like Brabant into our cause again. Tell him not to despair for me because I now join my enamorado, Inés."

Antonio then smiled at Edward and said softly, "And you, Edward, go back to your beautiful hija and tell her she's lucky to have a father such as you. I have been fortunate to call you my friend."

Edward's eyes became moist, and he said soberly, "No, it is I who have been honored by you." As his voice gained in strength, he said, "but, Antonio, your people need you to continue their cause."

Antonio grabbed Edward's arm, looked in his eyes and said, "Adios, mi amigo." With those words, Antonio Dega died.

Edward laid him down carefully, touched his hand, and said, "Antonio, my friend, there are not many times in our lives where people affect us so deeply as you have. Adios, mi amigo."

Edward heard a noise and quickly crawled over to grab the rifle Keitel dropped. Before he could get there, Alek came from the bushes.

"Alek, are you okay?" Edward asked.

"Yes, Mr. Amelot. It just took a few minutes for my head to clear. What happened here?"

"Antonio caught up to Keitel." Edward said dejectedly. "He had his rifle pointed at him, but Keitel tricked him and threw a knife into his chest and killed him. I saw it happen."

Alek walked over to Keitel, turned him over, and exclaimed, "Wow, who did this? It looks like someone gutted Keitel."

"You would not believe me if I told you the truth. For now, let's just say he was killed by a Mayan Indian. I'll tell you the rest later."

"Where is the Indian?" Alek asked.

"The Indian is gone," said Edward, as he walked over to Dega's body, "and so is Antonio Dega. He just died after a few words with me. He got into this because he was trying to help his people. He didn't realize how insidious the people were with whom he was joining forces. He didn't deserve to die this way." Alek then turned to Keitel's body and said with anger in his heart, "This man was diabolical. He deserved to die."

"Well, Mr. Amelot, we have to get out of here," Alek said anxiously. "It will soon be dark, and if we are caught in the jungle tonight, we will have to dodge the Mexican and the Guatemalan armies in the morning."

"Yes, you're right, but we have to mark this place so they may find the bodies of Antonio and his men before we go."

After a long, hard, forced march, they reached Alek's jeep. Suddenly, Edward gasped as he realized he had forgotten his artifacts. His mind was so full of Antonio and getting back to Cara, he had just forgotten them. He grew morose when he remembered they were probably blown to bits in the truck. All of his efforts to prove his theories were now only notes in his journals. He had no proof; however, the thing that was most significant in his mind was that the artifacts, which a short time ago were all-important, were forgotten when he had to face the loss of a friend. He suddenly felt very tired and fell asleep as they drove off into the night.

CHAPTER FORTY

The reunion with Cara was one of the happiest moments in Edward's life. In coming so close to death, he realized even more how important she was to him. The campaign against Brabant's army was successful, but only to a point. Most of the mercenaries were killed or captured, General Von Papen was killed, but William Brabant escaped and surfaced much later in South America. The Mexican and the Guatemalan governments were trying to have him declared an international criminal, but the Hague was still considering the case.

Edward told Camilo what Antonio had said to him. He thought about telling him about the Indian warrior as well, but he wasn't sure that he would believe him. There were some very tearful ceremonies held by the families and friends of Antonio Dega and his men. Because he had warned the Mexican Government about the plot by Brabant, Camilo Reyes wanted his ceremony to be carried out with full military honors. However, the Mexican Government only saw him as a leader of a revolutionary group, so he and his men were denied a military ceremony.

Edward, Alek, and Cara left Tapachula after the ceremonies and the government interrogations. They went to Puerto Vallarta on the plane Alek had charted. After staying a few days with Cara, Edward realized she kept finding excuses to see Alek, so he packed his suitcase and told Cara he would like to take her and Alek out to dinner because he would be leaving for Washington D.C. the next day.

At dinner that evening, Edward told Cara about some of their adventures. Edward made sure the more dangerous parts were left out. What he didn't realize, however, was Alek had told Cara everything that happened.

"Mr. Amelot, you never told me exactly what happened to Keitel. I know you said an Indian killed him, but there was no one there when I arrived. There was only one trail that led to the clearing, it ended there, and no one passed me," Alek said.

"Just as Keitel was about to shoot me, this huge Indian came from the brush. He looked like an ancient Mayan warrior. I have seen such a warrior in Mayan art. He killed Keitel. Before Antonio died, he told me it was the mythical warrior Jacatez, who was sent to avenge his people," Edward replied.

"Who is Jacatez?" asked Cara.

"There is a legend that the Sun God, Kinich Ahau, when needed, would descend as a warrior in the form of the Jaguar Lord, Jacatez, and would eviscerate anyone who defiled the temples or harmed the rulers of the Mayas."

"And based on how Keitel died, the legend is assumed validated," said Alek.

"Not assumed, I saw it and him." Edward said.

"That's an interesting legend," said Cara. "Is there more to it?"

"Yes, in addition, the legend says Jacatez could bring with him warriors from the Icono Ejercito."

"What is Icono Ejercito?" asked Cara.

"It is the stone army," Edward replied.

"What stone army?" Alek asked.

Edward said, "Keichi told me that the Icono Ejercito was a legend told by his people."

"And you believe it?" asked Alek.

"When we were camped by the river, Castillo was drinking, and I got him to talk about the temple we were trying to find. He said when he was in the temple, he went into a room that was full of Mayan warriors made of stone, which I think were the Icono Ejercito," Edward said.

"Really?" asked Cara.

"He said there were at least fifty in this room, they were very large, and were holding weapons."

"So do you think the legend of the Indians is true?" Alek asked.

"It sure sounds like it. But do you know what else this means? It is further proof of the Chinese connection."

"How?" asked Alek.

"The stone army Castillo described was similar to the well-known terra-cotta army of the Emperor Shihuangdi of the Ch'in Dynasty. They were made to guard the emperor's crypt," said Edward.

"And you think this is the same thing?" asked Alek.

"Yes. I think the Mayas learned of the protector warriors from their ancient visitors, and they decided to provide a stone army of their own to protect their temple," Edward said.

"Well, what can you do now?" asked Cara.

"Not a whole lot, I'm afraid," Edward said dejectedly.

"But why? You know all these things," said Cara.

"Maybe, I will write a book about my adventure, but it will have to be fiction since I can't find the missing temple or even the artifacts I had."

"Well, father, I'm sorry all of this didn't turn out as you wanted," Cara said. "But, maybe, I have a conclusion to your story. Alek and I are going to be married. Are you surprised?"

"No, Cara. I have watched the two of you gazing at each other like your mother and I used to do before we were married. Also, this Alek of yours would never call me anything but Mr. Amelot, even after I told him repeatedly to call me Edward. Only one reason for that. He intended to keep me on his good side. Besides, I already called my friends in Washington and told them there would be a wedding soon."

Cara smiled. "You always were a clairvoyant, father. So what are you going to do when you get back to Washington?" she asked.

"Well, I have to update my journals and fill in the parts that are missing. Then, I plan to resign from my position and become a consultant to the museum," Edward said.

"What!" Cara exclaimed. "You are giving up your position as director?"

"Yes," Edward sighed.

"But you worked your whole life to get there. Why would you give it up now?" Cara asked.

"I have discussed this with the Board of Directors and they agreed: I'm tired of sitting in the museum waiting for someone to bring in something new. There are archaeological excavations taking place all over the world, and I'm going to see some of them, after I to return to Chiapas, of course."

"I thought you said you didn't think you could find your missing temple, Mr. Amelot," said Alek.

Edward shrugged. "I'm not sure of that, but I'm not giving up on proving my theory. Maybe, there is someone else in Chiapas who knows something about the temple. I certainly have a lot of contacts among the Mayas. Maybe, Reyes can help. In addition, after thinking about it, I decided to see if I could find a boat route from Chiapas to China through the Pacific that could have been traversed in increments two thousand years ago. It's only about 18,000 miles. Then, I may see if I can find some archaeological digs in China that might lead the Mayas. There's always more than one way to find what you want. So, Cara dear, let me know when the wedding is, and I will be back for it, barring any interruptions from the Ancient Ones, of course. And, Alek, you are about to take on the greatest adventure of your life, so please call me Edward."